THE PEOPLE EATERS

THE PEOPLE EATERS

a novel from the author of MOCTU AND THE MAMMOTH PEOPLE

NEIL BOCKOVEN

RARE BIRD

Los Angeles, Calif.

THIS IS A GENUINE RARE BIRD BOOK

Rare Bird Books
6044 North Figueroa Street
Los Angeles, CA 90042
rarebirdbooks.com

Set in Minion
Printed in the United States

10 9 8 7 6 5 4 3 2 1

Publisher's Cataloging-in-Publication Data available upon request.

To my wife, Denise.
Your love and respect mean everything.

Acknowledgments

In ADDITION TO THE people mentioned in *Moctu and the Mammoth People*, whose help and support has continued through the writing of *The People Eaters* (for which I remain very grateful), I'd like to give further thanks to:

Jeff Eckert, Kim Shelton, and Steve Vealey, for close critical readings of the book and for their feedback and support. Jeff, in particular, read and commented on the book several times—and I've incorporated a couple of his ideas into the storyline. My publisher, Tyson Cornell, has been encouraging, and his associates, Hailie Johnson and Natalie Noland, suggested changes that made the book better.

Karen Weidenaar and Pat Shipman read sections of the book and offered feedback and supportive comments. Marti and Paul Sturm sent me the makings of a spear thrower that I built and then practiced using. I've realized that I'd starve if I had to hunt with it.

Scott Busby has been encouraging, as have many of my Facebook followers at authorneilbockoven.

Most of all, my wife, Denise, has been a huge help, very supportive and willing to look the other way from my piles of notes and reference books.

Finally, thanks to all the scientists doing the fantastic breakthrough research in ancient DNA analysis.

Author's Note

WERE NEANDERTHALS CANNIBALS? THE short answer is yes—a fair percentage of them were.

Life was tough for most Neanderthals. To paraphrase Thomas Hobbes, they had lives that were nasty, brutish, and short. At Krapina Cave in Croatia, portions of eighty Neanderthal individuals have been found, and the typical age at death was between fourteen and twenty-four. Most show evidence of periodic malnutrition or starvation.[2,48] Some of the individuals had been cooked and eaten.[2,70] Clearly, some Neanderthals were cannibals.

Krapina is by no means an anomaly. There is strong evidence of cannibalism in at least seven other European sites as well (Goyet, Belgium; Gran Dolina and El Sidrón in Spain; Moula-Guercy, Combe-Grenal, and Les Pradelles in France; and Vindija in Croatia).[1,2,3,4,11,67,68] According to noted paleogeneticist Svante Paabo, human bones with cut marks or percussion breakage to extract marrow are "typical of many, even most, sites where Neanderthal bones are found."[12,13,67,69]

Perhaps the saddest case is that of the Neanderthal remains recently found at El Sidrón Cave in Spain. There, about 43,000 years ago (roughly the time of our story), thirteen members of a clan, including men, women, and children, were eaten.[11] The bones indicate intense nutritional stress from a diet of moss and mushrooms. The overall evidence has convinced many researchers that the cannibalism was by another group for survival, not just one group eating its own dead. Life doesn't get much worse than that— starving on moss and mushrooms, then being killed and eaten by your neighbors. Nasty, brutish, and short.

Putting the best spin on it, some, perhaps most, Neanderthal cannibalism was likely done in times of famine only after the individual died of natural causes. And it's also true that we Homo sapiens have a rich history of cannibalism as well.[13,14,15,16,17,18,74] A fascinating study by Simon Underdown even speculates that Neanderthal cannibalism of modern humans may have contributed to their extinction.[15] Probably due to widespread cannibalism in our past, modern humans carry a gene (the 129 variant of the PRNP gene) that gives us some immunity to dangerous prions when we eat our dead. Neanderthals didn't have the gene, and they may have contracted kuru-like spongiform disease when they ate us.

So, much of the Neanderthal cannibalism probably happened only during what Effie (from my first book of this series, *Moctu and the Mammoth People*) called the "hungry-hungry times," when people were starving, and only after they were dead. But similar to certain modern-day human cultures, it's likely that some Neanderthals developed a taste for the practice.[3,16]

And how about warfare? Weren't the scattered, hunter-gatherer tribes mostly peaceful? Well, no. As it turns out, war is pretty common in hunter-gatherer cultures.[18,19,20,21,22,26,81] It's especially common between groups with different ethnicities, religions, and/or languages.[23,24] We can only imagine how pronounced it was between different *species*.

There were probably a lot of different languages in Paleolithic Europe. A more recent example is instructive. By the time of European contact, there were already at least 1,000 mutually unintelligible languages in the Americas and perhaps as many as 3,000 if dialects are included.[25] Those all developed during a blossoming of the population after a few groups migrated in just 16,500 years before.[31]

Some of our understanding of Paleolithic peoples and cultures has changed since I wrote *Moctu*. This is largely due to the rapid pace of breakthrough discoveries coming from the study of ancient DNA. A good example is the research around what Neanderthals looked like.

Although Neanderthals had lighter skin, hair, and maybe eye color than we did, new studies suggest that they were quite variable, similar to modern-day Europeans.[8,9] Recent analyses of the nuclear DNA from two Croatian Neanderthal females indicate that they were probably brown-haired with tawny skin coloring.[5,6,7] Red hair may not have been as common as earlier thought. In this book, you'll find the Neanderthals have a wide variety of characteristics. You can find other new learnings and understandings (e.g., about the domestication of wolves)[27,28,29,30] in the annotated references and notes at the end of this book.

Before diving into the novel, I'd encourage you to skim those references. They'll show that, while this book is fiction, it's solidly based on fact. I've bolded key parts, so scanning them only takes a few minutes, and it adds depth to the reading experience (and where else will you find references from Pliny the Elder and Julius Caesar?). I appreciate authors that apply extensive research to their historical fiction, and I've worked hard to do so.

Finally, some hidden things to look for: As in *Moctu*, I've used many Basque words or derivations for the Homo sapien people's names,[51,66] and there is a Neander verse[76] buried somewhere in the last few chapters.

I hope you enjoy this story.

PART ONE
SHIV RISING

Main Characters and Places

- **Moctu**—Young man of the Nerean people (Homo sapiens)
- **Nerea**—Name of Moctu's tribe (means mine or my people in Basque)
- **Etseh**—Large rock overhang that the Nereans use for shelter (means home if spelled etxea)
- **Nuri**—Young, dark-haired woman of the Nerea
- **Elka**—Hybrid daughter of Moctu (elkartu means unite in Basque)
- **Avi**—Young, fair-haired woman of the Nerea
- **Jondu**—Young man of the Nerea, who is Avi's mate
- **Nindai**—Lame shaman of the Nerea
- **Krog**—Tribe of Pale Ones (Neanderthals)
- **Uhda**—Shelter of the Krog
- **Shiv**—Fierce tribe of cannibalistic Pale Ones (Neanderthals)
- **Mung**—Tribe of Pale Ones allied with the Shiv
- **Shaka-Nu**—Leader of the Shiv
- **Lion People**—Large tribe similar to the Nereans (Homo sapiens)

Map of Shelters and Territories

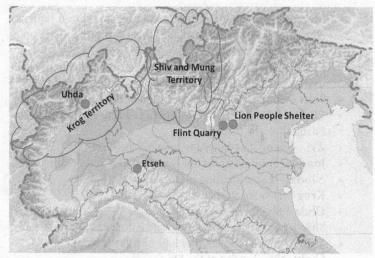

(Map modified from "More Images of Northern Italy")

1

(Flash-Forward)

Smoke rose from the roasting human tongues and lingered in the recesses of the walls of the shallow cave where it was protected from the breeze. The hair was completely singed from two fire-darkened heads that had been placed upside down near the flames to cook the brains. After a series of grunts and signings, three of the group of Shiv men got up from where they sat on stones near the fire. While two of them stood and waited, one turned the two heads so they would heat on their other side. Then the three moved toward the darker part of the shelter.

Nuri stopped breathing and kept her eyes downcast at the floor of the cave where she sat with several others, her hands tied behind her. She could hear the men coming to take another of the group, and she was terrified it would be her. Last time, they'd dragged a struggling young man out toward the fire, and his screams still echoed in her ears. The cries of "No! Spirits, no!" had become blood-curdling shrieks, then choked whimpers and gasps, and finally silence. Although she couldn't see it, the crackling of the fire and a new wave of smoke told Nuri they were roasting the man—or portions of him.

Her drive to protect the baby within her was overwhelming. "Don't pick me, oh, Spirits, please, don't let them eat me," she

whispered, her fear overwhelming the self-revulsion she felt for
hoping they would take someone else—anyone else. There was a
pause while the standing men spoke among themselves in hushed
tones. Even looking down, she could see the crude leather wraps
around their feet. Her pulse began to pound in her head as the
conversation stopped and the feet moved directly toward her. Nuri's
heart seemed to bulge into her throat, and waves of nausea swept
over her as powerful hands roughly pulled her to her feet.

2

Peaceful times at the Krog shelter...

THE TRIP TO UHDA was arduous for Nindai and Nuri, but both
remained cheerful and excited. The young shaman's lame right leg,
nearly a finger's length shorter than his left, had swelled to twice it's
normal thickness from the exertion of the long journey. His right
underarm was raw—the blisters had broken, and smears of blood
showed on the top of his crutch. In the end, Moctu fashioned a
travois to carry him at least half of each day along the muddy trails
and remnant snowbanks.

Although Nuri was sick each morning, she was thrilled to be
carrying Moctu's baby. Her belly was only slightly rounded, but her
normal endurance had abandoned her, and during the final two days
of the trek her head swam, and nausea threatened her on all of the
uphill stretches.

But now they'd been here with the Pale Ones—the Krog—for
more than a moon, and the elation of the reunion with Elka, Rah, and
Hawk had given way to a satisfied peacefulness as Moctu watched
Nuri twirl Elka around, and his beautiful hybrid daughter shrieked
with delight. The bond between Moctu and Elka's grandmother,
Rah, was as strong as ever, even though there had been several times
Moctu's eyes met Rah's as something reminded them of Effie. Elka's
mother, Effie, had been tragically slain by Moctu's people in an act of

mistaken vengeance. The huge, red-haired Krog warrior Hawk and Moctu were as close as brothers. Hawk, in fact, usually referred to his friend as "Brud Moctu," which meant Brother Moctu.

"You grow since last time," Hawk said, looking at Moctu and holding two thick fingers together sideways. "Two, maybe three fingers."

As they stood close together, Moctu realized he was now a shade taller than his powerful friend, and it surprised him that he had grown that much.

"And you eat much meat too," Hawk continued, chuckling as he patted Moctu's stomach.

Now in his sixteenth year, Moctu had developed into a tall, well-built young man. His shoulder-length dark hair just touched his broad shoulders, and he moved a thick strand of it behind an ear as he looked down at his stomach.

"I—"

Still chuckling, the big red man cut him off. "You too skinny back then. Now good."

Hawk slapped his back, and Moctu laughed, enjoying his friend's high spirits.

Moctu had brought a treasure trove of goods with him as gifts for the Krog. Hawk and the other men had been especially pleased with the flint spearheads, awls, and bone needles, and the Krog healer, Rah, was delighted with the assortment of herbal medicines that Nindai had provided. Nuri carried in her tunic pocket the beautiful children's hatchet blade that her uncle Samar had given her as a child. Expertly made from black glass which encapsulated small, white snowflakes, it was exquisite, and she'd given it to Elka. Since it was razor sharp, she'd keep it for her until Elka was a little older.

Four moons had come since the long nights of winter, and the snows were rapidly receding as new foliage in every shade of green burgeoned on the hills. The air smelled fresh, perfumed with the scent of new life. People, both Krog and Nereans, spent as much time as possible in the open, soaking up the sun's rays. Although the early hunting had been meager, the dried mammoth meat had held up well. Hawk and Da, the nominal Krog leader, and Da's best friend Ronk, were prepared to set off on another hunting expedition in the morning, and Moctu planned to go along.

Evenings were still cold, and Moctu and Nuri huddled affectionately, a large fur wrapped around them both. Moctu prodded the glowing embers of the fire into a pile as they sat on a log in Rah's hearth. Night was falling quickly, and bats carved arcs through the starry, moonlit sky. Recently fed by her nursemaid, Lok, Elka was already asleep in soft furs next to Rah.

"Brud Moctu," Hawk called out as he approached the group. "Change plan," he said, frowning slightly while widening the opening in the hanging skins that marked the hearth entrance. "Morning we trade with Mung for woman. Mung bad tribe, but good womans. Lok from Mung," Hawk said, referring to the younger of his two mates, his frown softening.

A signal fire had been seen from a hill to the north, and from a distance, the outline of a potential trade had already been worked out—the woman for two skins of dried meat. In normal years, it would have been a woman for woman trade, but sickness and the fierce hiss-gaw saber-tooth cat had thinned the ranks of Krog females this past year. And typically, two skins of meat wouldn't have been enough, but the Mung were hungry.

"I'd like to see that—the Mung and the trade," Moctu said with interest. "How will it happen?"

"We...um..." Hawk's forehead and large brows furrowed, then he pantomimed setting two large skins down. "Leave two skins meat in meadow. Girl come us, Mung take skins."

"That sounds pretty simple. And you've got plenty of dried mammoth meat, so it seems like an obvious deal."

"What means obvious?"

"Obvious...um...it's clear, hard to argue against."

"Obvious. Good trade is *obvious*," Hawk said, stressing the word, plainly pleased with it. "We go first light to make trade—is obvious," Hawk said.

Moctu smiled and good-naturedly rolled his eyes. "I'll be ready."

***

IT WAS LIGHT, BUT the sun had not yet crested the eastern mountains when the four men set out the next morning. It was a hard morning's walk, up hills and down. Hawk and Ronk each carried a large skin loaded with dried mammoth meat. Da was especially excited because the woman they were trading for was to be his mate, a replacement for Zat, his former mate, who'd been killed by a saber-tooth the year before. Moctu grimaced as he recalled finding Zat's partially eaten body. Trying to rid his mind of that image, he said, "Will the Mung be on that next hill over there?"

Hawk, breathing heavily after a steep uphill climb with the heavy pack, just nodded.

The area was heavily wooded with huge boulders strewn between the trees. Halfway down from the crest of the far hill they saw smoke from a small fire and they could see two Mung traders with the woman standing in a landslide meadow. The traders waved at them, and pointed to a broad meadow in the valley between the two hills, and Hawk and Da waved back in understanding. Moctu again noticed that Da was missing the ends of several fingers, probably the result of frostbite. Moctu smiled as he studied Da's happy and expectant expression. He was perhaps the fiercest-looking man that Moctu had ever seen—as strong as Hawk and even bigger, but with teeth that had been filed into fangs, giving his open mouth the look of a snarling wolf. Today, his ferocious appearance couldn't conceal his cheerful excitement.

They proceeded toward the meadow following the quick-moving, enthusiastic Da. They arrived at nearly the same time as the

Mung group did on the far side of the meadow, even though they'd traveled almost twice as far.

Da's best friend Ronk, a brown-eyed, barrel-chested man with long, tangled brown hair, put down the heavy skin of dried meat and expelled a loud breath through his two missing front teeth. In Krog he said, "The woman looks good, Da!"

Da smiled and nodded in agreement. From this distance he could see that she was light-brown-haired and a little thin, but she looked strong enough, and healthy. Although he tried to hide it, Da's eagerness was barely contained.

The Mung men across the meadow looked expectant and nervous. The young woman looked terrified.

By signing, the Mung indicated that the two skins of dried meat on the ground near Ronk looked big enough and would suffice as trade for the woman. Everything looked set for the trade to be completed. That's when the attack came.

3

THE ASSAILANTS HAD HIDDEN on Moctu's side of the meadow long before they got there. Hawk heard something just before a shrill whistle sounded, and he'd already pulled his spear from behind him when the forest seemed to erupt with movement. In his peripheral vision, Moctu saw the two Mung charge toward them with their spears held ready, but his group had more pressing problems close at hand. The nearest attacker, a huge Pale One covered in leaves and dirt, and with charcoal-blackened eye sockets and red tattoos on his temples and forehead, slashed Ronk across the shoulder as he swiveled to avoid the spear thrust. Ronk lunged at the man, and they tumbled to the ground, fighting savagely. Ronk grabbed the man's brown beard with one hand and hit his face and gouged at his eyes with his other. The snarling, dirt-covered man dropped his spear and slugged Ronk's jaw a vicious blow with his right and pulled out a bloody handful of Ronk's hair with his left.

Hawk and Da were holding their own against at least three attackers who wielded spears and clubs. Pivoting and absorbing the blow of a club to his shoulder, Hawk sliced the dark-haired man holding the club across the face with a lightning-fast swing of his spear. Blood sprayed from the face and Hawk's spearpoint, and the man screamed and drew back in pain. The swing had left the butt end of Hawk's spear up, and he thrust it at the next closest attacker, hitting him squarely in the lower neck.

Moctu had long ago realized he couldn't fight Pale Ones spear to spear—they were too strong and powerful—so he pulled his atlatl and quickly fitted a shaft. He knew his group was barely holding off the nearest assailants, and they'd soon be overwhelmed by the two charging Mung. He threw hard at the nearest one, and although he rushed the shot, it hit the man with force in his midsection. The man grunted, grabbed at the shaft, and veered off. Moctu had a momentary flashback to his engagement with the wolves long ago. These were wolves too—wolves with spears.

Da's eyes and beard were covered in blood, but Moctu couldn't tell if it was his or an attacker's. Da was snarling, shrieking, and baring his fangs while he fended off a rock-tipped cudgel with his spear and then slashed at the man.

The wounded Mung had broken off the attack, and the other one's charge faltered as his attention moved to his partner, who groaned and went to his knees as he gripped the shaft in his stomach. Moctu was fitting another shaft when a second shrill whistle sounded, and the assailants stopped their assault and began to melt back into the forest. Even the man battling with Ronk pushed away and fell back. From chaotic turbulence and screaming, the forest went immediately and eerily quiet except for the slight rustling of leaves as the attackers retreated. Moctu threw a shaft but missed as the Mung helped his hobbling friend move away.

The group were breathing heavily as they assessed their injuries. Ronk's shoulder was badly slashed and blood drained from his temple where the hair had been ripped away. Da's cheek was sliced to the bone from near his eye to his earlobe. Except for the shoulder bruise, Hawk was uninjured, as was Moctu. The young woman, their whole reason for being there, was gone.

"Shiv." Hawk said simply. "Shiv and Mung." He scowled and spit.

Da's facial cut pulsed blood, which seeped through his red beard, darkening it and dripping a steady stream onto the skins draping his chest, which were now covered with it. Da didn't seem to even notice. He glowered, showing his fangs, and said in Krog, "We follow Mung. Catch, kill wounded one."

"We need to have Rah tend your wound," Moctu said, his eyes transfixed by the pulsing blood.

"We get Mung," Da said more forcefully, and Moctu realized the big man was as angry about losing the woman as he was with the Mung betrayal.

Ronk's wounds weren't as bad as Da's cheek, so all of them moved out following the trail of the two Mung, cautious of the threat of another ambush. It was an easy trail to follow—two men, one shuffling, the other supporting him, and lots of blood spatter. The group came upon the wounded man sitting against a downed tree by himself. His partner was gone. The man had both hands gripped around the shaft in his belly and was trying to pull it out, although he was in great pain and weakening fast.

Da raised his spear, but both Hawk and Moctu stopped him from killing the man right away.

"Let's figure out why the Mung and Shiv are working together," Moctu said.

Dark red blood oozed in a steady stream where the shaft protruded from the Mung's intestines. It was clearly a mortal wound. Hawk knelt and began questioning the man, speaking with a mix of Krog, Mung, and signing. The man at first refused to answer, but Hawk shook the shaft, eliciting shrieks and a rapid stream of conversation. Mostly for Moctu's benefit, Hawk gave the group a summary as he learned details from the dying man.

"It was Shiv," he confirmed. "Five Shiv tribes and Mung together."

"Shiv tribes had winter sickness. Many womans die."

After a few more comments, Hawk stood, looking stricken. "We go now—fast."

Da and Hawk quickly nodded at one another, and Da efficiently stabbed the man in the throat with his spear. The Mung died instantly.

As Hawk turned and started to run in the direction of their shelter, he yelled, "Shiv attack Uhda!"

4

NURI SHIVERED AS SHE arose from her sleeping furs and rekindled
the fire. Moctu had left early this morning, careful not to wake Elka
and the others in the hearth. Rah, normally the first one up, was
still asleep. After others had retired to their sleeping furs last night,
she and Nindai had stayed up well into the dark hours, talking
awkwardly but excitedly about medicines and remedies. Earlier that
day, Rah had shown Nindai a green, fan-shaped fungus that kept
wounds from festering and helped with tooth rot. Two days before,
she'd found a patch of Jin, yellow-brown mushrooms with a bell-
shaped cap that intoxicated people and allowed them to glimpse the
Spirit world. Around the evening fire, she described their effects and
passed the mushrooms around, but all had decided to wait until later
to try them. Moctu had felt his chest tighten as he remembered Effie
giving him some shortly after he was first brought to the Krog shelter.
It had led to wild dreams...and to other activities that ultimately
produced Elka.

Conversations between the two healers were mostly pointing and
pantomiming, but it seemed to work for them. They were learning
so much from one another. Rah was entranced when Nindai played
long, haunting notes on his flute, which she learned had important
roles in some of his remedies.

Elka began to stir, and Nuri worked faster to get through some
of her chores before needing to tend to the toddler. As soon as she

awakened, Elka would need to be cleaned up quickly and then whisked to her nursemaid Lok to limit her crying. Like Nereans, the Krog frowned on extended crying as it brought out evil spirits. Nuri and Rah were splitting the childcare, and this was Nuri's day. She put her hand to the gentle bulge of her abdomen and wondered if Elka would soon have a brother or a sister. Smiling at the thought, Nuri reflected happily on how her life had changed. Here she was—sick most mornings, and many days travel from her family and friends, living in a Pale One camp, not understanding the language or their customs. And yet she was as happy as she'd ever been. That was mostly because she was here with Moctu, and she was carrying his baby. But there was more. She was fascinated by these people, and she was learning so many new and amazing things.

Elka made waking noises, and Rah groggily sat up, pushing her sleeping furs to the side.

"Good morning," Nuri said, smiling. She spoke in Krog, using one of the few phrases she knew.

Rah, still sleepy, smiled, waved, and yawned.

Although they got along well, and although Rah was obviously pleased to be learning so much from Nindai, Nuri sensed a level of anxiety in her. Nuri was sure that Rah dreaded the day she'd lose her granddaughter when Moctu and Nuri left with her. That day should have come already—Moctu, Nuri, and Nindai had been away from their people for far longer than planned. But their time here at Uhda was relaxed and pleasant, and Nindai was still learning wonderful new remedies, so they kept postponing their departure.

The Gathering of the Tribes was to be held early this summer near the Lion People's shelter, and that would force the issue in the next day or so. They had to leave soon to have enough time to prepare themselves and their people for the big event. One of the elders, Ono, was filling in as leader while Moctu was gone.

My mate will be leading our tribe, and he'll be taking his daughter—our daughter, Nuri thought proudly.

"But it's going to tear Rah up to have her granddaughter leave here," she murmured to herself, shaking her head. "I know how I'd feel if the roles were reversed."

Neighboring hearths began to bustle with activity, and Nuri was likewise industrious, getting Elka cleaned up and to and from Lok for nursing, and many of her other tasks underway or completed. Rah left to find Nindai, but soon returned after she learned that the young medicine man was already out looking for the plants he needed to show her how to make a toothache remedy.

As Elka contentedly puttered nearby, Nuri expertly twisted conifer-bark fiber into three-ply cordage to make a net that could be used in catching frogs and fish. She wanted to try it down where the creek fed into the lake where she'd seen a number of medium-sized fish. If the Krog had nets, she hadn't seen them. If hers worked well to catch the fish, they'd likely want to learn to make one like it.

The morning was clear and warming up to a pleasant temperature as the sun fully crested the eastern hills. It was tedious, repetitive work, and Nuri's mind wandered, first to Avi—she really missed her best friend—and then to Moctu. She smiled again, thinking of how good it felt when he held her. It was so different now than it had been with Jabil. Moctu was incredibly passionate, and he was tender, caring, and patient. She sucked in a small breath as she remembered the best parts of the previous night.

Then the Spirits overturned her world.

5

NURI HEARD A MAN'S shout followed by women screaming and yelling, and she went to the hearth entrance to see what was happening. Rah, who had been in the neighboring hearth visiting, was also immediately out to determine what was causing the commotion at the far end of the shelter. Nuri couldn't understand the language, but she recognized the look on Rah's face—fear. Instincts took over, and she grabbed Elka and began running away from the noise and pandemonium. But where to run to?

With Nuri pregnant and carrying Elka, it was just moments before Rah had caught up with her. The healer still looked frightened, but it was masked by determination. She carried a spear with an ease that made it clear—she knew how to use it. From what Nuri had seen, she was sure Krog women would make formidable foes.

Pointing to the southeastern forest, Rah said, "We go there." Then, pointing behind her, she said one word that sent chills through Nuri: "Shiv." From Moctu, Nuri knew the Shiv were a fierce group of Pale Ones, and they'd earned the name of People Eaters. Even the Krog feared these savage cannibals.

Glancing back toward Uhda, Nuri was shocked to see the bedlam. Painted men—with white stripes on their faces and arms and blackened eye sockets—were ransacking the hearths and fighting with the few individuals that had not run. Worse, she saw several of the hideous, painted men following not far behind them. And they were gaining.

The two women entered a trail into the forest, and they were soon out of sight of their pursuers. Both Nuri and Rah were sprinting, but Nuri was breathing heavily and her legs felt leaden. Rah sensed her failing endurance, and she motioned to a scrub oak and buckthorn thicket to the right where they could hide. They plunged into it, the branches and thorns clawing at them as they progressed. Elka had been quiet to this point, but now she started crying in earnest. Still moving fast through the thicket, Rah and Nuri looked at each other worriedly—Elka's crying would give them away. They might as well not even hide.

Stopping to face Nuri, Rah commanded, "I take Elka." Not waiting for agreement, she gave the spear to Nuri and put the crying baby to her chest, rocking and cooing while she and Nuri once again began wading through the brush as fast as they could. Elka continued to cry and the women anxiously looked at one another as they heard the Shiv enter the thicket.

Rah knew the thicket well, and she weaved from small trails to nonexistent ones while Nuri found the spear difficult to maneuver through the underbrush.

"We need to split up," Nuri said breathlessly. "I'll lead them away."

But Rah grabbed her forearm and motioned, "No." Nuri was shocked as Rah covered the toddler's nose and mouth with one hand, snuffing out her cries, but not allowing Elka to breathe. "All dead if they find us," she said, her lips pursed and tears in her eyes. She turned and ducked farther into the thicket. Nuri stood motionless, her mouth open, her brow furrowed and her mind racing.

The nearby sound of their pursuers roused her, and she silently followed Rah through the wall of vines and underbrush. Rah had hunkered down in a dark corner of the deep thicket, her hand still covering Elka's nose and mouth. Nuri settled beside them, worriedly watching as Elka's big blue eyes widened in shock, and her arms moved in protest at not being allowed to breathe. They could hear the men talking and calling to one another. They had split up to better search through the underbrush.

Elka's arm movements slackened then stopped, and her tiny arms fell to her sides. One of the men was close enough that they could see his movement through the tangled vegetation. Nuri's eyes moved back and forth from Elka's motionless body to the flashes of movement of the nearby Shiv.

Rah still held Elka's mouth and nose, and seeing the tiny, slack body, Nuri knew she had to act or Elka had no chance. She lay the spear at Rah's feet, and their eyes met. Rah almost imperceptibly shook her head from side to side, but Nuri answered with a slight nod, her jaw set. Alarmed, Rah shook her head more forcefully.

The matter was settled as one of the Shiv began moving closer toward them. Nuri broke and ran, leading the man away from Rah and Elka. He barked out a call to the others, then whooped and yipped bizarrely as he followed in pursuit.

Nuri crashed through the underbrush following one tiny game trail after another, the branches and thorn vines ripping at her skin and clothes. The weird, yipping noise came from several directions now, and she knew all of the Shiv attackers were pursuing her.

Sounds like a pack of hyenas, she thought, moving even faster. Can't let them hurt my baby! She was breathing hard through clenched teeth, making split-second decisions about which small break in the foliage to take. Although her arms and legs were bleeding from scratches and there were thorns lodged in both her feet, she took pleasure from the thought that her pursuers likely were suffering similarly—and they didn't sound like they were gaining on her. Her head was throbbing and she was nauseous, but she pressed on, looking for a place to hide. Have to stop—can't keep going, she thought.

"Spirits, please help me keep my baby safe," she whispered.

6

THE GRIM-FACED MEN RAN with purpose, Moctu leading the way.

I will never forgive myself if something has happened to Nuri or Elka, Moctu thought as he sprinted down a steep slope. Or Rah or Nindai, he added, and picked up his speed even more.

Da's face still oozed blood, and the front of his clothing skins were covered with it, staining them a dark scarlet. All the men were winded and breathing heavily through their mouths. Looking back, Moctu caught sight of the huge, fanged, blood-soaked warrior, and he was glad the man was not *his* enemy.

Because of their urgent pace, and their stashing of the meat skins under some fallen logs and leaves, they had covered the return trip in less than half the time it had earlier taken them.

"Please, Spirits, don't take Nuri, Elka, or Rah from me," Moctu whispered as he ran. "You've already taken…" he trailed off. The men rounded a hill crest, and they could see smoke from Uhda—too much smoke.

"I see body," Hawk said, squinting his eyes, his large brow furrowed. "Look like two."

All four men picked up their pace, catching glimpses through the trees of the scene at Uhda while focusing on the uneven trail that they pounded along.

They were soon close enough to see that Uhda was abandoned. No one was there except for the two bodies—Nug and one of the

Shiv, a large warrior with white lightning bolts painted on his arms, darkened eye sockets, and the distinctive red tattoos on his forehead. It was eerily quiet. The shelter was normally bustling with activity and noise, but now there was ghostly silence punctuated by the occasional popping or crackling of the burning skins, grass bedding materials, and fallen wood poles. The place had been ransacked, with most of the skin walls pulled down and the vital meat stores plundered.

Hawk knelt by Nug, who was lying face up near a smoldering pile of furs. He was not only dead, but his body had been mutilated with every part of it stabbed or slashed. Scowling and gripping his spear so tightly that his knuckles were white, Hawk raised the spear high above him and screamed, "Aaaarrrrrrr!

Da and Ronk likewise raised their spears and roared, "Aaaarrrrrrr!" They stabbed the dead Shiv warrior in the midsection, then spat on him.

Moctu desperately scrambled between the ravaged hearths for signs of Nuri, Elka, or Rah.

"Oh, Spirits…Spirits, no…NO!" he said, his panic building ever higher. "The People Eaters…Spirits, no. Please, no. Nuri! Elka! Rah!"

Behind him, Hawk let out a cry that became a mournful wail.

"Naaaaaaa!"

Moctu rushed back to find his friend kneeling by the body of Cha, his older mate. Cha was dead from many stab wounds, but her right hand still gripped a spear.

Hawk shook his head and kept repeating, "Naa, naa," in an ever-softer voice until his lips moved and no sound emerged.

Moctu put his hand on Hawk's shoulder, and the big, red-haired man turned to him with glistening eyes. Moctu had never seen his fierce friend so devastated. The burly warrior tried to say something, but no words came out. Hawk had shown anguish before, when his friend, Sag, died of the spotted lekuk disease, but this was much worse. He looked back down at his dead mate and continued to shake his head, not believing what he was seeing. The quiet desolation of his Krog brother was deeply moving but also unsettling.

"Hawk, I'm so...so..." Moctu felt a choking sensation in his throat and couldn't finish.

The two men were quiet for a long moment before Da and Ronk approached, each silently patting Hawk's shoulder, then kneeling beside Cha. Da reached over and felt the edge of the spear that Cha still held, then showed the blood on his fingers.

"Blood," he said in Krog. "Cha fought. She hurt them."

Hawk nodded but remained silent.

Worries about Nuri and Elka resurfaced, and Moctu cleared his choked throat.

"I'll come back, Hawk. I need to look for Nuri, Elka, Rah, and the others."

The comment stirred the men to action.

"Mik and Lok," Hawk said, rising, now even more worried about his son and younger mate.

All four men moved out, hoping to find evidence of their loved ones and friends. Wary of another Shiv ambush, they were cautious as they began searching the edge of the forest. Disturbingly, they found few fresh signs of their kinfolk. The main set of tracks indicated that most of the Shiv had moved east after the raid. How many captives had they taken with them?

7

RAH WAS TREMBLING AS she took her hand away from Elka's mouth and nose. Even though the Shiv were still close enough to hear a baby cry, the little girl's body was limp—either unconscious or dead.

She's not breathing—if I don't try to bring her back now, she doesn't stand a chance. But if she does come to and cries, we may both be dead, Rah worried and delayed.

Have to risk it, she thought finally. Rah pushed twice on Elka's abdomen.

Elka remained motionless, not breathing, her skin a sickly gray color. Rah continued to push and prod the little girl, but to no effect.

With every one of my heartbeats, she moves farther into the Spirit world, Rah thought desperately, and she pushed more vigorously on Elka's abdomen. She paused and watched Elka's chest to see if she was breathing or still moving into the darkness.

"Oh, Elka, come back," she moaned softly. "You are loved here. I'm so sorry—I was...I was trying to save both our lives." As Elka lay lifeless, her small arms sagging limply at her sides, tears welled in Rah's eyes. She put the small, slack body to her chest and squeezed her in a warm hug. "Live," she whispered in Elka's ear. "Live!"

Rah could no longer hear the Shiv, and she cursed herself for covering Elka's mouth too long. "I should have tried to bring her back sooner. If only I had started sooner... Oh, Spirits! Please bring Elka back to me! Spirits, please!"

Rah lay Elka on the ground and pushed on her chest and abdomen with more force. She knew the chest had to move in and out for life to come back. She stopped to see if there was any life returning, but the small form lay motionless, her arms splayed to the sides and her mouth slack and open.

Rah bent close to Elka, her mouth next to the little girl's. "Breathe!" she pleaded. "Live!" She pushed on Elka's chest. "Live!"

Rah's heart leapt as she thought she felt a small shudder. "Live!" she hissed louder and pushed again. The little girl shuddered and a wheeze escaped her mouth. Rah's heart swelled, and huge tears rolled down both her cheeks.

"Thank you, Spirits...thank you," Rah whispered, her eyes closing, expelling more grateful tears.

The little girl's chest began moving in and out, her gasps gradually easing toward normal breathing. As Rah patted Elka, welcoming her back from the edge of the Spirit world, she found her hands were shaking uncontrollably.

8

Meanwhile, back at Moctu's home shelter, Etseh...

I WONDER WHY NURI and Moctu aren't back yet? And Nindai," Avi said to Jondu as they sat in their hearth at Etseh. "I hope the Krog aren't mistreating them, or that a saber-tooth didn't get them. I really miss Nuri."

"I know Alta's worried sick," Jondu replied. "Father says if Moctu doesn't get back soon, we'll have to assume he's dead—that they're all dead. And we'll have to elect a new leader."

"Ono just wants you to be leader. That's the only reason he won't lead us to the Gathering of the Tribes. He wants you to take us there."

"He has a bad knee."

"Come on, Jondu," Avi said, rolling her eyes. "He gets around fine. It's funny how that knee seemed to get worse only after Moctu didn't get back here on time. He wants you to be leader."

"And what would be so wrong with that?" said Jondu, bristling.

Avi frowned. "Because you're trying to get it the wrong way. You can't just take over as leader because Moctu's a little late getting back from a trip. Everyone's worried, I know, but there are so many possible reasons for why they're late. And most of those don't involve needing a new leader. One of them could be sick...or...they're learning something new and important like how to make fire...something like that," Avi said. "Don't go raising yourself up to be the new leader.

Not yet anyway. That'll just look disloyal—to everyone. And don't let your father get too hasty about pushing you into it, either."

It wasn't what Jondu wanted to hear, and he scowled. "Well, at some point...some point soon..." He shrugged, then turned and left to prepare for tomorrow's hunt.

Avi shook her head, rolling her eyes again. Jondu's ambition would get him into trouble. Indar, her baby, began to cry, and Avi expertly placed him to her breast and pushed her nipple into his mouth. He took it and sucked eagerly.

"They're alive," Avi murmured confidently. "Nuri's...well, she's like a sister to me. I'd know it if she were dead." A chill went through her, and she gazed worriedly at the distant mountains to the north. "But something *is* wrong."

9

THE WOODS HAD OPENED, with far less underbrush and fewer places to hide. Nuri continued running, but her head swam, and she gasped for air. She could still hear the weird, excited yipping of her pursuers, but they hadn't gained on her.

"Why can't I breathe?" she muttered. "Why am I so weak? I've got to keep…have to save my baby."

Nausea overtook her, and she went to her knees and vomited violently into a pile of leaves at the base of an oak sapling. She could feel her pulse throbbing in her ears and still could not get enough air. She spit to rid herself of the trail of saliva that hung from her mouth, then used the sapling to help her stand. Her head swam, and her stomach was sick, but she felt a surge of energy as she recognized that the yipping was closer, much closer.

The hyena pack, Nuri thought. I have to get away from the hyena pack chasing me. She set out again, running hard, heading north, as best she could tell, toward where the trees had boulders interspersed between them.

Her burst of energy faded rapidly, and she was gasping again. "Have to find a place to hide—can't keep running," she whispered to herself. "Maybe I can hide there." But desperately dashing between rocks and trees, she found nothing suitable.

"They'd find me there. Have to find a cave or crevice—Spirits— help me find a hiding place!"

Her eye registered a flash of movement in the trees, and the eerie yipping got louder.

Terror surged through her. If I can see them, they've seen me, she thought, and waves of adrenaline flooded her veins. She gave up looking for a hiding place and ran flat out. Oblivious to any possible hiding spots, she raced away from the People Eaters, zigging and zagging through the forest, trying to get out of their sight line. She passed a group of small boulders and trees that might have offered a hiding place, but her only thought was to get farther away.

Once again, her legs began to feel leaden, and she struggled for breath. Gritting her teeth, she felt frustration swell within her.

"Have to...oh, Spirits! Keep going. My baby... Got to keep running," she coaxed herself onward.

The creepy yipping of the People Eaters was always there, not far behind her.

They're relentless—just like hyenas, she thought. "And now they're off to the side over there." She swerved away from the new source of the yipping. The forest to the north seemed to erupt with new yipping and excited barking.

More of them, she thought in horror. Are these people or hyenas?

For the first time, her new horror didn't translate into new energy.

"Can't outrun them... Have to find a place to hide. Those big boulders will have to do."

She raced to the boulders and spotted a crease between the two largest ones. Scooping an armful of dead leaves, she wedged herself in the depression at the base of the parting. She hunched down and spread the leaves over her head and body.

She was breathing heavily, and she could feel the leaves move as she desperately tried to still her body. The yipping came closer, and it sounded like there were dozens of them.

"Oh, Spirits, please. Don't let them find me. *Please.*"

They were close. Although her head was bent downward, she peered upward and could see movement—several of the beasts milling around, still yipping, but sounding confused. Some yipping was farther away, apparently a few of them still pursuing in the direction she'd been going. A nearby group seemed focused on the spot where she'd scooped up the leaves. Nuri saw a large man look toward the two boulders, and her heart ballooned into her throat. She quit breathing, but she worried her trembling would betray her.

The man was fearsome—hideous, with painted white cheeks, blackened eye sockets, and red tattoos that looked like fire on his forehead. The black around his eyes was elongated down his cheeks, making them seem to bulge and droop downward. White lightning bolts traced down his huge arms.

Nuri closed her eyes, worried that he or the others would see the tiny flicker of her eyes beneath the leaves. She could feel the footfalls as the group searched the area, getting ever closer to her. They were almost next to her. Her mouth was dry, but she resisted swallowing for fear of moving or making noise. Desperate to breathe, she took tiny sips of air, and she was pleased that some of the noises and footsteps seemed to be moving away. They hadn't seen her!

Nuri screamed as a powerful hand wrenched her by the hair from her hiding spot. She was dragged outward into the open by the huge, hideous man, and a cheer went up. The group heightened their eerie yipping, which soon transformed into loud barking and howling.

10

GRADUALLY, PEOPLE BEGAN TO return to Uhda. Hawk had found a group to the west as they emerged from their hiding places after he called out for his mate, Lok, and his baby son, Mik. But Lok and the baby were not among them, nor did either show up in the other small groups as the Krog straggled back to their hearths in the ruined shelter.

Moctu scrambled along the edge of the woods neighboring Uhda, continually calling for Nuri, Elka, and Rah. He was pleased to see Nindai show up, but the lame young man had not seen the others. Nindai tried to help in the search, but couldn't keep up with Moctu's frenetic pace. By late afternoon, a heaviness had descended on Moctu—his pace slowed and the world seemed to darken. His emotions had swung wildly from hopefulness to regret, and from anger to depression. His voice was raspy, but he still loudly croaked out calls for Nuri, Elka, and Rah.

Near dusk, Moctu crossed paths with Hawk, who was similarly distressed by not locating his loved ones.

"Shiv take them," Hawk said, his eyes steely. "We go tomorrow. Find and kill Shiv. Maybe get our peoples before they eat."

"I'm with you," Moctu said, his jaw set. "Nothing I want to do more now than kill Shiv." The fiery rage was back. He was mad at the Shiv, at himself, and especially at the Spirits who were toying with him once again. They'd stolen so much from him before, but this time they'd gone too far. They'd taken his mate, his daughter, and her grandmother—and the loved ones of his friends.

The Spirits aren't toying with me, he decided. They've declared war. They're either pure evil, or they don't exist at all. He knew the Spirits might punish him for such thoughts, but what more did he have to lose? The question was soon answered. He heard the crying before he heard Rah's call.

"It's Elka! And Rah! Is Nuri…?" He let out a whoop and bounded toward their sounds.

"Elka! Rah!" he shouted as he saw them and swallowed them in a bear hug, lifting Rah off the ground. Elka, even though very hungry, briefly stopped her crying.

"Find Nuri?" Rah asked anxiously.

The elation drained from Moctu, and his brow wrinkled. "No. Nuri's not back. I thought she'd be with—"

"No, she run to…to keep Shiv from finding Elka," Rah said, looking at the little girl who began to cry again. "Elka need milk from Lok."

"Mmm…" Moctu frowned. "Lok's gone…still not back."

Rah smiled bitterly and shook her head. "Two other womans have milk. I find."

Moctu saw movement in the trees to the west. He thought it was a woman, but she moved behind some brush as if to hide.

"Nuri? Lok? It's safe…come on out." He moved toward the trees, but he pulled his atlatl out and had a shaft ready to fit. "It's safe—come out," he said in Krog a little louder. As he studied the place where he'd last seen movement, a head of long, light-brown hair showed itself. It was the Mung girl.

With the atlatl still in his hand, Moctu smiled tightly and motioned for the girl to come closer. He didn't think this was another ambush, but he was taking no chances. His eyes scanned the nearby forest and brush piles. The girl showed more of herself, but hesitated. She tilted her head and seemed to weigh her choices.

Holding Elka, who was wailing, with one arm, Rah motioned with her other for the girl to come, and she finally did. With her hands held low and outward, like she might bolt at any time, the Mung girl slowly moved toward Rah who likewise moved toward her. Rah extended her free hand, and the shy girl took it. Rah nodded toward Uhda, and without a word, they began walking together.

Moctu warily watched the forest for a while, then he, too, turned and headed for Uhda.

Tomorrow, I leave to find Nuri, he thought. And kill the Shiv.

11

SMOKE ROSE FROM THE roasting human tongues and lingered in the recesses of the walls of the shallow cave where it was protected from the breeze. The hair was completely singed from two fire-darkened human heads that had been placed upside down near the flames to cook the brains.

As three of the Shiv men neared her, Nuri stopped breathing and kept her eyes downcast at the floor of the broad, deep overhang where she sat with several others, her hands tied behind her. They were coming to take another of the group, and she was terrified it would be her. Last time, they'd dragged a struggling young man out toward the fire, and his screams still echoed in her ears. Now, they were roasting him.

Her drive to protect the baby within her was overwhelming. "Don't pick me, oh, Spirits, please, don't let them eat me," she whispered soundlessly, her fear overwhelming the self-revulsion she felt for hoping they would take someone else—anyone else. There was a pause while the standing men spoke among themselves in hushed tones. Even looking down, she could see the crude leather wraps around their feet. Her pulse began to pound in her head as the conversation stopped, and the feet moved directly toward her. Nuri's heart seemed to bulge into her throat, and waves of nausea swept over her as powerful hands roughly pulled her to her feet.

She wanted to scream, but her chest and throat didn't respond. "No, no," she moaned, shaking her head. "Spirits…Oh, Spirits, no…no." She clenched her eyes shut, and tears rolled down her cheeks as the men dragged her out into the dusky light. The sun was almost below the horizon, but the area under the overhang was well lit by two large fires. The smell of roasting meat—roasting people—sickened Nuri, and she was convulsed by waves of fear and nausea.

The blond brute pulling her the hardest cuffed her on the side of her face, stunning her. Nuri quit her resistance, and stumbled toward the men gathered around the fires. There were a lot of them—easily more than two hands. She recognized the man sitting on the highest rock at the far end of the largest fire. He was the huge, hideous one who had found her and wrenched her from her hiding spot earlier in the day. After that, her hands had been bound and her head and eyes covered until they got to this shelter. Although unable to see much as she stumbled along the trail, she knew they had walked a long way that afternoon.

The hideous man's face was still painted with the nightmarish, dark eye sockets, and Nuri could tell he was the leader or a man of stature by the way the men addressed him. He stood and waited for her to be brought in front of him. She sensed that this man would decide her fate.

Am I to be eaten tonight? she wondered, as if in a dream. Although her pulse raced and her lower lip trembled, she managed to raise her eyes and stare at him defiantly. She allowed him to stroke her long, luxuriant black hair, and he did it a second time, apparently liking its feel. With a strong hand, he raised her head higher and studied her face. She twisted and jerked her head from his hand and he laughed. The men around the fire, largely quiet to this point, also laughed and made raucous-sounding comments.

As she twisted, Nuri caught sight of the two fire-blackened heads near the fire. Her eyes widened, and her knees almost buckled. She let out a soft moan, and the man laughed again, this time reaching to grab her breast. Although she twisted again, he grasped her bottom and pulled her closer to him. He seemed pleased by what he felt, and Nuri suddenly realized that he was evaluating her—was she to be food or kept for sex. As horrified and repulsed as she was, a sense of hope swept over her.

Maybe I won't be eaten! My baby... Maybe... Nuri remained motionless as his hand moved between her legs and explored her wetness. He sniffed his fingers appraisingly and then, with a jerk of his head, motioned that the blond man should take her away from the fire to a different part of the shelter.

I'm going to live! she thought. My baby's going to live! At least for now.

12

THE KROG REPLACED FALLEN poles and salvaged partially burned furs, and Uhda was gradually returning to a semblance of the bustling shelter it had been before the Shiv attack. The tribe's immense sadness at their losses was deepened by a crushing humiliation. The Shiv had surprised and beaten them this time, but they would retaliate. A palpable rage simmered just below the surface in men and women alike.

Da sent Ronk back to retrieve the two skins of dried meat they'd left at the trading site. Since the Shiv had ransacked their food stores, the two skins represented most of the food that the Krog had left. They would need a successful hunt very soon.

People gathered briefly but solemnly as Nug and Cha were buried. The dead Shiv that was found close to Nug had been hacked on, partly dismembered, the pieces then dragged to the refuse pile and left to be feasted on by birds and rats.

Rah and Nindai attended to Da and the other, mostly minor, injuries the Krog had suffered. The Shiv had inflicted a few of these, but the bulk had come as people frantically escaped. The Mung girl, who called herself Sima, had fallen while running away, wrenching her back and lacerating her knee. Nindai massaged her back and put a poultice on her shoulder. Then he carefully cleaned the knee wound, put a sphagnum moss dressing on it, and tied it off with a strip of soft leather. Da was delighted by Sima's arrival, but his fangs, the huge gash across his face, and his bloody clothes terrified the young woman.

"No," Rah said forcefully as she faced off with the fierce warrior who wanted to take the girl back to his hearth. Sima cowered behind Rah.

"Sima stays with me," Rah insisted, and added, "for now," when she saw Da's menacing eyes. "Your face heals, and Sima gets more comfortable with Uhda—and you...then."

Da relented, but he decided that he wouldn't accompany Moctu, Hawk, and Ronk, who planned to leave in the morning to go after the Shiv and their captives. Da would stay and guard Uhda and let his wounds heal.

The other pressing need was meat. All the Krog knew they needed a successful hunt—and soon.

"We need good hunt, but first kill Shiv, get Lok, Mik, Nuri, and the others," Hawk said. "All fast-fast." He frowned and pulled on his disheveled red beard. None of it was likely to be easy—or fast.

***

THE MORNING WAS COLD, and the sky was a mottled, dull gray. The dreary sky mimicked the mood of the small group as they set off in pursuit of the Shiv marauders.

"We're chasing a well-armed, much larger group of warriors than us. And they have hostages...hostages that we can't allow them to harm," Moctu said to Hawk. "Once we catch the Shiv, what do we do?"

Both Hawk and Ronk, who had only understood a few words, nodded. Hawk's eyes locked on Moctu's. "Catch them," Hawk said, his facial muscles tight. "Then make plan." And with that he was off, setting a quick pace.

The tracks were easy to follow until they came to a place in the forest where the Shiv group had stalled, split up, scattered widely, and then reformed and continued on their way, this time with more people. Moctu was convinced that this was where they had captured

Nuri, and perhaps others. There were no bodies or signs of blood, so maybe she was still alive.

"Less than one day ahead," Hawk said after studying tracks in a muddy portion of the trail.

"How many of them are there...how many hands?" Moctu asked.

Hawk put a fist up and opened and closed it three times. He closed it again, shook his head a little, then opened it slowly again.

Moctu's eyes widened. "Three hands, maybe four?"

"One hand prisoners...maybe more," Hawk said, shrugging off the concern.

As they continued tracking the larger band, Moctu's mind raced, trying to envision a good outcome, trying to formulate a plan that might work. He could think of nothing that ended well.

Late in the day, they saw carrion birds circling in the sky not far ahead. They hastened their pace and came to where the Shiv had camped the night before under a broad overhang on a layered, gray-brown rock wall. They were stunned at what they found after they dispersed the brown buzzards which had gathered there. Bones—human bones, and lots of them, including two skulls that had been split open after cooking.

Could one of those be Nuri's...could those be Nuri's and Lok's? Moctu wondered. For some reason, he was almost sure they weren't. Maybe it was just an unwillingness to believe otherwise.

Hawk, who was looking at the area around where the smaller fire had been, let out a choked groan, and Moctu moved to his side. Hawk clenched his spear in one hand, while his other one alternately opened and closed in a tight fist. Moctu followed his gaze down to a group of tiny bones—the bones of a baby.

"Spirits, Hawk, I'm so sorry. Maybe it's not..." Moctu said, putting his hand on Hawk's shoulder.

Hawk pulled away and said through clenched teeth, "We go. Go now...catch." His voice was low and malevolent, and Moctu worried about what would happen if the rage boiled over.

Not if, Moctu thought, but when.

Hawk had led the group all day, but now his pace was even faster, almost frantic. But they quickly encountered a problem. The Shiv had split into two roughly equal-sized groups, one going north, the other south.

"Well, it makes our odds better when we do catch them, but what if we follow the wrong group? Moctu said.

His mouth pursed, and Hawk shook his head. He closed his eyes for a long moment, lifting his face to the sky. "We go south," he said finally, and he was off.

13

As THE BLOND SHIV roughly directed Nuri toward an isolated, dark part of the rock shelter, he leered at her, and even through the white paint on his cheeks, she could see that he had a pockmarked face. He had buck teeth, an upper one of which was missing. There was someone already in the space—a woman, and she was sobbing quietly.

"Lok! Oh, Lok, I'm sorry they—"

The blond man shoved her away and forced her to the ground. He began tying her legs, but then stopped and touched the smooth skin of her inner thigh with the back of his hand. She twisted away, and the corners of his mouth came up and his buck teeth showed again. He said something Nuri didn't understand, then spread her legs and knelt between them.

"No!" Nuri shouted and drew her knees together, but the man was fumbling with his lower wrap. He forced her knees farther apart, and she found it was hard to keep her balance with her hands tied behind her. Even so, she managed to kick with her left leg, and her ankle connected with the side of his face. It had no effect other than to make him laugh.

"No. No!" she cried, trying to jerk away as his fingers probed her.

A force hit him from the side, and he became partially unbalanced, an elbow going to the ground, but his knees maintained their position between Nuri's legs. It was Lok, and even with her hands and feet tied, she was attempting to knock him off of Nuri. He clouted her jaw with the back of his hand and sent her sprawling.

"No!" Nuri yelled again, and he raised a hand, threatening to hit her if she made further outcry. "Stop it," she said through clenched teeth. "No! Stop it," she continued, writhing and pulling away.

He hit Nuri hard on the ear with a balled fist. Her head swam, and both ears rang. He lay on top of her, and his rigid shaft had just begun to penetrate when there was a roar of outrage behind him, and he was pulled off her by powerful hands. It was the man with the nightmarish face, and even in the dim light she could see his lips pulled back and his teeth bared as he snarled and shoved the blond man to the side. The men yelled at each other, and the blond warrior attempted to rise, but the standing man slugged him hard in the mouth, jolting his head sideways. The man went down on his knees and backed away, one hand cupping his injured mouth.

The shouting and fighting attracted a crowd of interested Shiv behind the standing man, and they began jeering the downed man, pointing at Nuri and laughing. Suddenly cold and shivering, Nuri edged as far into the shadows as she could, and she saw that Lok was doing the same across from her. After another angry exchange between the two men, the standing man barked a command and two burly Shiv roughly grabbed the injured man and dragged him away. Another barked command and a wave of his arm elicited two more Shiv, who lifted Lok and carried her a short distance away behind the lip of a rubble wall that compartmentalized the shelter. The authoritative commands and tone made it clear to Nuri that this man was indeed the leader of the Shiv.

Still deeply shaken, Nuri collected herself and appraised the leader. He seems to be the biggest of the group, she thought, and he's…Spirits—so fierce and…creepy. Make's my skin crawl to look at his face. But he… She realized she felt grateful to him, but she couldn't bring herself to complete the thought. "He's a Shiv," she whispered to herself, "and a cannibal."

In low tones, the leader addressed the remaining group and they quickly dispersed, leaving him alone with Nuri. He approached her slowly, and she cowered away from him. He held up a hand, swiveled, and left her alone, returning shortly with two sleeping furs. He draped one around and over her, and he placed the other close by and lay down on it.

Still shivering, Nuri once again felt conflicted—despising this man for being a murderous Shiv, a cannibal, but appreciating his small attempt to comfort her. The man lay on his back, eyes open, saying nothing, staring at the lip of the shelter and the overcast, dusky sky beyond. From the neighboring area, Nuri heard Lok's voice raised in protest followed by the sounds of a struggle. Nuri bit her lip and looked pleadingly to the leader lying next to her, hoping that he would intervene. Although he obviously heard the struggle, he made no move and continued to stare outward into the darkening nightfall.

Nuri's legs were still untied, and she began to get to her feet to help Lok, but the man next to her put out his arm. No words were exchanged, but Nuri knew it was pointless to try. After the sound of a sharp slap, it was quiet in the next compartment, soon followed by the rhythmic sounds of penetration and a man's heavy breathing.

Nuri was now sure the leader would soon turn her way and come for her, and she considered whether to fight or submit.

"If I fight too hard," she muttered, "he'll just have me eaten at the next meal. I have to stay alive for my baby...and I have to escape. But how? Moctu and Hawk—and maybe others—are looking for us right now. I know it," she continued hopefully. "But there are too many of them. The Shiv will just kill them, and I'll still be...I need to decide what to do tonight...I need a plan." She brooded over that for a while, and was surprised and relieved to hear gentle snoring from beside her.

14

As AFTERNOON PROGRESSED TO dusk, the overcast skies darkened further and the easterly wind began whipping the trees. Like Hawk, Moctu was driven to catch the Shiv, and at their pace, that might happen before nightfall. Throughout the day, Moctu's hopes for finding Nuri had faded, but he pressed on determinedly. His mood swung wildly from desperate gloom to rage, and since he ran faster during the angry stretches, he concentrated on what he would do to the Shiv when he found them.

He could outrun either of the burly Krog, but Hawk was still leading their small group, consumed with a murderous fury, convinced that the Shiv had eaten his son and maybe his mate. Although Ronk ignored his wounds, he found it difficult to keep up with Hawk and Moctu, and he trailed far behind, often almost out of sight. It was only the times when they stopped for water that he momentarily caught up with them.

It began to rain, a cold, slanting rain that muddied the trail and made each step more burdensome. Because of the clouds and rain, darkness fell quickly and completely soon after the sun went down. With no moon or stars, they had no light and could go no further. Using a torch to follow the trail would be foolhardy—they couldn't risk blundering into the Shiv camp.

"No fire," Hawk advised, and the others agreed. "Surprise Shiv tomorrow."

The night was cold, wet, and miserable as the three men huddled under a skin they placed over two springy saplings that they'd bent and tied down with a leather strap. Although the rain let up in the middle of the night, none of them got much sleep, and they were even more ill-tempered as a gray dawn broke.

"Today we find Nuri and Lok," Moctu said in a low growl, "and kill some Shiv."

Hawk snarled and nodded.

The rains had obscured the trail, so their pace was not as fast as the day before. Even so, by midday they found where the Shiv had camped the previous night and a fresh trail thereafter. They proceeded more carefully, aware of the possibility of ambush. The forests of oak, conifer, and elm gave way to lower but denser sedge of beech and scrub oak that could easily hide assailants.

After restudying the trail, Hawk frowned and faced Moctu. "Five Shiv," he said, then paused, his lip pressed tight. "Only one woman."

Moctu's heart sank. Either Nuri or Lok was dead. "So...then..." He couldn't finish the sentence. He felt guilty for desperately hoping that it was Nuri, not Lok, who was still alive. "Let's get her back—whoever it is," he said finally.

They were still headed south toward the lowlands, and at midafternoon when they crested a hill, they surveyed the brushy terrain before them.

"There," Hawk pointed. Moctu and Ronk nodded, seeing the tiny figures moving along a trail through the brush. But Moctu couldn't make out any details. Hawk shaded his eyes with his hands to see better.

"Who...which one is it, Hawk?" Moctu bit his lip, expecting the worst.

Hawk's shoulders slumped. "Not Lok. Look like Nuri." Hawk raised one hand to pat Moctu's shoulder half-heartedly.

Moctu's elation was swamped by sadness for his friend. "Oh, Hawk, I'm...I'm so sorry."

"Tonight, we get woman...Nuri. And kill Shiv," Hawk said, his nostrils flaring and a savage look in his eyes. Moctu felt rage swell inside him as well, but he knew they would have to be careful—and lucky—to get Nuri back alive.

They followed a safe distance behind the Shiv as they waited for them to make camp.

"Once the Shiv make camp, we can make a plan to get Nuri—before we kill those stinking hyenas," Moctu whispered to the others.

Well before dusk, the Shiv stopped and made preparations to camp on a low, boulder-strewn hill with a marshy pond to the north. The Shiv stationed a guard among some boulders and low brush on the west side of the camp in their direction, and as some men built a fire, others went to the pond to drink. Moctu was suddenly aware that Nuri could be what they planned to eat at their evening meal.

Swallowing hard, he said, "We need to get Nuri out soon. They may kill her for food. Hawk, can you make it to the guard and take him out?"

There was a gleam in his eye as Hawk nodded.

Pointing and using sign language, Moctu said, "Ronk and I'll circle to the south, which will take longer. When I give two dove calls, you answer with one, then you kill the guard. I'll throw some shafts, and Ronk and I will rush the camp and get Nuri. With any luck, some of the Shiv will still be down at the pond. Anyone have a better plan?"

After a brief exchange in Krog, where Hawk translated to Ronk, the two warriors shrugged and shook their heads. Both seemed excited about the chance to kill Shiv. Moctu and Ronk left immediately, and Hawk began a slow crawl through the brush toward the guard.

The sun was halfway behind the hills when Moctu and Ronk were in place. They could see Nuri kneeling while preparing the meal, facing away from them, her long, dark hair cascading down her back. There were only two Shiv near her, so at least a couple were apparently still down by the pond. Moctu's heart was beating wildly, and he wiped sweat from his hands as he placed a shaft in his atlatl, put one between his teeth, and had another ready in his left hand. He questioningly eyed the powerful man beside him, and Ronk nodded. The big Krog raised his spear slightly and smiled with his tongue partially protruding between his missing front teeth.

It was time for the two dove calls, and Moctu rolled his eyes as he realized he couldn't make a dove call with a shaft between his teeth.

Spirits, I'm nervous! he worried. Can't let anything happen to Nuri. He removed the shaft from his mouth and made two quick dove calls, then replaced the shaft and tensed to spring forward. Nothing happened.

"What the...?" Moctu whispered from clenched teeth.

Ronk frowned, put his left hand partway toward his ear, and said in Krog, "Hear something."

Moctu heard it too—commotion. "Do we go?" he whispered, more to himself than to Ronk. His stomach churned as he hesitated.

"Can't wait any more—they'll kill Nuri." Taking a deep breath, he surged ahead, and Ronk followed. They had not gone more than a few steps when he heard a single dove call.

"There it is," he mouthed in relief, his teeth still clenched around the long shaft. A surprised thickly-bearded, dark-haired Shiv turned to meet him, and Moctu threw his first shaft—and missed.

"Don't rush the throws," he chided himself. He slowed his run and followed easily with another shaft that took the Shiv in the midsection as he was raising a heavy spear. The burly man cried out, dropped his spear, and turned and ran. Moctu let him go and saw Nuri safely crouched down, looking away from the conflict. He focused on the only remaining Shiv in the camp, a shorter, dark-haired man who was facing a rush by the bigger Ronk. Ronk was bellowing a deep roar as he ran toward the Shiv, and the smaller man's eyes were wide with terror. He turned to run, but Ronk's heavy spear took him in the side, lifting him completely off the ground.

Momentum carried Ronk forward as the man fell, and Ronk's spear pinned him to the ground. He writhed in pain, clutching the spear as Ronk calmly withdrew a long, flint knife, grabbed the man's short beard, and expertly cut his throat. Blood sprayed out, covering Ronk's forearms, chest, and beard. With a gleam in his eye, he looked up at Moctu, dripping blood and crooning through the gap in his teeth.

Moctu's heart was still beating fast as he felt the glow of a battle gone well begin to dissipate. He looked to Nuri but was distracted by Hawk running into the campsite. He was breathless and excited.

"Shiv run. I kill guard, chase two by pond. They run." He looked at the dead Shiv on the ground, from which Ronk was trying to extract his spear without damaging the point. "No Shiv here?" he asked, looking around disappointedly. "I change plan...couldn't call dove sound. Guard look where I hide. Had to kill first, then call."

Moctu nodded and turned to Nuri, who was crying softly, her hands to her face. He knelt beside her and stroked her shoulder.

"It's all right, Nuri...they're gone...you're safe now."

Still sobbing, she let down her hands, and Moctu's jaw dropped. It wasn't Nuri. She looked like Nuri with long dark hair, and she was one of his people, not a Pale One. But it wasn't Nuri.

15

RAH'S HEARTH WAS CRAMPED, with nearly a quarter of it covered by medicinal plants that she and Nindai had gathered. The lame shaman had learned enough rudimentary Krog to allow the two healers to discuss uses and preparation techniques for dozens of potions and poultices. The two of them and Sima, the Mung girl, spent most days together in the forests and meadows gathering special leaves, roots, and fungus to make their remedies.

Each evening, Nindai played haunting melodies with his flute, and both Rah and Sima listened, spellbound. Every night before each of the three retired to their separate sleeping furs, Nindai massaged Sima's injured back and applied more herbal ointment to it. Enjoying the warmth and intimacy of the act, Sima hadn't told Nindai that her back was healed days before.

Morning dawned, and it was so cold that, as Rah got up, she blew out a breath to see if it fogged. Although it didn't, she shivered as she rekindled the fire from embers. As the fire brightened the skin walls and interior of the shadowy cubicle, Rah saw Sima's head of long, light-brown hair protruding from the furs where Nindai usually slept. Then she saw that Nindai was there too. Both were still asleep.

Uh oh. Dung! I hope Sima is just huddling with him for warmth. But as the room continued to lighten, Sima yawned, her eyes opened, and she met Rah's gaze. Her shy, embarrassed smile told Rah everything. "Dung," Rah hissed as she looked away, rolling her eyes.

She looked back at the girl and blew out a breath while running a hand across her forehead and through her hair.

"You are Da's woman," Rah admonished in Krog. "You…oh, dung, this isn't good." She shook her head. Speaking slowly, and using a mix of Mung, Krog, and signing, she said, "Da not happy. He kills Nindai or maybe both of you."

"Not Da's woman," Sima said in Mung, grimacing. "I don't like him…he's—"

"You *are* Da's woman," Rah insisted.

Now awake, Nindai pulled Sima closer and said, "Sima is my woman. I'll speak to Da."

"And he kills you," Rah said, her palms outstretched. "Da's not… not calm man. Da is fierce…our leader, and he gets what he wants."

Having understood most of what Rah said despite the language difficulties, Nindai put up a hand and responded, "I'll talk with him…I'll convince him. I'm not afraid of Da. I can trade for her…we can work out something."

"No," Rah said, frowning and shaking her head. "Say nothing. Da leaves tomorrow on a hunting trip. He's told me that he'll come for Sima today…he may be here this morning. He wants her before he leaves on the trip." She rubbed her face with her hands. "Let me think…let me think."

Although Nindai understood only half of her words, he comprehended all of their meaning from her tone and expression.

She knelt at the wall beside the fire and began grinding something hard, mixing in water and spit. Rah motioned for Sima to come to her, and the Mung girl complied.

Rah's eyes widened on hearing Da's voice as he approached her hearth. Rah frantically applied the mixture to Sima, then pushed her away. "Sit in the corner," she hissed.

Da pulled the skins far enough apart to see in. A long, reddish-pink scar, now healing well, accentuated his fierce appearance. His fangs showed as he smiled at Sima, and she shrank into a corner.

"I come for Sima. Now," he said. His mouth tightened, and he motioned with his head for her to get up and accompany him. His manner indicated that he had waited long enough, and now he expected obedience.

Terrified, Sima mutely shook her head, and Nindai cleared his throat to object. He stopped as he saw Rah's eyes, warning him off. Rah rose with a flaming stick and moved toward Sima, encouraging her to get up. She stopped midway and put her hand to her mouth.

"Oh, no," she said, pointing. "Sima has her menses." All looked to see streaks of red exuding from beneath Sima's loin skin.

Da's eyes narrowed, and he took a step forward to better see Sima's legs. Smiling bitterly, he blew out a sharp breath and turned and left without a word.

The corners of Rah's mouth went up, and she put a finger to her mouth, cautioning the others to silence.

"What...? How did—" Nindai said as Da moved out of earshot.

"Ochre," Rah said with a gleam in her eye, holding up some red powder. "Ground and mixed in water. But we still have a *big* problem. We just gave ourselves a little time."

16

In the darkness, next to the sleeping Shiv leader, Nuri desperately tried to formulate a plan. *I have to escape, but how? My legs are free, and he's asleep. I could probably slip away, but my hands are tied, and I don't know where I am. If they catch me escaping, they'll probably eat me. I need to save my baby—I need to survive. But how? If they use me for sex, their essence will affect my baby, and it'll be part Shiv. When Mother was pregnant with me, Father encouraged her to have sex with Samar several times to impart his creativity and craftsmanship into me, and that seemed to work. If the Shiv mate me, will my baby be a cannibal? Spirits! What do I do?*

Nuri didn't sleep at all, but by morning, she had a plan. *It's not perfect,* she thought, *but it'll have to do. Stay alive, and limit the effect of these beasts on my baby. Need to get his trust—the leader—so that he'll untie my hands, and I need to figure out where I am—at least roughly. And Lok and her...* Nuri realized Lok didn't have Mik, her baby with her. *Where was he? Spirits—I hope he wasn't...* She couldn't bring herself to finish the thought, but she guessed he was probably dead. *Poor Lok! I've got to help Lok get free too, but that may have to wait.* She could help Lok, but saving herself and her baby had to be the first step.

The sun had crested the eastern mountains, and it streamed through broken clouds as the Shiv broke camp. They headed north into more mountainous country, and the going was hard for Nuri. At mid-morning on an uphill stretch, she went to her knees and vomited. They had fed her almost nothing, so it was mostly dry heaves with a little stomach acid. Her hands were still tied behind her, so she wiped the strands of saliva which dripped from her mouth and chin on the leaves of a bush. Lok was allowed to come to her side, and although her hands were also tied, she offered up the skins that draped from her shoulder for Nuri to wipe her face.

"Lok, thank you…I'm so sorry that you…about what happened last night," Nuri said. Lok only understood a few of her words, but the full meaning came through from Nuri's eyes and tone.

Lok looked at the ground, shook her head sadly, then shrugged in resignation. Knowing a little of Moctu's language through Hawk, she nodded first at Nuri, then herself, and said, "You…I…live."

"Thanks for what you did last night. I wish I could have helped you when that man…"

Again, Lok understood most of what Nuri said. She grimaced and diverted her eyes. In a soft voice she said, "Three mans."

"Oh, Spirits!" Nuri said. "Oh, Lok—I'm so sorry."

Lok made a choked sound as she took a breath, then shrugged again. "I live."

Nuri nodded in agreement, and her eyes welled with tears. "And Mik…is he…?"

Lok lowered her head, and her stoic resignation broke. She let out a soft moan, and huge tears rolled down both her cheeks.

"Oh, Lok! Spirits—I'm so sorry." She touched her head to Lok's, and both women sobbed quietly as they walked.

By the time they reached the top of the hill, Nuri's anguish had turned into a seething desire to hurt the Shiv. Her teeth clenched tightly and her jaw out, she smiled tightly as she thought about her plan and the one small advantage she had.

"They will pay. I will make them pay…for everything."

The Shiv allowed the women to walk together, and they didn't take issue with them whispering between themselves. Nuri and Lok took the time to learn more of each other's language, and it helped lessen the sadness and strain of the journey.

From Lok, Nuri learned that they were probably two to three days from the lowlands to the south, and the Krog shelter, Uhda, was a similar distance to the west. Lok thought they were probably headed toward the main Shiv camp, which wasn't far from the Mung camp where Lok had grown up. The Shiv and Mung languages were similar enough that Lok could understand most Shiv.

"You be Shiv...maybe this night," Lok said softly.

Nuri's eyes narrowed and she cocked her head, sure that she was missing something.

"What?"

With her elbow, Lok motioned to Nuri's belly. "Keep safe... Must become Shiv. You, baby safe."

When Nuri shook her head in confusion, Lok continued. "Woman pleasured by Shiv leader...she is Shiv. No fight...show pleasure. Then you and baby safe...Shiv won't eat."

Nuri grimaced, but understood. To even contemplate pleasure with these cannibals just seemed...*wrong*. Nuri scowled and shook her head.

Lok pursed her lips, but nodded. "Live," she said, then closed her eyes and nodded again.

The women walked in silence, and Nuri's thoughts returned to the suffering that Lok had endured the night before. Three men—three Shiv! Her pace slowed, and her queasy stomach threatened to convulse again as she realized the same thing might happen to her—maybe tonight.

Oh, Spirits, she thought. I don't think I...Oh, Spirits—my baby!

She went to her knees again and vomited a small amount of bile. The blond-haired, buck-toothed Shiv warrior growled and prodded her with the base of his spear, and she rose, coughing and spitting, trying to get the acid taste from her mouth and throat.

Although Lok stayed behind with her, the Shiv began to walk between them, and they drifted apart to distance themselves from the man. Nuri was once again lost in contemplation about how she might escape.

I have to get away, she thought, and it has to be soon. Have to protect my baby!

17

MOCTU WAS SO STUNNED he couldn't focus as the woman, once she realized she was safe, joyously embraced him. She burst into tears, gushed a torrent of words, then cried some more. His head swam with questions, worries, and dramatically changing plans.

Nuri must have gone with the other group that split off to the north. Is she all right? Is she even still alive? Have they eaten her? How will I find her? We were supposed to be back with our people by now getting ready for the meeting of the tribes. I'm supposed to lead our tribe. I've got to find her. Spirits! What do I do?

The girl's name was Siduri, and she looked a lot like Nuri. She was a similar height, and she wore her long, dark hair the same way Nuri did. She was of the Lion People and had been captured in the late fall about six moons before. Like Nuri, she was about three moons pregnant, but her baby would be a Shiv. Siduri had been speaking fast in the tongue of the Lion People, which was similar to Moctu's language. But already distracted, he had difficulty following it. Now she slowed, and her voice lowered to a whimper.

"The day after they caught me, their leader…he…" She sniffed and continued, "he took me—and that happened…many times." She put a shaking hand to her mouth and sobbed quietly. "Then he… he let the other men have me." Suduri covered her eyes and looked down as she sobbed. "Sometimes…four different men in one…" she trailed off, her hand dropped, and she looked dully at the ground. "All in one day."

Kneeling beside her, Moctu patted her shoulder. "You're safe now. We'll get you back to your people."

"I…I don't think they'll want me now," she said, putting both hands to her face and rocking back and forth while weeping loudly. "I'm…ruined. I'm carrying a…a cannibal—a *Shiv*." She said the last word like a curse. "Who's going to want me?"

"It's going to be all right," Moctu said, but his mind was filled with the atrocities that Nuri was likely enduring—if she was alive.

"Listen," he said, "did…did you see any other women captives while you were with the Shiv?"

"Several days back, they brought in two that had skins over the heads, but I never saw them," Siduri said. "But one had darker skin and hair like mine."

Moctu looked at Hawk, who had been listening closely, and they nodded at one another. Hawk cleared his throat and said, "Camp here tonight. First light, go north. Find Lok and Nuri. Trail old."

The overcast skies shrouded the stars and moon, so the group's fire was the only light in a sea of blackness. Even the distant thunder brought no flashes of light. A gloom fell over Moctu as he felt the spark of hope inside him swamped by a darkness devoid of it. He could tell that Hawk felt the same. Still, aware of the risk of a Shiv attack, the group decided that two men would stay on guard while one slept.

Nervous about the Pale Ones, Hawk, and Ronk, Siduri stayed close to Moctu, bedding down next to him when it was his turn to sleep, and sitting next to him while he was on guard duty. Moctu knew Hawk was right—they had to go north after Nuri and Lok. But even if they didn't have Siduri with them, it was days back to an old trail that had been rained on heavily.

How can we track that? he wondered. And Nuri and I should already be back at Etseh, ready to leave for the Gathering of the

Tribes. He shrugged and shook his head. "That has to wait," he whispered to himself. "We have to find Nuri…and Lok."

Even before sunup, the group was off, and Hawk once again set a brisk pace. Moctu stayed back with Siduri, encouraging and talking with her. He was impressed with the pretty girl—she was intelligent, and she'd been able to learn much of the Shiv language while she was there.

"The Shiv developed a terrible disease while I was with them— they called it the 'Spotted Death,'" she said. "Most of their women and children died."

Her words brought to mind the lekuk—a spotted disease that had swept through the Krog while Moctu was with them, probably about the same time the disease had afflicted the Shiv. Thoughts of Effie surfaced, and he smiled, remembering how he had helped her treat the Krog, saving many of them. Most of the Krog that died had also been women and children. Moctu remembered Nindai once telling him that women die of disease more often than men because women tend sick men better than men tend sick women.

"That's the main reason the Shiv are raiding our camps and the camps of other Pale Ones—they need women," Siduri continued.

Moctu brightened at the comment, realizing that meant Nuri and Lok were likely still alive. He told Hawk, who seemed equally pleased, and the big Krog picked up the pace even more. The skies continued to darken through the morning, and in the late afternoon it began to rain again. Hawk caught Moctu's eye, and they both nodded, acknowledging their ability to track the northern Shiv group was getting more difficult by the moment. As the rain pelted harder, they looked for shelter, settling for where a large, slanted boulder provided a small overhang. They had no time to gather wood, so they weathered the night without a fire.

Up at first light, and retracing steps they had taken just days before, they were distressed to see little of their own tracks—two hard rains had obscured them. By the afternoon, they were back where the Shiv had divided into two groups. They knew they were in the right place. They knew this was where part of the group had gone north. But the trail had vanished.

18

Nuri and Lok with the Shiv…

IT WAS COLD AND windy. They had hiked along a barren, rocky ridge
for most of the afternoon, avoiding large stretches of ice, but well
before the sun began to edge below the western mountains, the
group began a descent toward the green trees below, which bordered
a turbulent, fast-rushing stream. As the sun moved lower, long
rays of light streamed through fragmented clouds seeming to offer
brilliant pathways up to the heavens.

Nuri was exhausted, tired from the day's walk, and ravenous. She
needed food, and so did her baby. She dreaded the evening, because
the Shiv would want sex, and she and Lok were the only females.
Could she fake pleasure? Should she? Nuri was less concerned now
about being eaten, but she worried about the impact of Shiv seed
on her baby. She was resigned that it would happen, and almost
certainly tonight. But she knew that the more times it happened, the
more effect it would have on the baby.

I can't let him—or her—be affected…become a cannibal. I have
to do something…something soon.

The Shiv were in familiar country because they didn't hesitate
at trail crossings but moved with purpose, arriving before dusk at a
well-used overhang shelter.

This is their territory, Nuri noted anxiously. If I escape, they know this area far better than I do.

The roar of the stream indicated that it was not far below them, and all of the Shiv began shedding their equipment and much of their covering skins. As the men began filing down a trail toward the rumbling noise, Nuri and Lok were ushered in that direction as well. A winding, rocky trail, bordered by vines and low growth, led to a pool of calm, milky water, which lay behind a giant boulder in the stream. Farther out, the stream thundered by, savagely pushing large rocks and huge chunks of wood downstream.

Many of the men were naked now, and even though several were close to Nuri, she didn't feel an imminent threat—their interest was not in sex. They looked to their leader, who was completely naked, and he began to speak in a loud voice.

As Nuri watched the huge, well-built man harangue his men, Lok whispered a translation, most of which Nuri could follow.

"Shiv have great victory. Spirits with them." Lok spoke some words Nuri didn't understand, then said, "Ah, this is Cleansing Ceremony." There was more translation that Nuri couldn't follow, then Lok stiffened. Her eyes became hard and her nostrils flared. "He say they take much meat."

Nuri knew Lok was thinking about her son, Mik, who was part of that "meat."

Then Lok translated words that made Nuri's heart skip. "He say all animals and people not Shiv...are food."

"So, I'm either food, or..." Nuri didn't finish the comment. She felt bile rise in her throat and fought the urge to retch. The worry about being eaten was back.

One by one, the Shiv charged into the icy water, rubbed themselves clean of their warpaint, blood, and grime, then bounded out, breathless from the cold. Last came the leader, and he too plunged under the water, staying down for a long moment before bursting to the surface with a whoop, at which the other men cheered.

With his creepy warpaint gone, the leader was surprisingly attractive—for a Pale One. He was smiling, and his white teeth were nearly perfect. As he came out of the water and got closer, Nuri was stunned to see that he had Avi's eyes—green eyes. Avi was her best friend, and the only person with green eyes that she had ever seen. His green eyes were accentuated by the red tattoos on his forehead that bent toward his brows. He had light-brown hair that streamed down onto broad, powerful shoulders. His skin was smooth and unblemished, except for a long scar on the right side of his chest that only served to make him look even more robust and masculine.

The leader approached the two women, untied their hands, and motioned for them to disrobe and go into the water. His men started shouting, "Shaka-Nu, Shaka-Nu," but neither Nuri nor Lok knew what that meant. When Nuri and Lok failed to respond, the still-naked men behind them roughly pulled their clothes off and pushed them toward the water. With the men still shouting, "Shaka-Nu, Shaka-Nu," Lok grabbed Nuri's hand and together, they plunged into the water.

The cold was intense, so overwhelming that for moments, getting out was all Nuri could think about. A numbness came over her as she dazedly followed Lok's lead in rubbing herself clean. Lok again took her hand and mercifully led her out of the icy water as the men cheered, raising their fists and shouting, "Shaka-Nu."

The shouting died down, and Nuri sensed something had changed. As she and Lok fumbled with their clothes, Nuri saw that the men, including the leader, were leering at them hungrily. She was trembling now, partly from the cold, but also from their predicament.

We're surrounded by naked savages—cannibals, who will either rape us or eat us tonight, she thought. Spirits, my baby—please protect my baby!

At a barked command from the leader, most of the men hurried up the trail, with some of them prodding Nuri and Lok in that direction as well. The men clothed themselves and took positions around two fires, which sprang up quickly. Meat began to be passed around, and Nuri was directed to the base of a large rock upon which the leader sat. The fires grew in strength, and Nuri began to feel warm and drowsy. She was so tired, and the water had been so cold. Even though she was hungry, Nuri felt her head bob as she fought the urge to nod off.

Her eyes were closing when a piece of meat was passed to her, and she gratefully took a bite, chewing quickly and swallowing, then biting off another large hunk. She was on her third bite when she caught sight of Lok, wide-eyed, grimacing and shaking her head from side to side. Realization set in, and Nuri gagged, coughed, and spit the meat from her mouth.

The men around the fire had been watching her, and now they laughed uproariously.

"Oh, Spirits! What have I done? That was meat from…I'm a…I'm a cannibal. Spirits, I'm a cannibal." She put her hands to her face, and her head sank in shame.

The laughter died down, and the men went about eating, mostly quiet except for an occasional belch or fart, some of which were followed by a quick comment and laughter.

Nuri kept her head down, shaking it slowly. She raised an eye to glance at Lok, who was looking at her, but Nuri immediately lowered her gaze.

After the men finished eating, there was a short period of what appeared to be story-telling, then the men began to leave for their sleeping furs in portions of the elongated overhang shelter. The buck-toothed blond took a reluctant Lok by the arm and led her to the northern end of the shelter. Nuri felt a strong hand take her arm and help her to her feet. She looked into the face of the leader, and from the gleam in his green eyes, she knew exactly what his intentions were.

This is it, Nuri thought. Spirits, please protect my baby. I have to do this…have to. She remembered Lok's earlier comments and wondered if she should fake pleasure. If I submit, I have a better chance of escaping…think of that. But I despise this…this savage, even though he hasn't been as awful as the others. Focus on the plan. She looked around and was encouraged that no guard had been posted. This is their territory. They feel safe.

Her shoulders slumped, and she felt numb as he led her to the far, southern end of the shelter. She noted that he had no spear or knife with him, apparently realizing that if he fell asleep, she might use them against him. He scouted the space for rocks of any size, and threw the one small, loose cobble he found far outside into the night.

At the southernmost end of the shelter two large furs were laid side by side, and he indicated that she should take the left one. Her hands began to shake, and tears welled in her eyes. Stop it! She berated herself. Focus. Have to play along to gain his trust. Nuri's jaw muscles tightened, and a fierce determination took hold. I will protect my baby. And I *will* escape.

She knelt on the furs to the left side and looked away as the leader shed his clothes. He knelt beside her and gently undressed her. As Nuri took and carefully folded her tunic and lay it close to her, the realization of her situation flooded her mind. She was naked beside a huge, powerful man who was also naked. A man who was not her mate, who was instead a murderous cannibal who would soon rape her. She would submit, because for her plan to work, she needed to gain this man's trust. Nuri knew she couldn't leave, but she felt a compelling desire to let her mind drift to a different place. Trembling again despite her resolve, she set her jaw and looked into his face. He finished removing her footwear and tucked them under his furs.

He's going to sleep on them, so if I escape, I'm barefoot, Nuri realized.

He lightly took her shoulder, looked into her eyes, and with his other hand touched his chest, and said, "Shaka-Nu."

So that's what Shaka-Nu is…that's his name, Nuri thought. "Shaka-Nu," she said softly, and he smiled.

He looked questioningly at her and touched her chin.

What could it hurt, Nuri thought, and she pointed to herself and said, "Nuri."

"Nuri," he said, cocking his head slightly and smiling. He said some words that Nuri didn't understand, and then encouraged her to lie back on her furs. She could see he was fully erect, and she braced for him to move between her legs and start. "Nuri," he said again and moved a hand slowly and lightly from between her breasts down to her mound and down her thigh. A tingle went through Nuri, and she frowned and clenched her teeth. His hand moved again, even more softly, this time starting on her neck, circling her right nipple, tracing down her stomach, to just below her mound. He smiled broadly as Nuri's nipples hardened and goosebumps rose on her flesh.

Nuri scowled at the betrayal by her body. She despised this man, and she hated what he was doing. It was like the time that Alfer had tickled her. She'd called over and over for him to stop, but he kept going. She'd hated it, and she hated Alfer for mercilessly continuing, but she couldn't stop giggling and squirming.

"No," she said, and twisted away from Shaka-Nu. Her mind was in turmoil. This is wrong…he's a murderer, a cannibal, she thought. I need to gain his trust, but…

"No, Shaka-Nu. No."

He smiled and stroked her again, this time pausing to gently squeeze her nipple between his thumb and forefinger before moving down to the soft skin between her thighs.

Nuri shivered as an electric wave coursed through her. No, this is *not* going to happen, Nuri thought, and she clenched her teeth and turned her body away from him.

Shaka-Nu chuckled and gently moved his fingers down the length of her spine to the roundness of her bottom. A massive chill went through Nuri, and she shuddered involuntarily. She lay back to prevent that from happening again. Shaka-Nu leaned down, and Nuri could feel his hot breath as he brushed his lips beneath her ear, downward along her neck, and slowly toward her breasts. He ran his tongue around her areola, and then took her nipple in his mouth and sucked gently, while his hand moved down her thigh to above her knee. More chills swept through her, and Nuri's head began to swim.

No, this won't do. This can't happen. This…a huge, electric pulse went through Nuri as Shaka-Nu moved a finger between her legs and stroked her wet, erect nodule. Unwillingly, she arched her back, and a small moan escaped her. No! Focus on the plan. Focus on the plan. She writhed to get away from his hand, but it continued its steady, gentle movement. The *plan*, she thought, and it reoccurred to her that pretending to show pleasure—or even allowing it—might actually help gain his trust.

Shaka-Nu's lips followed a slow trail from her breast to her stomach and down to where his finger was still sending riveting pulses through her body. Nuri continued writhing, attempting to separate herself from this man, and she put her hand to his head to prevent him from moving farther. It was like pushing a mountain. His powerful shoulders maintained their position, and his tongue began to probe and taste her, taking over from his finger.

This astounding feeling was something she had never experienced, and she found she could not catch her breath. Although she had never orgasmed with Jabil, she almost always did with Moctu, and she could feel the sensation building. Her thoughts were foggy but desperate. This shouldn't… Can't let this… She gritted her teeth and tried to focus on something else, anything but the exquisite feeling. Think of the plan. Would it be so bad to pretend he's giving me pleasure? It could help. Have to escape, and that means killing this man. He's a cannibal…he's… She thought how she was now a cannibal herself, and shame swamped her.

She had fought it so long that when it came, it was overwhelming. Nuri's whole body stiffened, her mouth parted, and she was staggered by waves of pleasure. The pulses of ecstasy continued for a long time, then slowly began to ebb. As her body relaxed, giant tears rolled down Nuri's cheeks, and her teeth clenched as guilt and regret mixed with a building fury inside her.

19

"WHAT DO WE DO now?" Moctu worried aloud as they desperately searched for the tracks of the northbound group. "With the tracks gone, it could take us years to find Nuri and Lok in these mountains."

"No more meat. Need hunt," Hawk said, reminding them that their food was gone. "Uhda need meat too."

Moctu nodded, remembering that most of the Krog people's dried meat stores had been stolen by the Shiv. "I'm supposed to be back at Etseh by now, and I should be hunting with my people—they may need meat as well. And they leave for the tribal meeting soon. I'm their leader, and I'm letting them down."

Ronk touched his chest. "I go back Uhda," he said flatly.

"I can't give up on finding Nuri...I just can't. I have to keep going," Moctu said, shaking his head. Anxiety flooded him, as he realized his decision almost certainly meant he would no longer be leader when—or if—he returned to Etseh. "My people will get along fine on their own," he continued with a forced smile.

"I go with Brud Moctu," Hawk said firmly.

Moctu smiled and touched his shoulder. "We'll find them," he said with more confidence than he felt.

Moctu looked to Siduri, and she immediately said, "I go with you."

"You won't be safe, and it'll slow us down," Moctu responded. "You can go to Uhda with Ronk."

Panic showed in Siduri's eyes as she flashed a glance at Ronk. "No! I won't slow you down. I go with you."

"Ronk's not going to harm you. He'll get you to Uhda safely, and I'll come there after we're finished…"

"No! I come with you," Siduri said louder. "I come with you." She kept shaking her head. "I won't slow you down—I come with you."

Moctu eyed Hawk, who shrugged, then he looked back at Siduri and relented. "All right, but we're going to move fast, and it may be dangerous."

"I'll move fast," Siduri said, relieved. "I go with you."

It was late afternoon, and Ronk decided that he would stay with them tonight and head west for Uhda in the morning. The four were hungry as they walked north along the main trail, with the men constantly on the lookout for game. But it was Siduri who spotted the rabbit, and Moctu was able to hit it with a spear throw. Siduri was jubilant that she'd helped secure food for the group, and she was very impressed that Moctu hit the rabbit from such a distance.

"A great shot! Only Lehoy of our people could hit such a target."

It was a small thing, but it seemed like the Spirits were perhaps finally with them. The feeling was reinforced shortly before dusk, when Hawk excitedly called out that he had found some traces of the Shiv trail. They hadn't lost it, and maybe they could follow it after all.

The air grew cooler, and the clouds dissipated into small, scattered patches. They camped out in the open under starry skies and huddled around a small campfire, the four sharing the meager but tasty rabbit.

"Shiv with Mung. Maybe go to main Mung camp," Hawk speculated. "I know where it is. Lok from that camp."

"All right, if we can't find more of their trail, we'll head that way," Moctu agreed.

They bedded down, and Siduri once more positioned her furs close to Moctu, as far from the two Krog warriors as possible. The night was cold, and Moctu was not surprised to be awakened as

Siduri nestled in closer to him for warmth. Her back to him, she pulled his arm over her and snuggled in tighter. He was a little cold himself, and she felt good next to him.

Moctu's head jerked up and his eyes widened as he felt Siduri begin to stroke his manhood. It felt good, and by rights, he could take another mate, but somehow, it seemed wrong.

Who knows what Nuri is dealing with right now? he thought. *They could be eating her... This just can't happen...at least for a while.*

"Siduri..." He restrained her hand.

"You don't want Siduri?" she asked, twisting to face him. "You don't... What, I'm...I'm ruined? Because I carry a Shiv child?" She began to whimper.

"No...I do want you. You're very pretty, and you're *not* ruined. It's just..." She let out a small sob as he searched for the right words. "It's just my mate...Nuri...she's going through what you did. She's with the Shiv, and it seems wrong for me to..."

In the dim firelight, Moctu saw Suduri's face brighten. "We'll find her," she said confidently. "Then maybe..."

"Then maybe," Moctu agreed.

20

Moctu is dead," Ono said to the men seated around the council fire at Etseh. "We have to face facts. All three are dead. They went to a dangerous place, and they knew the risks. They were due back almost a moon ago, and there's nothing that would have kept them away this long. They know we're leaving for the tribal meetings soon. Any leader would be back with his people for that. Moctu is dead."

He paused, and the men around the fire erupted into loud argument and conversation.

Ono waited for the debate to die down. "Whether you agree that he's dead or not, I'm the leader while Moctu is gone, but I can't travel to the meetings. It's too far and my knee won't hold up. We need to elect a new leader for when we meet up with the other tribes."

There was more loud disagreement and protest.

Palo stood. "Everyone here thought Moctu was dead once before, and he wasn't. He's alive and he'll be back. They all will... they'll all be back." He looked at Ono. "I know you want your son, Jondu, to be leader, but it's unnecessary. Moctu will be back."

"I can see the council is split," Ono said. He looked around, getting nearly imperceptible nods from several of the men. He hesitated, seemingly counting to himself. Finally, in a strong voice, he said, "We should vote. Stand if you think we need a new leader for when we travel to the meetings."

Palo immediately sat, but Ono, Jondu, Alfer, and several others rose. Ono counted and said, "It looks like a tie. Does no one else think that we need a new leader…a leader to take us to the meetings?"

After a pause, Avi's father, Petrel, stood, looking at his feet. Although he used to despise Jondu, and tried to prevent him from mating Avi, Petrel's feelings had softened toward him. As mate to the new leader, his daughter would gain status and benefits.

"Ah," said Ono. "So, we vote! I nominate Jondu as leader."

It was over quickly. The same group of men voted for Jondu, and he became leader.

Palo stood again. "I leave for Uhda—the Krog camp—in the morning," he said brusquely. "We've made a mistake here tonight. Moctu is alive. I'll find him and prove it. Nabu, are you with me tomorrow?"

Nabu, always shy in large gatherings, nodded.

21

NURI HAD LITTLE TIME for remorse or tears. His green eyes, locked on hers, Shaka-Nu positioned himself between her legs, slipped his hand beneath her bottom, and with one thrust, he was deep inside her.

I had to do this. Had to win his trust. It's part of the plan, she thought, desperately trying to resolve the torment in her head.

It felt so wrong. She thought of Moctu and what he would think about what was happening right now. Where *was* he? She tried to ignore what Shaka-Nu was doing and drift to another place in her mind. I will escape, she thought. I will escape…even if it means killing this man. I will… It was difficult to keep her attention from Shaka-Nu's energetic thrusting. Her thoughts were completely disrupted as Shaka-Nu drew back partway and moved her left leg over his head. He swiveled her to a kneeling position with him behind her, all the while staying engaged with her.

I didn't know that was even possible, Nuri thought, and she wildly tried to move her mind to other matters. But it was impossible. Shaka-Nu held her hips and rammed into her again and again. He slowed and moved one hand to where he could caress her nodule while still thrusting, and once again she scowled. It felt good, and it shouldn't. But any pleasure was secondary to the rage boiling inside her.

Nooo! Nuri thought, and she gritted her teeth and grimaced, twisting her head to the side. But this time her feelings were dominated by the anger she felt—anger partly at herself, but mostly focused on the man behind her. She drew on that anger. He's experienced—sure, but he shouldn't… *He shouldn't be there!*

Shaka-Nu slowed, let out a groan, and then began thrusting with more ferocity. Nuri felt his member pulsing and was immediately worried about his poisonous seed impacting her baby. But a smile gradually came to her face, for she was convinced that this would be the last time. She'd follow her plan. She would limit the damage to her baby. This man would never do this to her again—or to any other woman.

Shaka-Nu withdrew and lay on his back, breathing heavily. Nuri lay down on her furs, her back to him. He patted her flank and said, "You…you Shiv now."

More anger flared in her. I am *not* a Shiv! she thought, but didn't respond other than to turn toward him. Follow the plan. Have to have his trust.

Harnessing her resolve, she murmured a soft sigh and stroked his chest hair with her hand. He relaxed, and his eyes closed. His breathing became regular. Nuri continued to gently stroke his chest, occasionally pulling softly on his short beard. Nuri listened for sounds from the neighboring parts of the shelter and was pleased to hear nothing. Shaka-Nu was sleeping, and even though she was rested, her heart beat rapidly as she reviewed her plan. Now, I just have to wait for deep sleep—Shaka-Nu and the whole camp.

The glow from the outside fires was almost gone, and Shaka-Nu was snoring lightly when Nuri decided it was time.

Can I really do this? she wondered. I'm to the point where there's no going back. If I fail, they'll kill and eat me—and my baby. Can I kill this man? She rubbed the back of her neck and bit her lip. The pleasure he'd given her came to mind, but it gave her more anger than anything else. Certainly there was shame and humiliation, but mostly she felt a constant and abiding resentment. Think of your baby. Do you want the baby to have more and more Shiv influence? And Lok's baby! Rage surged through Nuri as she thought of cute baby Mik. This man was responsible for Mik's death, and for him being eaten. *Eaten!* No, this man should die, and I can do it. I *will* do it.

Nuri felt for her tunic and for the small bulge in the tunic pocket. Her heart began to pound as she extracted the small, obsidian, toy hatchet blade—Elka's toy hatchet. She felt it's razor-sharp edge, and questioned once more, could she do this?

She focused on the thought that gave her the most anger. Think about Mik. She scowled and her teeth clenched. This man was responsible. They killed him... They *ate* him. Still lying on her back, she took a deep breath, trying to stabilize her heart rate. Nuri went through her plan one more time. This is the hardest part and the most dangerous. Move fast. There'll be noise. Have to laugh it off if the neighboring Shiv get suspicious. He's lying on my shoes. Make sure you don't lose the hatchet—you'll need it.

Her thoughts in place, she knelt and moved close to his body. His breathing was regular, loud, but not quite a snore. She closed her eyes and took one more deep breath through her nose, lifting her head upward. Spirits, help me—this is it, she thought. Here we go. But she couldn't move. She put her left hand to her forehead and wiped away sweat. I have to do this. I have to escape. Think of Lok, think of her baby. Think of mine.

Shaka-Nu coughed and shook his head, but his eyes remained closed. Nuri froze as her heart ballooned into her throat. Think of the two heads by the fire. Think! Think of Mik! Do you want your child to be a Shiv? Her anger overwhelmed her paralysis, and she grabbed Shaka-Nu's beard and pushed the hatchet into his throat, moving it sideways toward her. Hard! she thought. Pull it hard! She felt a warm spray on her chest, and saw Shaka-Nu's eyes open in pain and confusion. She quickly lay the weight of her body over his face, and she felt a fountain of liquid warmth on her belly. Have to keep him from shouting… Have to limit the noise, she thought desperately.

She was distressed at how fast and how powerfully he threw her off, and her body hit the side of the rock wall hard, knocking the wind from her. He rolled to his knees, his hands still on the ground, and a gurgling roar escaped him. Even in the dim light she could see blood spouting from his neck. Still kneeling, and pushing up with his hands, he tried to stand, but the strength was leaving him, and he only managed to stagger toward her before going to his knees again. He lunged at her and managed to grab her ankle with his hand. Fear surged through her, and she stifled a shriek, but she quickly realized that there was little strength in his grip. He put a hand up in the air and gurgled, and she moved to him and covered his face with her stomach. He writhed, but then slowed until convulsions shook his whole body. Then he was still.

They had made noise—too much noise, and there was commotion in the nearest part of the shelter not far from them. Was someone coming? Drenched in his blood, she moved beside Shaka-Nu, covered herself and him with a fur, then forced a giggle, and cooed softly as if they had just had wild sex. After a little more movement, the neighboring area went quiet again, and no one showed up to check on the disturbance. Nuri lay next to Shaka-Nu's dead body, pooled in his blood, her thoughts racing.

22

AT FIRST LIGHT, RONK departed for Uhda, and the others set a fast pace northward toward Mung territory. The trail they were on ran through mountainous terrain along the western side of a fast-moving stream. They kept to the lower elevations as much as possible, as close to the stream as they could, but even so, there were a lot of steep inclines to traverse. In the afternoon, at the start of another steep incline, Siduri begged for a rest.

"Need...to stop...rest...then I go...we go fast again," she said, between breaths while clutching her midsection.

Need to remember she's pregnant, Moctu reminded himself. He turned to Hawk and said, "How about you and I scout for game around here? Siduri can rest a while."

Hawk nodded, and the men were off, down a narrow side valley.

Siduri watched them go then carefully put a hand under her loin furs. She felt wetness, and when she pulled the hand out, she was shocked to see it covered in blood. Her stomach had been queasy all day, and she retched but nothing came up.

"I promised...promised them I wouldn't slow them down," Siduri murmured to herself. "Need some rest." She lay back, her legs in the sun, but her eyes shaded by trees. In moments, she was asleep.

It was late afternoon when the men got back. Moctu had killed a marmot, and Hawk had speared a good-sized trout. Siduri awoke as they arrived and stood a little wobbly.

"We got some dinner," Moctu said, showing her the marmot. "Are you rested enough to climb this hill, and we'll camp on the other side?"

"Yes, I've rested. I can climb this one."

The three of them were most of the way to the top with Hawk leading and Siduri lagging behind. Moctu held back to wait for her to catch up, and as she shuffled slowly toward him, he saw that she had both hands to the small of her back. Her eyes were almost closed. As she neared him, Moctu was appalled to see rivulets of blood running down her legs. Her loin furs were sodden with it.

"Siduri, stop. Stay there...Hawk!"

Moctu helped her sit on a knee-high boulder.

"My back...oh...feel weak...hurts," Siduri mumbled, still clutching her back.

"Hawk! Siduri...she's in trouble," he called.

Hawk was well ahead of them, and as he backtracked down the hill, Moctu's mind raced with worries, both about Siduri's health and about the delay this would cause in rescuing Nuri and Lok.

"Aaagh!" Siduri groaned, twisting her head and grimacing. "Oh, Spirits...hurts." She moved a hand from her back to her abdomen as she was overcome by a fierce cramp.

"Siduri loses baby?" Hawk asked as he approached.

"Maybe...something's wrong down there," Moctu said, rubbing his forehead. "Something's really wrong." He looked at the sky. "Doesn't look like rain. We'll camp here, and see how she does overnight."

"We lose two days...maybe three, four," Hawk said flatly.

Moctu was just as stressed as Hawk was over this blow to their rescue efforts. "Maybe...we'll just have to see. Can't leave her."

"I'm sorry," Siduri said, her eyes watering. "I didn't mean...I'm so sorry. It's—"

"Just rest," Moctu said. "We'll figure this out."

Severe cramps wracked Siduri's midsection throughout the night, but the bleeding slowed. Some willow-bark tea that Moctu brewed served to lessen the cramping pain a little. In the morning, however, the bleeding intensified, and Siduri delivered several bloody lumps, one a stillborn embryo—a baby boy. Holding her hand, Moctu tried to comfort her, but she continually burst into tears.

"I don't know why…" she sobbed. "Don't know why I'm crying… didn't want a Shiv baby. I'm sorry…I'm so sorry for holding you up. I can walk soon. I can."

"You just rest," Moctu said. "We'll…um…we'll figure something out."

While Siduri slept, Moctu and Hawk discussed their options.

"Leave Siduri…?" Hawk suggested. "Leave fire, firewood, spear, food, water. We come back…come back…soon," Hawk's voice trailed off as even he realized the plan would not work.

"She can't walk, but we can build a travois," Moctu said. "And she can probably handle that…maybe as soon as tomorrow? It's slow, but at least we'd make some progress."

Hawk nodded, and the two men had a travois built by midday.

When Siduri awoke, she tried to stand, but Moctu pressed her to stay down.

"I can walk…I'm not bleeding anymore. I can—"

"You're not bleeding as much, but you're still bleeding. If you're up for it tomorrow morning, we'll haul you in a travois. It'll be bumpy, but—"

"We can do that now. I'm ready. I don't want to…" Her face clouded. "I told you I wouldn't slow you down."

"Tomorrow, then," Moctu said. "Tomorrow."

23

NURI WAITED TO MAKE sure the neighboring Shiv were once again asleep, then she gathered the materials she would take with her. She'd maintained hold of the hatchet, and she replaced it into the tunic pocket and slipped the tunic over her blood-soaked torso. She wrapped her loin garment around her and found her footwear underneath Shaka-Nu's sleeping fur. Although she took care not to look at his face, Nuri did momentarily catch a glimpse of it, and she took a few heartbeats to consider it. She was pleased that it didn't have the emotional impact on her that she feared it might. She felt no remorse. He was a murderer who kidnapped and raped women and killed and ate babies. Now he was gone, and that was good.

Two furs were too bulky, so Nuri only took the least blood-soaked one, wrapping it into a tight bundle. Looking around, she found Shaka-Nu's clothing skins, and she took the long, loin-skin wrap which she could use for leather straps. It'll come in handy, she thought.

Each moment that goes by, I'm taking more of a chance on being discovered, she worried, biting her lip. Listening for any sound of activity, she edged out toward the open and peered through the darkness, now lit only by stars. Hearing nothing, she crept southward, careful to make no noise. After some distance along a brushy path, she picked up her pace and moved as quickly as she could over the rough ground in the dark. Even so, it was slow going in the unfamiliar terrain.

"I'm free...I'm free!" she whispered to herself, at times almost bouncing from foot to foot with the exhilaration of it. Her joy was tempered by thoughts of Lok. "I have to get her out. Spirits, please help her and keep her safe until I can figure how to save her." Nuri was almost certain the Shiv would not kill Lok, because she was the only woman in their group, and they'd want to save her for sex. That was an awful thought, and she knew she had to help Lok soon.

But her mood was upbeat. She'd struck a blow against the Shiv, and her baby would likely be fine. "Shaka-Nu is dead...I did it...and my baby..." Nuri murmured. "Well, I've done the best I can...with luck, my baby won't be a Shiv. And they're not going to eat—" her words were cut short by a distant, but still too-close, wolf howl that was quickly joined by several others.

Images of wolf packs and the saber-tooth that Moctu faced came to mind, and Nuri stopped to cut and fashion a sharpened staff.

Stay focused on getting away for now—the Shiv are still the big worry, she thought. I'm not that far away yet...not nearly far enough...and they're going to be furious about Shaka-Nu. They'll want revenge, and they'll come hard after me. But...there's also lots of animals I can't afford to run into. Nuri decided to move west, away from the rumbling stream. As the roar of the stream receded, she began an uphill stretch and startled a large animal—a deer? It likewise startled her, abruptly crashing away through the low underbrush of the forest. Her staff up defensively, she paused to let the hammering of her heart slow. That's when she heard it.

Is that real, or my imagination? Nuri remained motionless, closing her eyes to focus on the barely perceptible sound. No, that's real, she decided, swallowing hard.

It was the yipping sound. The Shiv had discovered Shaka-Nu dead and Nuri missing. And they were coming for her. Even knowing they weren't near, the thought of the Shiv once again chasing her like a pack of hyenas made her breath catch, and she froze in terror.

Not remembering how she started, Nuri found she was running, the trees and brush scratching her arms and legs. Get away, she thought desperately. Run!

The added exertion helped focus her thoughts. Moctu said the Pale Ones are great trackers—they have better eyesight than we do, she remembered. Can they see in the dark? Can they smell better, too? Need to be careful not to leave a trail. Think! This is their ground—they know it far better than I do. How did Moctu leave misleading trails?

She slowed as she recalled some of the tricks Moctu had described from his escape attempt long ago. Coming to a creek, about as wide as she was tall, Nuri waded upstream until she found a rocky outcrop on which she could climb out of the creek without leaving tracks. There's more light now, she noted. Is dawn coming, or is the moon out and I just can't see it yet through the trees? As she moved away from the burbling creek, she could hear the yipping more clearly.

Spirits, they're gaining! They're closer! she thought as her pulse quickened. Hide! No...got to get farther away. Then hide. But first, leave a few more misleading trails. As the darkness gave way to a flat, gray light, Nuri realized dawn was breaking, and she could see trails and potential hiding places more clearly. Remembering another trick, she left tracks into a dense thicket, then backtracked in her footprints until she reached a downed tree. She walked along the tree as far as possible, then jumped to a pile of rocks. After a number of such maneuvers, Nuri felt confident that even the best Shiv tracker wouldn't be able to follow her.

"Now, to look for a place to hide," she whispered to herself.

24

Back at Etseh...

As LEADER, JONDU DECIDED the men would make a final hunting trip before most of the Nereans journeyed to the meeting of the tribes. Etseh needed meat, and hunting would be limited during the time of the meeting and games. Palo and Nabu had left several days before, heading north toward the Krog shelter, to find out whether Moctu, Nuri, and Nindai were alive and what had happened to them. Jondu decided his hunting party would head north, then swing east toward Lion People territory, scouting ground that the tribe would soon be taking to get to the meeting. The initial hunting to the north had been poor, so they veered east as planned and crossed the tracks of a small herd of caribou.

Squeezing a piece of dung between his fingers, Alfer said, "The caribou are two days ahead of us, maybe less."

The men picked up speed, and after a hard day of travel, they spotted the caribou far to the east. Exhausted but excited, the men camped for the night and, around the fire, inspected and prepared their shafts, heavy spears, and other gear for the hunt tomorrow. They moved out before daylight, and shortly after midday, they attacked the herd, not killing any, but seriously wounding two. The herd broke to the east, and the two wounded caribou struggled to keep up. The hunters followed, certain they would be enjoying fresh caribou meat by that evening.

The herd crossed a broad, shallow stream spotted with brush-covered sandbars. The wounded caribou, one with a shaft in the shoulder, and the other with two shafts in its side, were now far behind the main herd, and only a few atlatl throws ahead of the hunters. The animals paused on the stream bank before they too crossed. Both caribou were weak, having lost large volumes of blood, and they made the crossing with great difficulty. The twice-wounded caribou became stuck in loose sand most of the way across the steam, and it made loud, plaintive, croaking grunts before it finally made it to the far side.

Jondu was the first of the hunters to the stream, and he readied an atlatl shaft to throw at the closest of the beasts, which already had two of his shafts in its side. It was a long throw, and he barely missed, a little short.

Not to worry, he thought, smiling. We'll have them both soon.

He and the rest of the hunters were almost across the stream when the faltering animals stopped together, exhausted, a long atlatl throw away. As Jondu got to the far bank, his twice-wounded caribou went down on its front knees and then steadied itself, managing to stand again. Jondu excitedly readied another shaft, as did Sokum, who was also across.

Jondu twisted his head in confusion as several shafts hit the two caribou from the far side while a few others missed. His eyes narrowed, and he frowned. Someone else is killing my caribou, Jondu thought, stunned.

It was the Lion People. Jondu's band of five hunters cautiously approached the two downed caribou, their atlatls at the ready, as did a larger group of men wearing the distinctive necklace of two white shells with either a lion canine or claw between them. All warriors of the Lion People wore the necklace, with the more experienced and better hunters wearing the longer, finger-length canines.

"Thank you for finishing our kills for us," Jondu shouted. "You can feast with us tonight before we take our meat back to Etseh."

"You are on Lion People land," a smiling, well-built man with two long braids of dark hair said loudly. Striding easily toward Jondu's group, he waved his hand dismissively. As he got closer, Jondu could see that the tall man wore one of the biggest lion teeth that he had ever seen.

"We didn't expect to see Nereans for another half-moon…at the tribal meeting," said the Lion warrior. "I am Lehoy, of the Lion People, and you are welcome to feast with us on *our* meat tonight before leaving in the morning."

"Now, wait—" Sokum began to protest, but Jondu waved him off.

Although Jondu struggled to understand the man's dialect, most of his meaning had come through. Barely managing to control his own anger, Jondu studied the man briefly before replying. As an adolescent, he had seen Lehoy win the atlatl tournament at the last tribal meeting, and the man looked even more muscular and confident now. Lehoy's mouth seemed to linger constantly on the edge of a smirk. Forcing a tight smile, Jondu pointed and said, "You'll find two of my shafts in that caribou there, and one from my hunter, Sokum, in the other. We hit them on Nerean land, and they were mortally wounded. The caribou are ours."

"Two nights ago, our shaman Devu foretold that we would kill caribou on the edge of our land, and so we have," said Lehoy. "The caribou are ours. You are welcome to resume your hunt on Nerean land across the stream."

Sokum, Alfer, and the other Nerean hunters bristled, and Sokum raised his atlatl, causing the seven Lion warriors to raise theirs.

"It saddens me that the great Lehoy feels the need to take credit for kills made by others," said Jondu. "But no matter, we Nereans have made plenty of kills. Think of this as our gift to the Lion People."

Lehoy's face blanched, but his smile quickly returned. "It sounds like you won't need or want to feast with us tonight. Good luck with your hunt back on *your* land, and we'll see you at the tribal meeting," he said while motioning with his arm, encouraging Jondu and his men to leave.

Jondu gritted his teeth and turned, directing his hunters to recross the stream. As they grudgingly forded the stream, Jondu was glad his back was to the Lion warriors so that they couldn't see his barely contained rage. This isn't over, he thought. This is *not* over.

25

MOCTU AND HAWK TOOK turns pulling the travois, and Siduri gamely pretended that the nearly continuous jolting over the uneven trail didn't bother her. The travois slowed them considerably, especially on the uphill stretches, of which there were many, but at least they were making progress. Neither Hawk nor Moctu had seen any trace of the Shiv trail for two days, but they were almost certain the group was headed north toward the main Mung camp, or northeast toward Shiv territory.

At the top of each peak, they would stop to rest and survey the surrounding area. It was at one of these stops that they saw Pale Ones—two of them, either Mung or Shiv. They were walking slowly southward on a lower trail across the valley on the far side of a small but swiftly flowing stream.

"Kill," Hawk snarled. "You stay Siduri. I kill."

"Wait, Hawk," said Moctu, raising both hands slightly. "Let's think about this. First of all, there are two of them, so you're not going alone. And there could be more… Maybe we should follow them, or capture one of them for…for questioning."

"Siduri?" Hawk asked Moctu.

"I can walk," Siduri said. "Or you can leave me…for a while, anyway. I'll be fine on my own."

Moctu ran his hand across his forehead and through his hair. "If we capture or kill them, we could be kicking a hornets' nest." He paused, thinking. "If there's a lot of them and they chase us, with the travois, we'll leave a trail that baby Elka could follow. But it's probably the best way…maybe the only way to find out where Nuri and Lok are." He took a deep breath. "Let's go get those Shiv…or at least one of them."

They carefully lifted the travois and moved it and Siduri to a secluded spot farther into the forest. They left her with Moctu's heavy spear and the meager food that remained, then they were off, moving fast but silently downslope toward the men. Anticipating the men to continue their southward course, Moctu and Hawk glided quietly through the low trees and brush to intersect them. The rushing, rumbling stream masked any noise they made, but it took them some time to find a crossing site that didn't jeopardize their lives.

Hawk found a downed tree that angled out into the stream, and they were able to walk along it, then jump to a large boulder. From there, they could jump to smaller rocks, and they finally made it to the far side of the roiling water. As Moctu followed Hawk's fast strides upward toward the path, he readied his atlatl and shafts. The got to the path and set up their ambush behind two pine trees that had stopped a large boulder from moving downhill. Then they waited. And waited.

"Where are they?" Moctu hissed. "Did we miss them? Did they stop?"

Hawk shrugged and motioned for them to move northward along the trail to check for the mens' tracks or meet up with them. With Moctu leading, they cautiously moved that way, careful of an ambush and looking for evidence of the men.

They were Shiv, not Mung, and they obviously became aware of Moctu moments before the two friends heard their sounds. Moctu's eyes widened, and his heart leapt into his throat as the two brawny men charged him with heavy spears, howling and yipping like crazed hyenas. They were only several paces away, and every instinct told him to bolt, but he managed to get a quick shot off before Hawk was beside him. Seeing Hawk's heavy spear raised and his scowling, fearsome presence, the charging Shiv slowed. Moctu's shot was wild, but it hit the lead Shiv just above the left knee, and he immediately swerved to the side, limping badly.

The uninjured Shiv, a dark-haired, full-bearded brute of a man, looked to his partner and his advance also faltered. Both stopped their yipping, and as Hawk roared in fury and charged at them, the dark-haired one broke and ran. Hawk chased him but, seeing he was too far behind, turned back to dispatch the wounded man. The battle rage was in Hawk, and it was all Moctu could do to keep him from killing the injured Shiv. Hawk feinted with a thrust then followed by wheeling on his front foot and hammering the butt end of his spear on the man's forward arm, knocking the spear away from him. Pivoting again, he slashed the Shiv's forearm as the dark-haired man attempted to protect himself.

"Hawk, don't kill him," Moctu shouted. "We need him! We need him alive. Don't…"

Hawk's fury waned as reason returned to him. The Shiv went to his knees clutching the shaft in his leg. As Moctu fitted a shaft in his atlatl to throw at the retreating Shiv, the man rounded a bend in the trail and was gone.

"We'll regret letting that one get away," Moctu said, frowning.

Hawk knew little Shiv, but in Mung, he questioned the wounded man, who was surprisingly talkative. Hawk's bushy-red eyebrows furrowed, and he had the Shiv warrior repeat himself.

"They send out messengers to all Shiv tribes and Mung for more warriors." Hawk pointed at the man and continued. "He go south to get Mung shaman and more warriors to help fight black-hair sorceress," Hawk translated. "He say sorceress opened throat of Shaka-Nu…Shiv leader…bleed him…dead. Then vanish like Nightwalker."

A Nightwalker was a Spirit or person who could see and navigate in the dark like a leopard.

Moctu's heart beat faster, and he said, "Ask him what was the name of the sorceress. Where did she come from?"

After several more exchanges, Hawk excitedly said, "Shiv take two womans from Uhda. No names. One had baby...Krog...I think Lok." He paused, looking down at the ground, his mouth tight. His steely eyes returned to the kneeling Shiv, and he growled, "Baby dead." He fixed the Shiv with an intense stare, his teeth gritted, and the wounded man's face whitened in understanding.

"I'm so sorry, Hawk. Spirits—"

Hawk went on. "Sorceress not Krog...look like Dark Ones...like you. Kill Shaka-Nu, leader of the Five Clans. I think Nuri."

Moctu's pulse raced, and he found it difficult to catch his breath. "And she's escaped? She's...on her own?" He looked northward. "Out there somewhere?"

26

AT TIMES THE SHIV were close enough that Nuri could hear them calling to one another. There were a lot of them hunting for her, but she was well hidden in a dense thicket. She'd passed up an ideal site for fear the Shiv would know about it and come there looking for her. That shelter was small, where a large, flat boulder had fallen across a larger rock, leaving a tall but narrow space big enough for one or two people. It was shrouded by underbrush and a stand of medium-sized beech and oak trees. She'd use it later if she could confirm that the People Eaters didn't know about it.

The thicket she was in had a few patches of nettles, yarrow, and grapevines, all of which were edible. Before she found this hiding spot, she'd eaten some red clover, which lessened the gnawing hunger she felt. In that meadow, she also collected a small deer antler, which might come in handy. Nuri used a skin to pick the nettles and set them aside. Once they were drier, they'd lose their sting. There were no grapes, but still ravenous, she ate the leaves, and she even chewed some bitter yarrow leaves. Nuri cut and saved the grape vines for cordage. Later, she could set snares to catch small animals. For now, she just needed to avoid getting caught herself.

Sitting quietly gave her time to think and plan. She needed to free Lok, and that was going to be difficult and dangerous. Now would be a good time to do it because most of the Shiv were out looking for her. But they knew this region, and she didn't, and the risk of being caught was too great.

Tomorrow, I'll scout portions of the area, and that'll help me make a plan, she thought. And I can't let them move on, so I need to give them an occasional glimpse of me to keep them looking. Even the thought of them seeing her made her clutch her arms to her chest. Moctu, where are you? I miss you…and I need you. But there are so many Shiv—Spirits, please protect him.

Although she was an excellent fire-starter, Nuri hadn't collected any related materials, knowing she couldn't have a fire for fear of discovery. But she had furs, and she lay back to rest and began to reflect. I killed a man, she mused, wondering why it didn't bother her more. I was drenched in his blood. A man I'd just had sex with, who'd given me… She frowned and shook her head. I just don't… She paused, curious how she could be so callous and feel such a lack of regret. Her jaw set and she clenched a fist as she thought of Mik and the brutal treatment of Lok. Shaka-Nu was a kidnapper, a rapist…and a cannibal—they're all cannibals, all killers. Her lips pressed together. I regret nothing…*nothing*. I did what I had to do to save my baby…and myself. And now I'm free. And I will hurt them, she thought, scowling. And free Lok. I *will*.

A mix of anger, fear, hunger, and forest noises kept Nuri awake most of the night, but by morning she had a plan. It had big holes in it, but she had a plan. I'll free Lok, she thought, but first, I'll set traps, lots of traps—mostly small, but traps that'll injure and annoy them. I'll keep them from moving on…they'll be desperate to get me…to kill me. Oddly, that last thought didn't upset her. The corners of her mouth turned up, and there was a gleam in her eye.

Nuri scouted the surrounding area, paying special attention to the terrain northeast of her, toward the shelter where Lok was being held by the Shiv. She was careful to leave no tracks, and she stayed, as much as possible, concealed in deep foliage. It was afternoon when she found what she wanted. It was a narrow trail that led to a small peak, relatively close to the Shiv camp to the east. An even smaller trail led away to the west. She could build a signal fire on the peak. Moctu might see the fire, but the Shiv certainly would, and they'd be there quickly to investigate. Before she built it, she would lay some traps. Nuri left the trail as it was, and on the way back to her thicket, she collected an armload of sapling poles about as thick as her thumb.

She was hungry—so hungry, and her stomach rumbled loudly in complaint. Nuri drank deeply from a small creek, then looked for something to eat. She found no fish or frogs, so she settled for carving the outer bark off a mid-sized pine tree and eating the white, inner bark as Samar had long ago instructed her. She also found a small patch of wood sorrel and chewed the sour but fresh-tasting leaves until her hunger, while still there, was tolerable.

Nuri canvassed the area around the more ideal shelter in the boulders to see if the Shiv had been there to check on it. She was pleased to find no evidence of their tracks.

I'll check again tomorrow, and if they still haven't checked this place, maybe I'll move here, she thought. If it rains, this shelter will be so much better than the thicket.

Back at her thicket, Nuri set to work on the sapling poles, cutting lengths of them not much longer than her foot. On each, she sharpened one end to a hard, sharp point. Once she had about three hands of them, she smiled and took a deep breath. Satisfied, she lay back and was asleep in moments.

The sun was above the eastern mountains when a rush of wings brought Nuri fully awake. Something had startled the nearby flock of birds, and with both hands clutching her sharpened staff, all of Nuri's senses strained to determine the cause. Then she heard it distinctly— mumbled voices, Shiv voices—and her heart skipped a beat. There were at least two of them, and they were close.

Did they hear me? Did I snore or talk in my sleep? Nuri wondered, upset with herself for sleeping so soundly. I don't think I left tracks, but Moctu said Pale Ones are great trackers. Can they see things that we can't? Can they *smell* me? Can they smell the fresh wood shavings? Her palms were clammy with sweat, and she found it difficult to breathe. Her eyes widened as the Shiv began to beat the edge of the thicket with their thick spears. The urge to break and run was overwhelming her. Part of her just wanted to give up—she was so tired of feeling this fear. But the baby...no. Got to keep trying. I should have moved to the rock shelter. Why did I stay here? Please, Spirits! Don't let them find me. Don't let them...

Nuri cocked her head, and a tiny spark of hope kindled within her as she thought the men beating the brush were now moving away, not toward her. As the thrashing got farther away, she allowed herself a deep breath and whispered, "Thank you, Spirits. Thank you."

The close encounter shook Nuri, and she decided she needed to be even more careful. Maybe she'd left some tracks yesterday. When she was sure the Shiv were gone, she wrapped the sharpened stakes in Shaka-Nu's loin skin that she had taken, she hooked the deer antler on her loin skin, and she wrapped everything else tightly into her sleeping fur. Gathering all her possessions, she moved slowly—much more slowly than yesterday—through the forest, careful not to leave tracks or even move the leaves on the ground.

She scouted the area around the leaning-rock shelter thoroughly before going to it and leaving her sleeping fur bundle inside, covering it lightly with dry leaves. As Nuri was working, she made a happy discovery. The very back of the shelter was too narrow for a person, but the floor was covered with droppings—bat droppings. Looking up, she could make out perhaps two hands of the creatures tightly clustered together. She knew bats had a connection to the Spirit world, but they also represented something else. Food, Nuri thought, smiling. But later, when I have a fire.

The rest of this day is... The gleam returned to her eyes, and she shook her head. This is the day the Shiv will learn to watch *their* step. Taking the skin full of stakes and the antler, she started out, but a thought struck her and she returned to her new shelter with a large cobble. It took two throws, but with the second, she brought down a bat. The other bats screeched and a few fluttered around, changing positions, but the main group stayed in place. Nuri collected the bat and took her time getting to the narrow trail leading to the peak, ever careful not to be seen or leave tracks. She gathered fire-making tinder, pine pitch, and a good-looking, dry spindle on the way, as well as narrow, dry sticks she'd use to cover her traps.

At the trail shortly after noon, Nuri used the antler to dig three holes spaced along the trail, each about elbow deep and more than a foot across. She piled the dirt on the skin she'd brought and disposed of it inside the forest. Jamming a handful of stakes in each hole, she positioned their sharpened ends pointing up and slightly inward and then carefully laid a grid of small sticks across the top. Over the grid, she scattered leaves and dirt, then worked hard to match the look to the rest of the trail.

Nuri wiped sweat from her brow with a dirty hand and surveyed her work, pleased with the result.

"These are going to do some damage," she whispered to herself, smiling as she imagined the scene. "Wish I could stay to see it."

After a little more work building a trip snare on the other, smaller trail which led to the west, Nuri decided it was time to light the fire. She was exhausted and thirsty, and her right leg had cramped twice. Dusk was approaching, so the timing was perfect. In short order, she had a small fire started, but before building it bigger, she arranged the dead bat with its wings out on a branch not far from the fire. I'm sure they know that bats come from the Spirit world, she thought, almost chuckling. I'll bet this worries them.

It was time. Nuri piled wood on the fire until it was burning strongly, then put branches with green leaves on it. Smoke billowed into the air. She moved cautiously into the forest, then regained the west-leading trail farther down the slope. Then, as the Nightwalker, she passed into the darkness like a rustle of wind in the grass.

Halfway back to her shelter, Nuri heard screams of pain from the east, and she knew at least one of her traps had done its job. Exultant, she grinned and pumped her fist. Shiv, your time has come…now you'll feel it—you'll feel the fear. See how *you* like it.

Shelter, what is but she on man from the east, and she knew at least one of the maps had done its job wellnat she wished she'd prompted her to. "Oh, you'll time Hey Come," now say if that it—you'll feel the tick. See how you like it.

27

FROM THE WOUNDED SHIV, Moctu and Hawk learned that there were nearly two hands of warriors, and they were camped at an overhang shelter near the stream about two days ahead. And the Shiv were hoping to gather more from outlying clans.

"Two hands of warriors and maybe more?" Moctu worried out loud. "So this one's partner is racing back to tell them about us."

Hawk nodded, then pointed his spear at the Shiv and asked, "You have questions for him?"

Moctu paused, knowing what Hawk would do to the Shiv if he said no. "Now that this Shaka is dead, who'll be the leader of the Shiv?"

Even though Hawk translated the question, the dark-haired Shiv looked to Moctu as he answered, his eyes pleading with him for mercy. He was young, probably no older than Moctu. His dark hair was pulled straight back and braided, exposing the distinctive tattoos on the forehead that all Shiv warriors bore. Two red lightning bolts flashed above each temple toward his eyes, giving his face a menacing look. But kneeling now, gripping a shaft in his leg and with Hawk towering above him, the forlorn young man looked anything but ominous.

"Shaka-Teeb," Hawk said. "He say word 'Shaka' mean leader. Teeb is brud…um…brother of Shaka-Nu. Shaka-Teeb new leader of Shiv."

The young man continued to stare imploringly into Moctu's eyes.

"What's his name?" Moctu asked, pointing at the Shiv.

Hawk asked, then translated. "He is Ranu, oldest son of Shaka-Nu." Hawk looked at Moctu and closed his eyes briefly as he shook his head, indicating they needed to get going.

Even though this young Shiv had participated in murder, kidnapping, and cannibalism, Moctu felt a flash of compassion for him. Reluctantly, Moctu nodded at Hawk and turned his face, wincing as Hawk clubbed the man, then plunged his spear through the side of his neck.

Moctu's mind was racing as they recrossed the stream and headed back to where Siduri was resting. Two hands of Shiv warriors? How are we going to handle two hands of warriors? And they still have Lok. But Nuri's escaped, and she killed their leader. One side of his mouth turned up. That's my Nuri, he thought with pride. But he sobered as his thoughts continued. We're going deep into Shiv territory, way outnumbered... He bit his lip. We're leaving a travois trail everywhere we go, and carrying an ailing woman. How's that going to work out well?

It was late afternoon when they got back to her. The skies looked clear to the north, but storm clouds were rolling in from the south. They wouldn't be able to travel much more before nightfall, and they needed to find a good, safe camp.

Siduri was on her feet when they arrived. "I'll walk," she insisted as Moctu started readying the travois. "You can take the travois, and I'll use it if I feel weak...but just...not right now."

"Looks like it could storm, but we should make a little progress before we stop. There's water down the hill and big rocks...bound to be some good camp sites there. And maybe we can find one that'll keep us out of the rain," Moctu said.

Hawk was the one who saw it. He touched Moctu's shoulder and pointed to the north where, far in the distance, was a thin plume of dark gray smoke.

"That's a signal fire," Moctu said, his pulse quickening. "Is it the Shiv gathering warriors to come after us...? Or is it...maybe Nuri?"

28

Palo and Nabu searching for their friends...

STEALTH WAS KEY. ONCE Palo and Nabu saw the tiny trails of smoke from the Krog shelter far in the distance, it had taken them two days to carefully approach it. For all they knew, the Krog had killed Moctu, Nuri, and Nindai. Palo and Nabu didn't want to be the next victims. Finally in position, camouflaged by thick foliage, for the better part of a day they watched the activities of the Krog, hoping to see their friends, or at least learn something of them. Women were scraping hides, gathering wood, and bringing skins of water from the creek. Three men with spears had headed north.

"There's Nindai," said Palo, louder than he intended. "And he doesn't look like he's a captive...he's got a spear...and a woman—a Pale One?"

"I see him...and you're right...he looks like he's one of them. And she's with him," Nabu agreed.

"What is going on? Come on, Moctu, Nuri...where are you?" Palo wondered aloud, shielding his eyes and scanning the shelter.

An older Krog woman led a small child out from a middle hearth, and they joined Nindai and the brown-haired girl. The foursome headed into the western forest toward Palo and Nabu, who were much farther up the hill.

"Let's move down the hill and intersect them," Palo suggested. "Nindai can tell us what in the Spirit's name is going on."

Still using the brush and trees for concealment, the two men crept downhill toward Nindai and his companions until they could hear their voices.

"Nindai sounds normal," Palo hissed. He motioned for them to get closer.

As they converged on the group, Palo listened for any sign of duress in Nindai's voice. There was none, so he looked at Nabu, frowned in confusion, and extended a hand, palm up, questioningly. Nabu shrugged.

"Hello, Nindai," Palo said, stepping out of the brush.

Nindai's eyes widened and his mouth opened, but nothing came out. "Palo!" he said finally, and used the spear as a cane to hobble toward him.

Rah, fearful at first, relaxed when she saw that Palo was a friend of Nindai's.

"Nabu!" Nindai cried as the skinny man also emerged from cover. "Are you two alone? Oh, it's so good to see you...there's so much to tell you," he gushed. Turning serious, he said, "Nuri's been taken... The Shiv attacked. Moctu's out looking for her...he's been away...oh, there's so much to tell you."

"The Shiv took Nuri?" Palo asked, stunned. The Shiv were cannibals—People Eaters.

"Come with us...we'll sit and talk," Nindai motioned, turning to head toward Uhda. "Oh, this is Sima. She's my woman," he said, his chin rising higher. "And this is Rah, the Krog healer...she's great...a wonderful healer." He pointed, individually, at the two Nereans and said, "That's Palo, that's Nabu." Nindai paused, then using the spear for support, he knelt, put his hand on Elka's shoulder, and said, "And this is Elka, Moctu's daughter."

Palo noted that Elka had blue eyes and was indeed a very pretty child, but he was too absorbed in thoughts of Moctu and Nuri to think of much else. "Let's find a place to sit here," Palo said, pointing to a downed log. "I'm not sure it's a great idea for us to go into the Krog shelter."

"You're right," Nindai said. "Since the Shiv attacked, everyone's on edge."

"So when did all this happen?" Palo said as they found places to sit. Elka puttered with two pine cones at Rah's feet.

They talked all afternoon, with Nindai filling them in on the details of the assault and aftermath. His shoulders drooped, and he shook his head as he related what he knew about Nuri. "We thought they'd gotten Rah and Elka for a while...but they hid. Nuri led the Shiv away from their hiding place. But the Shiv got her. Our trackers say she was alive...she and Lok were both alive when the Shiv left with them. Moctu and Lok's mate, Hawk...you remember Moctu talking about Hawk...well, the two of them and another Krog warrior, Ronk, went after the women as soon as we were sure they weren't going to show up. That was more than half a moon ago. Ronk came back some days ago. Said the Shiv split into two groups, and they followed the wrong group. Killed some Shiv and recovered a woman...of the Lion People, but it wasn't Nuri...or Lok." He looked down at the ground and shook his head.

"Poor Nuri," said Palo, frowning. "And I'm sure Moctu is beside himself with worry...if he's still alive. He's been gone so long...and in Shiv territory. He may have been killed...my friend...my best friend. Spirits..." He shook his head with worry. "They both could be dead. But at least there's a chance they're still alive," he said, brightening a little. "That's better than many thought. I guess most of the tribe believed all three of you were dead. We were really worried."

"Yes, we're all worried about them," Nindai said. "We should have left for Etseh long before now. They'd be safe if we had." He glanced at Sima, and kept his thought to himself—that he wouldn't have met Sima if they'd left earlier. "When do our people leave for the summer meeting, and who's leading the tribe?"

Nabu fielded the question. "Jondu leads now, because Moctu was gone so long." He scowled. "So many believed he was dead…but we came here to…to prove he was still alive."

"Yes, and by now, most have already left for the meeting," Palo said.

"Well, even though I've learned so much here, I'm anxious to get back," said Nindai. "And I want to bring Sima with me," he continued, putting his hand on the pretty girl's shoulder.

Palo's eyes narrowed as he saw Rah grimace and shake her head at Nindai's comment.

"But what do we do about Nuri and Moctu?" the lame shaman continued. "If he does find her…and stays alive, he'll come back here for Elka."

Palo looked at Nabu questioningly, and Nabu shrugged. "We can't go after Moctu and Nuri," Nabu said. "We'd never find them."

Palo nodded. "I think we help Nindai…and the girl…Sima. We get to the meeting. And we tell everyone what's happened."

The next morning was overcast and cold, and it looked like it might rain. Set to leave, Palo, Nabu, Nindai, and Sima considered waiting a day, but Rah encouraged them to go. Finally, at mid-morning, the foursome left Uhda, heading for the main Lion People shelter where they'd join up with their own people, the Nereans at the meeting of the tribes.

Rah held tight to Elka's hand and bit her lip as she waved good bye to the others. She watched Sima, walking happily next to a limping Nindai, and she wondered how to explain this to Da. Sima was Da's woman…at least *he* thought so. And now she was leaving with Nindai, a Dark One who could barely walk. Da was going to be *furious*.

29

NURI WAITED UNTIL IT was raining hard to start her fire. Seeing the southern clouds rolling in, she'd gathered tinder, kindling, and firewood into her rock shelter. The rain would keep the Shiv from searching for her, and it would suppress the smoke and smells from her fire. And she couldn't bring herself to eat raw bat. She'd killed two of them, and she was ravenous for meat—even bat meat. She shuddered as she recalled the last meat she'd eaten. Human meat.

Am I a cannibal? she wondered. I didn't know it was... She shook her head, unwilling to finish the thought.

The fire gained strength, and its radiant warmth and flickering flames were sunbeams to her soul. It was her first fire—the first since her freedom from the Shiv, and its small but bright, undulating glow and the smell of roasting meat suffused her with well-being. There was so much more to do—rescuing Lok in particular—but tonight she would enjoy this feeling. She had gone from whimpering captive, afraid for her life, to killing the Shiv leader and hurting their warriors. She still feared them, but now they feared her too.

Nuri thanked the Earth Mother Spirit for her good fortune and promised to bury an offering of meat for Her when she had more to give. Picking the tiny bones clean, she savored the flavor and the richness of the meat and even sucked the morsels of fatty brain from each skull. It was a paltry meal, but to her it was a victory, further emphasizing her freedom and sense of control.

Her eyes became heavy as Nuri stared at the dancing, formless shadows on the rock wall beside the fire. I need a plan, she thought. How to rescue Lok? Warm, and satisfied from the first real meal she'd had in days, Nuri leaned her back against the wall. I'll rest for a moment, she thought.

It was light out, and birds were chirping happily when Nuri awoke. The rain had stopped, although she could hear water still dripping from the leaves of nearby trees. She yawned and raised her arms above her head, feeling her back pop comfortably as she stretched.

"I need food," Nuri murmured. "First food, then a plan for Lok. Got to get her out of there soon."

But how? she wondered. As Nuri stealthily ranged the nearby land for food, she pondered the question, but no answers came to her. There are so many Shiv, and even if I could sneak in at night, one is likely to be with Lok. She shivered at the thought of what the poor woman was enduring.

On a broad, southeast-facing landslide meadow, Nuri found a few stalks of edible grains and two hands of bright yellow lion teeth flowers. The whole lion teeth plant was edible, and she eagerly collected them. There was a great deal of dung from deer or elk, and she wished she had an atlatl and shafts. Maybe I can make them, she thought.

She crouched low and tried to limit her time in the open while she gathered her plants. It occurred to her, however, that the Shiv would know of the animals and hunt in this area, so she'd better be even more careful. Nervous now, she made her way toward cover, but she stopped when she saw the mushrooms with the bell-shaped caps. Jin, she thought. These are the Jin that Rah showed us! They're valuable… They give dreams of the Spirit world. I wonder if I can use them to trade for Lok.

The mushrooms were growing in groups, and Nuri paused, rubbing her chin. Not knowing exactly how she'd use the Jin, she quickly collected a large batch of it. Back at her shelter, she separated the mushrooms and lay them in the late afternoon sun to dry on rocks a short distance away. Rah had said you could dry them or eat them raw. Maybe she'd try one, but certainly not now. Hungry, Nuri ate a couple of lion teeth plants, then sat back to ponder how to get Lok away from the Shiv. She was confident that the Shiv would recognize the Jin as something of great value, but how could she set up a trade with them?

I don't even speak their language, and if they see me, they'll chase me and... She shuddered at what they would do if they recaptured her. No matter what, I have to get Lok soon. It's not fair... She helped drive Buck-tooth away that night even though her hands were tied behind her. A pulse of anger went through her as she remembered the blond, buck-toothed Shiv laughing as he forced her legs apart and knelt between them. After Lok barreled into him, trying to knock him away, he'd hit her and sent her sprawling. Nuri snarled at the thought and ground her teeth. I will make him pay, she thought. And I have to get Lok *soon*.

Always using the brush for cover, Nuri crept downhill to the creek and drank deeply. Her thirst quenched but still hungry, she was scanning the creek bed for anything edible when a twig snapped and there was a rustling not far away. Her breath caught—it was something sizable. Was it an animal or the Shiv? She silently withdrew farther into the brush and focused on the sounds. There was further rustling, a small splash, then something that made her heart sink—murmured voices. Shiv! At least two of them.

"Dung! They're here," she said under her breath. "Have they found my shelter?"

Using extraordinary care, she distanced herself from the men, and she angled back toward the shelter. Can't let them get my furs, my food...and my mushrooms, she thought. Need to watch the shelter from a distance... Can't go back yet. Got to make sure it's safe.

Nuri found a place where, through the dense oak foliage, she could see portions of the shelter and the rocks on which she laid out the mushrooms. It was only moments before she heard a shout, and there was clamor and movement about the shelter. The leaves blocked some of her view, but she saw a wiry, dark-haired Shiv raise her furs above his head and whoop. Several more Shiv cheered. Her shoulders sagged. More shouting came when they found the Jin mushrooms. The Shiv were exuberant, and several more men crowded the site. Dung, I've lost everything, she thought, sighing deeply. Well, I was right that they value the Jin. Spirits, how many Shiv are there? She counted at least a handful.

A feeling of hopelessness swamped Nuri. Everything…they got everything. My furs, my fire-making gear. My Jin. Even my sharpened staff. Her eyes widened in panic, and she quickly felt her tunic pocket. Relief coursed through her—it was there! She still had Elka's toy hatchet blade.

So many Shiv! It's too dangerous here, she thought, beginning to edge away. Nuri stopped as she saw that the men were eating the mushrooms. They packed some of them away for later, or for the Shiv back at camp, but they were eating them…now. She frowned. I thought they were for ceremonies and celebrations. Her head cocked in surprise and curiosity as she watched them. They were excited, laughing and talking animatedly.

I've stayed long enough…too dangerous here, she thought, edging away. Any moment, they might begin that dreadful yipping and hunt me down. Need a new sharpened staff and need to find somewhere to stay. Spirits, I've lost…I've lost everything. Her eyes filled with tears, but she fought them. Moctu, where are you? I need you. One tear slipped out, and she angrily wiped it away.

Nuri gritted her teeth and forced herself to press on. Dusk was approaching, and she was pleased to see a clear, nearly cloudless sky. Need to find a place to stay—far away from those men. At least it doesn't look like rain, she thought. She moved north and found a suitable thicket of birch, pine, and buckthorn. After cutting a sapling for a new staff, she settled in to sharpen it and reflect on the devastating events of the day. *I'll never be able to help Lok now,* Nuri thought morosely. She continued using the small hatchet blade to carve the end of the staff into a sharper point. Finally pleased with it, she set it aside and let her head drop to her hands. Her mind drifted away from the day's tragedies to the happier, more recent times at Uhda.

Nuri's head rose, and her eyes brightened as a thought came to her. For the first time today, the corners of her mouth turned up. She had a plan...and it just might work.

30

THE STORM HAD NEVER come to Uhda. Today was a gorgeous spring day, and the colorful butterflies and singing birds went about their business with apparent joy. But Rah was consumed with dread. She grimaced and bit her lip as the Krog cheered Ronk, who had returned early with a load of cave bear meat. The hunt was already successful—and finished. The hunting party had only been gone a handful of days, and they had killed a huge cave bear. Ronk was clearly euphoric, describing the fight with the bear, its great size and the rich meat and fat that it carried. Da would arrive later today with more meat. One hunter had been left behind to guard the carcass from scavengers until a group of women and boys could be sent to help with the butchering and processing.

While the crowd excitedly listened to Ronk recount the stalking and killing of the bear, all Rah could think about was how to tell Da about his woman, Sima. Da will arrive, happy and proud, bearing the meat our people need, she thought, shaking her head. It was a great hunt, and he'll want the praise and recognition he deserves… and he'll want Sima. That's the manner of men—one of the ways they like to celebrate. And I have to tell him that his woman left with a Dark One who can barely walk. She blew out a breath thinking about how that conversation would go. I'll be lucky to survive it, she thought ruefully.

Sima had left with Nindai and the other Nereans some days ago. Even traveling slowly because of Nindai, there was no chance Da could go after and catch them. Spirits, was he going to be angry! This kind of thing could start wars.

"I'm not even sure that Moctu is safe if…when he returns," Rah whispered to herself, turning to head back to her hearth. "Need to hide Elka—that makes sense. At least for a while, just to be safe." Her thoughts raced. I have to prepare for when he gets here and figure out what to say to him.

She didn't have long to wait. Da arrived in the late afternoon, pulling a travois heaped with meat covered by a skin. His chest was thrust out, his chin held high, and he looked as happy as Rah had ever seen him. His filed, fang-like teeth looked out of place as he smiled and waved. Even with his scarred face and the long-ago loss of the ends of several fingers, he looked robust and powerful—a huge warrior that no sane person would cross or challenge.

Rah waited nervously in her hearth, going over how she would break the news to Da. As expected, it wasn't long before she heard his approach, and he parted the skins that covered her entryway. His face fell as he quickly noted that Sima was not there.

"Hello, Da, congratulations on your successful hunt. Can I offer you something to eat?" Rah asked.

Da shook his head. "Don't need food—I've feasted two days on bear meat. I want Sima. Where—?"

"Sima is gone," Rah interjected, wanting to get the bad news out quickly. "She left with Nindai."

Da's thick brow furrowed, and his blue eyes narrowed in confusion. "Sima left with the crippled Dark One…the shaman? When…when does she return?"

"Um…I'm not sure." Rah swallowed hard. "She may be…gone."

"Gone?"

"Yes, I'm sorry Da. I—"

In a heartbeat, Da's confusion transformed to rage, and he lifted her with one hand by the neck and held her in the air. Rah's feet flailed, and she desperately supported her body weight by holding onto his powerful forearm.

Da's eyes were narrow and menacing, and he shook Rah as he snarled each word slowly. "Sima…is…my…woman. *My* woman." He threw her against the wall by her sleeping furs.

"I…" Rah croaked, holding her neck. Gasping, she tried to clear her throat, but she could get out no further words.

"When did they leave?" Da demanded.

Still wheezing and unable to speak, Rah held up four fingers.

Realizing they were too far away to pursue, Da clenched his fists and let out a loud, deep growl. He savagely ripped down the pole holding the entryway skins as he left.

Rah closed her eyes and shook her head. She had seen Da like this before. Each time, death had followed.

31

It has to be tonight. This is my best—really my only—chance to save Lok, Nuri thought. I can get close and watch. If there are too many guards, I'll call it off.

With that, Nuri grabbed her new staff, and she was off, cautiously moving through the forest and brush toward the Shiv camp. By the time she got to where she could see the camp, the sky had turned a dusky purple and was sprinkled with tiny silver stars. Frogs, crickets, and other insects filled the night with an incessant background cacophony. Nuri could track the movement of bats as they swept in dark arcs across the points of starlight. A quarter moon occupied the horizon just above the mountains to the east, but at least for now, it offered little light.

The camp was active and vocal. Some of the men sat around two closely spaced fires while others boisterously danced and shouted. There was a lot of laughing and good-natured rowdiness. They've definitely eaten the mushrooms. As Rah described it, they'll be delirious or at least distracted for a long time. Tonight's the night, Nuri thought, her pulse quickening. If I can find Lok.

She smiled as she noted that two of the seated men had bandaged feet. So my pit traps worked, she thought with a small glow of pride. That's two less Shiv to chase us. Nuri kept scanning the area. Come on, where are you, Lok? She scrutinized the group and the surroundings for evidence of her friend, but she saw nothing to help locate her. Spirits, they haven't killed Lok, have they? Oh, please let her be alive. Did I wait too long? Have they eaten her? Spirits—I'll never forgive myself.

The moon was a hand's breadth farther up in the sky, and the men had quieted measurably when Nuri noticed a man adjusting his loin skin while leaving a darkened part of the overhang shelter. "That's the second one who's come out of that space doing that," she murmured. "That's where Lok is…she's got to be there." Nuri shook her head, imagining what Lok had endured these last few nights. "It ends tonight, Lok. Don't give up—I'm coming for you, friend."

Nuri focused on the northern edge of the camp, closest to the space where she believed Lok was being held. A group of boulders and sapling trees formed the boundary of the shelter there. "Do they have a guard? Have to know where he is." But she couldn't see one. "Where are you? Show yourself," she whispered, hoping to see a figure or some movement. But if he was there, he remained out of sight. "Maybe there's not one." That was almost too much to hope for.

The campfires burned down to glowing embers, and the men became ever quieter, lost in their inner visions as they scouted the edge of the Spirit world. Many retired to their sleeping furs, and two had fallen asleep near the fires. It was a cold night, and Nuri shivered as she continued to wait, anxious for all the men to be in deep slumber. It was almost time. The night sky was now a deep, bluish-black, and the quarter moon had risen to where she could see its glittering reflection in the stream through a break in the brush. Shivering as much from nerves as the cold, Nuri could see only one of the Shiv who still appeared to be awake. He was sitting placidly by the fire, and even his head drooped occasionally. Nuri's pulse quickened as she began her move—a slow descent down the hill toward the camp, being ultra-cautious and alert to every sound.

Within a stone's throw of the northern end, Nuri stopped to control her heartbeat. It was throbbing so hard that she was worried the Shiv would hear it. She was a woman of two minds—two voices, with one screaming at her that if these men caught her, they would eat her and the baby she was carrying. The other voice was resolute, almost calm, saying she was the Nightwalker, a creature no one could hear, and her friend needed help. She focused on that one.

I am the Nightwalker, and Lok needs me. I am the Nightwalker. Nuri analyzed each step before putting weight on it. Even though the air was cool, her brow beaded with sweat. Far away, wolves howled, and she momentarily thought of Moctu since his totem was of the wolf. What would he think of me doing this? Nuri wondered. I'm risking his child. Her progress stopped as her determination wavered, and she put a hand on the bulge of her abdomen. She shook her head. No, Moctu would do this to rescue a friend. I am the Nightwalker. I *will* do this.

In the murky blackness, Nuri could make out the boulders that bounded the northern edge of the shelter. I'll make it to that large one by the two stacked boulders, then skirt around it toward the spot where Lok is, she thought. Where I *think* Lok is, she corrected herself.

The camp was now completely quiet and still, and even the background insect noise had slackened. Nuri was grateful that, apparently, no guards had been set. Everyone must have eaten the mushrooms, she thought, smiling. Edging soundlessly toward the large boulder, she was almost there when a snort came from the two stacked boulders next to it. Nuri's eyes widened, and her heart bulged into her throat as the top boulder moved! It wasn't a boulder, but a man—a very large Shiv. She barely stifled a shriek of terror.

Run! the inner voices screamed in unison, but she was paralyzed with fear. Nuri continued to stare at the top boulder, expecting it to leap on her. Her heart beat wildly, and a wave of nausea swept her. But the man-boulder didn't leap, and she realized he must be asleep. Nuri's feet began to work again, and she edged around the large boulder, away from the sleeping guard. She paused to collect herself and let her breathing become more regular.

Too close. That was too close, she thought. Should I quit? She patted her belly. I'm risking...I'm risking everything. But Lok...she's right over there. I've come this far. You can do this, Nuri, she coached herself. You're the Nightwalker. She closed her eyes and took a deep breath. Her racing heart slowed, and she found her feet moving again, creeping ever closer to where she thought Lok lay.

She'll likely be bound, Nuri thought, so she retrieved the tiny hatchet from her pocket. With it in her right hand and her staff in her left, she snuck forward a few more steps. The glow of the fire's embers gave enough light that Nuri could discern the outlines of two sleepers in the area where she believed Lok to be, both covered by furs. Which one is Lok? she wondered frantically. One had to be a Shiv. Since she had never seen Lok tonight, they both might be Shiv.

Swallowing hard, Nuri shifted the hatchet head to the hand carrying the staff, and squatting, she felt for a suitably sized cobble. I'll club the Shiv if he wakes while I'm getting Lok, she thought. If they're both Shiv, I'm dead.

There was a noise from behind her, by the fire, and she froze. She waited several moments, but nothing came of it, and again, she tried to bring her pulse and breathing under control. The two sleeping figures had their heads farther under the ledge of the overhang, and she desperately looked for Lok's straw-colored hair in the shadowy murk. She moved within a step of their feet, and from what she could see, both figures had blond hair. Spirits, why do so many of these folks have blond hair? As she crept even closer, she was thrilled to recognize one of Lok's shoes. So, one of these two *is* Lok, she thought happily. But which? Did the Shiv lie on her other shoe like Shaka-Nu did to mine? She shook her head. Have to get closer to see. Both figures continued to breathe heavily but regularly. Nuri hefted the cobble in her hand and decided that she would kneel by the left figure, raise the cobble to striking position, then lean in to see the facial features better.

Her hands were trembling, but they stabilized as she went to her hands and knees to crawl forward. She left her staff behind and sidled quietly, a thumb's width at a time, toward the head of the left sleeper. Her heart beat so wildly that she thought she might pass out.

It's Lok! It's Lok! I've found Lok. She was so stunned at her good fortune that she took a moment for a deep breath. She focused on the man lying next to Lok. It would be a stretch, but she could club him if he awoke while she got her friend up. Nuri shifted the hatchet to the hand with the rock, freeing up a hand to cover Lok's mouth to prevent her from screaming or making noise. She placed her mouth near Lok's ear and, covering her mouth, she began to soothingly whisper, "Shh, shh, shh, shh, shh." Lok's eyes opened wide, and she stiffened.

"It's Nuri, it's Nuri," she whispered, then put her face in front of Lok. Lok's eyes registered surprise, then recognition. Lok nodded, and Nuri removed her hand from her mouth and put a finger to her own lips. Lok nodded again then extended her hands, which were bound in front of her. Nuri moved the cobble to her left hand and quickly cut the binding with her right. Lok quietly arose and gathered her sleeping furs and looked for her shoes. Nuri retrieved the one she'd seen, and Lok found the other one. The sleeping man's breathing continued, deep and regular. Nuri motioned with her thumb for them to go.

We've done it! Nuri thought, allowing herself a smile. Now we just have to get out of here quietly. We are the Nightwalkers. We…

She was startled as Lok grabbed the cobble from her hand and, with lips curled, she clubbed the man hard on the head. The Shiv let out a loud moan before Lok clubbed him again, and he was still. Lok raised her hand to club him again, but there was commotion in the nearby hearth area, and Nuri forced Lok up and the two began moving quickly away from camp. They were just gliding past the large rock where the guard was sleeping when a cry went up behind them. The guard rose groggily to a sitting position on the rock and yelled at the women who began to run. He sluggishly clambered from the rock and stumbled after them, still yelling. With Nuri leading, the two women crashed into the forest and fled into the night.

32

MOCTU BIT HIS LIP as he studied the band of Shiv from their lookout on the hilltop. There were at least four of them, and they were moving south. They looked well armed and formidable. Hawk glanced at Moctu, pursed his lips, and shook his head.

"I agree," said Moctu. "We need to avoid those warriors. Too many of them. And we have Siduri."

Siduri bristled. "I can fight, and I won't slow you down."

"I didn't mean…" Moctu responded. "You're…not completely healthy yet, and there's too many of them."

"They look for something," Hawk said, still studying them. "Maybe Nuri."

Moctu's eyes met Hawk's, and he nodded. "I know…I know. She's out there somewhere with these savages looking for her. We have to find her, and save Lok."

For the first time, Hawk's resolve cracked, and he said, "There are so many."

Moctu wasn't feeling any more confident, but he said, "Let's try this. If we can get around this group…behind them, we'll go to where they came from. There can't be that many more of them. They lost a warrior at Uhda, we've killed two, and Nuri apparently killed one. If we get past these four, maybe the odds will be more even when we find their camp. And we can get Lok, find Nuri, and get out of here."

He made it sound simple, but they all knew it wasn't. Hawk smiled thinly, then chuckled and said, "Is obvious."

Moctu laughed for the first time in many days. "Right...obvious."

Siduri was feeling much better, and with her blessing, they left the travois behind. Keeping well-hidden and staying away from the main, south-trending drainage, the threesome made their way north. Besides remaining alert for the Shiv, Hawk and Moctu also watched for opportunities to procure some meat. All were hungry—starving, really—and it was Siduri who supplied the bulk of their food from the plants and roots that she gathered along their way.

They traveled far enough to be certain they were behind the Shiv warrior party they'd earlier seen, then they scouted for the tracks of the group. They wanted to backtrack the Shiv trail to find the camp that the warriors had come from because there they'd likely find Lok.

Finding Nuri's going to be harder, Moctu thought, biting his lip. With luck, she's heading west to Uhda, the Krog shelter—that's the safest direction. But she may come south toward us, trying to get to her family and friends at Etseh. In this country, with us each moving quietly, we could pass a few trees apart and never know it.

Hawk easily found the tracks of the Shiv, which suggested they were in a hurry and had made little effort to conceal their trail. Were the Shiv following Nuri as she headed south? Had they gone to get help from the Mung who lived in that direction? Would they soon be doubling back? All of those were troubling questions, and Moctu liked none of the answers.

Taking pains to mask their own tracks, Moctu, Hawk, and Siduri continued northward throughout the day. By late afternoon, they were tired and extremely hungry. Siduri was holding up well, but the rigorous travel and lack of food was taking its toll. Crossing a creek, they stopped to drink, and Siduri found a calm, clear pool which was loaded with medium-sized trout. Excited, the trio quickly cut three saplings and split the ends of each into three parts, between which they jammed small pieces of wood. They sharpened the three ends on each pole to make tridents, then they all waded into the cold water. Spacing themselves and moving slowly, they worked to herd the fish into a smaller section of the pool, then started stabbing at the darting fish. Siduri got the first one, and by the time the last fish had escaped around them, they'd speared four trout. The cold water, the successful fishing, and the thought of a good dinner was exhilarating, and they were in good spirits when they got to the bank.

"This is a good omen," Moctu said happily. "Maybe the Spirits are with us."

They collected their fish and started uphill, still moving north. Halfway up the hill, Hawk's smile faded, his eyes narrowed, and he pointed to the next hill north of them. There, at a lower elevation, were two closely spaced wisps of pale-gray smoke.

"It's the Shiv camp," Moctu said in a low voice. "It has to be."

33

As Nuri and Lok bolted through the forest, tree branches scratched their faces and arms, and low brush clawed at their legs. It was uphill, and both women were winded by the time they realized the guard was no longer chasing them. The camp was in turmoil, with lots of commotion and shouting. Nuri noted that the yipping had not yet started.

Maybe they're worried that I left more pit traps for them, Nuri mused. Would have been a good idea…but I didn't have time.

With no Shiv in close pursuit, the women stopped to catch their breath and take stock.

"How…how are you?" Nuri whispered, touching Lok's shoulder.

"Happy…free from Shiv," Lok answered.

The quarter moon was fully up, and Nuri saw something she hadn't noticed before.

"Your face. Oh, Lok, how'd you get those bruises?" Nuri moved her hand toward, but didn't touch, the bruises on Lok's cheek and eyes for fear of hurting her.

"Shiv chase you…come back very mad. Two hurt." She pointed at her feet. "Hurt foots."

"Oh, no, you poor woman. I'm so sorry they beat you because of my traps!"

Lok shook her head. The corners of her mouth turned up, and she hugged Nuri briefly. "Hate Shiv." She scowled and spit. "You hurt Shiv…make Lok very happy."

Nuri twisted her head, and her eyes widened as she heard the sound she dreaded. The yipping had started. They were being hunted.

"Come on," Nuri said, motioning with her hand. "We should get going. From here on, we need to leave no trail. The Shiv…they're good trackers…and they're like hyenas."

The two women moved quickly but carefully along narrow trails, with Nuri leading. Both walked delicately, trying not to break branches or leave footprints. They couldn't see the ground, but they tried not to disturb the fallen leaves.

Should we go back to my thicket? Nuri wondered, or should we just head west for Uhda? I should have put more thought into this, but I guess part of me didn't believe I'd get this far. They'll probably expect us to head west, so maybe we should head south instead. No real reason to go back to the thicket…don't have anything there. Is Lok healthy enough to keep going?

In the darkness, as they neared the thicket—her thicket—the yipping sounds were getting distinctly closer. She decided they should pass it up and keep going if Lok was able. Nuri put her face close to Lok's so she could better see her and, motioning with her head, she whispered, "That's where I hid out recently, but we'll keep going if you're able."

Lok touched Nuri's shoulder, and her eyes signaled that she didn't understand.

"Right," Nuri nodded quickly. "Can you keep walking? How are you?"

"We walk…walk far far," Lok said, pointing to keep going.

The yipping was much closer, and panic welled up in Nuri. Spirits, I hate that sound! How are they…? It's so dark. How do they know where to go? Can they smell us? My thicket's west of the Shiv camp… Maybe that's it. We've been taking our time hiding our trail. Maybe they're just assuming we'll head west, and they're charging out in that direction. Let's go south and see if they keep going west, she decided.

They set out moving faster, less cautious about leaving tracks, just anxious to put distance between themselves and the barking Shiv. As the moon arced farther across the night sky, the yipping noise became fainter, then it stopped altogether. The Shiv had continued west, and Nuri and Lok were well south of them.

The night was cold, but they had no need for the furs that Lok carried bundled under one arm. The country was nothing but ups and downs, and their exertion kept them warm.

Dawn began to melt the darkness, and in its still beauty, Nuri allowed herself a deep, satisfied breath. I did it, she thought. I'm free, and Lok's free. We're going to make it back...back to Moctu and Hawk and away from these...these horrible Shiv.

She looked at Lok, who was walking beside her. "Well, at least the Shiv did continue west, and we're south of them now," Nuri said, a little more relaxed. "But now that it's light, they'll figure things out pretty quickly, and they'll be back on our trail."

Lok seemed to understand. She nodded and said, "Now we hide tracks."

Nuri's mouth dropped open as she got a better look at Lok's battered face. "Oh, you poor woman," she said, softly touching her shoulder. Anger set in as she surveyed the damage—two black eyes, a scuffed cheek, and a split lip. "Who...which of them did this to you?" Nuri seethed.

"Two mans. Blond...um," She put two fingers near the front of her mouth pointing down.

"Buck-tooth," Nuri growled. "He did this? Who was the other one? What did he look like?"

"Shaka-Teeb," Lok answered. "Big." She put her hand up in the air, indicating the man was tall. "New leader of Shiv." She pulled on a strand of her hair and said, "Brown."

"We need to get away now, Lok. But someday...someday, we'll be back, and we'll..." Nuri shook her head, scowling. "We'll hurt them. They'll be so sorry they did this."

Lok nodded her head, not fully understanding, but appreciating Nuri's anger. She rubbed her stomach and said, "Eat?"

"You must be starving. I'm hungry too. Don't have any food, but we can look for some while we're walking. Look, there's a meadow down there," she said, pointing. "We can usually find something in a meadow, or on the edge of it."

It wasn't long before they'd located a few lion's teeth and yarrow plants, which wasn't much, but it dulled their hunger pains. They would have gathered more, but Lok suddenly cocked her head. Her eyes widened, and she said, "Shiv...not far."

Nuri heard it too. The Shiv were back and on their trail again. And the sudden revival of their excited yipping meant the Shiv knew they were close.

34

Cautiously making their way to a rocky outcrop from which they could get a better view, Moctu, Hawk, and Siduri studied the Shiv camp. It was dusk, but thus far they'd seen no sign of Lok. Moctu's prediction was right that many of the Shiv were gone, and there were few left at the camp. From what they'd seen, it was guarded by only three men, two of which had bandaged feet.

"We go to camp, kill three Shiv, and get Lok," Hawk said, indicating they should leave immediately.

"It feels like a trap," Siduri said. "There were so many more of them. Where are they all?"

Moctu frowned. "I know you want to get Lok as soon as possible, Hawk…I do too. But we don't even know if she's there. And I agree with Siduri…something just doesn't seem right."

"I do by myself then," Hawk said in Krog, his jaw set. He began to make preparations to go, and Moctu put up a hand.

"You're not going by yourself…I'll go with you. But let's watch the place until dark at least. Maybe we'll see Lok, or figure out if there are other Shiv waiting for us. Once it's dark, we'll sneak down there and attack them at first light."

Hawk nodded, and all three focused their attention on the camp and its surroundings. Sure enough, as darkness fell, two more Shiv came in from the nearby woods to sit by the fires. Outnumbered five to two, Moctu and Hawk decided to get closer to the camp to better scout for Lok. If they saw her, they'd attack at dawn or even before if the opportunity presented itself.

Not wanting to risk a fire, they ate raw fish, then left Siduri with their furs and Moctu's heavy spear. Siduri was willing to stay behind, and she made no pretense at wanting to be part of the possible attack. Moctu and Hawk made their way quickly but furtively downhill toward the fast-moving stream, where its rushing turbulence would mask any noise they made. Well before dawn they were in place, on a knoll slightly above the camp and a long atlatl throw from it. In the dim light of the fires and the quarter moon, they scrutinized the dark recesses of the overhang for any sign of Lok.

"I don't see her, Hawk. I'm beginning to think she's not there," Moctu whispered.

"No, she must be there," Hawk insisted in Krog.

From his tone, Moctu could tell his friend was distraught. If the roles were reversed, he'd feel the same. Nuri wasn't safe, but at least she was free from the Shiv. Who knew what miseries Lok was suffering as a captive? Then it hit him.

Spirits, they may have eaten her, Moctu thought. That's why Hawk is so upset. I didn't even... Crap...how could I not have thought about that? Is Lok dead...*eaten*? Anger surged through him, and he fought the impulse to charge the shelter and kill Shiv. Any Shiv. All Shiv.

"We're going to find her, Hawk," he hissed. "And if we don't, we'll kill every dung-filled one of these hyenas we can find."

Hawk nodded but remained quiet.

The night was clear and cold, and both men were tired and chilled. Neither man slept as they continued to focus on the camp, hoping desperately for a glimpse of Lok. As morning approached, and the dark-black hues of night began to lighten, one of the Shiv warriors stoked the fires, and the blazes lit more of the shelter.

"If she's there, she's got to be in the northernmost part of the shelter," Moctu whispered, pointing. "That's the only part we can't see much of."

Hawk nodded and motioned for them to move to a location where they could get a better look into the dark recesses of that part of the rock overhang. They took their time since they were edging even closer to the Shiv camp, and by the time they got into place, it was full dawn.

"Can't see clearly, but I don't think she's there," Moctu said. "Spirits, I know you're worried, Hawk. But I don't think they've killed her... If she's not here, maybe they took her with them somewhere else."

It was not what Hawk wanted to see or hear, and his lower lip went out. "Where, then? How we find? I want Lok...I thought..." He didn't finish his comment and just stared at the ground, shaking his head.

Moctu touched his shoulder. "How about this? It's a bad idea for us to attack the camp with so many of them. But maybe when they send out a lookout or a guard, we can capture him and find out about Lok."

Hawk brightened and nodded, and the two men waited for an opportunity to capture one of the Shiv. Not long after that, they heard it...the weird yipping sound that Rah had described. There were Shiv to the southwest, and they were hunting something.

"Siduri!" Moctu said, alarmed, rising up to leave. "That's coming from where we left Siduri."

Hawk stared at him for a moment, unwilling to leave Lok—or at least word of her, then he, too, rose.

"We'll get Siduri safe, then we'll come back here and find out where Lok is, I promise," Moctu said hurriedly. "But let's go... fast-fast."

35

SIDURI HAD HEARD THE Hunt Sound many times before while she was a captive of the Shiv. They used it to instill fear in those—both animals and humans—that they were hunting. From experience, she knew it worked well.

Were the Shiv now hunting Moctu and Hawk? She didn't think so. The sounds came from farther west than where she thought the men were. Siduri's pulse began to race even though she knew the Shiv weren't hunting her. But what—or who—*are* they hunting? It's got to be Moctu's mate, Nuri, the one who escaped.

Moving to the nearby lookout, she scanned the far hill and the slope below her and soon saw movement. It was a person on the far hill—no, two people. Shading her eyes with both hands she studied the figures. A dark-skinned woman with long, dark hair like hers was being chased by a blond-haired Pale One! Spirits! They've almost got her! Grabbing the heavy spear that Moctu had left her, Siduri abandoned the rest of their gear and charged down the hill to intersect Nuri and her nearest pursuer.

Siduri's mind was racing as she tore through the brush and low trees that surrounded a mélange of small boulders. I don't stand a chance against a Shiv warrior unless I surprise him, she worried. Can't see either of them anymore, but I ought to meet up with them if I keep going this way. When I hear them, I'll hide and set up an ambush. The Hunt Sound is still pretty far away, so the rest of the

Shiv… It occurred to Siduri that, oddly, the nearest Shiv wasn't yipping to alert the others.

Near the base of her hill she heard the thrashing of Nuri and her pursuer coming toward her. Choosing the small path that Nuri was likely to take, Siduri hid behind a gray boulder and readied herself to thrust the spear into the Shiv after Nuri went by. She'd never killed a man before, but this was a Shiv, and she would use all the power she had and all the vengeance she felt.

Siduri could hear the close rustling of brush and Nuri's footfalls. She gritted her teeth and braced for a hard thrust with the spear. I'm only going to get one thrust. If I don't kill him, he'll kill me. Siduri could hear her heartbeat in her ears and her focus narrowed as Nuri rushed by in a blur.

Nuri gave a small yelp of surprise as she passed by the crouched figure with the spear. Still running, she turned to see this new threat lunge out with a spear thrust toward Lok. Hearing Nuri's yelp, Lok looked up from the uneven trail to see a spear headed for her midsection. She swiveled to avoid the thrust, but she was too late. The thrust had force behind it, and it knocked Lok to the side, causing her to fall into the brush that bordered the trail.

Siduri felt the thrust penetrate, and she saw the Pale One fall. She let go of the spear and pivoted to run with Nuri, calling to her that she was a friend of Moctu's, and the Pale One chasing her was no longer a threat. Running a few steps, she saw that Nuri was stopped, her eyes wide with horror.

"That was Lok! That was a friend!" Nuri shrieked. "Who are you? What have you done?" She brushed past this dark woman who knew Moctu's name to go to Lok's downed body.

Siduri was stunned. "But…but he was chasing…"

"It's not a he, it's not a Shiv. It's a woman…Hawk's mate, Lok. Spirits, what have you done?"

Suddenly it made sense why this Shiv wasn't calling the Hunt Sound, and why he…she had stayed close behind but never quite caught Nuri. Siduri's face went ashen.

"Oh, I'm so sorry!" Her eyes widened. "I'm a dead woman. Hawk will kill me."

The two women looked to see Lok begin to struggle in the brush, trying to get up.

"She's alive!" Nuri said, helping her up.

Lok stood, holding her left bicep, which was bleeding from being grazed. But the spear was not in her. Scowling, she reached down and picked up the spear, which was deeply impaled in the rolled furs she'd been carrying. Unable to free the furs from the spearhead, she raised the butt end and came at this new person who had tried to kill her.

"No! Lok, no. She was trying to help. She thought..." Nuri interposed herself between the two women, and Siduri cowered behind her. "She's on our side, Lok. She's a friend."

The malevolent look in Lok's eyes made it clear that Siduri would never be her friend.

"She try kill me," Lok said, unwilling to put the spear down.

"She thought you were chasing me. She thought you were a Shiv," Nuri shouted, an arm raised, motioning for Lok to lower the spear.

A new pulse of barking and yipping indicated the Shiv were close—way too close.

"This way...our camp...Moctu and Hawk—they'll come there," Siduri said, regaining her composure and beckoning them to follow.

All three women were winded by the time they made it up the slope to the small camp. Moctu and Hawk weren't there, so they immediately went to the nearby overlook where they began scanning the hills for the men. They also watched for the Shiv, whose barking sounds were getting ever closer.

"There!" Nuri pointed to a spot on the far northern hill, east of where the yipping sounds were emanating. "I saw movement... Is it them...or is it Shiv?"

Lok had also seen the flash of movement through the trees, and she had a hand to her split lip because her broad smile hurt. "Is Awk," she said, using Hawk's earlier Krog name. "Awk and Moctu."

With uncontained joy, Nuri and Lok began jumping together and hugging one another, and Siduri happily joined in. Only the intensifying sound of yipping caused them to stop. The Shiv were at the base of their hill.

"The Shiv are closer than... Can't wait. Just grab the furs... hurry! We'll swing eastward and meet up with Moctu and Hawk. I know they hear the Shiv too," Nuri said breathlessly.

The women gathered their paltry possessions and fled to the east, then down the hill toward their men. Excitement filled Nuri as she raced down the hill, oblivious to the scratching branches and brush.

Moctu...I'm going to see Moctu, she thought, almost incredulous that it would happen soon. It was an event she'd wished for and dreamed about for days, an event she'd worried would never happen again.

Nuri was just beginning to wonder if they'd missed the men, gone by them in the dense brush of the forest, when Lok said, "There," and pointed. "Awk!" she called out.

Nuri saw Moctu at the same time he saw her. Hawk had just stopped, and now Moctu did too. For a moment, both men had their mouths open in just the same way, and a laugh burst out of Nuri at the same time tears streamed from her eyes. Lok, too, was crying and humming a throbbing, happy sound as she ran toward Hawk.

Moments later, both women were in their men's arms, and Moctu was whirling Nuri around and kissing her between one-word questions. "How...? When...?"

The nearby yipping of the Shiv brought them to their senses.

"Quick...I've been thinking about this," Moctu said, putting Nuri down and facing the group. "The Shiv don't know we're here, or how many we are. Everybody, start howling like a wolf," and looking at the women, he said, "The deeper you can make the sound, the better." With that he let out a deep, barking howl, and Hawk followed suit. Confused, the women joined in after a pause, and soon all five were howling lustily.

The effect was immediate. The yipping stopped completely as the Shiv realized that reinforcements had arrived in support of the prey they were chasing—and they were facing a large force. Still howling, following Moctu's signals, his group began moving back up the hill to a more defensible position, where they might see the Shiv better if they came.

They didn't come. It soon became clear that the Shiv had not liked the odds, and they'd left. After some time, with his finger to his lips, Moctu encouraged the group to move cautiously and quietly to a hillside farther west. He held Nuri's hand the entire way, unwilling to lose connection. Hawk likewise stayed close to Lok, repeatedly embracing her with his powerful arms. There was no talking as the group listened for any sound that could indicate a Shiv ambush. Only after they were safely away to an even more defensible site did the group begin to talk and celebrate their reunion.

They hugged one another and laughed and cried and traded stories well into the night. Only Siduri was quiet as she studied the interaction between Moctu and Nuri. Lok and Nuri were shocked to hear of the deaths of Cha and Nug. Everyone, especially Hawk, was filled with hatred and disgust for the Shiv as Lok described their barbarity and her mistreatment by them. Working backward, she recounted the beatings and rapes, and then got to that first, horrible night.

"The first night," she said softly in Krog, "they...took Mik and..." Her voice caught, and she looked at the ground, shaking her head. Several times she tried to speak, but no words would come. In a choked voice, she said, "They...they..." A sob escaped her and she couldn't continue. Tears streamed down Nuri's cheeks, and Moctu clenched his fists and put them to his forehead. Hawk barely contained his rage, getting up and pacing, his whole body taut, his hands tightly clenching and unclenching.

The group was silent for a long time, and Hawk sat back down. Moctu said, "I think the Shiv likely regret attacking us." Pointing at

Hawk, he continued, "We've killed several, and you women killed one, and—"

"Two," Lok said, and looked over at Nuri, who nodded back at her.

The men looked at Lok questioningly, but she offered no further explanation.

"Uh huh," Nuri said. "Lok clubbed another Shiv last night… I don't think he's getting up again."

Hawk looked over at his mate with admiration. She returned his gaze, the corners of her mouth coming up imperceptibly.

"And you," Moctu said, looking at Nuri, "are the 'black-haired sorceress' who magically opened Shaka-Nu's throat."

Nuri was dreading talking with Moctu about Shaka-Nu and what he had done to her—and to their baby. She still felt guilt and shame even though she kept telling herself that there was nothing else she could have done. Now she was stunned. "Where did you hear that?"

"That's what the Shiv call you now," Moctu said, with a gleam in his eye. "We heard it from Shaka-Nu's son before Hawk killed him. I was so proud of you… I still am."

Nuri blushed, very pleased by the comment. But she cringed at the thought of Moctu ever learning the details about what had transpired earlier with the Shiv leader.

36

As his large group approached the streambed, Jondu scowled, recalling his recent encounter here with the Lion People. This was where it happened, he thought. This is where the Lion People hunters took *my* caribou.

Jondu's early tenure as leader of the Nereans was not starting well, and he was bad-tempered and sullen. Hunting had been poor—very poor—and his people were rapidly eating through their stores of dried meat from past hunts. Jondu feared a winter of starvation for his tribesmen. Nereans had suffered so much misfortune that he worried the Spirits had turned against them.

Anger welled within him as he remembered returning to Etseh empty-handed from the earlier hunt in this area, even though his group had killed two caribou. The meat had been claimed by the Lion People because the beasts had crossed this stream into Lion People territory before they died. It especially galled him that one of the beasts had two of his shafts in it. Two!

Now he was leading a large group of Nereans to the summer meeting at the flint quarry near the Lion People shelter. These events happened every handful of years, and they were always exciting. There was so much to do and so many new people to talk, trade, and hunt with and to learn from. The games and competitions were challenging and fun, sometimes even thrilling. And the social interactions usually led to trades for females—and a host of unexpected pregnancies. But this year, Jondu thought, it'll be difficult to even be civil to the Lion People—especially Lehoy.

"He stole...*stole* meat that we needed...that we had killed. It's going to be hard not to spit when I see him," Jondu grumbled to himself.

About five hands of people were making the trip to the meeting, a smaller group than usual. The other Nereans were staying at Etseh, except for Palo and Nabu, who were off looking for Moctu, Nuri, and Nindai, who were missing. Those three had—in Jondu's mind, unwisely—gone to the Krog shelter and were long overdue to return. Jondu was pretty sure that they were dead, and he hoped Palo and Nabu, two of his best hunters, would not also be killed while looking for them. The Nereans had suffered so much over the past two years.

Jondu considered what would happen if Palo and Nabu returned with the three. Would Moctu try to take over from Jondu and resume his leadership?

"I'll worry about that when, and if, it happens," Jondu murmured, shrugging it off as unlikely.

Another concern was how to handle their new knowledge. Moctu had learned from the Krog how to make fire with sticks, and most of the Nereans had learned how to do it. Everyone—man, woman, and child—had been instructed over and over not to show or discuss the new technology with people of other tribes. Jondu and the elders would determine how to use this new knowledge in their trading and relationships with the other clans.

"No way are we just giving that knowledge to the Lion People," Jondu muttered.

After crossing the stream, Jondu knew it was another half day's walk to the flint quarry where his group would camp. From there, it was an even shorter walk to the Lion People's shelter, which some of them might visit tonight. About halfway to the flint quarry, the Nereans were met by Jondu's least favorite person, Lehoy, who waved, then walked confidently—but with a distinct limp—toward them.

"Welcome, Nereans! Our scouts saw you yesterday, and we've been looking forward to your arrival." The tall, muscular man scanned the group, his eyes passing over Jondu and settling for a long moment on Avi, who stood next to him, holding Indar at her side.

"You're limping," Jondu said, ignoring the greeting.

"Yes, a fall from rocks as we were chasing a bear. Should be all healed soon. Just sorry that the bear got away," Lehoy said, flashing a good-natured smile. "We're sorry that you couldn't bring more people," he continued while surveying the group, "but we're very pleased for the ones of you who did make the trip." His smile broadened, and his eyes sparkled as they lingered on Avi, taking in her unusual light-brown hair, which flowed loosely around her shoulders and neck, restrained only by a delicate headband braid. Avi noticed his interest and looked away shyly.

Jondu also noticed his gaze, and his poorly suppressed irritation flared.

"We'll get settled near the flint quarry and maybe we'll see you this evening," he said brusquely.

Avi was embarrassed but pleased by Lehoy's thinly disguised interest in her. Glancing up, she noted how tall and confident and handsome he was. The well-made tunic he wore made of soft, brown, and cream leathers reminded her of the beautiful tunic that Nuri had made for her to wear at her mating ceremony. On his neck he wore a splendid necklace of two white shells with a huge lion canine in the middle. Avi knew that the size of the lion claw or canine indicated the hunter's prowess, and she also knew that Lehoy had easily won the last atlatl competition. Clearly this man was an awesome hunter.

"We're having a feast tonight for those of you who visit," Lehoy said.

"A small group of us will be there, then," Jondu said curtly, galled by the thought that they'd probably be eating the caribou meat he and his hunters killed a half moon before.

"I hope it won't be too small a group," Lehoy said, starting the sentence while looking at Jondu and finishing it with a glance at Avi.

37

THEY HAD ONE FISH left, which they gave to Nuri and Lok. The group had decided it was too dangerous to have a fire, so the two women ate the fish raw…and they savored every bit of it.

All were still hungry and anxious to get home, so they decided to head west for Uhda at first light and hunt along the way. Moctu and Nuri planned to get Elka and Nindai, then journey with Siduri to her Lion People shelter and the meeting of the tribes. If they hurried, they could still make part of the event. Because of the Shiv threat, two people would stand guard at all times during the night. One man and one woman were to be on each shift, starting first with Moctu and Siduri, then Hawk and Lok, then Moctu and Nuri.

It was a cold night, and after some time guarding the camp from separate areas, Siduri came to warm herself next to Moctu.

"Nuri is very beautiful," she said.

"Yes…she is."

"Am I…am I beautiful too?"

Moctu nodded, then realizing she couldn't see, he squeezed her slightly and said, "Uh huh, you are too."

"Well…so…will I be your second mate?" she asked, holding her breath, waiting for the answer.

"Siduri, you're beautiful…and smart, and you'll make a wonderful mate. But Nuri just got back from a horrible time with the

Shiv... You both did. And it's...it's too early to be thinking of all that. Let's get you back to your people, and we'll see."

Siduri was quiet for a long time, and Moctu listened to the uninterrupted forest sounds, wondering what she was thinking.

"Nuri didn't talk about her time with Shaka-Nu other than to say how she killed him with the toy hatchet. Sometime ask her about him. He was...very...um, skilled at some things.

Moctu's brow knitted as he wondered exactly what she was getting at, but he let the remark pass. Bone-weary, he knew there would be little sleep tonight since he had to do another guard shift with Nuri. He was pleased when Hawk and Lok came to take over.

Moctu made his way to the sleeping furs and folded himself around Nuri. Still half-asleep, she snuggled in closer to him. A short distance away, Siduri frowned as she settled into her furs alone.

It seemed like just moments to Moctu before Hawk was waking him for his second guard shift.

"I can guard more," Hawk said, suggesting Moctu continue sleeping.

"No, it's my turn," Moctu said, getting to his knees. "And Lok needs more sleep. Nuri and I will take this shift."

Awakened from the deepest sleep she'd had in many days, Nuri shook off her grogginess and arose with Moctu. Sitting on a boulder at the edge of the camp, wrapped in a large fur, they stayed together until dawn, whispering between themselves.

Nuri told him of her time on her own, of her improvised camps, the Jin, and the pit-traps. On hearing of the pit traps, he told her of seeing two Shiv with bandaged feet. She had seen them too, but it was satisfying to hear about them from him.

"There were times when I thought...I'd never see you again," she said, her voice catching. She held Moctu closer. "The first few days with the Shiv were the worst. I was so scared for the baby. I thought they were going to eat me, and you would never...never get to see your child, our child." She shivered and was silent.

"I'm so glad to have you back…so glad you're safe," he said, tightening his embrace. "And I'm so proud of you. You just…can't imagine. I rushed here to save you—Hawk and I did, wondering how we would save you and Lok. But you not only saved yourself, you rescued Lok. And you have the Shiv fearing you."

Nuri glowed with Moctu's praise and hugged him. "The Shiv weren't fearing me yesterday when they were chasing Lok and me." She shuddered, remembering it. "Then you came."

It was dawn, and the sky lightened even though the sun had yet to crest the eastern hills. Hawk and Lok got up and prepared to leave, hoping the others would quickly follow suit. All in the group were happy to be heading west, but Hawk and Lok the most. Today, they would make their way toward Uhda! Moctu and Nuri were likewise eager—to get Elka, then travel quickly to the meeting of the tribes. Moctu felt guilty that he'd been away so long, and he hoped the tribe was doing well. He knew Ono, or whomever was leader, might be unwilling to return the leadership to him. That was a risk he'd been willing to take…and getting Nuri—and Lok—back had been worth it. Although anxious to leave the Shiv territory, Siduri was oddly quiet.

Ever watchful for evidence of the Shiv, the band made good progress throughout the morning. The country was extremely rugged, and by midday they were very tired and hungry. Because of her pregnancy Nuri had the least stamina, but Siduri had yet to fully recover from her miscarriage, and she typically lagged behind as well. Moctu had stayed by Nuri's side for much of the morning, but now he and Hawk ranged to either side of the trail, searching for game.

The two trailing women ended up walking together, and as long as they spoke slowly, they could understand one another well. "I'll bet you're looking forward to seeing your people again…your family and friends," Nuri said, eying Siduri. She had noted the connection between Siduri and Moctu and wondered about it.

It was Moctu's prerogative to share furs with Siduri if he wanted to, but she didn't have to like it. And she despised the hypocrisy she felt, knowing that she'd experienced pleasure with Shaka-Nu just days before, even if it was forced on her.

"Part of me is looking forward to it, but part of me is dreading it," Siduri replied softly. "I...I think many will believe that I've been tainted...ruined by the Shiv." She looked down and rubbed an eye.

Compassion welled in Nuri, but she had a flicker of fear for herself...that some would believe her tainted, or worse, her child. "I can't imagine that your friends and family won't be thrilled to have you back. None of us chose for this to happen."

"But it's like...if you fall and break your leg, and you can never walk again. You didn't choose for that to happen, yet no man will want you for a mate."

Siduri had spoken wisdom, and Nuri was suddenly even more worried that she and her child would seem tainted in the eyes of some. Still, Nuri thought most people would understand. "You're young, you're pretty, you're healthy, and you no longer carry the Shiv child. You can start over. There'll be lots of men who want you...I'm sure of that."

"Thanks for those kind words, but your mate didn't want me. He's rejected me several times. That tells me a lot."

A mix of emotions swept Nuri. She was relieved that Moctu had not been with this woman, yet, oddly, a small part of her was disappointed that Moctu had spurned the poor girl.

Just then, they heard a call from Moctu. He and Hawk had spotted game of some sort. Tonight, they might feast for the first time in a moon.

38

As soon as Lehoy was gone, Jondu could no longer contain himself, and he spit in the direction the man had gone.

"Such an arrogant hyena!" he muttered. "He takes food from us, caribou that we've killed, then acts like nothing has happened when he sees us."

Throughout the afternoon, Jondu struggled with whether to even attend the Lion People feast—if it was caribou, that really would irritate him. And if he did go, who should travel there with him and how many? Avi noticed his restiveness.

"You seem very troubled. Is there anything I can do?"

"You can leave me alone…I need to think," he snapped.

In the end, he elected to go, and he took Avi and three others with him. He had said they'd attend, so it would look weak not to. All five dressed in their finest clothing, and baby Indar was left with his grandmother. Jondu wore a finely made deer-skin tunic, and he had his wavy black hair tied back smartly. Avi looked resplendent in the tunic that Nuri had made for her. Her light-brown hair was braided at the temples, and the braids were joined together in back. Avi's hair and the ivory ringlets on her tunic accentuated her fiery green eyes. Although they had quarreled a lot since Jondu became leader, he was proud to have her with him not only as his mate, but representing the Nerean people as well.

On arrival, Jondu was immediately glad he'd decided to come, as he saw Marco, Ordu's oldest son, who led another clan. He needed to tell Marco about the death of his father and all that had happened. It would be painful, but it was important. Jondu went to the big, broad-shouldered young man and hugged him, not knowing where to start.

The other three Nereans had taken seats by the fire, so Avi was left by herself. She watched apprehensively as the two men talked, then Marco gasped, pushed away, then put his hands to his face, covering his eyes. Avi was flooded with sorrow, remembering the deep pain that the news of Ordu's, Samar's, and Tabar's deaths had brought her and the rest of the Nereans. She watched as Marco turned and left, and Jondu followed him. She shook her head. The past two years had brought great sadness to the Nereans, she reflected, and this tribal meeting was likely to have many such moments as this.

Avi's thoughts turned to Nuri, Moctu, and Nindai. If they, also, were dead, then the Nereans truly were cursed. But she didn't think they were dead. Avi had a strong bond with her sister-friend Nuri, and she just *knew* that she was still alive.

"You look so sad and thoughtful…and a little lonely," a deep voice said from beside her.

Avi looked up to see Lehoy smiling at her. She knew Jondu hated this man, and she probably should too. But from all she'd seen so far, he seemed friendly and pleasant.

"I…I'm waiting for Jondu. He had some unhappy news to deliver to Marco, our kinsman."

"Why don't you come sit with me…you and Jondu. We'll be with Rolf, our leader, and Devu, our shaman. As you can see," he said, smiling and pointing to the disheveled shaman, "they're not very attractive, and we need your beauty for balance." He chuckled, and his eyes sparkled as she blushed.

Avi found it hard to dislike this man. He was the perfect balance of danger, charm, and confidence. Lehoy was tall and attractive—muscular, but not too muscular, and his face had just enough imperfections to be interesting. He was no longer limping. By the look of his clothes and adornments, he was very prosperous—a great hunter. His dark eyes seemed to dance, but lingered often on Avi.

With his hand gently on her back, Lehoy ushered her toward the two men, then made introductions. As Avi took a seat, she noted that Rolf was an overweight, dignified older man—reasonably well-dressed, but not what she would expect for the leader of the Lion People. Devu, the shaman, was appalling. He was unkempt and thin, almost skeletal, and he continually ran his fingers through a scraggly, graying beard which did little to hide his sunken cheeks. His fingers occasionally caught in the beard where it was caked with dried spittle and flecks of food. Even seated, she could tell Devu was tall and cadaverous. He wore a necklace similar to those of Lion warriors, but instead of a lion's tooth between the two shells, there was a jagged piece of lightning-struck wood. All the objects had been stained with red ochre to look bloody. His first words to Avi were as creepy as his appearance.

"The Earth Spirit is hungry."

Avi felt her skin crawl. Confused and repulsed, she frowned, and her head drew back slightly.

"Yes, the Earth Spirit is hungry," he said again, nodding and leering at her.

"Forgive him, Avi," Lehoy said, putting a hand on her shoulder, his ever-present smile a little tighter. "Devu sometimes forgets his courtesy."

Avi saw Jondu return and motioned for him to join them. When Jondu came over, Lehoy once again made introductions, whereupon Jondu looked for a place to sit. The largest space available was between Avi and Lehoy. Noting Jondu's momentary hesitation, Avi slid over, making more space on her other side, and Jondu gratefully sat there.

The feast was indeed a caribou stew, but Lehoy at least had the grace to call it deer stew. Throughout the evening, he went out of his way to be nice to Jondu, which Avi appreciated. It had been difficult living with Jondu lately, and Avi was glad that he held his temper and seemed to enjoy the evening. Jondu was particularly taken with the shaman.

They learned important news, horrible news—that the Pale Ones had attacked the Lion People and carried off some of their members. Fear swept through Avi as she and the other Nereans recognized the implications for Moctu, Nuri, and Nindai.

Could I be wrong? Avi wondered, biting a fingernail. Maybe they *are* dead. She shook her head, unwilling to accept it. No. I just don't believe that Nuri's dead. No.

During the meal, Jondu elbowed Avi and motioned with his head for her to look at Devu. Avi's eyes widened as she saw that Devu was drinking a thick liquid from a human skull—the skull of a Pale One. The shaman's eyes met hers, and he smiled lasciviously, causing the hair on the back of her neck to stand up.

As the Lion People finished their meals, their eyes turned toward Devu, and soon the crowd had quieted expectantly, and all looked to him. He started off by recounting in vivid detail several heroic hunts of lions and mammoths. His voice was deep and powerful, and his words carried wisdom. With each story, he subtly emphasized that he had foretold of the animals' location and of the outcome of the hunts. Even Avi was spellbound by the shaman. He had amazing powers.

Devu was quiet for a long time, and the crowd grew anxious, almost breathless, waiting for his next words.

"We all know," Devu said finally. "Everyone knows that souls can wander during dreams. My soul traveled last night. It ran with the wolves. It saw game...great herds of game. Then it left the wolves and soared with the eagles. It traveled from the edge of the sea to the farthest mountains. And that's where I saw them." He took another drink from the skull cup, and it appeared that he was finished speaking for the night.

"What did you see?" came from several in the audience.

Again, Devu waited until the crowd was nearly breathless with anxious curiosity, then he said, "The night bends down and speaks to me in silent languages. I learn and see much." He stopped, enjoying the tension he was creating.

"What did you learn?"

"What'd you see?"

He again scanned the crowd, and his eyes settled on Avi and Jondu. "Three ghosts…I saw three ghosts. Ghosts of Nereans."

A chill went through Avi, and she looked around, first at Jondu, whose jaw had dropped, then the others across from her. Everyone that she could see was as stunned and transfixed as she was. The ghosts of Nuri, Moctu, and Nindai? she worried. She soon had an answer.

"The ghosts are gathered with us tonight." As shocked people in the crowd looked around, Devu continued. "Yes, they are here with us. One has an injured leg."

Nindai! Avi thought with horror.

"But the Earth Spirit is hungry," Devu said loudly. "It will take more." He looked slowly around the crowd, his eyes lingering on Avi, then moving on. "Death stalks you in your sleeping furs or wherever you set foot."

39

EVERYONE IN MOCTU'S GROUP was ravenous. Other than a few roots, some tree bark, and a few yarrow and lion teeth plants, they'd eaten nothing of substance for two days. The deer that Hawk and Moctu had seen on their first day of travel toward Uhda had disappeared into a forest thicket.

They were less than two days from Uhda when Lok saw movement in the rocks on a hill south of them.

"Leopard," she said in Krog, "with something in mouth."

Even though leopards were dangerous prey, Hawk and Moctu set out to try to kill it. They had only gone a short way when Lok, who had her hands shielding the sun from her eyes while she studied the distant scene, called to them.

"Leopard has wolf pup in mouth."

Moctu looked at Hawk and he frowned, then shrugged. Now they had two dangerous beasts to worry about, and maybe multiples of each. Leopards sometimes hunted in pairs, and wolves commonly gathered in packs. Hawk shrugged again and pressed on.

He's even hungrier than I am, Moctu thought as he followed the big, red-haired man. They crossed a small creek between the hills and started up the slope. They could no longer see the beast, but they occasionally looked back to Lok, who directed their heading with hand signals.

They were winded, having climbed most of the way up the hill when they saw her. It was a wolf bitch, and she was in a bad way. She was lying nestled against the base of a large boulder panting, her legs sprawled in front of her. The fur at her neck was covered in blood, and she had a severe wound to her abdomen. As the men cautiously approached, they could see a loop of her intestine protruded from the stomach wound, near the uppermost of her enlarged teats. A small pile of regurgitated meat lay beside her. As they neared the wolf, her lip went up and she growled briefly—almost half-heartedly, then went back to panting.

The wolf barely moved as Hawk stepped quickly forward and, with one thrust of his spear, ended her pain.

"Wolf not good meat, but better than nothing," he said, kneeling to begin processing the carcass.

Moctu heard a high-pitched noise from beyond the boulder and scrambled over the boulder to investigate. Dirt had been dug away from under a smaller, neighboring boulder. It was a den, and he could hear tiny yips coming from within it. Moctu looked around for other wolves, and he apprehensively touched his wolf tooth amulet.

The leopard—or leopards—he thought worriedly, had attacked the wolf den and carried away a pup before the mother attacked and defended them. In the fight, she'd been mortally wounded, but she'd driven the leopard away. At least for now.

Watchful for the returning leopard or male wolf, Moctu moved closer and peered into the shallow den. He could make out only two more pups, and since the typical wolf litter was about six pups, he figured the leopard had gotten the rest of them. It would probably be back for these two as well.

The pups were about one moon old and full of energy. As he watched, the larger one, gray, with dark ears and a white tuft on his forehead, came partway up the incline of the den entrance to investigate him. It was almost to him when the other pup grabbed it playfully by a back leg and dragged it back. Moctu chuckled as the first pup tumbled over the other one and the two happily mauled one another.

They were cute, and it would be difficult to kill them, but the pups represented a food source for his group. Moctu reached into the den and extracted the nearest one by its back legs. It let out a high-pitched squeal, and he held it by the scruff of the neck so that it wouldn't bite him while he got the other one. Their fur was softer than he thought it would be, much softer than adult wolf fur. Once out of their den, neither seemed inclined to bite him, so he held one under each arm and worked his way around the large boulder toward Hawk.

Struggling to get over a medium-sized boulder in his path using no hands, his eyes widened, and his heart bulged into his throat as he saw the leopard eying him from a higher position, two rocks away.

He stopped and stared back at the big leopard, who was crouched, ready to spring. His hands were occupied with the pups, so he couldn't reach for his atlatl.

Without moving, out of the side of his mouth he hissed, "Hawk. Hawk! I've got problems!"

The pups recognized the danger and began squirming vigorously with their ears flattened. Moctu worried that putting them on the ground might trigger the leopard to action. The cat continued to study him, weighing its odds.

"Hawk," Moctu hissed louder. "The leopard…it's here."

Moctu's mind raced as he watched the leopard creep a finger's length closer, until it was at the edge of the rock it was perched on. He was close enough to see its muscles tensing, readying for its assault. I'll swivel when it leaps, he decided. I'll turn my back to the beast and protect my neck and face. I'll drop the pups…maybe I'll…

"Arrrrarrrr!" Hawk roared as he charged into sight, his heavy spear upraised and ready.

Suddenly, the odds had changed, and the cat didn't like it. In a flash of movement, it turned and disappeared behind the rock it was on. Moctu closed his eyes in relief and blew out a breath.

"Brud Hawk, you…you saved my life. Spirits, that was close."

Hawk eyed the squirming bundles of fur that Moctu held and looked at him questioningly.

"Uh huh, we can…um…" He looked down at the cute, soft pups and said, "We can eat these later…if we get hungry before we get to Uhda." He already knew, however, that there would be no way he'd be able to kill these cute, wiggling little balls of fur.

40

BACK AT THEIR MAKESHIFT camp of huts fashioned from sapling poles and hide, Jondu told the Nereans gathered around the main fire what they had seen and heard from the shaman.

"The Lion People shaman, Devu, he's very powerful. His visions are...amazing. At night, his soul travels far, and he sees game...lots of game. We'll be hunting for it soon...with the Lion People hunters. Now for the bad news...he saw ghosts—three ghosts, Nerean ghosts—and one was Nindai." Although it was more tragic news for their tribe, this story suited Jondu, because it cemented his role as leader—Moctu was gone.

The crowd gasped, then let out a collective moan. Nindai was gone! And if Nindai was one of the ghosts, then the other two were probably Nuri and Moctu. Avi was glad that Alta was back at Etseh so she didn't have to hear that her son, Moctu, was dead—at least not yet. It had almost broken her before when she thought he was dead. Maybe, just maybe, it would prove untrue this time as well.

"There was more bad news," Jondu continued. "The Lion People have been attacked by the Pale Ones. Some have been killed, and some of their women and young men were carried off. Even the Lion People leader, Rolf, lost his son. I'm afraid the Pale Ones have turned on Moctu, Nuri, and Nindai. I'm afraid they're gone."

The moaning and wails of the crowd grew louder.

"We'll join with the Lion People to fight the Pale Ones and avenge our dead," Jondu said loudly. He saw Avi frown, and he was surprised at the muted cry of support he got. Avi and many in the audience remembered that, last time, the vengeance against the Pale Ones had not worked out well.

"After a feast tomorrow evening to which all are invited, our hunters will leave in the morning and travel north with Lion People hunters. Devu has seen large herds of game there as his soul wandered during dreamtime."

A cheer went up from the Nerean hunters as they envisioned a successful hunt.

"We may also encounter the Pale Ones, and we'll need to be ready. While the hunting party is gone, the rest of you will gather flint at the quarry."

***

AT DAWN THERE WAS a mist in the air which gradually gave way to beautiful, rose-colored beams of sunlight that exploded from the eastern hills. It was a good omen, and Jondu wished the hunting group was leaving this morning instead of tomorrow. Tonight there would be another feast, and he would get to hear more from Devu, the impressive shaman. Today would be spent making new atlatl shafts. There was an almost unlimited supply of high-quality flint for spear points, and yesterday women had gathered cedar, ash, and fir branches for the wooden shafts.

All day long, the clinking of flint being struck could be heard over the low, background buzz of sandstone being used to grind knobs and irregularities off wooden branches. Men did all of the flint shaping while women did the woodwork. One woman used sand in a rawhide bag to polish the well-ground shafts while two others expertly bent branches over fire to straighten them.

By evening, the tribe was tired and ready for a feast. All were excited, especially the younger Nereans. For many of them, this would be the first time they had met anyone outside of their tribe. Everyone was again instructed not to mention their newly acquired fire-making ability.

Jondu and Avi again sat near the shaman, along with the Lion People leader Rolf and Lehoy. During the meal, Jondu was extremely pleased to hear that Lehoy would not be participating in the upcoming hunt because of his injured leg.

"The Spirits are favoring me," Jondu whispered happily to Avi.

His mood changed as he listened to Devu speak once most had finished eating.

The shaman, looking even creepier than the night before, first recounted an exciting tale of an extraordinary year-ago hunt in which more than two hands of animals had been killed. That hunt alone had provided the Lion People with nearly a full year of meat.

"I foretell similar results for this hunt," he said loudly, to cheers from all present. Then his face grew serious, and his voice changed to a tremorous hiss.

"But Nereans," he rasped, staring at Jondu and Avi, "who will be hunting in the same area, will have poor results…because they are cursed."

Jondu's head jerked back as if he'd been slapped, and his mouth fell open. Similarly shocked, other Nereans looked to him for his reaction.

"Why have so many Nereans died over the past two summers? Why have their hunts failed? They're cursed because they believe in the wrong Spirits," Devu continued. "They believe the Earth Mother came first, but every thinking person knows the Earth Spirit is *male*. It is the sky that is female. It is the mountains that thrust into the sky, not the sky into the mountains.

"Each year, women make new life that looks like them. Only women can do this, not man. The earth is different…as different as a moonbeam from a lightning bolt, or a snowflake from fire. Mountains do not produce a new mountain each year. So, the Earth is male." The forests are female, yes, because they produce new life each year, and the moon is clearly female, because, like women, it has a moon cycle."

Avi looked nervously at Jondu and saw his head was cocked and his mouth pursed. He's considering this! she thought. I wish Jelli or Ono were here…someone to confront…to dispute this…

"There's only one way for Nereans to break the curse, or further misfortune will follow," Devu intoned loudly. "The Earth Spirit is hungry… *He* is hungry for more dead." Devu looked fixedly at Jondu and continued. "Their leaders need to fast…a long fast that will thoroughly cleanse them. And their key women," he paused and cast lustful eyes at Avi, "need to be purified…by me."

Avi could tell that her "purification rite" would include sex with him, and her lip curled in repulsion. She looked away from the shaman, her eyes finding those of Lehoy, who appeared embarrassed by the shaman's words. He shook his head imperceptibly, which she appreciated. Maybe not everyone here was crazy. She looked to Jondu for support and instead found him staring at the shaman, entranced.

41

WHILE HAWK FINISHED GUTTING and cleaning the she-wolf carcass, Moctu fed the pups from the food that the mother had regurgitated. The pups did not seem to recognize or mind that their mother was dead not far from them, and they hungrily ate the chunks of slightly digested meat.

The men kept a careful watch for the leopard or for returning members of the wolf pack, but none showed. It was mid-afternoon by the time Moctu and Hawk got back to where the women were, and they already had a fire burning. Everyone was hungry, ready for a meal even if it was wolf meat. During her moons of captivity with the Shiv, Siduri had seen them make fire many times, so she was not surprised that Nuri could make one.

All of them were completely charmed by the playful pups. The larger male loved to ambush and maul the other, a solid-gray female who was a little smaller but feisty and active. The female happily reciprocated, falling on her back and pushing with her paws while softly biting and play-fighting. When the male finally tired and lay down, the female crouched nearby, wagging her tail, and gave three high-pitched barks, trying to coax him to further brawling. Everyone laughed.

The roasted meat of the mother wolf was the most nourishment that any of them had gotten in a half moon, and it did much to reinvigorate them. Nuri fashioned a pack in which to carry the pups, and she and Moctu split the duties. The energized group made good progress, and by evening, Hawk recognized landmarks that indicated they would reach Uhda late the next day.

It rained hard the next morning, but the group decided not to wait out the storm. Rather, they slogged through it, and by the time it ended in the early afternoon, all were soaked and exhausted. They pushed on, however, and by evening they were thrilled to see the fires of Uhda winking in the distance.

As they neared Uhda in the dark, they heard excited cries, and soon Da, Ronk, and several women were whooping and jumping, embracing both Lok and Hawk, and chattering rapidly in Krog. Moctu and Nuri glowed with happiness at the scene, but it was not long before Moctu perceived a distinct iciness from Da.

What going on? he wondered. Da's not even acknowledging the rest of us. Is it the pups? Not sure he's even noticed them. He sure doesn't like something.

Rah arrived to the growing group, and while smiling and warmly welcoming Lok and Hawk back, she quickly made her way to Moctu. "Come," she said to Moctu, taking his hand. "Elka sleeping. You, Nuri," she paused, eying Siduri, not knowing what to make of her. "Her," she said finally, nodding at Siduri. "All come with me. Much to tell."

When they got to Rah's hearth, Elka was stirring, and with the commotion, she awoke. Sleepy and tired, she began to cry and whine. Elka continued crying while Moctu hugged her, then stopped suddenly as he discharged the wiggling pups from their carrying pack. Anxious to talk with Moctu, Rah had been in the middle of a sentence, but she, too, was now transfixed by the squirming pair of wolf pups. The pups seemed to recognize the young girl as another pup, and soon they were tumbling over her while she giggled and unsuccessfully tried to corral them.

After hearing a little about how they came to have the pups, Rah came back to her matter at hand. "Da mad-mad. Very mad. Two

Nereans come...Palo and...um...another one. They help Nindai. He takes Sima, Da's woman. Big trouble...you maybe not safe. Elka maybe not safe."

Moctu closed his eyes and rubbed his forehead. "Nindai," he said, shaking his head. "Oh, Nindai. Dung. Dung!" He remembered Da's happy and expectant eagerness when they were trading for the young woman, and his utter despondency—and fury—when the trade fell apart. The big man's emotions had been further whipsawed. They soared when Sima was recovered after the attack, but then fell when he was made to wait while she adjusted to Uhda and his horrible face wound healed. Now, she'd been taken away completely.

"You go tomorrow. Take..." she paused, and had trouble finishing her sentence. "Elka," Rah said finally, her sad eyes meeting Moctu's. Sorrow welled in both Moctu and Nuri as they realized how much Rah would miss her granddaughter. Rah smiled thinly and pointed to the corner of the hearth, where the three pups—the two wolves and Elka—lay curled up together, asleep.

42

You can't be serious," Avi said, scowling. "I'm not—"

"We'd only have you do it if the hunt goes as he forecasts... Then we'll know his power is real," Jondu interrupted. "Devu has power, Avi. You have to admit that. And if he's right, and we're being cursed, then it's the only way."

"There is no way I'm—"

"Look, Avi, our hunts have been poor, and we're facing a bleak winter this year...a starvation winter. If we're cursed, and we don't... correct things, then we're not going to kill enough game, and people will die—our people. I'm leader, and I have to do everything I can. And I'll gladly do the fasting part. You...you may need to..."

"No. Just the idea of it makes me want to vomit."

"Let's just see how the hunt goes. Maybe we'll kill a lot of game. We might not need to...well, we'll know soon enough." Hunters from all the tribes would head out tomorrow morning. They'd move north to where Devu had seen large herds of game in his nightly dream travels.

Lying next to Avi in their tiny skin hut, Jondu turned on his side and put an arm over her. She angrily pushed it away.

"Come on, Avi. I'm leaving on a long trip tomorrow." Jondu didn't like the whiny tone in his voice, and he shook Avi to reestablish his control. Without a word, Avi turned to him, and Jondu climbed between her legs. In the darkness she lay there, still scowling, as Jondu strained and grunted above her.

Morning came, and the sky had already lightened as the sun peered over the eastern mountains like a giant, golden eye. Hunters from all the tribes had gathered at the muster point, and all were ready and excited about what Devu had said would be a great hunt—a great hunt for *most* of the tribes, anyway. A signal was given, and the hunters started walking north with their right foot because all knew that successful journeys and hunts had to begin with that foot.

Avi tended to baby Indar, then left him with her mother and collected her daily firewood. After that, she headed for the flint quarry to help with the effort there.

"Hello, Avi," said Lehoy, smiling at her while walking with a very slight limp in her direction. "You look lovely, as always."

Avi felt her cheeks flush. "Good morning, Lehoy. You look nice too. I hope your leg continues to get better?"

"Ah, it's much better, thank you. I almost went on the hunt, but for now, I'd rather stay around here." His smile broadened roguishly.

Avi could feel the blood heating her face and ears, and she looked down. She should send him off. Jondu didn't like him, and he certainly would not approve of Lehoy's flirting. Instead, she said, "Maybe you can help me locate some good flint."

"I'd like that. I'd like that very much, and I..." He nodded and touched her shoulder lightly. "I know some good places."

"I'm talking about flint...some good places to find flint," Avi said.

"Oh, I am too. Good places to find flint...I'm a good flint hunter. Come this way." He pointed east and smiled innocently. "Don't worry, there'll be people nearby." They talked easily while they walked, and Avi enjoyed his company and attention. They were several atlatl throws from the main group, and there were, in fact, no people nearby when they got to a small cliff face. Along its base was a rubble that included large quantities of high-quality flint.

"There's so much here," Avi said happily. "I'll have to make many trips."

"And I can help you…I'd be glad to help you," Lehoy said. His words were innocent, but his tone was mischievous.

Avi ignored the tone and said, "You certainly are a good flint hunter."

"I'm a good hunter of everything…a very good hunter. And this time," he said smiling, one eyebrow raised, "I'm after you."

"Oh, Lehoy…that's not—"

He pulled her to him and kissed her deeply. It was a warm, rich kiss, and Avi found herself kissing him back before she abruptly pushed him away.

"No. This is wrong," she said, but her thoughts went back to the night before. Jondu wants me to have sex with that…that horrible—

Lehoy kissed her again, and it was a long time before Avi reluctantly pushed him away.

"No, wait…wait."

"Wait? Wait for what?"

"I…I need some time to think. I just…need some time."

"Avi, I want you…you're all I think about. You're my sun and my moon and my stars."

She studied his face, which looked sincere, almost sad. He drank in the green fire of her eyes, then bent to her and kissed her softly. When she didn't pull away, passion overwhelmed him, and he became more aroused and forceful, his tongue finding and deeply exploring hers. She melted into his embrace, and he pulled his lips from hers only long enough to kiss her neck below her ear and under her chin. It sent exquisite waves of warmth through her. She quivered, powerless in the tumult of her feelings. Conflicting emotions played havoc through her.

Lehoy held her close to him while his left hand slowly roamed her body. Both delighted in the raw power and texture of sensuality. Avi could *feel* the blood pump in her veins. Still kissing her, Lehoy swept Avi up into his arms and carried her a short distance to a leafy thicket, where he gently laid her down.

"No," Avi said, but her voice lacked resolve. Lehoy slowly kissed all parts of her neck and caressed every part of her body with his hands, and Avi drank in the sensations. "Wait," she managed finally, gasping for breath. "Wait."

Lehoy drew back in mild surprise. His voice was husky with desire. "What...why?"

"I just..." Avi took another breath. "I...I need time...time to..."

"Please, Avi, I need you. It's never been like this before...you are so..." Before he could come up with the right word, he was kissing her again, and she was kissing him back, running a hand through his hair and holding onto his powerful back.

He was mostly out of his clothes, and now he undid the rawhide straps that held hers together. He nuzzled and fondled her large breasts, aware that any sucking might initiate milk flow. When Avi adjusted her position to allow him to remove her lower garment, he realized that she'd made her decision, and it inflamed him with a desperate need for her. He forced himself to slow down, however, and he continued kissing her breasts and neck. When his fingers found the wetness between her legs, he let out a soft moan of desire. Avi arched her back and gasped.

This is different, Avi thought, as Lehoy stroked her gently. Jondu saw love between a man and woman as a conflict which the man had to—and by the Spirits was ordained to—win. This man, Lehoy, she realized, is *sharing* pleasures, not just taking them. She arched her back again as Lehoy's fingers brought her close to the edge. It feels... oh, Spirits, it feels so good...Spirits...then she was there.

"Gaaaaa..." She let out a sound that was half gasp and half moan. Her body heaved and bucked as waves of ecstasy swept her. Lehoy smiled, happy that he had brought her such enjoyment. He was rigid with desire, and as her pleasure ebbed, he looked into her green eyes questioningly.

"Yes," she said breathlessly, pulling him to her. As he moved atop her, she could feel his strong chest against her breast, his heart beating wildly. "Yes," she said again.

He thrust inside her, his breath catching with the pleasure of it. Her hips moved like waves on the ocean, undulating wildly, as he plunged into her depths again and again. He was near the brink when he noted the change in Avi's breathing and felt her pushing harder into each of his thrusts. He forced himself to slow, desperately delaying his pleasure until Avi tensed, then relaxed, still thrusting.

"Aaaaaa," she moaned again, and then he was over the edge himself. The power of it was immense, towering, like nothing he'd ever experienced before. He pounded into Avi like a savage, wild animal. They continued to move together but gradually slowed as the feeling subsided for both of them. Both were breathing heavily as they lay together, enjoying the intimacy that sharing pleasure brings.

For Lehoy, a contented drowsiness set in, and he was soon asleep. As the pleasurable feelings and warmth subsided in Avi, conflicting emotions returned. Guilt up to the feather-edge of nausea bubbled forth and receded, then bubbled up again. Focusing on the sleeping man next to her helped diminish her remorse. She stared at Lehoy— the curls in his hair and on his chest. Avi breathed in his rich, earthy, masculine smell, and she happily relived their love-making. She had never enjoyed anything as much—nothing with Jondu had even come close.

But I have a child with Jondu, she thought. And I have responsibilities. She bit her lip as guilt swamped her again.

Her eyes widened as she heard a nearby commotion. People! Or someone, anyway. She covered Lehoy's mouth and nudged him. "Someone nearby," she hissed, and they both quietly scrambled to reclothe themselves.

It was Leuna. Twice-widowed Leuna, who was now Seetu's mate, was collecting flint from the rich piles of it in the rubble at the base of the cliff face. Avi shook her head at the irony. She and Nuri had long ago viewed—and scorned—a tryst between Leuna and Jabil. How the Spirits toy with us, Avi thought. The lovers were dressed, and they needed to move before Leuna saw them together in the thicket, which had no flint.

"I think there was more flint back this way, Lehoy," Avi said loudly, pretending he was some distance away. She walked calmly out into the open. Leuna looked up and said, "Oh, Avi, I didn't know you were there. There's a lot of good flint—" She stopped in mid-sentence as Lehoy walked out of the thicket, following a little behind Avi. She studied Avi, who saw her gaze and immediately looked down, becoming engrossed in looking for flint. With her peripheral vision, Avi could see Leuna continue to stare in her direction. She knows—or suspects, Avi thought, mortified.

43

THE MORNING WAS COLD and windy, and the sky was mottled with both dull-gray and dark-gray clouds. After heartfelt goodbyes to Hawk, Lok, and Rah, the foursome of Moctu, Nuri, Siduri, and Elka—along with the two wolf pups—left Uhda.

Elka, who had been getting solid food as well as nursemaid milk, would have to be fully weaned on this trip since no lactating females were accompanying the group. The little girl didn't like it, not one bit, and she screamed for milk again and again. She was nearly inconsolable the first night. It was the pups that made the difference. They, too, were being weaned, and over the first couple of days, the three of them seemed to forge a bond. They began to sleep together every night, and they would eat together as well. When Elka saw the wolf pups eat the finely diced, dried mammoth meat that had been rehydrated with stream water, she ate it too.

The trip through the mountains took longer than any so far. Moctu was extra cautious about ambushes from either Shiv or fierce animals like saber-tooths. Furthermore, both women were not at full strength, and they had the toddler Elka and the two wolf pups to care for. But the group encountered no dangers, and they made it into the lowlands in four days. On the last day in the mountains, they'd come across the tracks of a travois, several days old, which Moctu assumed was Palo carrying the lame Nindai the last portion of the trip.

They considered swinging by Etseh, but that would cost them several days, and they were already very late for the meeting of the tribes.

"What are we going to find when we meet up with our people?" Moctu asked Nuri. "We have so much to tell them—so many stories. And they'll meet Elka for the first time. I wonder if her aunt Zaila is there, or if she stayed at Etseh? They'll get along great. I wonder if I'm still leader? Probably have to fight for it...been away so long. Ono's probably decided that he wants to be leader after all."

Siduri was close enough to hear, and Moctu continued. "And the Lion People will be thrilled to have Siduri back."

"Maybe," Siduri said. "But I know some will say that I'm tainted, contaminated by the Pale Ones." Her lower lip went out, but she went on. "Our shaman, Devu, has spoken often of how the putrid Pale Ones corrupt the earth. He—and many others—will think that of me."

Moctu grimaced and whistled apprehensively, pointing to the travois tracks they'd been following toward Lion People territory. "And Nindai is arriving there before us, bringing Sima, a Pale One, with him. That can't be good."

"And we're bringing Elka, who's half Pale One," Nuri said. She didn't give voice to her fears that she and her unborn baby would also be considered tainted.

Thinking of Jondu, Moctu said, "Some in our tribe, too, have never been...comfortable with the Pale Ones. And especially now— I'm sure the Lion People are at war with the Shiv. We are as well, or will be soon. But they likely don't know the difference between the Krog and the Shiv. They think all Pale Ones are a threat." An image of an angry Da came to mind, and he shrugged and said, "And even some of the Krog may no longer be friendly."

The group was silent for a long time as they walked.

"We may be walking into a hornet's nest," Moctu said finally, and the women murmured agreement. "But we have to keep going— Nindai and his woman, Sima, may be in danger."

44

PALO LOWERED THE TRAVOIS and grimaced as he arched his back, slowly stretching out the cramped muscles. Just a few days out of Uhda, Nindai's leg had swelled grossly as he gamely tried to walk on his own with a crutch. Finally, Palo and Nabu forced him onto a travois, and they took turns carrying him through the mountainous country and into the lowlands. Unfortunately, the swelling had yet to go down, and the whole leg was red and inflamed.

Sima had walked alongside the travois most of the way, smiling and talking with her mate in stilted language and hand signs. Now, the young Pale One girl stepped forward, pointed to herself and then the travois handles, and, without waiting for approval, lifted and started carrying it. She was robust and remarkably strong, and she pulled the heavy contraption with an ease that astonished the men.

As they neared Lion People territory, they came across the tracks that the Nereans had taken many days before. At least three hands of people pulling several travois had left an easy trail to follow.

"Who are you?" called a young man, using the dialect of the Lion People. Palo could see at least two other men who remained partially hidden.

"We're Nereans. We come to be with our people…and take part in the summer meeting of the tribes," Palo called back.

All three young men approached cautiously, weapons at the ready, and Palo could see that each wore the necklace of two shells and a lion's tooth that marked them as Lion warriors.

"Who…or *what* is that?" said the apparent leader of the young men, scowling and pointing at Sima.

Nindai attempted to get up to address the man's insult, but Palo waved him off and replied, "She is Sima. She is of the peaceful Krog tribe, and she's the mate of our shaman, Nindai. Now please direct us to our people."

The young men had seemed shocked to hear the name Nindai. They conferred briefly, clearly still troubled by Sima.

The leader of their group finally responded. "We heard reports of Nindai's death…obviously he was only wounded." He pointed northeast and said, "Your people are just over that hill near the flint quarry. You may continue, but Devu, our shaman, will hear of this…" He frowned and nodded at Sima. "And her." He and his two companions turned and quickly left.

"Well, that wasn't particularly friendly," Nabu said sarcastically. He put away two atlatl shafts that he had surreptitiously drawn. "And what's this about Nindai dying?"

"I know of Devu," said Nindai. "He's powerful…and not 'particularly friendly,' either. This feels like trouble."

Palo pulled the travois, and the group was quiet as they trudged up the hill where they, at last, saw the meager skin huts that temporarily housed their people. Carrying a spear, Petrel came to meet them.

"Palo! Nabu! It's so good…" Petrel's jaw dropped as Palo lowered the travois and he saw Nindai. "Nindai?" His wide eyes lasted only a moment, narrowing as they encountered Sima, the first Pale One he had ever seen. He pointed at her and said, "Who is…this?"

With Sima's help, and grimacing from the pain, Nindai stood and said, "This is my woman, Sima."

Petrel's face reddened, and he said, "Oh, now I see why you're so late. Spirits, we've been worried...we thought you were dead." He scowled. "And now we find that you were just enjoying the Pale Ones' women. So where are Moctu and Nuri? Did Moctu take another mate...another Pale One?"

Nindai's nostrils flared, and he glared at Petrel. "No, we were attacked. And Nuri was taken...by the Shiv. She's in great danger... the Shiv are horrible...they're People Eaters. And Moctu's gone after her. He's in great danger too."

Petrel winced and rubbed a hand across his face. "I'm sorry. The Lion People here were also attacked. They lost several young women and men to the Pale Ones."

Palo brightened and said, "We heard from the Krog people...a returning warrior told them that Moctu was able to rescue a young woman from the Shiv. It wasn't Nuri, so I'll bet it was one of the Lion Clan women that was taken. She's free and with Moctu...if he's still alive."

The group was quiet as they contemplated the danger that Moctu was in and the atrocities that Nuri was undoubtedly suffering. The quiet was broken as other members of the tribe saw the group and rushed to greet them.

"It's Palo...and Nabu," they shouted. "And Nindai. Nindai's alive!" Soon the temporary camp had emptied, and the group was surrounded by people greeting and hugging them and asking questions. They were ushered to the central fire ring, where they answered questions and told their stories. Most of the questions centered on Moctu and Nuri, but people were also curious about—and suspicious of—Sima.

"Are the men on a hunt, or are they visiting the Lion People?" Palo asked. "Where are they all?"

"Most of them are on a hunt. A few of us have been left behind to guard and protect the camp," Petrel said. "The Lion People shaman, Devu...he's very powerful. He says there are large herds to the north.

It's really exciting—he saw them in a dream." He trailed off, thinking. In a softer voice he said, "But he also saw the ghosts of three dead Nereans...one with a bad leg. So we thought Nindai was dead, which meant you *all* were dead—Nindai, Moctu, and Nuri." He paused and put a hand to his beard, thinking how the shaman had wanted his daughter, Avi, to be "purified" by a sex rite with him. Like Jondu, he'd been enthralled by the shaman. Now, he was having second thoughts. "Maybe he's not as great a shaman as we thought."

As Petrel and the group considered that, there was a commotion behind him, and he swung around to see three young Lion warriors. One of them pointed to Sima as Devu strode forward.

Devu's lip curled as he looked at Sima, then he scanned the crowd and said, "Which of you is the shaman Nindai?"

Seated next to Sima, with his swollen leg extended before him, Nindai raised one hand and said, "I'm Nindai...and you must be Devu."

Devu's eyes narrowed as he scrutinized the man sitting next to the Pale One. "Yes, I'm Devu. I see you're cursed with a swollen leg. It looks painful...and infected."

Embarrassed, as most in the crowd turned to stare at his leg, Nindai shrugged it off. "It's an old injury, and this happens when I try to walk too much. I'll be fine with some rest."

"No, you're cursed. You Nereans not only believe in the wrong Spirits," he paused as his eyes settled on Sima, "you bring filth to your shelters."

Even though many of the Nereans were uncomfortable with Sima's presence, they bristled at Devu's incivility and his aspersions about their beliefs.

Petrel took a step forward and said, "You had us believing Nindai was dead...all your talk about three ghosts, one with a bad leg. That turned out to be garbage. Now you challenge our beliefs and insult our guests?" Petrel was backed by several in the group that nodded their agreement.

"*You* were the ones that thought of Nindai. The ghosts I saw were all bigger men…much bigger. And my visions are never wrong."

Nabu, who had only just heard about the visions, whispered something to Palo.

"Uh huh," Palo nodded at Nabu. And to the crowd, he said, "It could have been the ghosts of Ordu, Samar, and Tabar. Ordu had a bad leg."

Petrel's chin dropped, and he backed up and sat down, lost in thought. The other Nereans were quiet as they, too, considered this new possibility.

"You fight the truth," Devu said. "Each person has a spirit…a soul that's born and nourished in the darker and slower corners of our being—not like the body which we see develop every day." Once again, the small crowd seemed spellbound by Devu's eloquence and imagery. After a pause, he went on. "Most pay no attention to their souls. They're unwilling to think on darkness and death. Not me…I dwell there. I travel on the edge each night."

The shaman's voice was commanding and confident, almost hypnotic, and his words carried wisdom beyond the group's full understanding. The recently rebellious Nereans were quiet, largely won over, and even Palo and Nabu could see that this man had power.

"Now, if you accept that the world is dominated by the Earth *Father*, and you rid yourself of filth," Devu paused, looking again at Sima, "then all your curses will be broken. Your hunts will be successful, your tribe will prosper. Death will not stalk you as often. Life will be good again."

It was a wonderful vision that all desperately wished for, and Devu was offering a simple way to get it. Sima cowered against Nindai as more and more in the group looked at her disapprovingly.

Seeing that he had persuaded most in the crowd, Devu motioned to the three warriors, and they turned and left with no further words.

Nindai put a hand to his throbbing leg. Was it getting hotter?

PART TWO

MOCTU AND THE LION PEOPLE

45

As MOTTLED GRAY CLOUDS continued to darken into towering, bluish-black thunderheads, the temperature dropped and the wind picked up. The darkest areas occasionally flashed with lightning and rumbled ominously. Moctu had been on the lookout for shelter, but now he became desperate for it. The mountains, which offered large trees, boulders, crevices, and caves had been left behind days ago. Now the foursome was in the lowlands, which had no large boulders and few trees.

"Let's head for those trees on that far knoll…maybe we'll make it before the storm hits," Moctu said, raising his voice over the blustery wind. He could see rain falling on the brushy grasslands behind them where the clouds touched the ground. It was moving toward the group and gaining on them.

The foursome was tired from days of travel and an especially hard morning as they pushed to stay ahead of the storm. Nuri struggled to keep up as her endurance failed her.

I should have more energy than this, she thought worriedly. I'm in my fifth moon…it shouldn't be like this. She remembered her mother telling her that pregnancies last for two hands of moons. The first three moons are the sickness ones, the middle four the mild ones, and the last three are the awkward ones. I should be doing better. I'm holding the group back—I have to move faster.

A huge bolt of nearby lightning underscored the threat, and Nuri, Moctu, and Siduri all broke into a near-run. Elka, who was strapped to the front of Moctu, started to wail, and the wolf pups that he carried in his backpack began to whimper and squirm.

A wave of nausea and dizziness swept over Nuri, and her ramped-up pace faltered. Huge drops of cold rain began to pelt down, just a few at first, then coming in droves.

"We're not going to make it," Moctu yelled over the whipping wind. He pointed to the biggest sapling he could see, a young pine not much taller than a man. "Let's huddle under some sleeping furs there."

The rain came hard, cold, and slanting, and they were drenched in a few heartbeats. A veil of near darkness cloaked the area as they threw their sleeping furs over the spindly pine, which bent double under the weight. Crouched in the darkness under the furs, and with their teeth chattering, the three adults tried to calm Elka.

"Shhh, shhh, shhh, it's going to be all right," Moctu told Elka over and over. Bright flashes of light sporadically lit the huddling group, who clenched their teeth each time, anticipating the almost immediate thunderous explosion. The pounding rain not only continued, it increased, and the furs became sodden and heavy. Moctu helped hold them up as the small sapling was more than doubled over, and he thought it might snap. Moctu grimaced as, added to the steady drumming of the rain on the furs, came a popping of sleet or small hail.

"Uh oh," he said as the popping increased in frequency and strength. "It's hail."

A huge crash of lightning and instantaneous thunder indicated to everyone that they were in the middle of the storm. Siduri began to pray aloud.

"Spare us, Storm Spirits, please spare us. We see your great power, and we're awed by it, but we trust you to protect us through..." Another huge crash blotted out her words, and the popping of the hail became louder, more like the sound Jelli made when she beat the hollow log with a stick during the "Song of the Tribe." The hail was much larger and stung Moctu's hands as he held up the furs. Pieces of it bounced under the furs, and Nuri could see that it was acorn sized.

"If we didn't have the furs, that could kill us," Nuri said, whistling softly.

The hail increased in size, and each strike to the furs made Moctu wince. He shifted from holding the furs with his hands to using his forearms.

This is a test, he thought. As a warrior, I can't cry out…must be stro… A huge block of ice hit directly on his wrist where it held up the furs, and a groan escaped him. "If the furs shred, we're all going to die," he muttered to himself. "Spirits, please protect us. Please."

There was one more pulse of heavy hail, which Moctu weathered without a sound, then the storm's fury lessened as it moved on, and the hail abated. Moctu sank to the ground and took a deep breath while gently rubbing his throbbing hands and forearms. "Thank you, Spirits. Thank you," he murmured, shaking his head with relief. "We're going to live."

The sky lightened as the storm moved on, thundering violently to the northeast of them. Behind the storm came a penetrating cold. The adults shivered with both easing fear and the drop in temperature. The pups still cowered in their backpack, trembling with their ears pulled back. Kept warm next to Moctu's chest, Elka stopped crying. Siduri pulled up a lower flap of the furs to see the ground white with hailstones, some the size of pine cones. It was still drizzling lightly, but she ventured out to collect one of the bigger stones and determined that it was actually two stones which had fused together. She hefted the stone, feeling its weight, and grimaced.

"It's about half the weight of a cobble of this size…could've killed us."

"I've never seen anything like it," Nuri said, turning to Moctu. "You must be bruised and hurting." Pulling the furs up higher let in more light, and she could see Moctu rubbing his hands and forearms. They were covered with red welts. "Oh, Moctu, that looks really painful. How can I help...what can I do?

Still stunned by how closely they had dodged death, Moctu said, "Cold...we need a fire. Everything's soaked. Get my horse-hoof fungus and dry kindling and spindle from the pack. Don't think I can do it right now." He shivered involuntarily.

While Siduri searched the nearby area for wood that wasn't completely soaked, Nuri stayed under the fur lean-to and gathered the key materials from Moctu's pack. She found the concentric-banded, disc-shaped fungus and shredded it. Moctu had learned from the Krog that it was the easiest tinder to catch fire, and he'd collected a handful of it from fallen trees. He now always carried tinder and kindling that had been dried by his most recent fire, but he didn't have much.

Siduri returned with some damp, dead grass and an arm-sized log she had found partially buried. She knocked the bark from it, exposing wood that was not green or wet. All of them knew that they'd only get one shot at this, and they were all wet and cold. Siduri went to look for more wood while Nuri prepped the spindle and flat fireboard.

"Sorry, I can't help...my arms and hands—"

"Don't worry, we'll get this. You rest." She paused and smiled at her mate. "You saved our lives, Moctu...all of us. You rest."

Nuri splintered the relatively dry log, and she began turning the spindle as Siduri returned with an armload of wet wood. Although Nuri worked expertly, the air was too damp, and she couldn't produce an ember. Nearly exhausted and totally frustrated, she stopped to rest. "It's going to get colder tonight...we really need this fire," Nuri said, wiping her forehead. "I'm just not...I just don't know what..."

"Siduri, you push down on the spindle while Nuri turns it... let's try that," Moctu offered, upset that he couldn't help. His swollen hands felt like they'd been stung by dozens of wasps.

Siduri pushed down on the top of the spindle while Nuri turned it rapidly back and forth. The tip got exceedingly hot, but no smoke emerged. The rain had let up, but the temperature kept dropping and the wind was buffeting the wet furs. Everyone was cold except for Nuri, who was breathing heavily and sweating from her exertions.

"We're not going to have a fire tonight," Nuri said finally, wiping sweat from her eyes and shaking her head. "I just can't get it. I'm sorry...the wood and air...they're too wet. Can't get an ember."

Siduri's teeth began to chatter, and the dejected group huddled for warmth. As night fell and a wolf pack began howling to the northwest, the adults chewed dried mammoth meat that Rah had given them. Both pups' ears lifted, and they were riveted by the far-off sounds. The grim mood of the group was broken when Mut let out a squeaky, high-pitched howl, at which they all chuckled.

Nuri chewed some of the tough meat for Elka and was surprised when she ate it hungrily. The pups likewise devoured the pre-chewed meat. Worried about the pack of wolves, Moctu gave his heavy spear to Nuri. It wouldn't be much use to him. The wolves didn't come, but they spent a miserable night wet, weary, and cold, bunched tightly under soggy furs. In the morning, Moctu had a fever.

46

DEVU'S PREDICTION IS PROVING true, Jondu thought disconsolately. In an eerie parallel to two summers before, the joint hunt had started out with a rhino kill. Unfortunately for Jondu and the Nereans, they were hunting to the west when the Lion People hunters, along with a few Gurek men, found and killed the beast. It was a huge amount of meat, but none of it could be claimed by Jondu's people. The previous rhino kill, when Ordu, Samar, and Tabar were still alive, had been wildly celebrated by Nereans, but that hunt had ended in tragedy. Was this an omen...were the Spirits presaging a similar, horrible outcome for this hunt?

Three days had passed since the Lion People had killed the rhino, and Jondu's hunters had yet to find, much less kill, any game. Perversely, Jondu hoped the Lion People were having no further success. His team of hunters were to rendezvous this afternoon with their hunters at the pass between the twin snow-capped mountains to the north.

"I'm not sure I can stomach more of their success," he muttered, shaking his head. "Is Devu right? Do we honor the wrong Spirits?" He considered that. "I'm willing to fast, but Avi..." He closed his eyes for a long moment. "It would kill me to let that hideous man have Avi for a night. But if it would cleanse us and make us successful again, then I need to put the welfare of the tribe first. Devu has a strong argument about the Earth Spirit being male, not female. Have we been wrong all this time? Why is it only now causing us harm?"

His thoughts were broken as Seetu returned excitedly from scouting to the northwest. He'd crossed caribou tracks—fresh ones… maybe six hands of them. It was a long trek to the rendezvous site, but following the caribou tracks was only a slight diversion, so Jondu and the hunters broke into a run. By late afternoon, the Nerean hunters were exhausted and dripping with sweat, but the tracks and dung were no fresher. The caribou were moving fast.

"Do we continue chasing these caribou and miss our meeting tonight with the Lion People?" Jondu asked the hunters. "They'll call us unreliable." He pulled on his short dark beard. "But this is as close as we've gotten to game since the hunt started."

"I've been thinking about this," Seetu said. "We can meet up with the Lion People, and if they haven't seen game recently, we can hunt these caribou together. It's the friendly thing to do, and we'll only lose about half a day."

Jondu sighed, knowing it was the right answer, but still desperate to catch up with the caribou. "You've spoken wisely, Seetu. We'll do that."

They headed north, and it was dark before the bone-weary Nereans saw the fires of the Lion People hunters. Jondu called out, not wanting to surprise them. He heard answering calls, and soon two torches bobbed in the darkness moving toward them.

"We were worried about you," said a small, wiry man holding one of the torches. "Come, have some fresh caribou meat with us. We killed three today."

Jondu's lips tightened as a wash of dissonant emotions swept him. He should be happy for the Lion People success, but he wasn't. He felt like spitting. The Spirits were not whispering to him, they were shouting. They favored the Lion People because the Nereans honored the wrong Spirits and had false beliefs. It was so clear. Devu was right, they'd been cursed, and he would need to fast soon. And Avi…she wasn't going to be happy.

47

AVI PULLED THE LAST piece of firewood from her gathering skin and stacked it with the others. She stared at the ground, lost in thought. *When I'm with him...I've never been happier. He makes me feel...* She struggled to find the right way to express the joy she experienced when she was with Lehoy. *It's not just joy and pleasure,* she thought. *It's contentment. I just feel fulfilled when I'm with him. He understands me and wants to know more about me...who I am. Every time I close my eyes, every time I dream, it's him. I'm living another life, different from my waking one.*

From inside the skin hut, Indar began crying lustily, and that took her thoughts in the other direction. *When I'm away from him, and especially when I look at Indar, I see Jondu's face, and I'm sickened by what I've done...what I've become. It's just not me—it's not who I am. Jondu's a good man, and he deserves better from me. He cares about me in his way. We've been together almost two years, and we have a beautiful son. What am I doing?*

As she tended Indar, she saw his face had Jondu's cheekbones and deep-set eyes. His eyes were hazel, sort of a cross between her fiery green eyes and Jondu's dark ones. Once again, she was swamped by guilt. And fear. *If Jondu finds out, he might reject me,* she worried. *I'd likely lose my position, my son, even my place in the tribe.*

Would Lehoy take me if that happened? Yes, I think he would. But I'd have to live with him here, and I might never see Indar again…or my friends and family. An image of Nuri came to her, and her spirits sank further. Avi had been stunned to learn that Nuri was a prisoner of the Shiv—if she was still alive.

With Indar fed and happily teething on a caribou bone, Avi went outside and knelt in the sun.

"Spirits, please bless Nuri. Keep her safe, and help her escape from the Shiv. Please bring her and Moctu safely back to us unharmed." Avi shook her head thinking of the atrocities and horrors that Nuri was undoubtedly experiencing. "Please, please help her.

"I miss her so much," she murmured. "If Nuri was here…she'd know what to do. I could trust her, and she could help me figure all this out.

"Please, Spirits," she prayed again, "help free her, and bring her—and Moctu—to safety." She touched her dove feather talisman, and an idea came to her. She dug a small hole, then took out her small flint knife and sliced the top of her left hand. She dribbled blood into the hole and said, "Please, Earth Mother. Accept my blood offering, and send Nuri and Moctu safely back to us." She rubbed blood onto her talisman and said the prayer to her totem.

She pulled off the leather strap holding the talisman, kissed the blood-stained, white feather, then placed the necklace in the hole and covered it. She sat back and closed her eyes, thinking of her beautiful, kind, and warm-hearted friend.

That afternoon, Nuri arrived.

48

THE WOMEN HAD WALKED in silence for a long time as they pulled the crossed-pole travois carrying Moctu, Elka, and the pups. It was exhausting work as the ground was muddy and clods of soggy dirt and vegetation bunched on the dragging ends, acting as natural brakes. The path they followed had been grooved recently by many other travois, all going eastward.

"We should check on Moctu soon…see if his fever has broken," Nuri said, breathless and knowing that Siduri would probably recognize the statement for what it was—a ploy for a rest. They'd earlier felt his forehead and determined his fever had lessened.

"Moctu and Elka are both sleeping. Let's push on to that next low hill," Siduri said.

Nuri was dizzy and her legs felt leaden. Where has my endurance gone? she wondered. Does Siduri know I'm exhausted, and she's just being mean, or is she oblivious?

Siduri's next words took away what little breath Nuri had left. "Does Moctu know about Shaka-Nu?"

"Yes," Nuri replied. "He knows Shaka-Nu raped me and that I killed him. But you know that, so what do you really mean?"

"Does he know *all* about Shaka-Nu?"

Guilt flooded Nuri as she remembered receiving pleasure from her captor. She looked behind her to see if Moctu was still asleep.

"What are you getting at?"

"Does Moctu know you became Shiv?"

Nuri bristled. "I am *not* a Shiv."

"Did you receive pleasures from Shaka-Nu?"

"I...I—"

"Did you eat human flesh?"

"I..."

Siduri chuckled bitterly and said, "I know. I know what Shaka-Nu could do...what he did to me. How he made me a Shiv."

"You're not—"

"I received pleasures from him...many times, at least before he gave me to his men." Her face clouded, and her eyes misted at the thought. "And I ate human flesh. I...I carried his child for more than two moons." A small sob escaped her.

Nuri felt like going to her, but she could not put down the travois pole. "Oh, you poor girl," she said, feeling close to Siduri for the first time. "You...you shouldn't have had to suffer that. And yes, it was suffering, even though there may have been some pleasure involved. It was not something you wanted."

A tear streaked down Siduri's cheek. "But that's just it," her voice choked. "I grew to want it." She tried to stifle a sob but couldn't. "I...I wanted to escape or be rescued, but I looked forward to my nights with Shaka-Nu. It was the only part of my days that wasn't...*awful.*"

Nuri motioned for them to lower the travois, and once it was on the ground, she went to Siduri and hugged her while the girl broke down.

"Does that make me a Shiv?" Siduri asked plaintively.

"No. You are *not* a Shiv. You're a young woman who was put in a horrible situation, and you did the best you could to survive. That doesn't make you a Shiv." Nuri thought about her personal encounter with Shaka-Nu, and some of her guilt melted away. Saying the words to another woman—a woman who'd experienced the same misfortune—helped reconcile her own conflicted emotions.

"I was there too," Nuri continued. "I had a similar time." She looked to Moctu again, and in a half-whisper, said, "There was some pleasure, and I feel guilt just like you. But those were pleasures neither of us wanted." She saw Siduri about to object, and she added, "At least at first. Neither of us should have been put in that circumstance… neither of us wanted to be taken by the Shiv. I'm sure, like me, you were terrified."

Siduri nodded, and her crying abated. "My people will think I'm tainted. No one will want me."

"Oh, come on…a beautiful girl like you? Trust me, there will be a lot of your people that are thrilled to have you back. And a lot of men that want you."

Siduri smiled up at Nuri and said, "You're very kind…" She paused and shook her head. "A beautiful and kind woman, and I see why Moctu loves you so much."

Nuri blushed, pleased by her words. "Thank you, Siduri." She squeezed the girl and said, "I think I have enough energy now to pull the travois to that next hill."

They were skirting the hill when Moctu awoke. "I can walk," he said.

"You've got Elka and the wolves, and you still have a fever," said Nuri. "You just rest and get better."

Still groggy, Moctu didn't argue. He lay back and was soon asleep. Nuri had refashioned the two packs that separately held Elka and the pups into one pack where they could be together. All three seemed more content that way.

The women pulled the travois to the east side of the hill where they could see a braided stream far ahead. Siduri recognized that Nuri was tiring again, so she suggested they stop to rest and scan the area for game. Nuri appreciated the gesture and smiled at how their relationship had transformed from an unspoken adversarial one to friendship in just one morning.

"Hellooo," yelled a familiar voice, and two men waved from the hill to the north.

"It looks like...that's Palo!" Nuri said, putting a hand to her chest as relief and excitement spread through her. "We're there...or close."

Soon Palo and Nabu were with them, hugging, laughing, talking loudly, and praising the Spirits.

"We've been so worried. Nuri, you were captured... How did Moctu get you away from the Shiv?" Palo ruffled Moctu's hair, waking him. "What are you doing, friend, relaxing while these women pull you? You have a bad leg?"

"Palo! Nindai!" Moctu said, slowly getting to his feet.

"Whoa... Where did all the bruises come from? You look like you took down a bison with your bare hands."

"Not myself right now...got beaten up by some hail," Moctu replied.

"We had that storm too, but it looks like you got it way worse than we did. You going to be all right? Sit, tell us everything. We have some news as well." Palo's eyes met Nabu's, and they nodded. His tone grew more serious. "And there's some things we should warn you about."

Nuri made introductions, and when Palo held Siduri's hand for an extra moment, Nuri winked at her and gave her a smile and a quick "I told you so" nod.

49

PALO AND NABU TOOK turns carrying the travois even though Moctu complained that he could walk. Nuri felt his forehead and worried that his fever was once again increasing.

Crossing the stream was accomplished easily, with Palo and Nabu keeping the travois mostly out of the low water and Nuri holding Elka and the pups in a pack at her front.

"Where did you get those, and what are they doing with Elka?" Palo asked.

Nuri laughed at his consternation. "Moctu and I have three pups now."

"I see that," Palo said. "Aren't you worried they'll bite her?"

"I'm more worried she'll bite them," Nuri replied, grinning. "They love being together. They really are like brothers and sisters."

"Moctu wasn't just talking like a proud father... Elka really *is* a beautiful child... Look at those eyes," Palo said.

As Nuri looked down at Elka's large, blue eyes, they heard a hailing call from the hill to the northeast.

"There they are... We're here," Palo said cheerfully. "That looks like Petrel. I'm glad we didn't have to deal with the Lion People... Their lookouts normally meet up with us by now." His face clouded. "And sometimes they bring Devu."

As they climbed the hill, Palo asked in a low voice, "So, Siduri... is she mated yet, or...?"

"No, and I think she likes you," Nuri said, raising her eyebrows and smiling at him.

"Nuri!" Petrel called as they got closer. "It's so wonderful to see you. And Moctu! You're both safe. Praise the Spirits!" Other Nereans were soon on the scene, and Petrel dispatched a young boy to run and fetch Avi. "Like the rest of us, Avi will be overjoyed to see you. I've heard her pray often for your safe return. But what's wrong with Moctu...? Why isn't he walking?"

"He saved us during the hailstorm. He took a real beating...and now he has a fever," Nuri said, casting a worried look back at her mate.

Once again, there was lots of hugging, loud, happy talk, and praising the Spirits as people showed up to welcome the new arrivals. All were very curious about Elka and the wolf pups, but Nuri held up a hand and started to make introductions. Palo cleared his throat and intervened, locking eyes with Nuri, the corners of his mouth turned up slightly. With his hand on Siduri's back, he said, "And this is Siduri... She's been rescued, and we're so pleased to have her back here with us and her people."

Siduri smiled warmly at him and dipped her head to the crowd.

Breathless, Avi flew past several people and hugged Nuri from the side, avoiding the large, wiggling pack at her front. The two women danced with happiness, laughing and squealing.

"I knew you weren't dead... I knew you'd make it back!" Avi said loudly, a happy tear rolling down her cheek. "I've prayed so often and so hard. My prayers...they're finally answered...! Thank you, Spirits." The two women rocked back and forth, hugging and laughing. Tears streamed down their faces, and many in the crowd wiped their eyes as well.

Seeing three little heads projecting from the pack, Avi finally stopped and said, "And who is this...and what are these?"

Palo held up a hand and said, "Here comes Devu." A hush fell over the crowd as the tall, bony shaman approached with the same three guards as before.

"Siduri, is that you?" he asked. "Your mother will be pleased. Your father is on the hunt." He eyed her. "Did the Pale Ones...did they soil you?"

Siduri swallowed hard and stuttered. "I...I..."

Nuri stepped forward and said, "This isn't the place for that. Siduri's story will be told soon enough. She's safe, and she's acted bravely and honorably."

The shaman's eyes narrowed as he took in Nuri and the three figures in her front pack. "Who are you? And what are these... these...?" He was left pointing at her pack, at a loss for words.

"This is Elka, daughter of Moctu, leader of the Nereans. And Elka is my daughter now as well. And these," she looked at the pups and couldn't help smiling, "these are her friends."

Devu scowled at the pups and Elka and said derisively, "We'll call her Lo-Otso, our word for Sleeps with Wolves." His lip turned up. "Well, where is this Moctu? I thought Jondu was leader of the Nereans. Where is this...*other* leader?"

Several in the crowd pointed toward Moctu, who was still lying on the skins of the travois. He raised his hand slowly and said, "I'm Moctu." After a pause, he added in a stronger voice, "Leader of the Nereans."

"Your face is red with fever, and your hands and arms are bruised. Clearly the curse of the Nereans carries on in you." Devu glanced at Elka's lighter skin and blue eyes and nodded back at Moctu. "You've been with Pale Ones. You need to be cleansed... You'll need to fast. The sooner the better." He turned to Nuri, who was standing between Siduri and Avi, and his gaze slowly swept from her face to her hips and down her legs. He licked his lips.

Nuri felt her skin crawl as the man undressed her with his eyes. After similarly scanning Siduri and Avi, the corners of Devu's mouth turned up, and he said, "The rest of you who have been with the Pale Ones...you'll need to be purified as well."

His meaning was clear, and Nuri's mouth opened in an appalled scowl as her head pulled back in disgust.

Not waiting for a response, Devu turned and left with the guards.

"Who does he..." Nuri started, then stopped, shaking her head and grimacing. "What an awful, creepy man."

"Don't underestimate him...he's powerful," Avi said flatly, and Siduri nodded solemnly. "He's convinced a lot of people that that he's right...maybe even Jondu. And maybe we *are* cursed. Sometimes I wonder." She brightened, looking at Nuri. "But not today. The Spirits have blessed us—you're here now—and maybe our luck has changed."

Nuri smiled at Avi, then watched the departing shaman and guards. "I'll just tell you, the earth and seas will freeze over before I am 'purified' by that man."

"Well, pray for a good hunt. For us, I mean. Women have already been sent to where the Lion People killed a big rhino, but none of that meat is ours. If Jondu comes back, and we haven't been successful, he may force us, or at least me, to be purified," Avi said.

Nuri stared at her friend, shocked by her words. "Jondu? No, I can't believe that."

Biting her lip, Avi nodded. "I need to talk with you privately— sometime soon...about that and...some other things too. I've missed you so much."

Nuri hugged her and said, "I want to talk with you too—soon." Turning to Siduri, she said, "Let's get Moctu and Elka settled, then maybe you'd like to go see your family and friends." Seeing the girl's trepidation, she added, "I'll go with you if you want."

With the help of Palo and Nabu, they quickly erected a skin hut over stacked poles. Still feverish, Moctu slept through most of the activity, even when they moved him inside. Nuri anxiously felt his forehead. It was no worse, but it was no better. Nabu said he would stay with Moctu and Elka while Nuri went with Siduri to the Lion People camp. Remaining attentive to Siduri, Palo insisted on accompanying the women.

They had just entered the Lion People camp when northern lookouts yelled that the hunters were back.

50

IT WAS AVI'S WORST fear. The news was bleak. Whereas the Lion People hunters had been wildly successful—as Devu had foreseen—killing a rhino and three caribou, the Nereans were coming back empty-handed.

Jondu will be so dejected, she thought. She let out a breath, and her shoulders slumped. And now there's the leadership issue with Moctu's return. Jondu won't want to give up being leader. How's that going to work out? Jondu will think Devu's right—that we're cursed... and maybe we are. First there were the deaths of the elders... She pursed her lips and stared at nothing as her thoughts continued.

We haven't had a good hunt in so long, and there's all of Nuri and Moctu's misfortune with the Shiv. And now Moctu's sick. Are we cursed? And what about Lehoy? In some ways, he's a blessing, and in other ways it's a curse. Do I need to be purified? She cringed, revolted by the thought of Devu touching her.

Avi went outside, where the clear, blue skies, bright sunshine, and gentle breezes were a tonic to her mental torment. Far down the trail, she saw Nuri, Palo, and Siduri walking back from the Lion People shelter.

"That's odd... They weren't there long. And it looks like Siduri's going to stay with us, not her own people," Avi murmured. She collected Indar and went to meet them.

"I didn't expect you back so soon. What happened?" Avi called as she got near them.

Nuri shook her head and didn't speak until they got closer. "Devu has the Lion People...stirred up. They're pretty upset." She looked offended. "Says they shouldn't let themselves be *infected* by us."

Avi's first impulse was to laugh, but instead she wrinkled her nose and said, "What?"

"Their hunters are openly mocking ours," said Palo, scowling. "I heard two of them say that Nerean hunters couldn't kill a wounded duck."

Siduri sniffed and wiped wet eyes. "My mother...would only hug me once the hearth skins were closed. She was ashamed...ashamed to hug me where people could see." Siduri's chin trembled, and her eyes welled with tears, but she fought them back. She took a moment to collect herself, then continued. "She said I was contaminated, and I need to be purified."

Nuri rolled her eyes at the word *purified*.

Palo put his hand on Siduri's shoulder. "Removing that shaman—that human piece of garbage—that's where we need to start purifying."

The group had neared Avi's hut when they heard a call from Petrel on the northern hill. The Nerean hunters were returning.

Avi blew out a large breath and said, "Jondu's back. He's not going to be happy." After a moment, she added, "I think he's going to want me to be purified."

Nuri's face contorted. "I heard you say that before, but I still can't believe it."

"He thinks that's the way to break the curse. He thinks we're cursed—like Devu says—and he believes if he fasts and I get... purified, that'll break the curse."

"Jondu? Jondu said that?" Nuri asked incredulously.

"No, but he...he was thinking that before he left on the hunt, and not killing any game will have him believing it even more." She shook her head. "I'm actually beginning to wonder myself."

Siduri whispered something to Palo, and he put his arm around her shoulder.

"No, you're *not* contaminated. You're…amazing. You—"

A tremor shook Siduri, and she swiped at her eyes, but the tears came anyway. She rested her head on Palo's chest and was unsuccessful in choking back her sobs.

Nuri put her hand on Siduri's back and said, to Avi as much as Siduri, "One man…one man with some confusing but persuasive words has done this. Don't be taken in. You're not contaminated, and none of us need to be *purified*."

Appreciating her words, Avi nodded and excused herself to go meet Jondu. Nuri likewise needed to check on Moctu, Elka, and the pups. Before she drew away from Siduri, she squeezed her shoulder and said, "As I told you earlier, you're welcome to stay in our hut."

Palo answered for her. "Siduri…um, she'll be staying in my hut tonight…more space." Siduri nodded, smiling shyly, and the corners of Nuri's mouth turned up.

She approved of the budding romance. Palo is just what Siduri needs right now, she thought.

Nuri found Nindai, not Nabu, tending Moctu. He grinned watching Elka roll on the ground, wrestling and play-fighting with the pups.

"Nabu's gone hunting, and I'm trying to get Moctu's fever down," he said while wiping Moctu's chest with a wet skin. "I put a poultice on the worst of the bruises on his arms. He was awake for a while, and I got him to drink some willow bark and yarrow tea. I think he's going to be all right if we keep the fever down."

Nuri nodded and mouthed a quick prayer of thanks to the Spirits. "Thank you, Nindai. That's wonderful news. And I'm pleased to see that your leg is better." She paused, wrinkling her brow, then said, "What do you know about this other shaman, Devu? He's…he's got me worried… He's causing a lot of trouble."

"He's very powerful, maybe more powerful than Jelli," Nindai said, referring to the old, female shaman who mentored him. "Devu foretold of the results of this recent hunting trip, which demonstrates his power. Although I don't agree with his views about the Spirits, his arguments are strong. He chooses his words wisely, and he'll convince many that we honor the wrong Spirits. Devu's dangerous... and he hates my Sima—that's obvious. I'm worried too." He paused, considering whether to say his next words.

"Avi says Jondu has been persuaded by him. That's one of the reasons I'm here. Moctu needs to get well—and soon—to reassume leadership. Otherwise, if Jondu leads us, who knows what Devu will convince him to do?"

"You're wise, Nindai. I agree. Moctu's illness comes at an unfortunate time. He needs to get better quickly."

51

AFTER TWO DAYS OF brilliant, sunny weather, thick clouds and much colder air rolled in from the north. The gray clouds hung heavy with misery, for with them came snow on the high hills. Everyone knew that early snows in late summer were harbingers of long, harsh winters. With no food stores, the cold season would be a starving time for Nereans.

"Hello, Avi," Nuri said, pulling on the skins to enlarge the opening to the hut. She peered in to see Avi, alone as she nursed Indar.

"Hello, Nuri. Come in…I've been hoping to talk with you. How's Moctu?"

"No change. He's no worse, but the fever still grips him. I'm worried."

"Moctu's strong. He'll get better soon." Indar had drifted off while suckling, so Avi laid him on a pile of sleeping furs.

"How are things with Jondu?" Nuri asked.

"He plans another hunt soon. If we don't kill some game this time, we'll have to trade with the Lion People for some of their dried meat. They'll want many of our furs, spear points, and probably a woman in return." The two women were quiet for a long moment. "Jondu wanted to fast and have me…purified, but I convinced him to have one more hunt before…" Avi's voice quavered on the last few words, and she stopped.

"Oh, Avi, I'm so sorry," Nuri said, moving to her side.

"Is Devu right?" Avi asked, her face contorted. "Why aren't our hunts successful? Why is Moctu still sick? Why have so many of our people suffered misfortune these past two summers? Are we cursed?"

"No, Avi," Nuri said, but, like Avi, her conviction was faltering. "We...we honor the Spirits that our fathers and their fathers did, and they were successful. Why would things change? Perhaps the Spirits are testing us."

"Maybe the Spirits are *punishing* us for...for pleasures we shouldn't have had," Avi said.

Nuri's mind flashed to the pleasure that Shaka-Nu had given her, and guilt welled inside her. Does Avi know? she wondered. Has Siduri spoken with her?

"I...I need to tell you something," Avi stammered. "I hope you won't think...I hope you'll still be my friend after—"

"I will *always* be your friend, Avi," Nuri interjected. "That'll never change."

"Well, I'm worried that something I've done has caused some of this hard time we're going through," Avi said, lowering her voice. "There's...um, there's been another...another man in my life," she whispered, dropping her gaze to the ground.

"Avi..." Nuri's eyes narrowed, and she put her hand on her friend's shoulder.

"It's Lehoy, and he's all I think about. We've only been together twice, but he makes me feel...alive...and happy. How can he mean so much to me in such a short time? Every part of me smiles when I'm with him, inside and out. And he feels the same about me." She paused. "There. I've said it. Can you still be my friend? Can you excuse this...?"

"Oh, Avi, of course we're still friends," Nuri said, covering the shock she felt. "But...this isn't like you. But...what caused...how'd this happen?"

"It just did. Jondu hasn't been himself lately. He's just...I don't know." She paused, frowning. "And before Jondu left on the last hunt, he said I'd have to lie with…be purified by Devu, and I couldn't believe he would force me to do that…that he would *want* me to do that." Avi's mouth tightened, and she shook her head, still feeling the sense of betrayal.

"And then Lehoy helped me look for flint, and it just…" she stopped, and her eyes softened. "And he doesn't think I should…that I need to be purified. Nuri, he's amazing."

Avi grimaced and her face clouded. "But I feel so guilty. Sometimes it overwhelms me."

Nuri tightened her arm around Avi's shoulder. "We all have things we feel guilty about. But tell me more about Lehoy. Isn't he mated?"

"His mate, Reva, died in childbirth. He lost the child too."

"That's so sad," Nuri said, unconsciously putting a hand to her abdomen.

Avi stared at the ground and bit a fingernail. "Sometimes when I look at Indar, I see Jondu's face, and the guilt just buries me. But since I've been with…him, never once have I been in the furs with Jondu that I wasn't thinking of Lehoy."

The women were both silent for a long moment, then Avi said, "But I know it's wrong, and I know Jondu can never find out. Jondu loves me…in his way. And believe it or not, I still love him." She pressed her lips together, then looked up, her jaw set. "I'll make this up to him…for what he doesn't know about me and for the things he hasn't seen—by the things I do for him that he does see."

Nuri's brow furrowed as she considered that. She nodded, then gave Avi's shoulder a squeeze. "I…I need to get back to Moctu and Elka, but Avi, I want you to know that there is *nothing* you could do to hurt our friendship." She paused, momentarily worried that such statements were sometimes taken as challenges by the Spirits, but she pressed on. "I know you, and I know that this must have been difficult for you. Are you going to be all right?"

Avi nodded and wiped an eye. "I'll be fine. You go be with Moctu. But first, let's hold hands and say a prayer to the Spirits—our

Spirits—for him." The women held hands, and each said a prayer aloud to the Earth Mother and to Giz, the Healing Spirit. Nuri hugged Avi once more then left for her nearby hut.

As Nuri approached the hut, she heard Moctu's raised voice.

"No! That's not for you."

Anxious as to what was happening, she quickly drew the skin entrance cover aside and looked in. Moctu was sitting up, holding a chewed leather sandal, trying to look angry at the dark-eared pup who cowered behind Elka. Mut had his head down, but his eyes looked upward sadly. Nuri stifled a laugh and refocused on Moctu. Stepping forward, she quickly put a hand to his forehead. Moctu's fever was gone.

"I need to go see Jondu," Moctu said seriously. It was obvious that he'd been thinking about this since he awoke. "I'm the leader of our people, and if there are going to be...problems about that, then the sooner I deal with them, the better."

"I'm so relieved that you're better," Nuri said, kneeling next to him. "We were worried about you...are you feeling *all* better?" She thought back to the prayers that she and Avi had just spoken. A deep, gratified sigh escaped her, and she closed her eyes. Our Spirits listened and answered. And they're strong, she thought happily.

"I feel..." he shrugged, "like myself. I feel great." He got to his knees and hugged and kissed her. It was a long embrace, and his hand moved slowly down her back and along the curve of her side. "And I've missed you...a lot. Sorry I caused you problems...that you had to carry me and tend me and all."

"Oh, that was nothing, Moctu. You saved our lives in that hailstorm—I'm convinced of that. And you got so beaten up. I'm just glad you're back to feeling good again."

As Moctu's hands continued to explore her curves, she winked at him and said, "And tonight I'm going to show you how much I appreciate you."

He smiled at her and held up a chewed bit of leather. "Someone destroyed a sandal, and I think it was Mut. The other one is Neska... I think she's innocent."

"You're using the old language words for 'boy' and 'girl.' I like that," Nuri said. "Mut and Neska. It fits them."

"Mut," said Elka, and Moctu and Nuri stared at one another. It was her first word. Excited, they both moved to Elka, and the little girl, liking the attention, said it again.

"These little beasts are definitely brother and sister to you, aren't they?" Moctu said to Elka. "Your totem's going to be the same as mine...the wolf." Moctu looked at Nuri for confirmation and reflexively touched the wolf-tooth talisman at his neck. "What do you think about that?"

"Oh, it's perfect for Elka," Nuri said. "It couldn't be anything else."

"Mut!" Elka said again, and they laughed.

52

"Hello, Jondu," Moctu said as he approached the man kneeling by the fire, straightening a shaft above the flame. "I think it would be good for us to talk."

"So you're finally up," Jondu said, standing. "We weren't sure you were going to make it."

"Yes, I'm fine, and I wanted to thank you for filling in as leader while I was gone."

"My father, Ono, filled in for you," Jondu said pointedly, moving closer to Moctu. "I was *elected* leader when you didn't return."

"But I did return, and here I am."

"It's not that simple, Moctu," said Jondu, his face now so close that Moctu could see dried saliva at the corners of his mouth. His breath smelled faintly of onions. "You left the tribe and stayed away while they...while we needed you. You can't just walk back in, many moons later, and think nothing has changed. Because things *have* changed. The tribe suffered for your lack of leadership. The Spirits began to curse us. As the new leader, it's my duty to regain the favor of the Spirits."

Moctu felt his temper rise. "I went after the Shiv who had taken my mate, Nuri, someone the whole tribe loves. If they took Avi, you'd go after her, wouldn't you?"

"Yes, but I wouldn't expect to walk in, many moons later, and be leader again."

The men stared at each other for a long moment.

"Well, I guess we'll have to have a council vote on this," Moctu said. "We can vote on war with the Shiv, too."

"The Lion People have already declared war on Pale Ones," said Jondu. "We'll join with them."

"But the Shiv are who we need to fight…the Shiv and the Mung. Not all Pale Ones."

"Maybe, but if we fight alongside the Lion People, no one can stand against us. We can sweep the country of them. We won't have to worry about Pale Ones again…taking our women and killing our people. Whether it's the Shiv or the Mung, or whatever."

Moctu realized he wasn't going to change Jondu's mind. He started counting in his head, only half-listening as Jondu spoke on. There's Palo and Nabu…they'll support me, Moctu thought. And Nindai, Nindai for sure. Probably Seetu. There were a couple more warriors who had come to the meeting of the tribes, but he figured they'd likely support Jondu.

"…and they kill our game," Jondu continued. "Game is so scarce…we won't have to share it with Pale Ones. And Devu says—"

"Devu is poison," Moctu interrupted. "From what I've seen and heard, he only cares about himself."

"Devu's powerful…and he sees and locates game," Jondu retorted. "If we follow his teachings and advice, our people will eat meat again. Otherwise, we'll starve on acorn mush and pine bark this winter. As leader, I can't let that happen. I've seen it—Devu has true powers and wisdom. He's asked to speak to our people this evening, and I've granted it."

Moctu rolled his eyes and looked away. "Well, then after that we'll have a council of warriors. We'll determine the leadership and who, exactly, we're at war with. Spirits!" He shook his head disgustedly. "Then we'll plan a hunting trip. That's the one thing I agree with you on—we need to kill some game…a lot of it, and soon." He turned and left, not waiting for confirmation from Jondu.

Although most of the men of the tribe were out hunting, Moctu spent the afternoon talking with the few who were not. Palo had not gone on the hunt, preferring to spend time with Siduri. Moctu was certain of Palo's support, but was nonetheless reassured by his comments.

"Nindai will be with you, especially if Jondu's for joining the Lion People in war on all Pale Ones. Spirits, he's mated to a Pale One. And Siduri...I'm not going to let that hyena of a shaman touch her. She doesn't need his *purification*."

"Yes, I've talked with Nindai, and he's worried about what might happen to Sima," Moctu said. "He's right to be worried...I'm even worried about Elka."

Long before dark, hunters began to filter back to the camp to eat a meager meal before hearing Devu speak. All had been unsuccessful except for Seetu, who had killed a goose.

Devu arrived with an entourage. Rolf, the leader of the Lion People, was with him, as were Lehoy and several warriors. All were dressed in fine clothes, but it was Devu's attire that was breathtaking. He wore a woven, plant-fiber robe which was stained with alternating stripes of red and black. On his head he wore the top piece of a lion skull, with its huge, canine teeth hanging down by his eyes. Around his neck was the lower part of the lion skull, with its massive front teeth projecting upward by his jaw. From his neck hung an enormous tooth nearly a foot long. The effect was riveting, making it appear that his head had been swallowed by the beast.

Devu carried a short staff, the large end of which had been carved into a half-lion, half-man figure. The crowd, including Moctu, was immediately spellbound. Rolf and the other people with Devu showed unmistakable reverence toward the shaman.

Moctu blew out a breath. "This is a powerful man," he said in a low voice to Palo, who stood next to him. Unable to take his eyes off the shaman, Palo simply nodded.

"The Earth Spirit is hungry," Devu said in a slow, deep voice that was almost a growl. The words seemed to come from the lion's mouth, and they sent a chill down Moctu's spine. Moctu could see the shaman was having a similar effect on those around him.

"He calls to me in Dreamtime. Yes, the Earth Spirit is a male, not female, and *He*…He will have his meal—that much is sure. Will it be our people or Pale Ones? Many moons ago, the Pale Ones attacked us. They killed and wounded our warriors, and they took Siduri and Penag, son of Rolf, our leader. They *ate* Penag." Devu let those words hang for a moment as he sympathetically nodded to Rolf.

Himself moved by the shaman's words, Moctu thought back to the hatred he had felt when he watched Hawk discover the cooked remains of his son, Mik. He had wanted to kill Shiv—any Shiv, all Shiv—at that time. He looked around and saw rapt attention from the crowd.

"They not only killed our leader's son, they ate him. These are not people. The Pale Ones are animals who have molded themselves to try to look like people. But their attempts have failed—they are deformed and monstrous." He motioned to a young warrior who brought him the Pale One skull, and Devu took a long drink from it.

Devu's eyes swept the crowd, settling on Nindai. Nindai was glad Sima was back at the hut. "Some of you," Devu's scornful eyes moved from Nindai to Moctu, and he raised his voice. "Some of you have… lain with the Pale Ones, and you are now unclean. You've brought these…". He shook his head. "You've brought this contamination with you. And you wonder these days why your hunts fail, why your people die, and why illness stalks you."

Anger rose in Moctu, and he was about to interrupt and say that, yes, the Shiv are evil cannibals, but not all Pale Ones are bad. The shaman's next words took his breath away.

Still staring at Moctu, Devu said, "Oh, I have heard your arguments—they come to me in the dreamtime. You say that not all Pale Ones are bad—only the Shiv. Your words are a smokescreen meant to blind us from the truth. Just as every dark cloud hides the sun, moon, and stars, they are still there. There is always the truth, the light behind the clouds."

Can he read my thoughts? Moctu wondered, drawing back, his mouth partially open.

"This land is ours, not the Pale Ones," Devu continued. "The time before man was on earth, before even the mountains were formed, is the Early Dreamtime. In this time, the Earth Spirit released two eagles from each edge of the world, and this is where they met. Here is where the Earth Spirit first made us, and He gave this land to us. This is sacred land...our land. He did not give it to People Eaters."

The people standing behind Devu, as well as many in the crowd, murmured their agreement. Moctu looked to see Jondu nodding and, more worrisome, Seetu was too. As Moctu continued scanning the audience, his eyes met those of Nindai. He looked stricken.

Devu's eyes fell on Siduri, who was standing next to Palo. A hint of a smile broke the scowl the shaman had maintained. "Others of you have been made unclean by the Pale Ones—unwillingly, yes—but you are still unclean. You'll need to be purified."

Siduri trembled, and Palo put his arm around her shoulder.

Devu's gaze moved to Avi and stayed there for a few moments, but he said nothing. Even so, she drew back a half step. His eyes settled on Nuri, and she looked back at him defiantly. His next words shook her, striking at the heart of her fears.

"The Pale Ones have not only made some unclean, but the unborn lives that women carry within them—they've been made part Pale One. The impact of this..." He struggled for a word severe enough. "This *infection* is deep. It can—and must—be purified."

Devu smiled as he saw the impact of his words on Nuri. Turning to address the crowd, he said in a loud voice, "I've seen the future." He paused, and the crowd leaned in, anxious not to miss his next words. "Last night I fasted. In the early morning, I ate. But not all nourishment is food. I ate rare herbs...herbs that nourish the soul. My soul left my body, and it merged with the Lion Spirit." He held the half-man, half-lion carving high in the air, and he looked at it reverently. "There were two other lions with me, and we were hunting, stalking something in the tall grass. Step by step, we got closer, and as the grass parted, we saw it was a large Pale One. The three of us leapt on him, and together, we killed him easily. We feasted on his liver, and as we ate it, I returned to my shaman form. The other two lions changed as well." The shaman turned to look behind him. "One was Rolf, leader of the Lion People, and the other was…" Devu took a long moment, looking first at Moctu then at Jondu. He smiled, enjoying the tension he created. "Jondu," he said finally.

The crowd gasped because the implication was so clear and so profound. The leader of the Lion People and the leader of the Nereans—Jondu—would be allies. Together, they would easily wipe out the Pale Ones, *all* Pale Ones. Devu surveyed the gathering and liked what he saw as most seemed both awed and persuaded. He nodded at Jondu, turned, and left.

53

THE COUNCIL OF WARRIORS was not going well. Most of the men appeared to have been won over by Devu's eloquent speech. For Moctu, this meeting was eerily similar to the one where Jabil was elected leader. And that meeting had led to disaster.

Seetu was the key—Moctu needed his vote—and it was a bad sign that he was avoiding eye contact with Moctu. The time had come in the meeting for Jondu and Moctu to speak, and Jondu motioned for Moctu to go first. Rather than motion back that Jondu should start, Moctu decided to comply. He stood and tried to look confident.

"Fellow warriors, it was only a year ago that I was made leader, the choice of every warrior in the tribe. I want to thank Jondu and his father, Ono, for filling in as leader while I was gone. Now, Jondu wants to be leader, and he'll make much of the fact that I was gone for so long. But you all know why I was gone all that time. We are at war...war with the Shiv and the Mung. No one disputes that. They attacked the Lion People, and they attacked us, killing people and taking prisoners that included Nuri.

"You're all brave warriors, and no one here would have done differently than what I did. I went after my mate, and I killed Shiv warriors. I'm the only one in this tribe who has fought and killed the Shiv and Mung. Any one of you would have done the same. Nuri did much to save herself," he said, smiling with pride for her. "But I was able to find her and bring her back here to safety. Along the way, I was able to rescue Siduri and bring her back as well.

"Jondu would, like Devu, have us war against all Pale Ones, not just the vicious Shiv cannibals, but also against the peaceful Krog." Images of Rah, Effie, and Hawk came to him, and he smiled tightly. "The Krog are not our enemies, they are allies."

A rise in commotion and muttering told Moctu that many of the warriors didn't agree. He raised his voice, speaking over the noise.

"As I pursued the Shiv who had Nuri, a Krog warrior was with me, and he killed at least as many Shiv as I did. The Krog hate the Shiv as much as we do. Just as the Lion People were attacked by the Shiv, and they're our allies, so are the Krog. They were also attacked, and they lost people to the Shiv, some of whom were eaten. The Shiv are sending messengers to bring warriors from many different clans, so there'll be a lot of them. Why should we battle people who, like us, want to kill the Shiv?

"We've gained a lot from our contacts with the Krog. Their healer has shown Nindai many new medicines and remedies, and, most importantly, from them we learned how to make fire." Moctu let that last comment settle for a moment. "If we need to, we can trade with the Lion People...our fire knowledge in exchange for food." Many in the crowd nodded at this, and Moctu thought it was a good time to end his talk.

"Keep me as your leader. We don't have to fight all Pale Ones, just the Shiv and the Mung." More of the men were nodding, so Moctu, likewise, nodded then sat. All eyes moved to Jondu, who rose and put a hand through his dark hair.

"Moctu is a good person," he started. "But after a short time as our leader, he left us for many moons. We didn't know if he was alive or dead. We needed him, but he wasn't there. So we moved on to new leadership. Now, after all those moons away, he wants to be leader again. But we have a leader," he said, touching his chest.

"You just heard Devu speak. Anybody who's seen him knows that he has powers...awesome powers, and he knows the Spirits better than anyone here. There's no doubt that he's right—ever since we've associated with the Pale Ones, our hunts have failed and more of our people have gotten sick. Moctu says that we've learned some things from the Pale Ones, but none of that will matter if we can't feed our people.

"I believe in our hearts we know that Devu's right. The Pale Ones are unclean, and we're cursed by the Spirits for our...association with them."

Moctu's stomach churned, and he unconsciously rubbed his wolf-tooth talisman as he watched more and more of the warriors begin to nod at Jondu's remarks.

"Devu says that we'll face a starving winter if we don't change our ways. We have to stop our contacts with the Pale Ones." Jondu looked around the circle, pleased to see many of the men agreeing with him. "Most of you were with me as we hunted territory alongside where the Lion People hunted. Just as Devu foretold, we got *nothing*. We got nothing because we're cursed, while the Lion People killed enough to secure themselves food through the winter."

He shook his head. "That was enough for me. As leader, I will do *everything* I can to feed our people." Jondu smiled as the warriors' nodding grew more vigorous, and there were murmurs of approval. "Even when the curse is broken, there may not be enough time to kill the game we need for this winter. Like Moctu, I plan to bargain with the Lion People...to show them how to make fire in exchange for food."

"As for the Pale Ones, Devu has seen visions...visions of a great slaughter and of our success against them. His visions see us as allied with the Lion People, and me as leader. Moctu says we should battle only certain Pale Ones. Some are bad while some are good." He gave a short, derisive laugh. "What would he have us do? As Pale Ones charge at us with spears, should we ask which tribe they're from?" Several of the men chuckled.

"No. It's clear that things have to change. We need food. We need to stop our contacts with the Pale Ones, and we need me," Jondu scanned the men, individually nodding to most of them. "We need me as leader."

Jondu sat, and for Moctu, the next moments were a dismal blur. It was over quickly. For the second time, Moctu lost an election for the leadership.

54

WHAT DO WE DO?" Nindai asked the small group gathered near his hut the next morning. "Sima and I can't stay here. Where do we go?"

"We're leaving," said Palo. "Not sure where we'll end up, but we're not staying here. Siduri doesn't want to be *purified*, and I don't want that either. But Jondu will be on the lookout for it, and will try to stop us."

The two other men of the group, Moctu and Nabu, remained quiet. Moctu stared off to the side, lost in thought, occasionally shaking his head as if to clear it.

"The atlatl competition is tomorrow," Palo continued. "If we leave tonight or tomorrow morning, no one will be expecting that. I say we head back to Etseh—there are a few men left there—some of them may join us. With one or two others, we'll have enough to start our own tribe," said Palo.

The fog seemed to lift from Moctu, and he said, "That's the best plan I can think of too. We can't stay—Elka's at risk, and Nuri's not going to put up with…purification either." He looked at Nindai. "Sima's probably the most at risk of anyone, being a Pale One. How's your leg, Nindai? Are you up to traveling again?"

"I can travel. The leg's fine…almost back to normal."

Moctu looked at Nabu and said, "How about you, Nabu? You're an elder, and you and Poza are safe. If we leave, are you staying or coming with us?"

Nabu considered for a moment, then nodded and said, "We'll come with you."

Moctu smiled tightly. "Palo's right. We have to keep these plans to ourselves. Jondu will do whatever it takes to stop us if he hears about this. We should leave before first light tomorrow...that's a good idea, Palo. We'll break camp quietly and be off before people get up." He extended a hand forward. "Everybody in?"

All of the men extended their hands, one on top of the other.

"Spirits, please guide us to a better future," Moctu said, and all murmured their agreement.

"No! No, you are not taking her!" Moctu heard Nuri shouting from their hut, a half atlatl throw away. He was up and moving quickly, followed by the other men, and they could see a sizable crowd gathered near his hut. Moctu arrived in time to see a heavyset, bull-necked Lion warrior use the blunt end of his spear to roughly club Nuri's shoulder, keeping her away from another warrior who had Elka in his arms. She was wailing, reaching for Nuri.

Fury overwhelmed him, and Moctu plowed into the man who had clubbed Nuri, knocking him down. Moctu followed the big man to the ground, landing on him, the spear horizontal between them. He slugged the man in the nose with his right fist and followed with his left, which was partially blocked as the man released the spear to shield his face.

People were screaming as Moctu felt the sharp prod of a spear from another Lion warrior, but that man, too, disappeared as Palo barreled into him. Yet another warrior pulled Moctu from the man he was on, clubbed his head, and restrained him at spearpoint. Palo was similarly quickly subdued by a fourth warrior. The Lion People had come in force.

Devu's voice cut through the tumult. "These men have been infected," he screamed. "Not only do they mate unclean women, this one," he said loudly, pointing to Moctu, "has a Pale One child."

Moctu's head cleared as he looked up at Devu, and for the first time, he saw Jondu standing next to the shaman. Jondu looked alarmed, but he was doing nothing to stop Devu's men.

The warrior that Moctu had attacked was up and angrily moved toward him with his spear. He raised the butt end to club Moctu, but Nabu intervened with his own spear, and the burly man backed down.

"Enough!" yelled Devu. "We have what we came for." He glanced at Jondu. "The Nerean leader was worried that some of you would leave and not...support our effort." He eyed Moctu for a moment, then cast his gaze to Nuri, smiling lasciviously. "We'll be keeping little Sleeps with Wolves with us for a while." He turned to leave, accompanied by his guards, but had a second thought and looked again at Moctu. "Don't interfere with us. You wouldn't want Sleeps with Wolves to be hurt..." The corners of his mouth came up, and he added, "So soon."

Chilled by Devu's last words, Moctu looked to Nuri, whose eyes widened with apprehension. As Devu and his guards left with Elka, Jondu cleared his throat to speak. Already incensed, Moctu's rage exploded. Fed by the powerlessness he felt as his baby girl was carried away, Moctu squeezed his fists tightly, and he let out a guttural roar as he charged Jondu.

Although carrying a spear, Jondu was unable to react in time before Moctu's body hit him. The pair were airborne for a moment before crashing to the ground, punching and tearing at one another.

"You!" Moctu screamed, landing a heavy blow to Jondu's mouth. Jondu released the useless spear and slugged Moctu in the ear. Moctu smashed Jondu's nose and heard a satisfying crack just as Jondu belted Moctu in his right eye.

The two struggling men were pulled apart by Palo, Petrel, and Nabu. As they were separated, Jondu threw another punch at Moctu, but missed.

Restrained by Palo with some help from Nabu, Moctu continued to scream. "You! You did this." He struggled to go at Jondu again.

"Elka's taken by that…that crazy hyena because of you," he snarled through clenched teeth.

Blood ran from Jondu's nose, and he glowered back, saying, "You made me do it. I know you…you'd leave." He broadened his gaze to include Nuri. "And you're the ones most infected by the People Eaters. You're the main reasons we're cursed."

Moctu lunged at Jondu again, but was deterred by Palo and Nabu. Together they pulled him farther away.

"We're not cursed," Moctu said and spit to the ground. "I can't believe you've been persuaded by that…that…" He shook his head. "And now you've let them take my daughter."

"I…I didn't know he was going to do that," Jondu said, contrition replacing most of his anger.

The men were pulled farther apart and led to their separate huts.

A hush fell over the Nerean camp as people processed what had happened and what it meant for the tribe.

55

GOLDEN BEAMS OF SUNLIGHT streamed through jagged clefts in the eastern mountains, and the rich chorus of morning birdsong began. Despite the beautiful sights and sounds, Nuri rubbed her red eyes and stared vacantly at the small fire. Even the pups had been distressed last night, letting off high-pitched, mournful howls. They clearly missed Elka as much as Moctu and Nuri did.

Moctu and Nuri had whispered long into the night, trying to figure ways to extricate Elka from Devu and the Lion People. At dawn, Moctu set off to see Rolf, the Lion People leader. Thinking about yesterday, when Elka was taken, filled Nuri with a bitter, near-violent indignation.

"Jondu…he set this up, or at least caused it," she muttered. "And I can do *nothing*." Nuri got up slowly from the fire and stretched her aching back.

She brightened. "I'll go see Avi. She didn't want this, and she doesn't like Devu. Maybe she can convince Jondu, and maybe he can get Elka back from Devu." The chances were slim, but it was better than hopelessly sitting around. "I have to do something."

She found Avi returning with water from the stream, carrying Indar in the sling that Nuri had made for him.

"Hello, Avi," Nuri said, feeling a strange lack of warmth for her best friend. She knew it was caused by the fight between their mates yesterday and the friction between the men as to who would be leader. But still, this was Avi...

"Hello, Nuri," Avi replied without looking at her.

So she feels it too, Nuri thought. Still, I have to try. Avi's probably the only one who could convince Jondu, and Jondu's the only one who might get Elka back safely.

"Avi, I have to do something to get Elka back. It was horrible yesterday when they took her, and now that awful man has her. I'm really worried."

"What would you have me do? I'm not going to go against Jondu."

"Oh, Avi. You've got to convince him. You have to. He's got to help get her back."

"Or what?" She looked at Nuri for the first time, her face a mix of fear, distrust, and anger. "Or you'll tell him about Lehoy?"

"No...no. I'd never do that to you, Avi." The women stared at one another for a long moment. "Never," Nuri said again.

Some of the tension left Avi. She shrugged and said, "Well, your mate attacked Jondu yesterday. He broke his nose."

Nuri felt anger rise in her. "And your mate was responsible for our little girl being taken from us...*taken*. I wanted to attack him too."

"He...he didn't know that would happen. He's just trying to do the best thing for the tribe."

"So taking our baby away and forcing me to have sex with that... that creepy shaman is the best thing for the tribe...that's what you think?"

"I think Jondu may be right...that we're cursed...and so maybe..." Avi's voice trailed off, and she looked away.

Nuri expelled a breath and shook her head. "You know he's going to want you too, Avi... Devu is. And he's going to take Nindai's mate, Sima. Who knows what he'll do to her? Avi, he has Elka...and he means to harm her. I heard it in his words yesterday. Don't let... Avi, *please* don't let that happen."

When Avi didn't respond, Nuri felt herself getting angry again, so she turned and quickly walked away.

"Nuri," Avi called after her, but Nuri didn't look back.

***

MEANWHILE, MOCTU'S RIGHT EYE was nearly swollen shut as he met with Rolf, the Lion People leader, seeking his help to get Elka back.

"Spirits, your eye...what happened to you? The atlatl competition is today, and Lehoy thought you were his toughest challenge. Can you even see?"

"Thank you, Rolf, for meeting with me. Some of your men and Devu did this. That's why I'm here...they took my daughter, Elka. I'd like your help to get her back."

"They didn't do that on my orders," Rolf said, still studying Moctu's eye. "Devu...he has a lot of power with my men. Sometimes it feels like he's in control here, not me." Rolf laughed it off, but Moctu could tell that his words were serious. Rolf's eyes narrowed. "Why did Devu take your daughter?"

"Elka is...special. Before I tell you about her, let me say how sorry I am to you for the loss of your son...to the Shiv. As you're aware, my mate Nuri was taken by them, and she suffered horribly. You'll be pleased to hear that she killed their leader, and I killed some of their warriors."

Rolf smiled and nodded, his eyes glistening. "Penag is..." He shook his head. "Was...was a good son." After a moment he cleared his throat and said, "You've brought Siduri back. For that, you have our great thanks."

"Thank you for your kind words, but all I want is my daughter back. Please help me. Devu holds her now because...because she's part Pale One."

Moctu saw Rolf stiffen. His eyes narrowed, and he stared at Moctu's damaged face.

"Not all Pale Ones are evil," Moctu continued quickly. "Elka's mother was a wonderful woman, and the Krog people...they were attacked by the Shiv, like us. They suffered and lost loved ones. And their warriors have helped me kill Shiv."

Rolf considered that, but then frowned and shook his head. "I will never trust any Pale Ones... How could I? I'm sorry about your daughter, but if she's a Pale One..."

Moctu saw Rolf's eyes harden, and the frown was frozen on his face.

"But she's just a little girl. And the Krog, they're our allies. They hate the Shiv."

Rolf turned his back to Moctu. "I'm sorry. Goodbye, Moctu."

Frustration swamped Moctu, and it quickly bled into rage. He clenched his fists, closed his eyes, and took a deep breath.

"I'll get my daughter. I'll get her...or..." But he could think of nothing—nothing to say or do.

56

ONLY THREE COMPETITORS REMAINED: Lehoy, Palo, and Moctu. Moctu's early throws had been far from the target, but his final two shafts had landed well, keeping him from elimination.

"You're getting used to only having the one good eye," Palo called encouragingly to him.

Moctu smiled, feeling the warmth of Palo's friendship. If he didn't win this, then he hoped it would be Palo. But he had to win. Maybe it would increase his standing, his renown enough to make a difference. Maybe a win would help him get Elka back.

It's not likely, he thought, *but maybe, somehow, it'll help. Anyway, it's all I've got…it's the only thing I can do that might help.*

It was the final, winner-take-all event, and each of the men had a shaft in their atlatls and two more shafts stuck loosely in the ground in front of them, readied for a quick launch. To aid the onlookers, Lehoy's three shafts had been darkened with charcoal, Palo's were uncolored, and Moctu's had been marked with red ochre.

The men were to individually throw the three darts rapidly at a rotten stump several tree lengths away. The stump had been outlined with white and yellow flowers to make it more visible. An adolescent boy beat a slow, steady rhythm with a stout wooden rod against a hollow log. The men had to get all three shafts launched within five beats. The excited crowd, which was dominated by Lion People, would loudly count out the five beats as each man threw.

Since Lehoy had won the earlier contests, he was allowed to choose the order, and he chose to go last. Moctu was picked to go first.

Moctu took a deep breath and studied the faraway stump. With the fingers of his left hand, he forced his sore, nearly closed-off right eye open to better ascertain the distance. Having practiced speed-throwing with Palo many times, he wasn't worried about getting his shots off in time. He just had to be able to see the target. Once again, he checked his shafts, then he nodded, signaling that he was ready.

Three beats went by then Rolf shouted, "Now."

Moctu fired off his first shaft and the crowd began their chant. "One... Two..."

Moctu's first shaft hit nearly the length of a man away from the stump, and Moctu cursed himself for missing by so much as he began his second throw.

"Three!" The Lion People were pleased by his miss, and they cheered more than counted.

Moctu's second shot was in flight as he quickly loaded his final shaft. "Four..."

Moctu was pleased to see his second shot hit the left edge of the stump as he threw his last shaft.

"Five."

The final shaft appeared to hang in the air twice as long as his previous shots before it came down a hand's breadth from the right side of the stump.

It was a good shot, and the Nereans cheered while the Lion People quieted noticeably.

Palo went next and performed well. All of his shots were better than Moctu's first, but he failed to hit the stump, and in aggregate, his shafts were not as close as Moctu's.

So Moctu or Lehoy would win the competition. The crowd was hushed, and the only sound was the steady, almost hypnotic beat of the rod on the log. Lehoy looked serious but confident as he readied himself for his throws.

Nuri looked across the crowd and caught Avi's gaze as she was standing next to Jondu and biting a fingernail. Avi's hand dropped from her mouth, and the two women locked eyes for a moment. Neither smiled, and Avi finally turned sideways to attend to baby Indar.

"I wonder who she wants to win?" Nuri murmured under her breath. She was pretty sure she knew.

Lehoy nodded that he was ready, and Rolf let five beats go by, building tension and excitement in the crowd.

"Now!" Rolf shouted.

Lehoy launched his first shaft gracefully and began to load his second.

"One... Two..."

His first shaft hit the middle of the stump, and the crowd of Lion People cheered. Even Lehoy paused to appreciate the perfect shot.

"Three..."

Lehoy's second shot was airborne as he picked up his final shaft.

"Four..."

Like Moctu and Palo, Lehoy had practiced speed-throwing many times. Now realizing he was half a beat behind, he rushed the placement of the shaft on the atlatl. He was in mid-throw when the Nereans in the crowd shouted, "Five!"

"Did he get it off in time?" some in the audience wondered aloud.

Lehoy's second shot hit the front edge of the stump, but the third and final shaft sailed long, missing by even more than Moctu's first shot. This was going to be close.

The crowd surged forward, wanting to determine for themselves who won. Two Lion People guards did their best to control the mass of people as Rolf made his way toward the stump.

"It was late...his third shot was late," Petrel yelled. "Moctu's the winner."

His statement brought an uproar from the nearby Lion People onlookers, and one of their warriors shoved Petrel. He shoved back, and the two men had to be restrained by others in the crowd.

Rolf held up his hand for silence, then yelled for everyone to be quiet. People gradually stopped talking and looked to him for the decision.

"The shafts of Moctu and Lehoy are of equal distance from the target, but Lehoy hit the stump twice, and Moctu only once. I therefore declare Lehoy the winner!"

Half a heartbeat later, the crowd erupted, cheers coming from the Lion People, and angry complaints coming from the Nereans. In the subsequent pushing and shoving, Siduri was knocked down. Palo, who was already making his way toward her, jostled past a warrior who indignantly threw a punch, grazing his shoulder and hitting him in the neck. Palo turned and hit the burly man squarely in the nose. Falling back, the man grabbed Palo's tunic, and they collapsed in a struggling heap amidst the crowd. Palo headbutted the warrior, again hitting his nose, which was bleeding profusely. With his left hand, Palo pushed the man's jaw to try to disentangle himself. His little finger slid toward the man's mouth and the warrior bit down hard, nearly severing the finger below the nail.

Palo screamed as much in rage as in pain, and he slugged the brawny man below a large wart on his right eyebrow. The man released his finger as he hit Palo's cheek with a massive blow. The men were finally separated by others in the crowd. As he was dragged from the man, Palo looked around to ensure Siduri was safe.

More Lion People guards arrived, and the tumult ended quickly. Scowling Nereans gradually moved away from glowering Lion People. The summer meetings, games, and competitions had, in the past, solidified and brought the disparate tribes closer, promoting peace, friendship, and goodwill. This time, it wasn't working.

57

"I'M AFRAID IT'S GOING to have to come off…just the last little part at the joint," Nindai said after examining Palo's mangled finger.

"Let's get it over with," Palo said, placing his hand on the block of wood beside Nindai.

Siduri stood over them, worriedly watching as the men knelt by the fire just outside Palo's hut. Nindai first placed a flat, smooth river rock on the hottest coals of the fire. He expertly positioned a slender but sturdy flint blade in the small depression of the joint socket, then picked up a short, wooden club with his other hand. Palo gritted his teeth and looked away, determined not to evidence pain.

Nindai struck the blade quickly, and the tiny digit was immediately separated. Palo's eyes closed, and he frowned, but he made no sound. Blood oozed rapidly from the wound, and Nindai used two sticks as tongs to pick up the red-hot rock. He quickly pressed the end of Palo's finger to the rock, cauterizing it. As his finger sizzled, Palo tried to look unconcerned, but his eyes narrowed as he grimaced, and the tip of his tongue showed between his lips.

Siduri knelt behind Palo and gently rubbed his shoulders. Nindai placed sphagnum moss around the fingertip, then bound it in place with a thin skin. Palo smiled at the result, and flexed his hand slightly to test the level of pain.

"Thank you, Nindai. This is excellent." He retrieved the tiny piece of finger and briefly looked at the fingernail on it before placing the segment in the small, leather talisman sack around his neck.

"We need to leave this place," Siduri said flatly as she moved to where she could see both men's faces. "I understand that Moctu and Nuri need to stay…for Elka, but we're in danger too…really all of us are. We need to leave—and soon."

Both men frowned, but they nodded in agreement.

"I've been thinking the same thing," Nindai said. "Sima's not safe here, and the longer we stay…"

"Let's talk with Moctu first…Moctu and Nuri," Palo said. "But I agree. We've got to get out of here."

It was evening before they connected with Moctu.

"How's your hand?" Moctu asked, motioning at Palo's bandaged fingers.

"Lost a chunk of the little finger. It'll be all right, though. Congratulations on winning, even though they gave it to Lehoy," Palo said, making a wry face.

Moctu shrugged. "It was close…but I do think I won."

"I'm sure of it," Nindai said. "Listen, we need to talk. It's getting serious here. We're almost at war with the Lion People from what I can see. It's too dangerous for me to stay here with Sima. If they try and take her, I'll be killing someone," he said, lifting his cane slightly.

Moctu and Palo knew that the bottom part of the cane, which was wrapped with a thick piece of hide, concealed a spear point. Nindai had used the cane before with deadly effectiveness.

"And if they come to try to *purify* Siduri, I'll probably kill someone too," Palo said. "Then we'll be at war with the Lion People for sure, and outnumbered like we are, I don't like our chances."

"No, you're right," said Moctu. "But Nuri and I have to stay. We have to figure a way to get Elka back. But you and your mates…I understand. You've got to leave."

The men talked long into the night, stoking the fire twice. As the fire died to embers a third time, they had determined a strategy that might work and a way to signal each other. The plan still had big holes in it, such as how Moctu would get Elka back, but by the time the half-moon would be full again, each man had important roles... and a lot to do to be ready.

Well after midnight, the men said their goodbyes and wished one another the blessings of the Spirits. Palo and Nindai returned to their huts, gathered their few possessions, and, with their mates, they broke camp and were gone before dawn.

The sun burst above the snow-crested eastern mountains like the explosion of a campfire rock sending bright, fiery rays in all directions. Consternation soon swept the camp as people realized that four of their group had left in the night. Jondu was especially displeased, but he held off from confronting Moctu.

An uneasy peace set in for several days as Nereans collected more of the high-quality flint and made small trades with the Lion People. Typically, the Nereans would have left the summer meeting by now with travois piled high with flint and trade goods. Several travois loads had been sent back to Etseh already, but much remained. Before moving everyone back, however, Jondu waited for word from the Lion People scouts about war. Small scouting groups had been sent out to determine the location of the nearest Pale Ones, and depending on what they found, a war effort might be launched soon.

Moctu and Nuri also waited, desperate to retrieve Elka. The reports they got indicated that Elka was well-fed and getting good care. They spent every night futilely devising plans to get her safely back.

It was a bright morning, much warmer than usual, when Jondu crossed paths with Moctu as he returned from the stream.

"You knew about them leaving," Jondu said accusatorially. "In fact, you put them up to it. They weren't supposed to leave. You—"

"I'm glad you showed up," Moctu interrupted, ignoring Jondu's words. "I'm planning to offer to show Devu how to make fire if he'll return Elka to me."

"No, no," Jondu said loudly, shaking his head. "We're saving that to bargain with them for food if our hunts continue to fail. We have to get food for the winter or our people will starve."

"I know that was the plan, but that was before they took Elka... before you brought Devu here to take Elka," he corrected himself.

"I didn't know Devu would do that."

"But you brought him to our camp, didn't you? And you stood by while he took Elka away."

"I needed you and the other men to stay...to fight the Pale Ones. I knew you'd try to leave, so I went to Devu for advice. You made it clear that you didn't want to fight the Pale Ones. But I didn't know he'd take your daughter."

"I'll fight the Shiv—they're our enemy. I've already killed some Shiv, and so has Nuri. But you actually expect me to go to war with the Krog too? What am I supposed to do? Slaughter my daughter's grandmother? Or my friends there?" He spit to the side.

"Devu says that the only way we'll prosper again is to—"

"I'm sick of hearing what Devu says," Moctu interrupted. "Everything he says and does is for his own benefit."

There was a pause as the men stared at one another. Moctu moved a step closer to Jondu.

"I'm going to get Elka back. If that means teaching the Lion People how to make fire, I'll do it. Then we're leaving."

"I can't let you do that," Jondu said menacingly.

Moctu felt a hot rage build inside him, but he took a deep breath and tried talking one more time.

"It was a year ago when I taught *you* how to make fire," Moctu said through clenched teeth. "And who taught me? Oh, that's right... it was the people you want to destroy—the Krog." He put his face closer to Jondu's. "I'll use fire-making to get Elka back if I want to, and you're not going to stop me."

Jondu took a step back, whistled loudly, and raised a hand high in the air. In moments, Seetu showed up with a spear in hand. It was clear he'd been nearby and was there to do Jondu's bidding.

"Really, Seetu? You'd threaten me with a spear?"

Jondu moved between the two men and motioned for Seetu to hold off.

"We'll have a council of warriors to decide what to do with you," Jondu said. "I think they're going to vote to have food this winter."

There was commotion near the edge of camp, and all three men turned to look.

"Oh, dung," Moctu grumbled. "Not Devu again."

58

"IF HE SAYS ANYTHING about making fire, club him," Jondu instructed
Seetu as he pointed at Moctu. "Teaching the Lion People about fire
is going to feed us this winter…and keep our people from starving."

Moctu looked at Seetu, and he didn't think the young man would
follow through on Jondu's command, but he decided to keep quiet
about fire nonetheless. It was an important decision, and the council
should get to decide.

"Cursed!" Devu shouted. "You Nereans are cursed. And now,
several of your people have left without being purified. The men are
cowards, unwilling to confront the Pale Ones. They took Siduri and
the Pale One female. For that, they're especially cursed."

Devu's voice was commanding and captivating, and he chose his
words carefully.

"Think back, Nereans. When have your hunts been so poor? Just
this last hunt, the Lion People killed enough game to survive the
whole winter. You Nereans who hunted the area next to us killed
nothing." Devu let those words settle for a moment.

"Are your hunters not as good as ours? No. You have excellent
hunters. The only difference is that your tribe has been…polluted.
Polluted with filth from the Pale Ones. Cursed! You're all cursed.
I ask you to think, Nereans. Think! When did your hunts begin
to fail?" He paused and was pleased to see the crowd was hushed,
breathless to hear more.

"Your hunts began to fail shortly after you made contact with the Pale Ones." Devu's eyes swept past Moctu and settled on Nuri, who had just walked up.

"Polluted! Your women have been polluted by Pale One seed." His gaze came back to Moctu. "And your men have lain with Pale One animals."

Rage flooded Moctu's senses, and he charged forward but was blocked by two Lion warriors with spears.

"No! You spout hate," Moctu shouted. "Nothing but hate. Some Pale Ones are good. And we've learned so much from them..."

Jondu grabbed the spear from Seetu's hands.

Moctu continued. "We've learned medicines and remedies, and most important, we've—"

Jondu clubbed Moctu from behind, and he crumpled to the ground.

Nuri's jaw dropped, and she was momentarily frozen with shock. Then, with a growling scream, she flung herself at Jondu, hitting him from the side. The nails of her left hand made two long, bloody claw marks from beside his eye down his cheek to the beginning of his short, dark beard.

Jondu swiveled and hit Nuri with the side of the spear, knocking the wind from her, and driving her toward Moctu's unmoving form on the ground. She collapsed beside him and tried to catch her breath. As it came back, she focused on her unconscious mate, checking his injury.

"See how the curse affects those who are polluted by the Pale Ones?" Devu shouted.

He pointed at Nuri and said to the crowd, "If your leader, Jondu, allows it, we'll take this one back for purification."

Jondu wiped his cheek and looked at the blood on his hand. He scowled, then nodded to Devu. The two Lion People guards quickly collected Nuri, who struggled wildly.

"No," she shrieked. "No! Get your hands off—"

One of the guards thrust the butt end of his spear into her gut, knocking the wind from her once again. Nabu moved toward the guards but was warned off by spear point. Avi was wide-eyed, with both hands to her mouth, but she remained rooted in place.

As much to Nuri as anyone, Devu said, "I will be asking the Spirits whether they demand the sacrifice of the Sleeps with Wolves child. That one act would do much to break the curse."

With that ominous comment, the corners of Devu's mouth turned up, and he motioned for the guards to head for the Lion People camp with Nuri in tow. He made a curt nod to Jondu, then turned and followed them. Still gasping for air, Nuri grappled with the guards and cast pleading eyes to the Nerean crowd. Moctu lay unconscious on the ground as Nabu's mate, Poza, tended to him.

"What have you done?" screamed Avi, staring unbelievingly at Jondu. She shook her head then knelt to help Poza attend to Moctu.

"It's...it's for the best," Jondu said to her and the crowd. "We had to do this...the curse...it's..." His voice trailed off as he saw cold eyes from the group.

His posture stiffened, and he said, "I did what I had to do for our survival." Jondu handed the spear back to Seetu and, trying to regain his authority, he motioned for the young man to follow him back to his hut.

"Come, Seetu. We have some planning to do."

59

DEVU'S HEARTH WAS DARK and full of animal skulls, piles of wilted plants, blocks of red ochre, and a huge bone of an animal that must have been twice the size of a mammoth. Nuri's hands were tied, and her stomach hurt. Across the hearth, Devu knelt near a pile of furs. As he removed his tunic and donned his red and black robe, Nuri could see his bony frame.

"Where is Elka?" she asked, scanning the room.

"She's with Ratna, my apprentice. Little Sleeps with Wolves is safe...for now," Devu said, turning toward her and trying not to sneer. "Her continued safety...well, that depends on you."

As Devu approached her, Nuri grimaced at his appearance. He was unkempt and skeletal. His beard was gray and dirty—caked in places with unidentifiable clots. Devu was unsuccessful in keeping a smirk from his face.

"You will be purified, and Sleeps with Wolves will live longer if you...cooperate."

With a finger, Devu moved a thick strand of hair from Nuri's face to behind her shoulder. As he pulled his hand back, he let his fingers slide across Nuri's neck, and she disgustedly jerked away.

"Oh, Nuri, you'll have to try harder than that. This is for your benefit too." He pointed to the bulge of her belly. "Your baby has been polluted by Pale One seed. This purification will remove the filth and foulness from your baby, and it will lessen the curse on your tribe."

Nuri momentarily frowned as her worries about the effects of Shaka-Nu's seed on her baby resurfaced.

Devu smiled as he saw that his words had impacted Nuri, however briefly.

He moved closer to her, but she retreated until her back was to the wall. He put his hand to the curve of her hip and moved upward along the graceful arc of her body. A mixture of fear, revulsion, and confusion swept her, and she tried to move sideways, but was blocked by the end of the huge bone.

"That's a bone we found in a riverbed along with some huge teeth. It's from an Aldak—a mutant beast of the Spirits. They're made of rock," he said, touching the fossil with reverence. "I've seen them in my dream travels. They're twice the size of a mammoth with sharp claws and teeth. They guard the entrance to the Cave of the Spirits at the eastern edge of the world."

He turned his gaze back to Nuri. "I can tell you of many such things…and teach you. But first, you must be purified." He reached a hand to her breast and stroked it. Nuri tried to pull away, but there was no place to go. Her hands strained to break their binding.

"You're very pretty," Devu said huskily. "And you'll be even more beautiful after you're purified." As he reached his other hand to her waist, his robe came open. His large, engorged member looked odd projecting from his gaunt midsection.

A half a head taller than her, Devu was looking down, beginning to remove Nuri's tunic when she headbutted him. It was a powerful blow, and Devu staggered backward, clutching his face, and tripped over the large blocks of red ochre. He fell with a cry into a seated position, and Nuri sprang for the hearth entrance.

Running with her hands behind her looked ungainly, and it drew the immediate attention of two kneeling women who were scraping the massive rhino skin. They called out and pointed, and soon Devu was at his hearth entrance screaming for a guard.

Since the attack from the Shiv, guards had been stationed at each end of the shelter, and Nuri recognized the bull-necked guard that quickly began chasing her. He was the one who had clubbed her a few days before, when Elka was taken. The man swiftly ran her down and brought her, kicking and struggling, back to Devu.

"Good work, Drogo," Devu said, still holding hands to his face. Blood dripped from his beard where it had run down from his nose. "Put her inside the hearth by the furs. I'll deal with her there."

Drogo smiled knowingly and roughly shoved Nuri to her knees on the furs. He frowned disappointedly when Devu said, "You can leave now."

Reluctantly, Drogo exited the hearth, but he turned and said, "I'll be nearby."

Devu waved him off, then wiped his nose with a thin skin. His eyes were cold and hard as he turned to Nuri and said, "You're more polluted than I thought. We may need to sacrifice Sleeps with Wolves before we begin your purification."

Nuri didn't think that Devu would harm Elka immediately. He'd use her as a tool to get what he wanted...at least at first. As she strained against her bindings, she fought back fear...fear for herself, for her baby, and for Elka. But with the fear was a confidence born of her recent history.

I've dealt with Shaka-Nu. I can deal with this man. Her thoughts moved to the toy hatchet blade she carried, now more as a good-luck charm than anything. I'll use it again...if I get the chance. I'd cut this man's throat in a heartbeat if I can keep my baby alive...and get Elka.

Devu finished cleaning the blood from his face and staunching the flow from his nose. He took two quick strides toward Nuri and slapped her face hard with the flat of his hand.

Momentarily stunned, Nuri shook it off. Although the blow had brought tears to her eyes, she stared upward at Devu with raw fury.

"Let me tell you about the last man to do this to me," she said, twisting her wrists against the ties. "His name was Shaka-Nu. He was leader of the Shiv, and twice the man you are." Nuri paused and stared into Devu's eyes. "I am the Sorceress. The Sorceress who left him dead in furs like these. You want to purify me? I purified myself—I bathed in his blood."

Nuri could see her words took Devu by surprise, and they had the intended effect. His head pulled back and his mouth opened in shock, if only for a heartbeat before he recovered his authority. He was used to submissive women, and this one was very different. Could she be a sorceress?

"You *will* be purified, and I'll do it," he said loudly. "The curse is deep within you, and we may need to sacrifice little Sleeps with Wolves *now* to lessen its power."

It was Nuri's turn to register shock, and Devu smiled. All women—all people—had weaknesses. You just had to know how to find them.

Nuri wracked her brain for a response…something, some tool to use to counter this man.

"Fire," she said. "I can make fire from nothing…and I'll bring it down on you."

Devu's eyes narrowed. Only the Spirits could make fire with lightning bolts from the sky. Nuri saw she had his interest, and she continued.

"Put me in an empty hearth with dry wood. Close the hearth entrance skins, and leave me there. Place as many guards as you want…I won't try to escape. I don't want to leave without Elka. If I can make fire, you let me go with Elka. If I can't, I'll submit to your…" she grimaced and almost spit the next word. "*Purification*… willingly."

Devu smiled, realizing that Nuri was just stalling. Only the Spirits could make fire, and he was already imagining the purification rites with this would-be sorceress. He pulled out a knife and held it close to Nuri's face. It was a long, sharp, wicked-looking blade of red flint. He ran it gently sideways along her cheek.

"We'll let you attempt to show us these powers and abilities, but I'll have Sleeps with Wolves next to me, and I'll sacrifice her immediately if you try to escape. I'll cut her throat from ear to ear and burn her polluted body in my hearth. If you can make fire in a cold, empty room, then you can go." He looked quickly from Elka to Nuri and shrugged. "If you can't, you'll be purified by me readily... and enthusiastically. Agreed?"

Nuri gave a slight smile and nodded.

60

RATNA WAS THE FATTEST person that Nuri had ever seen. As she lumbered into view bearing Elka, Nuri was entranced by the sight of her. She was easily the size of two women, maybe three. She wore a short, woven-fiber wrap around her huge hips, and Nuri could see that her inner thighs were red from rubbing against one another. A much-too-short tunic allowed rolls of belly fat to spill out and did little to disguise her fleshy, pendulous breasts.

The Lion People are certainly successful for one to eat so much, Nuri thought. Could Devu be right? Maybe their Spirits are—

Her thoughts were cut short as Devu barked orders to Ratna. The ponderous girl approached Nuri and untied her hands.

"I'll get some wood—" she began, but Nuri cut her off, and quickly described to her what supplies she would need. Ratna asked a few questions, and Nuri quickly recognized that although physically slow, Ratna was intelligent and good-natured. Her eyes were bright, her dark hair well-kept, and her face was pretty.

After Ratna left, Nuri smiled and waved at Elka, who seemed to have been well cared for. Needing to focus, she turned her back to Devu and the small but growing crowd of onlookers.

"I can do this," she murmured excitedly. "I'll get Elka, and when I get back to our hut..." She smiled broadly as she imagined how happy Moctu would be. "We'll leave in the morning...maybe even tonight...and we'll be away from this horrible place. And that man." She shivered with revulsion as she recalled Devu close to her, beginning to undress her.

Ratna returned with exactly the materials Nuri had requested. Devu checked to see what was included and to make sure there were no embers. Knowing she was just stalling, Devu said, "You don't have the rest of the day. You have to have your fire soon."

Nuri pointed to the sun and said, "The sun is there. I'll have fire before it moves..." She moved her hand a small distance. "to there."

Nuri retreated into the hearth and pulled the skin over the opening. She quickly set up, repeating the steps in her head. She used her tiny hatchet to carve a small divot in the flat board and a notch to the side. She expertly prepared her tinder and began the twisting of the spindle. The wood was dry as she'd requested, and she soon saw smoke trailing up from the head of the spindle. It was not long before she had a stable fire going in the tinder and small twigs. Nuri snapped off the charred tip of the spindle and put it into the burning tinder so that people could not determine how the fire had been made.

Nuri scooped her hands under the batch of flaming tinder and moved to the entrance.

"Open the hearth entrance," she said in her most commanding voice to those outside.

It was early—the sun had not yet moved to where Nuri had pointed, so Devu was perplexed as to why this girl had not delayed as much as possible. He was stunned as she emerged from the hearth with both hands holding high a large batch of tinder which was...*burning*! The crowd burst into clamor and commotion, most wondering how Nuri had performed this trick.

"I am the Sorceress," Nuri said loudly, looking at Devu's wide eyes. "I can bring fire, and I can bring death."

She laid the burning pile at Devu's feet and said, "Now give me my daughter, and I'll be on my way."

Although staggered by what he had just seen, Devu tried to regain his authority. He nervously motioned to a guard, who came quickly.

"As we agreed, you may leave," he said to Nuri. "But I'll be keeping Sleeps with Wolves."

Nuri's nostrils flared, and she said, "You told me that I could take Elka with me."

"No, I told you that *you* could go. I have plans for Sleeps with Wolves."

Nuri lunged toward Devu but was blocked by the guard, who shoved her away with the side of the spear.

"I am not leaving without my daughter," Nuri shouted.

Devu smiled as the power shifted back his way. "You can stay as a prisoner, or this man will escort you away."

Nuri hesitated, glowering at Devu.

At a murmured command from Devu, the guard began hitting and shoving Nuri with the shaft of the spear, herding her away.

"You'll regret this," Nuri yelled to Devu. "I'll make you pay…and if you hurt Elka, I'll kill you. *I'll kill you!*"

The guard continued his prodding and shoving past the edge of the Lion People shelter, where he was joined by two other guards who seemed to relish hitting Nuri with their spears. They suddenly stopped as one guard pointed down the path to a pair coming toward them.

"Moctu!" Nuri shouted. It was Moctu and Nabu, and she began running toward them and calling their names. The three guards whistled and motioned to lookouts for backup.

Both Moctu and Nabo carried their heavy spears, and their grim expressions turned to broad smiles as Nuri ran toward them.

"I'm free," Nuri said loudly as she neared them, "but they still have Elka."

She and Moctu embraced happily, but Nuri anxiously gushed, "Devu has Elka…he was supposed to let her go with me. He's bad… I'm worried about her. I didn't let him purify me, Moctu. But Elka… we've got to get her."

They approached the Lion People shelter but were blocked by the guards, who now numbered five.

"You're not welcome here," one bellowed to them. "Turn around...don't make trouble."

One of the guards had a shaft loaded in his atlatl, while the rest had heavy spears. Faced with the impossible odds, Moctu, Nabu, and Nuri finally turned and left.

On the way back to the Nerean camp, Nuri told them all that had happened to her.

"So, Devu met the Sorceress," Moctu said, smiling. "And they've seen fire made, but they don't know how to do it. You think we can get Elka back if we show them how to make fire?" he asked Nuri.

"I guess I agree with Jondu about that," Nabu interjected with a frown. "We need food. I think we need to trade that for food. Otherwise, it's going to be a horrible winter, and a lot of people will die. Even if we got Elka back, she might starve in the winter."

Moctu and Nuri both glumly nodded their heads. The group walked in silence for a long time before Moctu voiced the question on all their minds, "How are we going to get her back?"

61

MOCTU...MOCTU AND NURI," JONDU called as he approached their hut. His eyes narrowed as he saw that each of them had a small wolf asleep on their lap as they sat near the fire discussing something serious.

"Jondu," Moctu replied, barely keeping the scowl from his face.

"I...uh...there's some news," Jondu started. "The scouts came back and they've found evidence of the Pale Ones—the Shiv—not too far away. A war party will leave soon." He paused before going on. "There's no easy way to say this, but...uh...Devu's announced there will be a...sacrifice...at the full moon in several days—to ensure success with the war. He didn't say who or what, but I'm sure it's Elka. I've urged him not to...but he plans to go ahead. I thought you should know."

Moctu and Nuri both stood, displacing the sleepy pups. "No," Moctu said loudly. "We can't let this happen."

"Now, don't go doing something reckless. I'm going to talk with him again tomorrow. Maybe I can stop it. I'm leaving after that... we'll wipe out the Shiv and be back soon."

Moctu was pacing, shaking his head.

"No, no, no." He stopped, and through clenched teeth he said, "Devu." He spit, then picked up his heavy spear, but Nuri put her hand on his arm.

"Moctu, no." She looked at Jondu and searched his eyes. "Can you stop this?"

"I'll talk with him again, but…" He shook his head and looked at the ground. "This shouldn't be happening. Everyone's upset…those who've heard. I know you and Avi…you're not talking these days, but she's worried too."

Nuri scowled and looked away, remembering their last conversation.

"Well, I'm going to do something," Moctu said, hefting his spear. He glared at Jondu. "You started all this…are you going to help me?"

Jondu put a hand out. "Don't do that, Moctu. You'll get yourself killed and start a war."

"Well, I'm not going to stand around while Devu butchers my child." He blew out a bitter breath. "I knew you wouldn't help. Maybe I can get Nabu and Seetu. I wish Palo was here."

"Nabu and Seetu are going with the war group, but we'll be back soon. As you and Siduri have told us, they don't have atlatls. We'll slaughter them." He hesitated. "It'll be a big victory, but I'm guessing that you won't want to come."

Moctu cocked his head and stared incredulously.

"Are you serious? If Indar was about to be sacrificed…butchered, would you go to war next to the people that were killing him? The only good news here is that there'll be fewer Lion warriors to stop me from getting Elka."

"Moctu, don't do that. At least wait until I talk with Devu again tomorrow."

Moctu looked off in the distance with unfocused eyes. "I'll wait for a little while," he said finally. "But Jondu, I am *not* going to watch my daughter slaughtered by that…" He couldn't think of a word vile enough, so he spit to the ground.

"I'll do my best to…to stop it," Jondu said. He shrugged, turned, and left.

Nuri embraced Moctu, whose breathing caught while he tried not to show emotion.

"Nuri, what do I do? I can't let her…I can't let that man—"

"Whatever you decide, I'll be there next to you," Nuri said. "I can use an atlatl."

Moctu separated himself from Nuri enough to see her face. "No...no. No, no, no. You're carrying my child. I'm not going to risk you or this baby," he said, putting his hand on her belly. Visions of Effie being hit by an atlatl shaft came to him, and he squeezed Nuri tighter. "Please promise me that you'll stay safe. I can't lose you...or the baby. Please, Nuri."

After a moment, Nuri nodded, and they were both quiet for a long time, holding each other.

Moctu finally let go, saying, "Well, I've got a few days to come up with a plan to get Elka. I need to see Petrel and a few others. Maybe they can cause enough of a diversion that I can..." His voice trailed off, and he shook his head as the hopelessness of his situation set in.

"Moctu," Nuri said, and she paused for a long moment. "Don't die. Spirits, please don't just...waste your life."

"I'm going to get Elka," he said firmly. "And I'll kill Devu if he's hurt her." He smiled thinly, nodded at her, and left.

Moctu spent the day talking to the men he thought might help him, and by the evening, only Petrel had agreed. But even he had reservations. Any action he participated in had to have a reasonable chance of success. He wasn't willing to die pointlessly, however good the cause.

"You'll be with Nuri, creating a diversion on the north side—the bigger the better. I'll be at the other end of their shelter, and I'll try to get Elka from Devu or Ratna," Moctu said.

"There are guards all over that place," Petrel said, grimacing. "You don't stand a chance. And if you kill some of them, you'll start a war. Don't be doing that, Moctu. We'll lose that war...especially with half our warriors back at Etseh."

"I'll do my best not to kill anyone."

When Petrel frowned and cocked his head, Moctu amended his words to "I promise not to kill anyone."

"Well, you're going to get yourself killed, Moctu," Petrel said. "I'll help you with a diversion, but I don't like it. I think it's hopeless."

Moctu let out a deep breath and looked at the ground. Petrel was right—it *was* hopeless.

"I have to do something," he said quietly.

62

MOCTU WIPED AWAY THE sweat that was dripping into his eyes as he set the load of freshly cut green branches and leaves to the side of the fire pile. It was the second one he'd built, each at the top of two widely spaced hills.

"These'll give off good signals," he murmured, then blew out a sharp, bitter breath. "Probably won't be using either of them." The fire piles were for signaling Palo and Nindai after he'd secured Elka.

"I can't even think of a way that this'll work. But I've got to try." The corners of his mouth came up as he imagined what his stepfather, Tabar, would think.

"He'd approve," Moctu said, considering. "He always said to do the right thing. Live your best life, and die your best death." He nodded to himself, thinking there was no way that Tabar would have let him be sacrificed and not tried to stop it.

It would be a full moon tomorrow, and that's when he was to light one or both of the signal fires. That was also the day that Elka would be sacrificed.

A large contingent of well-armed men had left at dawn, including Jondu, Nabu, and Seetu, along with a few Gureks and a lot of Lion warriors. It was a surprise to Moctu that Lehoy had stayed behind due to a leg problem. The warriors were in good spirits, planning to exterminate the Shiv and return soon. Unfortunately for Moctu, there were still a lot of Lion men left at their shelter for defense.

Rescuing Elka would be nearly impossible, and Jondu had made matters worse. After he talked with Devu about halting the sacrifice, Devu had not only refused—he doubled the guard on Elka.

Moctu sat on a log and looked off in the distance toward the lowlands. I've had a good, long life, he thought. I've lived more than three hands of summers, and done so much. Mated two wonderful women and each has given me a child...or will soon. I met the Pale Ones and learned to make fire. I fought off a saber-tooth and killed a mammoth. Became leader of my tribe. It's been a good life.

Moctu would make the attempt to get Elka tonight, in the dark hours before dawn. Even though he was likely to die, he was oddly cheerful.

"I'm doing the right thing," he murmured. "Tabar, Jona...I'll probably be with you soon." He smiled at the thought, sure that they'd be proud of him for doing all he could to save his child.

The sun was low in the western sky, and he headed back to his hut. When he got there, he found Nuri painting her face and body with red and black ochre while trying to restrain the rambunctious pups.

"They've been wild today—chewed through the leather each time I tried to leash them."

"Your face," Moctu said. "What's the paint for?"

"You wanted a diversion. It's only going to be Petrel and me... I've got to look like the Sorceress. Petrel's taking a spear, which he'll beat on a small, hollow log. We're going to make as much noise and bedlam as we can."

Moctu grinned, but it faded quickly. Nuri was so creative, and he appreciated her effort. But it was unlikely to be enough. He went about his preparations, every now and then pausing to relish his life and wonder what the afterlife was like. As the sun set, the moon became visible, already high in the sky. Moctu and Nuri sat together near the fire as the stars rivaled the moon in intensity.

"Let's pray to the Spirits," he said, taking her hand. "Let's pray together."

Nuri's lip trembled as her forced optimism broke. She hugged Moctu tightly.

"Moctu, please...I know you have to do this, but please...don't die. Please." Tears welled in her eyes. "I can't...I can't..." She shook her head, unable to finish her sentence.

Moctu hugged her and said, "It'll be all right. You just make sure you stay safe." His eyes misted, and he fought to control his feelings. I don't want to die, he thought, but instead he said, "I love you, Nuri."

Nuri sobbed, and a tear rolled down her cheek.

"Hey, don't worry...I'm going to be fine," he lied. "Come on, you're messing up your face paint."

Nuri chuckled between two sobs, then sniffed and gathered herself. She knelt with him and dug a small hole in the dirt near the fire. From her tunic pocket, she took her good-luck hatchet blade, and she made a small cut at the base of the sacred finger—the longest and strongest—the middle finger of the right hand. Moctu extended his right hand, and she made a similar cut to his finger.

They dripped blood into the hole in the ground, and Moctu said, "Mother Earth, thank you for all your blessings. Please accept our blood offering and give us good fortune tonight. Please help us recover Elka, and keep us safe. We know we'll return to you one day, but please allow us more life."

They were quiet for a long time as each said silent prayers and reflected on their lives and the task ahead. There was commotion from the hut, and the two pups came out barking and howling.

"They've chewed through their restraints again," Nuri said, getting up to quiet them.

"Shhh, shhh, shhh," both she and Moctu said, trying to keep them from waking those in the nearby huts.

That's when Avi showed up.

63

Even in the dim light, Nuri could see Avi's face was flushed with excitement.

"Hello, Nuri. Hello, Moctu."

Nuri noted that the cold tone was gone, and she got up to welcome Avi. It soon became apparent why Avi was excited—the figure of a tall man that had to be Lehoy moved behind her in the murky darkness toward the group.

She's had sex with Lehoy while Jondu's away, Nuri thought.

"Hello, Avi," she said neutrally. "What are you doing up in the middle of the night?"

Avi was smiling broadly.

"I have someone I'd like you to meet…or get to know better," she said breathlessly. Avi turned as Lehoy moved into sight. He was strangely dressed with a cloak or cape around his shoulders. As he got closer, the pups went berserk, barking and charging toward him despite Nuri and Moctu trying to manage them and keep them quiet.

Nuri wondered what was it about Lehoy that agitated or worried the wolves so much. She didn't much like him either.

"I'm sorry…they're not usually like this," she said, scrambling to contain Neska, the female.

Like Avi, Lehoy looked happy, and his eyes sparkled in the firelight. He nodded at Moctu, who was holding the struggling Mut. Moctu nodded back solemnly.

This is the man who didn't really win the atlatl competition, Moctu thought, fighting a scowl. I don't have time for this…I have to leave soon for…

That's when Lehoy pulled open his cloak. There, nestled against his chest, was Elka.

Stupefied, Moctu stood motionless while Nuri gave a small shriek and moved to take Elka. The firelight, the pups barking, and the action as Lehoy moved his arms awakened Elka, and the toddler held her arms out as Nuri reached her. Moctu was there as well, and Avi and Lehoy beamed as the small family danced with the joy of reunion.

After a long moment of hugging and kissing from Moctu and Nuri, Elka held out her arms toward the pups and Moctu placed her on the ground. The little girl squealed with laughter as Mut and Neska cavorted about her, licking her face and wiggling with excitement.

Wordlessly, Nuri embraced Avi. Trembling and choked with emotion, she finally croaked, "Avi, you…you are—"

"I've missed you. I've missed my sister-friend," Avi whispered.

"Oh, Avi, me too. Thank you. Thank you so much."

Both women fought back sobs as happy tears streaked down their cheeks.

Moctu clasped Lehoy's hand and said, "I don't know how you did it, but I can never repay you."

Lehoy smiled, but then turned serious. "Get to safety soon—your whole tribe. A storm is coming…a storm between our tribes." He shook his head. "A very bad storm."

Moctu nodded. "We'll leave now—or as soon as we can." He touched Lehoy's shoulder. "Thank you again. If you ever…if you ever need…"

Lehoy dipped his head, thanking Moctu, understanding his unfinished offer for what it was.

"I need to get back before Elka is missed," he said, gently pulling Avi away from Nuri.

"You go with Moctu and Nuri," he said in a low voice. "It won't be safe here."

Avi nodded, then hugged him.

In a choked voice, she said, "Come with us. Lehoy, I…"

Lehoy put a finger to her lips and said, "I can't." He kissed her on the cheek and then vanished into the darkness.

Moctu stared after him for a moment, then turned to Elka, who was still playing with the pups. This seemed like a dream—it was too wonderful to be true. Only now was it dawning on him that he was going to survive the night. And they had Elka back. But they weren't safe yet.

"Devu's going to be furious, and he'll retaliate. We need to hurry—no one's safe here. Wake up everyone. We need to get out of here. All of us."

While Nuri and Avi alerted the other Nereans, Moctu dismantled the hut, separating the skins from the poles. Nereans were skilled at rapid decampment, and with few personal possessions and unfortunately small meat reserves, the tribe was on the move westward well before dawn. They pulled a handful of travois mostly bearing their skins, some weapons, cooking gear, and about half of the flint they had on hand.

The sun was just peeking over the eastern mountains as the group crossed the braided stream that divided their territory from that of the Lion People. Moctu and Nuri left briefly, each to a separate hill to light the signal-fire piles that Moctu had earlier built. Once the green branches and leaves were added, the fires belched dark clouds of smoke upward, and Moctu and Nuri moved quickly to rejoin their group. The Lion People would soon be investigating the signal fires.

Earlier, in the dark hours, Petrel had been surprised but pleased to learn he would not be helping Nuri make a diversion. Now, he joined Moctu as a rear-guard for the Nereans as they tramped westward. The group was well into their own territory when they first glimpsed the Lion warriors—moving fast and gaining on their straggling column.

64

JONDU'S EYES NARROWED. THIS was almost too easy. From their forest concealment, they could see into the Pale One camp far down the hill. It was a Shiv camp, where timber and skins had been added to jumbled boulders to define a series of small huts and chambers. Women and older children bustled through chores of firewood collection and processing hides while smaller children played games of chase. The one guard they could see was bearded, light-skinned, and had the distinctive red facial tattoos. Bored, he sat with a spear looking southward.

Men of the Lion People made up the bulk of the three hands of their war party, so one of their group, Drogo, was in charge. Although Jondu wanted to lead the effort, he understood that there were only three Nereans compared to more than two hands of Lion warriors. So far, Drogo had handled things the way he would. The forest was eerily quiet as Drogo sidled over to Jondu and courteously asked him if his men were ready.

"There'll be no prisoners…we need to kill them all," Drogo whispered. "Are your men up to it?"

Although Nabu had earlier told Jondu that he would kill no women or children, Jondu nodded to Drogo.

"Good," Drogo said. "We'll attack when I give the call of a crow."

As he began to move back toward his men, he grinned at Jondu and said, "Good hunting."

That's when the forest erupted around them. Men—large, burly men with spears and huge, rock-tipped cudgels—arose from leafy patches on the ground. Nearby bushes implausibly transformed into camouflaged Shiv warriors, powerful men adept at close-in spear work. There were lots of them, and all were howling and barking a weird, high-pitched, terrifying noise.

The surprise was total, as was the panic. The bulk of the Shiv force hit the right flank of the Lion warriors, and they immediately broke and ran. Many had prepared their atlatls for the assault on the Shiv camp, but in the dense forest, in a close engagement, the weapons were next to useless. Lion warriors dropped their atlatls and fled. The warrior next to Drogo got one shot off before he was speared in the belly by a brawny Shiv with brown hair and blackened eye sockets. Drogo was shocked to see the spear not only penetrate his companion, but nearly two feet of it extended out the man's back. As he dropped his atlatl and ran, Drogo saw the Shiv move behind the dying man and pull the wooden shaft all the way through so the shaft was covered in blood and gore.

Jondu and Seetu both threw shafts before they too dropped their atlatls and turned to run. Seetu's shaft missed badly, and Jondu's glanced off a small branch before hitting a broad-shouldered, red-haired Shiv in the upper arm. It didn't even slow the man. Nabu saw the nearest threat was a buck-toothed, blond Shiv swinging a cudgel. Releasing his atlatl, Nabu took up the heavy spear he carried just in time to see the warrior swing at Jondu. The Nerean leader raised his forearm to block the club, but the heavy cudgel's impact snapped Jondu's arm like a thin stick. It hung at a sickening angle with the bones protruding, spouting blood. Jondu screamed and staggered, and the Shiv began another swing which Nabu blocked with his spear. He followed through, slashing across and downward, slicing the Shiv's chest to the rib bones. The camouflaged, buck-toothed warrior grunted in pain, dropped his club, and fell back.

Nabu could have thrown the spear and killed the man, but he decided keeping the spear was more important, and he let the Shiv escape. He turned his attention to Jondu, who had stopped and was mumbling in shock as he tried to put his right arm back together.

"Come, friend—now!" Nabu yelled over the clamor of the yipping, the screams, and the clashing of spears and clubs.

To his credit, Seetu retraced his steps, returning to assist Jondu. As Jondu attempted to hold his arm together, his face showed more astonishment than pain. The men each took hold under Jondu's arms and rushed him away from the disaster.

A skinny, young Shiv with a freshly tattooed forehead gave chase, yipping loudly, but Nabu released Jondu and turned to face him with his spear. Unconsciously growling with rage, Nabu charged the boy, who recoiled, then turned and fled. Nabu let him go and returned to where Seetu was struggling to hold Jondu. Blood was pulsing from the wound down the dangling wrist and running in rivulets from the fingers. Jondu had passed out from shock.

"We need to get farther away—fast—then stop the bleeding," Nabu hissed. "He's going to die if we don't hurry, but we're all going to die if we stay here."

The men broke into an ungainly, half-running, half-walking gait, supporting Jondu's slack body, his feet trailing limply behind. While hauling Jondu's dead weight, Nabu did his best to pinch off the bleeding with his free hand. In the mountainous country it was a grueling effort, but they kept going until they were far enough from the battle site to begin to feel safer. On an uphill stretch, Seetu gasped, "Gotta stop...let's treat...his arm here."

They lay Jondu down and examined his arm. Seetu grimaced and turned away.

"I don't know much about healing, but I think at least the bottom part has to come off," he said.

Nabu frowned and nodded. "We should get the arm severed while he's unconscious. You build a small fire so we can cauterize it and slow the bleeding. But use dry wood—no smoke."

Although the bleeding had slowed, it was still flowing steadily, so Nabu tied a strip of leather around the end of the arm as a tourniquet. Nearly half of the forearm remained, but bloody, splintered bones protruded, so it would be best to amputate at the elbow. Nabu had worked on many deer and caribou carcasses, disarticulating them at joints, but he'd never cut off a human arm.

"Cutting off just the hanging part won't help—the arm should come off at the elbow. Should I try to do it, or should we wait for Nindai...?" Nabu paused, realizing Nindai was gone. "Should we have Devu do it?"

"I think you just answered your own question, Nabu. You've got to do it."

Nabu nodded and wrinkled his brow. Jondu moaned and stirred, so there wasn't time to deliberate.

"I need to do this fast while he's still unconscious," Nabu murmured.

He tied another strap below Jondu's bicep, pulling as much of the arm skin above the strap as possible. Excess skin would be needed to cover the stump and be sewn together over it.

"Get over here, Seetu. I may need your help holding him down if he wakes up when I start this," he said, scowling with distaste.

With his sharp flint knife, Nabu quickly cut a circle in the skin around the arm just below the elbow. He sliced through most of the muscle and severed the key tendons and was just positioning his larger spear blade to knock the joint apart when Jondu woke up, thrashing and screaming.

Even with Nabu kneeling on Jondu, and Seetu putting the weight of his body on the flailing man, it took three strikes to separate the joint. Although Nabu felt sorry for Jondu, he was more worried that his uncontrolled shrieking would bring the Shiv. Jondu fell silent, his eyes rolling back, exposing the whites. He began quivering, then went still, unconscious again. As Nabu feared, the yipping immediately surged in intensity, and some of it was close.

Nabu tightened the tourniquet around Jondu's bicep to slow the bleeding, then took a burning stick from the fire and singed the end of Jondu's arm.

"Need to sew it and stop the bleeding more, but we've got to get moving—now. That screaming's gotten them excited again, and they're coming," Nabu said.

With no time to bury the severed piece of arm, they placed it on the fire, then began an awkward run, lugging Jondu as before.

65

Moctu's group, as they retreat toward Etseh...

THERE WERE SIX OF them, heavily armed and coming fast from the east. When they got in range, Moctu sent a shaft that landed near the leader, stopping them temporarily.

"Stay back, or the next one doesn't miss," Moctu called.

"We have orders—to bring you, the Sorceress, and Sleeps with Wolves back. Come with us, and the rest of your people can go on."

Moctu studied the group, noting that Lehoy wasn't with them. Their leader was a sturdy, middle-aged but handsome man wearing a red, ochre-stained tunic.

"No one is coming with you," Moctu yelled.

"You have only two warriors, and we have six."

"Come closer, and that number will change quickly," Moctu threatened.

As the man conferred with his other warriors, Moctu whispered to Petrel. "They'll spread out and flank us. That's what I would do. You keep the column moving. Tell everyone to go faster. Any of these warriors that circle around to the north—they're yours. I'll keep the rest away."

Sure enough, the man in the red tunic motioned to the southwest, and two of his warriors went that direction. Then he motioned to the northwest, and two went that way. He and one other approached warily from where they were.

Moctu gave ground, staying close to the three, trailing travois of the Nerean column—two of them carrying the heavy flint. An uneasy equilibrium set in, with the Nereans moving ever westward, and the Lion warriors following, but getting no closer. Four men shadowed him, and he could see that two were tracking Petrel. The men were close enough that Moctu could study their faces. The easternmost man was not much more than a fresh-faced boy, slender with no beard.

The sun rose high in the cloudless sky, but the none of the six warriors came nearer. Almost bored, Moctu yelled, "We don't want war with the Lion People. Whose orders are you following?"

When there was no answer, Moctu called again, "Whose orders are causing war between the Lion People and Nereans?"

"Our orders are from the great shaman, Devu," yelled the man in the red tunic.

"So what does your leader, Rolf, think of this? Or does he even know?"

"Rolf defers to Devu on matters like this," the man called back.

"So Devu is the real leader of the Lion People," Moctu murmured to himself.

The leader of the warrior group whistled loudly, then held his right hand high in the air. After a moment, he moved it forward, pointing to Moctu, and his men began advancing.

Adrenaline surged in Moctu, more a mix of anger and excitement than fear. These warriors were coming to kill him and take Elka and Nuri.

Rather than wait for four warriors to close in on him, he decided to attack. Springing toward the fresh-faced boy, Moctu screamed, "Aaiiiyah!" and charged right at him. The boy had been advancing confidently, but now his eyes widened, his jaw dropped, and he broke and ran, dropping most of his shafts.

Moctu immediately rounded on the next closest warrior, a competent-looking man who wore his hair in multiple braids.

"Aarruuu!" Moctu yelled, his anger now replaced by a battle joy. He rapidly closed the distance to the warrior with a zig-zag run. Steadfastly, the man not only stood his ground, but launched a shaft at Moctu. It missed closely to the left, and Moctu threw his own shaft, which took the warrior in his upper leg. The man cried out, grabbed his leg, and went down.

Veering off again and still screaming wildly, Moctu ran at the leader of the group, who looked stunned to see two of his men out of action and the man he was chasing now berserk and coming for him. He threw a half-hearted shaft that missed badly, then he, too, ran.

The fourth warrior who had been advancing on him was already backing away when Moctu turned in his direction. When he turned and fled, Moctu slowed to a stop, his battle rage sated. He looked to the north to ensure that Petrel was not under attack. Petrel, who had watched the encounter, raised his atlatl high in the air as a salute to Moctu.

Keeping an eye on the Lion warriors, Moctu moved back toward the Nerean column, where he saw Nuri approaching with an atlatl and three shafts.

"Avi has taken an atlatl to help her father," Nuri said, smiling. "I see I'm too late to help here."

His heart still pumping hard from the rush of battle, the corners of his mouth came up, and Moctu nodded toward the warrior he'd hit with a shaft.

"They're gathering over by the one I wounded. Probably two out of action now—Tabar once told me that wounding an enemy was like wounding two. A warrior has to care for the wounded one. Maybe they're all going to leave, but it's too early to tell." He blew out a short breath. "You may still get to help."

Moctu had considered this earlier. Having already witnessed one mate killed by an atlatl attack, he didn't want Nuri endangered. But if he were killed or wounded, she and Elka would almost certainly be killed as well. Or worse, they'd be taken back to Devu for sacrificing.

He watched as two warriors lifted the wounded man and began carrying him away. The leader in the red tunic raised his atlatl high in the air and yelled, "This isn't over. We'll be back…with a lot more warriors. You'll die for this—we'll kill you *and* your men…and take your women."

"Come this way again, *you'll* be the ones to die," Moctu shouted back, his anger resurfacing.

"And the women here'll be killing you too," Nuri added loudly.

The man said something else that they couldn't understand, but he and his remaining warriors turned and began walking away.

Moctu closed his eyes and gave thanks to the Spirits. His band was safe for now, but he was sure the man was right. The Lion People had many more warriors than the Nereans, and this wasn't over.

66

"Jondu's lost a lot of blood," Seetu worried aloud.

Nabu just nodded glumly as together they carried his limp body. The threesome had traveled for almost two days, and they were now far away from the site of the ambush, but they needed to keep moving. The Shiv were pursuing, and they were close. Their excited yipping sound could still occasionally be heard as they hunted down Lion warrior stragglers.

Jondu needed rest and the care of a healer, neither of which Nabu or Seetu could give him. He remained mostly unconscious, and when he wasn't, he was delirious. A serious fever had set in.

"If we stop to allow him to rest, I'm afraid the Shiv will catch up with us," Nabu said.

Seetu nodded. "I wonder how many of the Lion warriors are still alive?" he said.

That question was partially answered as dusk approached. Seeing movement on the hill opposite them, Nabu put his finger to his lips, pointed to where he'd seen the movement, and gently lay Jondu down behind a stand of scrub oak. As he and Seetu watched, a group of Lion warriors emerged from a broad clump of trees and cautiously made their way across a mostly open stretch of hillside to the low forest beyond.

"There were four of them, right?" Seetu asked.

"Uh huh," Nabu said. "And I would have called to them if I could be sure that the Shiv weren't close behind. Let's head that way and try to meet up."

By dusk, they had met up with Drogo and three other warriors, one of them with a serious leg wound.

"We thought you were dead!" Drogo said, smiling broadly as the two parties met. His smile turned to a frown as he saw Jondu's limp body.

"We thought the same about you," Seetu said.

"How badly hurt is he?" Drogo asked. He grimaced as he saw that Jondu was missing part of his arm.

"He's lost the arm and a lot of blood," Seetu said. "And he's feverish. Needs a healer—soon."

"We're about a day from our shelter," Drogo said. "Devu can heal him. I sent two on ahead to tell them to be ready for some wounded." He scowled and shook his head. "How did they surprise us like that? They came out of nowhere."

"How many did you lose?" Nabu asked.

"At least three, and we're missing four others. I'm afraid some of them..." Drogo just shook his head and didn't finish the sentence.

Nabu could see the anguish in Drogo's eyes, and he patted him on the shoulder.

"I should have...should have been more careful," Drogo said in a choked voice. "My fault. But Devu had said the victory would be easy...and it looked like...like it *was* going to be."

The combined group of men trudged on, carrying their wounded in demoralized silence until late afternoon when they spotted three heavily armed men coming from the direction of the Lion People shelter.

"That's the two I sent ahead," Drogo said, squinting with a hand over his eyes to block the sun. "And Lehoy. Good...they can help us get the wounded to the healers faster. Both Jondu and my warrior aren't doing well at all."

As the three men got closer, Nabu could see Lehoy still suffered from his leg injury. But his limp was not too noticeable, and he was keeping up with the other two warriors. All of them wore grim expressions.

Less than an atlatl throw away, the youngest arriving warrior blurted loudly, "We're at war with the Nereans now."

Lehoy moved to stifle the fresh-faced young man, while Drogo looked at Nabu in confusion.

"Did he say...?" Drogo asked, frowning.

Nabu's eyes narrowed, and he nodded. He and Seetu took up protective positions around Jondu, their weapons ready, but not held threateningly.

Lehoy held up a hand to gain everyone's attention, then solemnly said, "Yes, we're at war with the Nereans."

"And Devu says to kill these..." The young warrior, pointing at the Nereans, stopped in mid-sentence as Nabu and Seetu raised their weapons slightly and scowled at the boy.

Lehoy cuffed the young man and said, "There'll be none of that."

It was then that Lehoy saw Jondu lying unconscious and bloodstained by Nabu. His eyes widened, and he took a few steps toward the Nereans.

"How...?" he started. His head drew back, and his mouth fell open as he saw that Jondu was missing his right forearm. He grimaced and said, "Is he going to...to be all right?"

"He's lost a lot of blood, and he has a fever," Seetu replied. "He needs a healer."

Lehoy's brow wrinkled.

"He's not going to be able to come to our shelter," he said slowly, as much to himself as to the others. "We *are* at war."

"They fought bravely," Drogo said, while rubbing the beard on his chin. He was still confused at being at war with men who were in his war party. "Jondu wounded one before...before that happened." He pointed to Jondu's missing arm.

"You'll have to go to your shelter—Etseh—and get help from the healers there," Lehoy said.

"He'll never make it," Seetu said. "It's days away, and Nabu and I are already spent from carrying him this far."

"I'll escort you…I'll help you carry him, at least until we get into your territory. We'll build a travois." Lehoy shook his head. "That's all we can do. We're supposed to be *killing* you."

67

Dusk was approaching, and the air turned cold. Dark clouds rolled in from the north, shrouding the mountains. A big storm was building there, and it would probably reach the retreating Nerean group by morning. Moctu had stealthily followed the Lion warrior band to ensure they were no longer a threat. The men stopped by a small creek, and after a long conversation, he saw their leader point to the east, toward Lion People territory. The young, beardless warrior immediately helped the wounded man to his feet, and they began to hobble in that direction. Moctu frowned as the other four warriors stayed behind, deep in discussion. They were planning something.

Moctu's concern rose as two men began trotting through the brush headed west—the direction his people were headed. The leader and another warrior also moved in that direction but at a slower pace.

"They're flanking us, and it'll be dark soon. Going to be hard to protect our group in the dark," he murmured. "Where are Nindai and Palo? What's taking them so long? Didn't they see the signal fires?"

Keeping low, Moctu scrambled back to the Nerean column, all the while scanning the landscape for a defensible campsite that they could reach before dark. He settled on a grove of pines on a low hill that overlooked lower brush and grasslands.

It'll offer a better view and wood for fires, he thought.

The tired travelers made it there well before dark and immediately set to gathering wood for fires.

"We'll have one fire for ourselves, and we'll set three outlying fires so we can watch for anyone trying to approach," Moctu said. "Petrel and I will take shifts guarding, but we'll need more lookouts during the night. Which of you women will volunteer?"

"Avi and I will help," Nuri said, raising her hand slightly. "Leuna and Poza say they'll watch over the children and pups."

"Great. Avi, you stay with your father and spell him. Nuri will stay with me and keep watch while I'm asleep."

With storm clouds to the north blocking out the moon and half of the stars, darkness fell quickly, and the outlying fires were lit. Although Moctu and the other lookouts saw movement all through the night, there were no assaults from the Lion warriors.

"Probably just trying to keep us awake all night," Nuri said to Moctu after she awoke him as he'd requested if she saw any warriors.

In the morning the rains came, and they were heavy and cold. The whole day had the grayness of dusk, and Nereans erected crude skin shelters in a largely unsuccessful attempt to stay dry and warm. The murky dampness affected everyone, and their sour moods were not helped by growling stomachs. The Nereans were running low on food, and they began rationing it. Lion warriors could occasionally be seen in the sodden brush—most of them west of the Nerean group, blocking their way to Etseh. An uneasy standstill ensued, with neither adversary moving toward the other.

"They're pinning us here, hoping more Lion warriors will come soon. But they don't know that we're waiting for Palo or Nindai to bring help," Moctu said, scanning the dim horizon. "Nindai's gone to Etseh, and Palo's gone to get help from Hawk and the Krog. I sure hope that our friends get here before their warriors do."

"At least they're suffering more than we are," Nuri said, nodding toward where they'd last seen one of the Lion warriors. "We have fire, and they don't. Leuna and the others have worked hard keeping the fire going—holding skins over it to keep the rain off and drying wet wood beside it. And the babies and children are safe and dry and not too grumpy. Hungry though. Everyone's hungry…they're even talking about eating the pups."

Moctu blew out a breath and shook his head. "Hope it doesn't come to that." He looked at the leaden sky. "Spirits, please help us. Send Palo or Nindai with the help we need."

That evening, his prayer was answered, but only partially, and not at all in the way he'd hoped. Palo slipped in…by himself. He was half-carrying, half-dragging a small red deer that he'd killed, but he was alone.

"The others?" Moctu asked hopefully. "Were you able to see Hawk? Are they coming?"

Palo's shoulders slumped. He shook his head and looked at the ground.

"Hawk wasn't there. He was out hunting, and I had to talk with Da. He's mad, I mean really mad. If Rah hadn't been there, I think he might've attacked me." He grimaced. "That Da—he's a scary-looking…fierce…" He paused, searching for the right word. "Those teeth…they're like fangs."

"So they're not coming," Moctu said, frowning and putting a hand through his hair. "I thought they would." After a pause, he cocked his head. "Where's Siduri? I thought she was with you."

"She went with Nindai's group to Etseh. I thought it was too dangerous…going to see the Krog." Palo's brow furrowed. "How many warriors are out there? I counted at least three before I slipped through."

"I think there's four," Moctu said, "but we're expecting more to arrive soon." He smiled bravely. "But you're here, and you've brought meat. That's a huge help."

"I'm sorry, Moctu. I tried to convince Da. Rah helped translate, and she tried too. Da wouldn't even consider it. He's so angry at Nindai for taking Sima, his woman. Says he'll kill him if he sees him."

"We'll figure something out. Hopefully Nindai's bringing help from Etseh." Moctu paused and grimaced. "Even so, we're going to be seriously outnumbered."

68

OTHER MEN HAD TOLD him about it, but this was the first time he'd heard the noise, and it was unnerving. The eerie, unrelenting yipping sent chills down Lehoy's spine and made him want to run. The Shiv were coming, and there were a lot of them.

"So many," he breathed, trying to calm himself.

"You get used to the sound," Nabu said. "The first time you hear it, it's…it's horrible."

Despite his casual tone, Nabu picked up his speed, as did Seetu. They had switched to carrying Jondu on a travois, and Lehoy would occasionally spell them. Jondu had come to only once in the past two days. Raising what was left of his arm to see what was causing the pain, he had started screaming, and he hadn't stopped until the screams weakened and he passed out again.

"Does he still have the fever?" Nabu asked Lehoy.

"It's no better…maybe worse," Lehoy said. "We have to get him to your healer soon. And to Avi. She should…see him, and maybe it'll help if he sees her."

This trip was a guilt offering for Lehoy. As strong as his feelings were for Avi, a sense of shame sometimes overwhelmed him.

Lehoy considered his situation. I never liked Jondu, he thought. Not from the start. And here I am risking my life and going against the wishes of my leaders to save him. He pursed his lips trying to figure out why he was helping this man.

"They're to the northeast," Seetu said. "We haven't gotten very far this morning. Once they cross our travois tracks, they'll pick up speed. We need to move faster."

"Rain coming from the north," Lehoy said, nodding to the dark clouds they'd all been tracking. "Maybe that'll slow them."

"How about your people?" Nabu asked. "Will Lion warriors hear the Shiv and come to fight?"

"That depends. We'll defend our shelter—that's most important. But we should also have enough warriors to go after them, if they don't outnumber us too much." He paused, listening. "Sounds like a lot of them, though."

"Let's try and make that hill before it rains," Nabu said. "We can set up a shelter to weather the storm. Looks like a bad one. Not even mid-morning yet, and it looks like dusk. Wouldn't be good for Jondu to get soaked. And the Shiv will seek shelter too, if they have any sense."

A nearby bolt of lightning underscored the point. The men had just reached the hill when the rains hit. Working quickly, they bent three young trees down and lashed them to a larger one. After spreading furs over the framework of bowed saplings, they moved Jondu under the shelter. The men were efficient, but even so, they were all soaked by the time they crowded under the skins. It was a cold, heavy rain, and the wind whipped at their paltry structure as lightning crashed around them. Without a fire the men shivered and huddled around Jondu.

Each time the thunder died off, the men listened for the ululating yipping of the Shiv, but they heard none.

"At least the Shiv have taken cover as well," Seetu said.

"As soon as the storm lets up, we need to get going again—fast. If we can hear the Shiv, then they're..." Lehoy stopped as Jondu stiffened, then began to shake violently.

"He's seizing," Nabu said, holding Jondu's head to prevent it from banging on the ground.

"Spirits! Is he—?" Seetu began.

Nabu cut him off. "No, he's not dying…not yet. But it's not a good sign. He needs a healer. Need to get him to Jelli or Nindai—soon."

The three men held Jondu and tried to comfort him as the shaking intensified, then began to abate. Nabu pulled up one of his eyelids, exposing only white cornea.

"It's bad," he said. "I wish Jelli was here. The storm is mostly past us. Let's load him back on the travois. I'm with Lehoy—let's get out of here."

The sky was still dark, and it was still raining, but it was getting lighter to the west, the direction they were going. They covered Jondu with their driest furs, then set out in the light drizzle. Pulling the travois was harder than before as it grooved two large furrows in the muddy ground and clods of grass and mud caked the trailing poles. Every small depression, every gulch was full of water. The storm had dropped a great deal of water in a short time, and it slowed their progress. Lehoy carefully watched their rear for signs of the Shiv. He saw nothing and was pleased not to hear their dreadful yipping.

The sky continued to lighten, and the rain stopped. They were wet, and the air was colder, but their exertion kept the men warm. Although they were all tired, none of the men would allow himself to ask the others for a rest.

"Aiaiaiai. Aiaiaia!" they heard ahead.

"Stop," Lehoy directed quickly. "That's the Lion warrior call for help. They're…ahead of us."

"No farther!" called a voice in front of them.

"I recognize that voice," said Lehoy. "It's Mica, one of our youngest warriors."

"Mica! Mica…it's me, Lehoy."

"Who are those with you?"

"Friends. Let us pass, Mica. You've done your job well."

"They're Nereans, aren't they? We can't let them pass. Why are you with them?"

"One of them's hurt…very badly. He fought the Shiv with us, Mica. He needs a healer." Lehoy's voice took on a tone of anger, and he stressed each of the next words. "Now, let us pass."

The warrior was more a boy than a man, and Lehoy's words clearly unsettled him. Still, he swallowed hard and made a show of authority, moving his atlatl to a more ready position.

"My orders are to let no one pass…in either direction."

Lehoy took out his atlatl and put a shaft in it.

"Mica, I taught you to use an atlatl. Do you really want to threaten me…to go against me?"

The young man fidgeted, then lowered his atlatl. He looked relieved as another Lion warrior ran up. The man was older and looked competent. He immediately recognized Lehoy, and Lehoy smiled and called him by name.

"Gerlari, welcome. We were just passing through. There's no problem now."

Gerlari had his atlatl ready, but now his eyes narrowed, and with his free hand he scratched at his beard. He saw Nabu slowly give the travois weight over to Seetu as he, too, made his atlatl ready.

"So you're with the Nereans now, Lehoy? Is that how it is?" Gerlari asked.

"These men fought with us against the Shiv. One of them is seriously wounded, and he needs a healer. We *will* pass through and be on our way," Lehoy said. When Gerlari started to object, he interrupted. "The Shiv are close behind us. They're the enemy, not these men. There's a lot of them…and they're coming."

With that, he pressed forward, motioning for Nabu and Seetu to follow him. As he passed the two Lion warriors, he said, "There's a lot of Shiv. Either join with us or head back to our shelter for more support. Otherwise, you're dead."

69

A RUSH OF HAPPINESS overtook Moctu as he recognized some of the men pulling the travois.

"Nabu! Seetu!" Moctu's eyes narrowed. "Lehoy? Oh, Spirits... that's Jondu. What's happened?"

"Is Nindai with you?" Nabu asked. "Jondu's...bad. He needs a healer."

Nuri hurried over to see the newcomers and, like Moctu, was thrilled to see Nabu and Seetu. The figure of Lehoy was so incongruous, so implausible, that it took her a moment to process. For the last two days, they'd been threatened with an attack by Lion warriors, and here was one of their best, standing among them.

"Lehoy?" Then her eyes fell on Jondu, and in bewilderment she called out, "Avi. Avi!"

As both Moctu and Nuri moved to care for Jondu, Avi rushed up. Her mouth fell open as her eyes met Lehoy's, and she advanced uncertainly toward him.

"It's Jondu here," Nuri said sharply, and Avi's hand rose to her mouth as she registered her mate's body on the travois.

The sudden whipsawing of her emotions took Avi's breath away, and she stood motionless for several moments before rushing to check on her mate.

"Nindai," Nabu repeated. "Is he here?"

"No, but we've been expecting him," Moctu said. "We set signal fires—days ago—and he's going to bring warriors from Etseh." His voice trailed off. "At least, that was the plan."

"We'll need warriors," said Lehoy. "The Shiv...they've been chasing us. And there's a lot of them."

As he said those words, a far-off Lion warrior raised a fist in the air and shouted, "We'll be back...and you'll pay for this!" With that, the man and his three companions turned and headed southeast toward their distant shelter.

"I hope they don't run into the Shiv on their way back home," Lehoy murmured.

"Lots of them, huh?" Moctu said, still worried about the size of the Shiv warband. "We've only got six capable warriors to slow them. That's if you're staying, Lehoy?"

Lehoy looked at Avi, then nodded at Moctu.

"Then we need to get the children to safety...and Jondu," Moctu said. "All the men are needed here. So Nuri, Avi, can you lead the group back home? You'll have to be on guard in case those Lion warriors double back. You'll be on your own, but you may meet up with Nindai's group coming this way.

"I'm going to stay and fight," Nuri said, her jaw set.

"And so will I," Avi said, looking up from Jondu.

"Me too," said Poza.

Moctu shook his head. "We need to get the children and Jondu to Etseh. And it'll need to be protected too, if Nindai is coming this way with warriors. There won't be many left at Etseh."

"I've killed Shiv, and I can use an atlatl," said Nuri. She moved toward Moctu and looked directly into his eyes. "Let me help here, Moctu." In a soft voice only he could hear, she added, "I don't want you to die." Her dark eyes misted, and Moctu smiled at her.

"Nuri, Nuri." He drew her to him and held her tightly. Lowering his voice, he said, "You're carrying my baby...and there's Elka. I'm not going to risk that. Please, Nuri." His lips close to her ear, he whispered, "I love you...*so* much. And I know you could help here, but you're needed with the group. I'll be careful...I'm not going to die."

Nuri's tough exterior gave way, and Moctu felt her tremble.

"Don't die, Moctu. You be careful...and come back to me."

Moctu smiled and nodded.

Leaving both of the heavy flint travois behind, the women gathered the children, and, hauling Jondu, they headed for Etseh.

After seeing them safely off, the handful of men gathered around Moctu. All of them, including Lehoy, looked to him to say something.

"We have two worries—the Shiv are coming, and the Lion People may send warriors against us." He looked at Lehoy. "If that happens, what'll you do?"

Lehoy pursed his lips, then said, "I'm here."

Moctu's eyes narrowed, and he was about to ask what, exactly, that meant, when Lehoy continued.

"I'll do my best to talk them out of attacking, but if they come..." he touched the atlatl at his waist. "I'll convince them another way." He smiled thinly as some of the men chuckled. "Our enemy is not one another...it's the Shiv. And they smashed us the last time we met."

Moctu nodded, satisfied.

"All right, we're way outnumbered by the Shiv, but we do have some advantages. This is our territory, and we've walked and hunted every part of it. We know it like we know each scar on our hands. And we have atlatls—they don't. So here's my plan."

Moctu took some time to lay out the details and assign roles, but after he'd finished, the men were nodding, some even smiling.

"Might work," Lehoy said. "Just might work."

70

IT WAS LATE AFTERNOON the next day when Avi spotted them. Warriors—four of them—coming their way. Had the four Lion warriors doubled back? They were a long way off, but they were moving toward them from the south. A mix of fear and excitement swept through the women as they corralled the children and positioned the travois containing furs near some low trees. It was a crude barricade, but it would have to do. They could hide behind it and still throw their shafts.

While Leuna looked after the children, the other three women would use their atlatls. Maybe they could inflict enough injury that the warriors would leave them alone. Nuri's hands were trembling, and she fumbled getting the shaft registered in the right position.

She blew out a breath and shook her head. "I don't need to stop them all," she muttered to herself. "I just need to hurt one of them." She tried to remember what her uncle Samar had taught her. "Wait for a good shot. Stay calm. Watch your target and the tip of your shaft. Nice, easy throw and follow-through."

Jondu was in bad shape, still unconscious on the travois behind them. If the warriors start throwing shafts, we can hide behind this travois and the trees, she thought. But Jondu's exposed...and so are the children. With that last thought, her jitters disappeared, replaced by a cold fury. Nuri's eyes turned flinty hard, and she clenched her teeth. That Elka or any of the children might be harmed or killed filled her with a rabid ferocity. She wanted to hurt these attackers.

Poza and Avi saw the change in Nuri, and they, too, moved from anxiety to resentment. As they waited, the slim breeze died, and even the birds quieted. Long moments went by until Avi let out a shriek.

"It's Nindai! I recognize his gait!"

Nuri squinted, and her eyes confirmed it too. She began to take deep breaths while Avi waved her arms and yelled to the group of warriors—their warriors.

"Nindai, hurry! It's us...we've got Jondu. He's been hurt. He's in really bad shape."

Nuri could see the individuals now. The group had been coming slowly, warily, but now most of them broke into a run.

"There's Ono," Nuri murmured, watching the older man's limping sprint. "He's going to be devastated to see his son this way." As adrenaline drained from her, a complex mix of relief and deep melancholy brought her close to tears. She looked at Jondu's motionless body and imagined her feelings if it were Moctu instead. Something like that could very well be in her future. A horde of Shiv were coming. And there was still the threat from the Lion People.

The next moments were a blur, with Avi and Ono kneeling at Jondu's side, both with tears streaming down their cheeks. Alfer arrived, then Nindai hobbled up, helped by Sokum. Nindai went immediately to Jondu, checking his fever and his wound. The smile he had when he saw his friends was quickly replaced by a deep frown.

"Water," he directed. "We need water to cool him down. And a fire...to brew some willow bark tea...willow bark and yarrow." He began stripping Jondu's clothes from his torso.

"Is he going to be all right?" Ono asked Nindai.

Nindai glanced at Ono, then finished opening Jondu's tunic.

"It's bad."

As he applied a cool, wet skin to Jondu's chest, the young man let out a soft moan, and Avi winced, holding tight to his remaining hand. Her green eyes brimmed with fresh tears and her face showed the tracks where earlier ones had trailed through the dust on her cheeks. Waves of guilt swept her. Were the Spirits punishing Jondu for her misconduct?

Looking around quizzically, Alfer said, "Where's the rest? Where's Moctu...and the others?"

Sokum nodded, wanting to know as well.

"The Shiv are coming," Nuri said. "And maybe the Lion warriors. That's who we thought you were...Lion warriors. They've attacked us—we're at war. But the Shiv—they're the main threat. There's a lot of them. And Moctu and only five others...they're a day north of here."

"Did Palo come with the Krog?" Nindai asked, looking up, hoping they had yet to show up.

Nuri shook her head and grimaced.

"Palo's there, but the Krog—they're not coming. It's Da. He's..." She paused.

"Mad at me," Nindai finished her sentence and looked away.

He was quiet while he checked Jondu's amputated arm.

"It's infected. A lot of pus." He looked to the side, momentarily overcome by anguish.

"Nindai, please help him. Please...please make him better." Avi's voice cracked, and she sobbed. "I can't lose..." She trailed off, overcome by wracking sobs.

Sokum cleared his throat. "So, Seetu and Moctu...and the others—they need our help. Some of us should head that way."

Ono looked up from his stricken son and took charge.

"It's late today. First thing in the morning, Sokum, you and Alfer go north to help our warriors there. Nindai and I'll help get Jondu and this group to Etseh."

71

IN THE MORNING, JONDU died.

Nuri sat quietly with her devastated friend, caring for baby Indar as best she could. Avi's eyes were vacant as she stared at nothing in the mid-distance. She had cried all while Nindai worked to save Jondu, and over and over she'd beseeched the Spirits for her mate's recovery. Since the moment that Nindai's shoulders drooped, and he looked at her and shook his head, she hadn't cried at all. There had been a sudden intake of breath, her eyes closed, and her lips tightened. Since then, she'd been stony-faced and withdrawn.

Ono, too, was shattered. Jondu was his only son, the pride of his life. Ono's puffy eyes remained mostly closed, and he intermittently shook his head as if to clear the nightmare from it.

Since the group was only a day away from Etseh, Jondu would be carried there and buried near where Ordu and the other heroes of the tribe were interred. Sokum and Alfer were set to leave to join up with Moctu, but they stayed until mid-morning, paying their respects to their fallen leader and friend. Alfer knelt beside Jondu's body and touched his lifeless shoulder and murmured a prayer.

Nuri watched her friend closely, trying to think of anything that she could do or say to help. "We all love you, Avi. Let me know if you want to talk," she said quietly. "I'll take Indar downstream to wash—"

"I never got to say goodbye," Avi murmured. "I never got to tell Jondu that I was proud of him...that I loved him."

"He knew, Avi."

"He had his faults…we all do. I was so mad when he was going to let Devu…purify me. But I shouldn't have betrayed him. I…still feel guilty…*so* guilty about that. And I never got to make it up to him."

"You were good to him, Avi, and you gave him a beautiful son."

Avi was quiet for a long time, staring off to the horizon.

"And there's Lehoy. I was so shocked when I saw him with Jondu that I never thanked him for risking his life…to bring Jondu to me."

"And he risked his life to bring us Elka, too," Nuri said. "He did that for you, not for Moctu and me. He loves you, Avi."

Avi looked at the ground. "I know he does. And I…" Rather than finish the sentence, she shook her head and was quiet. "I'm just… confused. And *so* tired."

"You need to rest," Nuri said. "When we get to Etseh, you stay with me, and I'll take care of Indar, and you can rest. And I'll keep people away for a while."

"That sounds good," Avi said softly, once again lost in thought and staring into space.

72

Moctu had just about given up hope of getting any help from Etseh when Sokum and Alfer arrived. Neither group had good news. Moctu was shocked to hear about Jondu's death, and it added to the pervading sense of doom. Everyone was quiet, and several of the group walked away to collect themselves. After some time, the men gathered again, and Moctu explained their precarious situation.

"But we have a plan," Moctu said. "Now there are eight of us to face all the clans of the Shiv." He gave a short laugh. "We've got them right where we want them."

The men chuckled, and some of the tension was broken.

They filled the newcomers in on the plan, and now it was time to execute it.

"Palo, Nabu—you two are the most important. You're the fastest men in the group. We need to find out where they are without you getting surprised and killed or captured. Remember how good the Shiv are with camouflage. Be really careful."

Nabu and Palo, both excited, smiled and nodded and they were off. The rest of the group followed them, but at some distance. Although they hadn't heard any of the creepy yipping of the Shiv, thin trails of smoke rose from the low foothills to the northeast, and that had to be them.

It was a day and a half later, a bright, sunny afternoon, when Palo and Nabu were investigating a brushy but treeless valley. Nabu saw movement on the other side of the creek, and suddenly even the bushes on their side began to move—in the shapes of men—big, burly men. Palo and Nabu each threw a quick shaft, both missing their targets, then they broke and ran. The eerie yipping sound erupted, and a mass of camouflaged men bounded after them.

Driven by adrenaline, the two men sprinted up a low hill, down the other side, and they were crossing a broad meadow toward another hill when Palo turned his ankle as he stepped on a cobble. They had outdistanced the Shiv, but now those warriors were catching up, and the yipping escalated into a feverish intensity.

As Nabu helped Palo hobble up the slope, the meadow was covered by at least three hands of Shiv warriors, many of them camouflaged, some with painted faces, and some unadorned except for their red facial tattoos. All were making the horrifying, other-worldly yipping and yelping, their voices clearly excited with the thrill of the chase.

A heavy spear thudded into the ground just behind Palo, and he looked back, eyes wide with alarm.

"I didn't think they threw their spears," he said anxiously.

The two picked up their ungainly pace, but it was clear that they weren't going to get much farther. Nabu and Palo were near the top of the knoll when their eyes met. They both smiled grimly, and without a word spoken, it was clear that this was where they'd make their stand. Turning while loading their atlatls, they faced the oncoming horde, each throwing a shaft. Palo's hit a huge, brown-haired Shiv in the shoulder, spinning him sideways, but not stopping him. Nabu's shaft also hit, his taking a still-camouflaged warrior in the hip. But on the Shiv came—there were so many of them!

"Now!" A shout rang out from just above them on the top of the knoll. Moctu stood and threw a shaft, and five other men followed suit. Shafts began to rain down on the Shiv, and their progress faltered. A shaft took one of the nearest Shiv in the throat, piercing all the way through and abruptly ending his keening howl. The yipping stopped, and a shrill whistle sounded. The Shiv warriors began to fall back, two of them helping wounded companions.

Lehoy loosed a shaft that hit a retreating warrior at the base of his skull and penetrated through, its flint tip breaking teeth and protruding from his cheek. The man's momentum carried him one step before he crashed to the ground like a rotten oak tree and lay still. As the Shiv got farther away, Seetu managed to hit one of the camouflaged men in the back of the leg. It was a long, hard-thrown shot, and the shaft didn't pass through the leg, so it must have hit bone. Even so, the burly warrior merely wrenched the shaft from his leg and moved on with no apparent limp.

"Let's go collect our shafts. We need to be ready for them to return...maybe with more warriors," Moctu said.

"This one's alive," Palo yelled from lower on the hill.

"Your ankle got suddenly better, Palo...great performance," Moctu called.

Palo smiled slyly. His injured ankle had obviously been a ruse to let the Shiv catch up. Now he was moving with ease over the hillside.

"Do I kill him?" He was standing over the warrior who had come the closest—the one that Nabu had hit in the hip. The Shiv's face was painted a mottled gray and brown, and he had small branches of greenery strapped to his arms and back.

"Wait," Moctu said, moving that way. "I wish we had Hawk here to question him—none of us speak Shiv."

He approached the man who was pulling on the shaft in his hip. The shaft was broken, but there was enough extending for the man to grab it with two hands. The pain must have been immense, but the warrior made no sound as he pulled on the blood-soaked end, trying to dislodge it.

Palo prodded the man with his heavy spear, and he looked up with no apparent fear. Two red spiral tattoos started on his forehead, the end of each trailing off below his eyes.

Moctu pointed in the direction the Shiv had retreated and asked, "How many?"

He started touching his fingers, counting for the man, then pointed in that direction again. "How many?"

The Shiv smiled, understanding. He let go of the shaft, and held two fists in front of him. He opened the fists showing ten fingers, then he did it again. He paused, and then with a laugh he did it twice more. He sneered as they registered shock. He swept his index finger slowly around, pointing to each of the assembled men. Then smugly, with his mouth wide open and his teeth clenched, he slowly ran his finger across his neck. He chuckled at their alarm, then continued his efforts to dislodge the shaft.

Although stunned, Moctu felt rage well up inside him. These were the people who raped his mate and who killed and ate his friend's baby son. And now, this man was mocking them.

"Kill him," he said, and he watched as Palo quickly dispatched the man.

The men were quiet as they hurriedly collected their shafts, then moved west. They had killed three of the Shiv and wounded several more without suffering an injury. Their elation at winning a battle, at stinging their enemy, was countered by the sobering news. If the Shiv was telling the truth, how could they stand against such a force?

73

THEY CAN SEE BETTER than we can," Moctu said to the group around the small fire. "And they can set ambushes...they're so good at camouflage."

Palo blew out air, whistling softly and nodding.

"That was too close. Even though we were on the lookout, Nabu and I almost walked in on them. Didn't even see them until it was almost too late."

"Even with many more victories like we just had, they'll still outnumber us," Seetu said.

"We need to move southwest and make sure they can't attack our people at Etseh," Moctu said. He glanced at Lehoy. "I'm also worried about the Lion People. They might threaten Etseh as well."

Lehoy nodded. "I think that could happen. Devu...he won't back down."

Moctu ran a hand through his hair. "We're outnumbered by the Shiv. We're outnumbered by the Lion People. We have no food stores for the winter." His lips tightened, and he shook his head as he stared at the darkening western horizon. The sun was behind the hills, and the rose colors of the billowing cumulus clouds were dimming to gray.

After a long silence, Lehoy said, "If we encounter my people—the warriors, I mean—maybe I can convince them..." He paused. "I don't think they realize how big a threat the Shiv are."

"They've raided you, taken some of your people, and your war party just got thrashed by them," Palo said. "What's it going to take for Devu to realize they're the threat?"

"Devu thinks that sacrificing Elka will ensure victory...and that's why our war party was defeated. But he hasn't heard the numbers," Lehoy answered. "If my people knew that the Shiv have eight hands of warriors, maybe we wouldn't be fighting among ourselves."

The men were mostly quiet for the rest of the evening, each lost in their own thoughts. In the morning, before the sun crested the eastern mountains, they headed south.

It was late afternoon when Palo spotted them.

"Warriors. Looks like Lion People, not Shiv. But there's a lot of them."

"Those are my people," Lehoy confirmed. "I recognize Drogo. And Koby always wears the red tunic."

"Maybe three hands of them," Palo said.

"I'll go talk with them," Lehoy said. "Maybe once they know the facts..."

"I'll go with you," Moctu said. "I can speak for my people."

"That would be good," Lehoy said. Then he smiled broadly. "I may need someone with me who's good with an atlatl." His smile widened further. "Almost as good as me." He laughed when Moctu's mouth dropped open and slapped his shoulder. "Just kidding, Moctu—I know there was some...disagreement on all that. We'll have a rematch when this is all over. If we live that long."

"Deal," said Moctu, smiling. "You know, I'm beginning to like you, Lehoy."

Waving a green tree branch high in the air, the two men approached the group of Lion warriors. When they got within an atlatl throw, both parties stopped.

"Well, it's the traitor, Lehoy," Drogo said loudly to his men. "Devu wants us to bring you to him. We know it was you, Lehoy. Ratna has told us you took Sleeps with Wolves. That was your first treachery. Then, you helped three enemies escape. That was your second disloyal act. Are you here for a third?"

"I'm here to warn you," Lehoy said, grim-faced.

"And Moctu, you're the other one we want," Drogo continued. "You started this war by hitting Donal with a shaft."

"I started this?" Moctu said, disbelieving his ears. "You took my daughter…you were going to sacrifice her. Three of my warriors who fought the Shiv with you…you were going to kill them. Then six of your men came at my people who were traveling home. You're lucky all six didn't get shafts."

"You're the two that Devu wants now," Drogo said, ignoring Moctu's comments. "Come with us, and your other men can go."

Angry, Moctu loaded a shaft while muttering, "That's not going to happen."

As many of the Lion warriors began fitting shafts in their atlatls, Lehoy held up a hand.

"Lion warriors, we have much bigger problems than these little disagreements. The Shiv are coming, and there's a horde of them… maybe eight hands. *They're* our enemy. We shouldn't be fighting among ourselves."

"You lie, Lehoy," Drogo said dismissively. "You'll say anything now to protect yourself. The Shiv can't muster that many warriors. We've seen their shelter. They had only two or three hands when we encountered them."

"And they savaged your war party, Drogo, didn't they?"

"Yes, so they're good at camouflage. We'll be more alert the next time we attack them."

"They are attacking *you*, Drogo…or will be soon."

Drogo shook his head. "Just come with us, Lehoy. Don't make this difficult."

Now it was Lehoy's turn for anger. He closed his eyes, clenched his teeth, and bent his head down trying to control it. Moments later he looked up and said, "Fellow warriors, you know me well. Some of you are my cousins. I've trained many of you on how to use the atlatl. I don't want to hurt any of you, and I don't want you hurt or killed by the Shiv. Listen to my words. The Shiv are coming…a very large force of them. Moctu and I are leaving now. Focus on the Shiv, not our group."

Drogo ignored his words. "Just come with us, Lehoy," he repeated. "We'll give you until tomorrow morning. Then we're coming for you, and people *will* get hurt."

74

It was dark, and the men sat around the embers of a fire that gave off less light than the stars overhead.

"I won't kill my own people," Lehoy said, as much to himself as the others.

"I know what I said, but those are my friends and relatives." He stopped clasping and unclasping his hands long enough to run one through his hair.

"Well, they seem willing to kill you," Palo said.

"It's Devu," Lehoy said. "We've never gotten along. And now, if he knows about Elka…" He blew out a breath. "I've seen him become incoherent with rage."

"I'll always owe you for that…for getting Elka away," Moctu said. "How can I help?"

"I need to leave…or turn myself over to them."

"For Spirit's sake, don't do that," Palo said, rolling his eyes. "Devu will kill you and say it's in the name of beating the Pale Ones. What we really need is your atlatl alongside ours."

"I'm with Palo," Moctu said. "Turning yourself in is just pointless."

"Well, then I've got to go." With that, he began gathering his few possessions.

Moctu watched him for a long moment, then said, "Slow down, Lehoy. We'll go with you. It's a gamble, because they might go on to Etseh. But I think they really want you…and me. So I think Etseh's pretty safe. They'll come after us, and they'll follow our trail. But we'll have a night's travel between us and them by morning. Like Palo said, we're going to need your atlatl to have any chance against the Shiv."

After stoking the fire to give the appearance that they were still there, the men walked all through the night. They headed north on the west side of the Iba stream, which was running high from the recent big storms. Lehoy walked alone, lost in thought and perhaps regret. The men were quiet, carefully listening to the moving water and the buzzing and croaking of insects and frogs, constantly on the alert for sounds that might suggest the presence of the Shiv.

"What're we going to do when we meet up with the Shiv?" Moctu whispered to Palo and Nabu, who were walking with him. "With the Lion warriors on our tail, pushing us north toward the Shiv, it's going to happen soon."

"I've been considering that," Palo said softly. He moved closer to the two other men. "Our one advantage is that we know this area better—than either group. Here's what I'm thinking."

After Palo had finished laying out his plan, Nabu nodded and said, "I like it."

"It's the best idea I've heard," Moctu said. "And the only one so far that might work."

At the first gray of dawn, they came to a bend in the Iba, caused by its confluence with another, slightly smaller stream. They crossed it, being sure to leave enough disturbance for easy tracking.

Chilled by the frigid water, they built a small fire to gather around and dry out. The sun had just peered over the eastern mountains when they were off again, most of the group going north, and Palo and Nabu moving east…toward the Shiv.

By early afternoon, Moctu's group was on a high, forested hill with a good view of the distant stream crossing site they had used that morning. Moctu paced and chewed his lip as he watched the site.

"Where are the Lion warriors? Spirits, I hope they're not on their way to Etseh," he murmured.

But the wait went on and on. It was long enough that Moctu had decided they'd need to backtrack and rush to Etseh to protect it.

"There they are," Seetu exclaimed, pointing.

Moctu smiled and took a slow, deep breath as he saw the Lion warriors arrive at the stream and immediately begin crossing. "Thank you, Spirits."

The pursuing warriors didn't stop for a fire to dry themselves out. The sun was up, so they trudged on, drying out along the way. They were gaining on Moctu's group.

"There're a lot of them," Moctu said worriedly.

"We need to go faster," Lehoy said. "I'm not going to fight my own people."

"I understand," Moctu said. "We'll stay ahead of them."

It was high sun the next day when Moctu saw the smoke.

"Seetu, you have the best eyes. That's Palo's signal. Is it one fire or two?"

Seetu framed his hands around his eyes and studied the far-off trail of dark gray smoke.

"It's one. It's only one. So what's it mean?"

"It means we're going east for a while," Moctu replied cryptically with a tight smile. "And be on the lookout for one more signal fire."

75

Back at Etseh...

JONDU WAS BURIED NEAR Ordu, just a short way downslope. Nindai sprinkled his body with the sacred red ochre and placed him facing up so he could view the noon sun. While they covered the body with earth, Avi wept uncontrollably, and many of the other women of the tribe did as well. Jondu's father, Ono, was silent and stoic, but his swollen face and red eyes betrayed that he mourned more fully in private. A sense of gloom and melancholy suffused the entire tribe. Nereans were having more than their share of misfortune, and with threats from the Shiv and the Lion People, more was undoubtedly coming.

With Elka and Zaila by her side, Nuri held Jondu's son, Indar, while Avi mourned atop the grave. Moctu's mother, Alta, who had lost two mates over the years, sat beside Avi, patting her back and murmuring condolences and encouragement.

The settlement was on high alert, and women took their turns at sentry and lookout duties along with the men. Nuri and Poza split Avi's workload so that she could mourn and rest.

That evening, as Nuri readied Indar and Elka for sleep, Avi broke the silence she'd maintained through the afternoon.

"Thanks for helping, Nuri...for being here."

"I'm so sorry this happened, Avi. I wish I could do more."

"You've been great. Just being here...it's helped." She looked into the small fire that burned in the hearth and shook her head. "The worst part is the guilt. I mean the sadness is there, but I just feel... empty, worthless."

"Oh, Avi, don't be talking like that. You're a wonderful woman, a wonderful mother."

"There were times...times when I was with Lehoy..." Avi stopped and covered her eyes with both hands, and a small sob escaped her. She shook her head while keeping her hands to her face, and the sobs increased. Nuri knelt beside her and put her arm around Avi's shoulder, and the crying abated just long enough for Avi to choke out, "Times when I wished Jondu..." Her last two words were a whisper, "...was dead."

The statement served to amplify the sobs, and soon Avi was shaking and gasping convulsively. Nuri hugged her tightly, and rocked her, cooing softly as sympathetic tears streamed from her eyes.

After a long moment, Avi quieted. She sniffed, wiped her eyes, and took a shaky breath.

"Avi, thoughts like that...they happen sometimes," Nuri said. "My mother told me she felt that way about Father—several times— but she never stopped loving him. And Jondu had just told you that he was going to let Devu purify you...that's when Lehoy came along. It was the timing."

"But—"

"Avi, you had nothing to do with Jondu's death. It was the Shiv, pure and simple."

Avi remained silent, but Nuri saw her head nod.

The two women were still for a long time, each gaining strength from the other's presence. Nuri's thoughts drifted to Moctu, and she shuddered.

"Avi, I know this is the time for me to support you and be strong for you. But I'm really worried. There's so much stacking up against us. Right now, the men...they're out there facing off against the Shiv *and* against the Lion warriors. And there's so many of them, and so few of us. I just don't see…"

"I know, it doesn't look good. I'm sure you worry for Moctu's safety." In a softer voice, Avi said, "I worry about Lehoy."

"If I didn't have Elka—and this baby inside me—I'd be there with them."

Avi nodded.

"But even if they…" Nuri started, but then shook her head. "If we all manage, somehow, to survive, we've got no food for the winter. A lot of us won't see the spring. I especially worry about the children."

"I know—everyone's gathering all those acorns—baskets and baskets of them." Avi scowled. "Even when you peel and soak them and cook them just right, they taste awful. And they won't last us very long. I guess all we can do is pray to the Spirits." She frowned and looked at the ground. In a soft voice she said, "But praying hasn't been working for me lately."

"Makes me wonder sometimes if Devu is right," Nuri said. "I mean, the man is despicable, but maybe we *are* wrong and not praying to the correct Spirits."

"Maybe," Avi said. "But I keep remembering the horrible winter when we were young and so many died. People were saying the same things back then. But my grandfather and Mago, the shaman, kept saying, 'We will honor the Spirits of our fathers.' Well, we did, and an early spring saved most of us."

"That was a bad time," Nuri agreed. "But things got better after that."

Elka whimpered in her sleep, and Nuri went to her side and softly rubbed her back. The wolf pups were on either side of the toddler, snuggled as close as they could get to her.

"Sometimes I wonder if Elka feels things that I don't," Nuri said. "I wonder if she can sense when Moctu's in trouble." Her face clouded. "When she whimpers like that it makes me worry. I wonder if I'll feel it if he dies."

Avi saw Nuri's eyes mist, and now it was her turn to comfort her friend. She put her arm around her.

"Hey, we're going to get through this, and we'll always be friends, Nuri. Try not to worry. Moctu, he'll find a way. And Lehoy…together, they're going to be tough to kill."

76

THE LION WARRIORS...THEY'RE GAINING on us," Seetu confirmed from his lookout. "And there's sure a lot of them."

"I won't fight—" Lehoy started.

"I know, you won't fight your people," Moctu interrupted. "You've made that clear, and I understand." The words had come out fast and harsh, and Moctu continued, trying to temper them. "I understand... I'd feel the same way in your position. But the Shiv are out there somewhere, and I don't want to blunder into them." Turning back to Seetu, he called, "Do you see any sign of a signal fire?"

"Nothing like that."

"Come on, Palo and Nabu, where are you?" Moctu pursed his lips and looked at the sun, high overhead. His group had moved a long way eastward, but if they didn't move faster, they'd soon be fighting the Lion warriors. Even if Lehoy stayed and fought, Moctu's small group didn't stand a chance against so many.

Now, the group was at the junction of two long valleys, and whichever direction Moctu chose, they'd be going that way for a long time. He closed his eyes and implored the Spirits to send him a signal. Nothing came.

"North. We're turning north," he said finally. "Seetu, you move along with us at the higher elevations and keep lookout."

They crossed a good-sized drainage and then moved fast on the eastern side of the south-trending creek, trying to put distance between themselves and the Lion warriors. The sun was still high when Seetu called out, "Signal fire!"

"Is it one fire or two?" Moctu yelled back.

After a pause, Seetu shouted, "It's one, only one."

Moctu closed his eyes and smiled.

"North," he murmured. "Thank you, Spirits." Maybe they had guided him without him even knowing it. "How close is the fire?"

"Not far. About twice the distance to that next hill to the north. But the fire's on a hill to the northeast."

"All right—let's build a signal fire to let Palo and Nabu know where we are so they can join up," Moctu said, getting out his fire-starting gear and motioning to Sokum to start gathering wood.

His mind on other things, it didn't occur to Moctu that Lehoy knew nothing of starting a fire without an ember. As he began working the spindle, he became aware of Lehoy's interest.

Too late to hide it now, he thought. And we've got bigger worries.

"Watch this, Lehoy," he said.

As smoke began to come off the wood, Lehoy sucked in a breath, and Moctu chuckled. It never got old, showing people how to make fire.

"That's impossi...how'd you do that?" Lehoy stammered.

As Moctu blew the ember into a blaze, then added more kindling to it, he grinned and said, "Magic. Show you later."

They heaped green boughs and leaves onto the fire, then set off briskly northward.

"No, really...how'd you do that?" Lehoy said, edging closer to Moctu.

"It's something I learned from the Pale Ones. The ones Devu wants to exterminate."

Lehoy nodded. "There *are* probably things we can learn from them."

"That's what I've been trying to tell your people. Not all Pale Ones are bad." He smiled, a vision of Rah coming to mind, then Hawk. "The Krog...they saved my life. I owe them a lot."

From higher on the hill, Seetu whistled, then pointed behind them to the south. He held his hands far apart, then moved them closer together. The Lion warriors were closing the gap.

"Pick up the pace," Moctu encouraged the group. "Seetu says they're getting closer."

It was late afternoon when, on the next hill, they heard a hailing call, and they saw movement. It was Palo and Nabu. Moctu threw both fists high in the air, partly to wave at them and partly in celebration. Palo and Nabu waved back, and began descending the hill in their direction. Moctu's group continued toward them, and it wasn't long before the two small parties converged.

"Palo! Nabu! It's great... We've been worried that the Shiv—"

"They're right behind us...not far anyway," Palo interrupted. "They've given up on their yipping noise. We haven't heard that this whole trip. And they're being more cautious. Not chasing us blindly. I think they learned their lesson from our ambush."

"Just glad you're safe. For now, anyway. And it looks like your plan is working, Palo. We've got our enemies to the south...Lion warriors." As he was talking, Moctu motioned Seetu down from his lookout higher on the hill. Once down, Seetu informed him that the Lion warriors were alternating walking and running, and still closing the gap.

"We're going a little farther north, then we'll cross over to the west side of this drainage," Moctu said, pointing at the nearby creek. "If we have to face the Lion warriors, at least we'll have the creek between us."

Moctu waved off Lehoy, who was opening his mouth to once again say he wouldn't fight his kinsmen. "I know, Lehoy." To the other men he said, "Look for a crossing where we won't leave tracks. But we're going to have to move faster and find a good crossing site soon."

77

THE SKIES WERE MOTTLED gray as clouds rolled in from the north. The wind picked up and the air was much cooler.

"We'll catch them soon," Drogo said, still panting from the recent interval of running. The periods of walking helped the Lion warriors catch their breath, but running in the mountainous terrain was sapping their energy.

"Tell me why we're doing this again," complained one of the younger warriors near Drogo. "Lehoy…he was one of us…and now we're supposed to—"

"He *was* one of us," Drogo loudly cut him off, turning to glare at the young man. "He took an oath, to always be a Lion warrior. And now he's broken it. He was given an order. That's why."

Drogo knew he had to be commanding—he'd been given orders, and he was going to get the job done. But even he was having misgivings. Lehoy had taught most of his men to use the atlatl, or at least to use it better. And the Nereans—some of them had, until recently, been his allies against the Shiv. But Devu, in the presence of Rolf, had given him an explicit order, and at his bloodletting ceremony, Drogo had taken an oath to follow the orders of his leaders. Moreover, that one Nerean, Moctu…he'd wounded one of his men. He'd pay for that.

"The trail's gone," Gelari, one of the young warriors, shouted. "It leads into those woods, but it's like they vanished."

Drogo knew this trick. "They set a false trail into the woods, but they've backtracked and crossed the stream. Check for a stream crossing."

It took a while because the streambed in this area was rocky, and there was no mud in which to find footprints. Drogo scanned the trees on the far shore, certain that the Nereans were watching them from behind cover. He could *feel* people eyeing his men.

Sure enough, with most of his men searching their side of the creek, one of them finally shouted, "Here! They crossed here!"

As Drogo's men congregated for the crossing, Lehoy emerged from behind a large pine less than an atlatl throw away.

"Drogo, Gelari, Koby, all of you Lion warriors, I won't fight you. But if you cross the stream, the Nereans…they'll use their atlatls, and some of you'll die. And I'm sure you'll kill some of them. But there's no need for us to fight among ourselves. We have a much greater enemy, the Shiv, and they're near. Forget our minor quarrels, and let's fight the Shiv together."

"There you are, Lehoy," said Drogo. "You're siding with people we're at war with, which makes you, once again, a traitor. But you may not know that Moctu wounded your friend Meeko. Did you know that? And there you stand defending them."

Lehoy shook his head and looked at the ground.

"I knew there was a fight when you were chasing them. I'm sorry Meeko got hurt. But no one else needs to get hurt or killed…between us, anyway. The Shiv are coming, and there's a lot of them. We'll need every warrior—Lion and Nerean—to fight them off.

"You're still using that tired ploy?" Drogo scoffed. "The Shiv don't have that many warriors. And we know their camouflage ambush tricks now. We can handle them." He held up his atlatl. "With these…Lion warrior atlatls."

"We don't want to kill you, Lehoy. Come peacefully with us, and I'm sure every warrior here will support you and speak on your behalf. Devu will be lenient."

"All right. All right. I'd rather do that than see a bunch of you killed by Nereans," Lehoy said, moving down the hill toward them.

Drogo smiled. The hardest part is over, he thought.

"Now, Moctu," he shouted. "I know you're up there. If you come too, then no one here will get hurt."

There was a long pause, then Moctu burst from the tree line, atlatl in hand, shouting, "Noooooo!" As Moctu flung a shaft, Palo and Nabu also emerged from the trees and threw shafts.

The Lion warriors were surprised and stunned. They crouched or dodged behind small scrub oaks for cover while setting shafts in their atlatls. Moctu's shaft sailed over them, landing in the brush between trees higher on the hill. Palo's landed in a bush near Moctu's, and Nabu's went long as well, landing in brush a treelength upstream. The anxiety of facing the Nereans drained from the tired Lion warriors.

"They couldn't hit a mammoth if it was right next to them," one of the younger warriors joked and several laughed.

"Turn around!" they heard Moctu yell, but there was no way they were turning from this fight.

That's when the bush where Palo's shaft had disappeared... *moved*. It got up and staggered, then fell forward. The tree line erupted with movement as dozens of camouflaged Shiv warriors sprang forward. For a moment it looked like the forest had come alive and was rushing downhill. A chill went down Drogo's spine as the shrill, yipping cacophony commenced...like a pack of hyenas descending on them.

78

ALL OF THE ATLATLS of the horrified Lion warriors were loaded, and to their credit, most of the men got a shot off, and several hit. But aided by the downhill slope, the quick-moving Shiv warriors were on them in a few blinks of an eye, and it was as if a huge wave had hit a bunch of children.

Drogo threw his shaft, hitting the shoulder of an oncoming Shiv who was wielding both a spear and a cudgel. The hit barely slowed the warrior, who swept past him while swinging the cudgel at his face. Drogo swiveled to avoid it, but the blow took him in the shoulder, spinning him in an almost complete circle and knocking him to the ground. Dazed and gasping for breath, he was astonished to see his bloody collarbone protruding from his skin and tunic. Wondering why it didn't hurt more, Drogo staggered to his feet just as another Shiv rushed up and plunged a thick spear into his midsection. The painted warrior followed through using his powerful shoulders, pinning Drogo to the ground with the spear point.

The Shiv wasn't camouflaged, but had blackened eye sockets and his dark hair pulled back, exposing red, zigzag tattoos on his forehead. The thickset man paused, pulling on the spear, trying to dislodge it while scowling at Drogo. Realizing that extracting the spear would take time, he released it, took up a cudgel, and moved on.

It was a rout. Lehoy watched in despair as his kinsmen were slaughtered. Koby, a seasoned warrior, was one of the last to fall. As he slashed a spear at the dark-haired Shiv in front of him, an untattooed Pale One, probably a Mung, lifted him off the ground with a powerful spear thrust. The spear pierced his red tunic, entering under his right arm and exiting through the left side of his neck. Blood sprayed an arm's length outward, showering the dark-haired warrior. The Pale One released the spear and let him fall, searching for others to fight. Koby was dead before he hit the ground.

The east bank of the creek was slick and gory with blood, brains, bones, and entrails. Most of the handful of Lion warriors who got away did so by jumping in the stream and letting the fast-moving water carry them downstream.

Several of the Shiv raised their spears in celebration while surveying the bodies of fallen Lion warriors. Moctu shuddered, realizing the beasts would likely feast on warrior meat this evening, and it would last them for days. Seetu threw a shaft and missed.

"Save your shafts," Moctu yelled as he nervously counted the handful he had left. "Look at their numbers...we'll need to make every shaft count."

Earlier, they'd each thrown a couple of shafts in support of the Lion warriors as the Shiv descended the hill. But once the close-up fighting began at the water's edge, they couldn't risk sending shafts into the wild melee. At one point, there had been so many Shiv descending the hill that Moctu's band managed to hit several even though they were moving fast. One of Moctu's shafts hit a painted Shiv solidly in the midsection, spinning him to the right. He swerved back and continued downhill, but several steps later went to his knees. Shiv were yipping and barking their eerie call, stabbing and tripping over bodies on the stream bank, almost all of which were Lion warriors. Eddies in the stream were red, and clogged with bodies.

When Shiv warriors began splashing their way across the stream and starting up the slope, Moctu's eyes widened, and he looked behind him. He saw the same fear he felt in the other men's eyes.

It's easy to fight when everything's going well, and you're filled with battle joy. There's a thrill when you sense victory's near. It's different when you see the enemy slaughtering their way toward you, and it's five against one.

"Take your time…throw one shaft. Make it count. Then run… south."

Forcing himself to wait and ignore the spine-chilling yipping, Moctu watched the nearest Shiv—a massive, camouflaged warrior— climb the hill toward him. He was wielding both a cudgel and a spear, which he used as a staff to help him scale the incline. The man got close enough that Moctu could see the mottled green and brown paint on his face and huge forearms. Green branches strapped down with leather bindings seemed to sprout from his shoulders.

Gritting his teeth as he pulled the atlatl back, Moctu flung the shaft hard and was pleased to see it bury just below the warrior's jaw, stopping him immediately. Another atlatl shaft hit the man's stomach a moment later, and Moctu cursed himself for a wasted shaft. From now on, they'd specify and call out their targets. Every shaft counted. The massive Shiv fell forward, the lower shaft snapping and his neck twisting grotesquely as the end of Moctu's shaft encountered the ground. Two more Shiv passed the body, one pausing to touch it respectfully, and Moctu realized it was time to run. As he turned, he saw another Shiv fall, taking a shaft in his eye that, with a spray of blood and gore, protruded through the skull near the opposite ear.

Lehoy and all the Nereans ran in a tight group, heading south and maintaining elevation along the hill. They could hear the yipping from the Shiv behind them, and that was worrisome enough. When they heard a second group of Shiv coming from the east, Palo yelled, "Another group…they're flanking us!" He swerved to a more uphill and westerly course, and the rest followed.

Moctu racked his brain as he ran, thinking about the best place to make a stand. This is our territory, he thought. We know it best. An idea came, clear as if the Spirits had whispered it.

"To the talus slope," he yelled. The Nereans knew it well, and several of the men nodded, liking the idea. It was a south-facing, rocky promontory with an apron of talus around and below it. A small spring ran in a cleft between two large crags. They'd camped there and used it many times as a lookout for game animals.

"How far?" Lehoy asked, gasping for air and limping more noticeably.

"It's on the south side of this hill…not far," Moctu said. "A little farther uphill. You'll make it."

Although the men were running fast, the eerie yipping sounded as close as ever, especially from behind them to the north. The group of Shiv coming from the east were having to climb the hill, so they were a little farther off, but still yipping wildly.

Nabu was the first to the talus pile, followed closely by Palo. Moctu was last as he helped Lehoy, whose leg problem had worsened. Climbing across the rough and sometimes sliding talus rubble was treacherous, so the men were only halfway across it when they spotted the Shiv coming from the north. They had just reached the promontory when they saw the other group of Shiv emerge from the tree line a short distance downhill and to the south of the first group.

Finally making it across the unstable talus, Lehoy looked back at their pursuers. "How many Pale Ones do you count?"

"At least four, probably five hands of them," Nabu said.

"Count your shafts…how many do we have?" Moctu asked.

A quick tally indicated that they had only six hands of shafts between them.

"We can't afford to miss much at all, so hold your shots until you're sure to hit," Moctu said. "And call out your targets…we can't afford double hits, either."

"Even with the talus slowing them down, we're going to miss more than that," Palo said, shaking his head. "There's going to be hand-to-hand spear work."

"We're not going to hold up long in hand-to-hand with those beasts," Petrel said gloomily.

"And they may come at night," Lehoy said.

The men grimaced at that thought and looked to the sun, which was nearing the western mountains.

"Dung—they're everywhere!" Palo cried, pointing that direction, his eyes wide. A distant, third group of Pale Ones was coming from the west.

79

THE SUN WAS HALFWAY behind the western mountains, and the cloud cover was a mix of grays and pinks with a spray of amber beams. The Shiv and Mung hadn't attacked yet, so it was likely they were waiting for dark. With overcast skies it would be a black, foreboding night.

At Palo's suggestion, the men had gathered piles of cobbles and small boulders to throw down the hill at their attackers. The stones would bolster their meager shaft supply, and they might even kill some of the attackers with them. A huge, blocky boulder with a diameter nearly the size of a man had been shoved near the edge of the promontory. It had taken four men to move it, but now it was in a position where a spear could lever it over the edge.

The men were mostly quiet, some praying to the Spirits, some thinking about loved ones they'd probably never see again. They made no fire because they wanted their night vision to be as good as possible, and there was little wood anyway.

The Pale Ones, on the other hand, had several fires, and the men could see figures—lots of figures—circulating around the light of the flames. After the sun went down and the glow of dusk died behind the far hills, the Pale One fires were the only lights on the mountain. There was no yipping, and several of the Nerean men dozed. It had been a long, dreadful day. Moctu stayed awake talking with Palo.

"Your plan worked, but not like we expected," Moctu said.

Palo nodded glumly. "We wanted the Lion warriors to fight the Shiv first, but not get surprised and slaughtered by them."

"Drogo never took it seriously," Moctu said, frowning. "That there'd be so many of them coming. And now, there are still almost as many Shiv and Mung as before."

"They killed some, and we did too. But you're right, it's not looking good," Palo agreed.

The two were lost in thought for a long time.

"What will you miss most?" Palo asked finally. "I mean, if we end up in the next world."

"Don't be talking like that," Moctu said, and the men were again quiet.

After a long moment, Moctu softly said, "Nuri…and Elka. How about you?"

"Siduri for sure," Palo said. Then he added, "And you."

A melancholy gratitude filled Moctu that he had a such a friend. He could see little of Palo—only slight motion in the inky darkness—but he reached across and found an arm and squeezed it.

"Me too, Palo. In the Spirit world, I'm sure we'll be as good of friends as we are in this one."

It was only moments later that they saw the lights of the nearby fires extinguished, and what little glimmers they'd provided were lost in a sea of darkness. Downslope, a slow beat began of a club on a hollow log.

On the promontory everyone was now awake and feeling in the dark for their spears, atlatls, and shafts.

"Are they coming? You think they'll come now?" Seetu asked in a higher-than-normal voice.

"Maybe they're just trying to scare us," Alfer said.

"It's working," said Palo, and the men chuckled in spite of their anxiety.

"I think they see in the dark better than we do," Moctu said. "So, focus on your listening…maybe we hear better than they do."

The men were silent and still, the whole of their attention centered on the sounds of the night.

It was so obvious that no one broke their silence to mention it. First, the trilling and buzzing of insects and frogs in the small pools downstream from the spring stopped abruptly. More worrisome, there were noises coming from above and to the sides of them where the talus apron was not as broad.

Palo finally spoke. "Hey, Lehoy, you there?"

"What is it?" Lehoy answered.

"Nereans," Palo said, addressing them in a louder voice. "I think we should each give one of our shafts to the man who's best with an atlatl." He paused, then said, "Moctu."

Everyone laughed, including Lehoy.

"But seriously, each of us should give up a shaft for Moctu and Lehoy to use. Face it, they're better than we are."

There was a murmur of agreement and the sound of shafts being handed toward where Moctu and Lehoy were positioned. Moctu smiled as three extra shafts came to him.

The men were quiet once again, straining to hear any sounds that would tell them where the Shiv were. The rhythmic thumping of the hollow log stopped, and for a long time, there was an eerie, total silence—the Shiv weren't moving. The men's nerves were on edge when Palo spoke again.

"Nabu, you're the only elder here. I think we'd better elect Moctu leader while we can."

Some of the men chuckled nervously, but there were murmurs of agreement.

"Good idea," Nabu said. "All in favor..." he started. "Wait," he said. "It's so dark...is anyone against it?"

There was silence that stretched for a long moment.

"Then Moctu is now leader," he said.

"Let's hope he—" Palo started, but stopped abruptly as they heard the unmistakable sounds of rocks grating and teetering on one another as bulky figures stepped on them. The Shiv were on the move again.

Adrenaline surged through the group as they all analyzed the noises, trying to determine the number and location of their enemy.

"I think it'll work best if we pair up," Moctu hissed. "One man with a heavy spear and one with an atlatl. There's eight of us, so four pairs. Palo, you're with me, all right?"

There were no complaints, so in the darkness Seetu and Sokum paired up, then Alfer and Petrel, and that left Nabu with Lehoy. Wondering when the morning light would come, Moctu looked to the stars but once again saw there were none. The men were standing, waiting for a charge from perhaps the most fearsome warriors in the world.

It's a lot like when the saber-tooth was stalking me, Moctu thought. But I was frozen with fear then. Why not now? Have I gotten braver? No, it's because Palo's here, and Nabu and the others. And as scared as I am, I want to protect them as much as myself. He remembered Tabar's words: "Live your best life, and die your best death."

Moctu gritted his teeth. "I will show bravery," he whispered to himself. "The death I die tonight will be a brave one." He gripped the atlatl tighter and focused on the night sounds. They were closing in.

80

WHEN THE EERIE YIPPING started, it was almost next to them. The closest was from the upslope areas where the talus rubble was not as extensive, but the noise came from all directions. Even the upslope attackers still had to cross a saddle, then move slightly uphill to the promontory.

The men began to throw cobbles at the closest and loudest yipping sounds, and a few grunts and cries indicated they were having an effect. Nabu and Lehoy levered the boulder over the edge, and it crashed down the hillside with a satisfying, pounding rumble that the men could feel reverberating up their legs. The yipping down the hill was replaced by cries of alarm and pain.

Guarding the upslope direction, Moctu focused on the nearest sound and threw a shaft, and he was rewarded with a quick thud of impact and a groan from the recipient. To the left, from where he'd last seen Lehoy, he heard a similar impact and another groan of a Shiv or Mung.

The Shiv that Moctu had wounded lurched forward, a shaft in his shoulder, but Palo stabbed him in the face with the heavy spear, and the man went down. Moctu loosed a second shaft and was again pleased to hear the thump as it connected with another assailant. An uninjured Shiv wielding a cudgel burst forward, and Palo said loudly, "Moctu, I need—" There was a loud wallop of wood on wood as Palo blocked a savage swing. Moctu could see no clear shapes, just flashes of movement. He dropped the atlatl and took up his heavy spear. Something hit his side—maybe the butt end of a spear—knocking the wind from him, but he maintained his feet and charged forward.

"Aauggh!" the attacker gasped as Moctu rammed his heavy spear into the man's side, and together, Palo and Moctu pushed him backward, where he fell on the rocks. Moctu quickly reacquired the atlatl he'd set down and readied for another throw.

"Got one!" they heard Seetu call out.

"Aim at the yipping sounds," Lehoy shouted. "It's working." From that same area, Moctu heard a cry from Nabu, followed by a loud, intense commotion. There was a howl of pain, and the tumult ended suddenly. Moctu feared Nabu was dead.

"Spirits, please…no," he murmured. "Nabu, Lehoy…you all right?"

A shrill whistle sounded, and the yipping ended. Moctu could hear some of the Shiv retreating.

"Nabu? Lehoy?" Moctu called again.

"Nabu's down," Lehoy cried worriedly, and Moctu's heart sank.

"I think they're leaving," Seetu yelled.

"Nabu?" Palo called.

"I'm all right," Nabu said with a shaky voice, and Moctu closed his eyes in relief. "Well, I'll live anyway," Nabu corrected himself. "Shoulder's sliced up."

"Anyone else hurt?" Moctu asked.

"Sokum's fingers…and hand…we can't see how bad they are," Seetu called. But they're bashed up pretty awful."

"Petrel," Alfer yelled. "He's down…hurt bad."

"Ahm a ive," Petrel choked out a muffled response, showing he wasn't dead.

"Bad leg wound, and I think his jaw's broken," Alfer called.

That was when Moctu checked the pain at his side, and his hand came away wet.

Dung, he thought, grimacing. I guess it wasn't the butt end of the spear. He gingerly felt the wound to determine how bad it was. It was deep and bleeding freely. As he moved, Moctu nearly stumbled over the body of the first Shiv, and he felt the shaft protruding from the man's shoulder.

"Recover any shafts that you can. We're going to need every one," he said loudly. "And make sure they're dead before you get too close to their bodies. They love ambushes."

"They'll probably be back soon," Palo yelled. "Let's be ready."

Moctu frowned at the thought, but Palo was right. "Spirits," he whispered, shaking his head. "Half of us are wounded now, and a large portion of our shafts are gone. How can we hold them off? Please help...tell me what I can do...some ideas...anything."

But no thoughts came.

81

THE CLOUDS HAD PARTED in a few places, giving a little starlight, and there was a vague glow in the east that indicated the dawn was near. But it was still very dark when the Pale Ones came again. They had learned their lesson, and this time they made no yipping noise, so it was harder to locate them to make shots.

The fighting was chaotic, pure pandemonium. Even knowing that he had few shafts left, Moctu found himself throwing at nearby sounds—and missing too often. A huge figure smashed into Palo, bowling him over and then stabbing downward. Palo rolled to the side and narrowly missed being pinned to the ground by a massive spear thrust. Moctu dropped his atlatl and stabbed with his heavy spear, completely missing the hulking figure that had been there moments before.

The Pale One wheeled around without his spear, which was still stuck in the ground, and barreled into Moctu, knocking his wind out and throwing him against a nearby rock face. Moctu dimly saw the brute fumble at his waist then raise a club or cudgel to strike him when Palo speared him in the back, severing his spine. The beast went limp and fell at Moctu's feet. Then another attacker was on them.

The others were having similar troubles. Above the ruckus, Moctu heard Seetu cry out, "Sokum!"

But then it was back to the matter at hand. Moctu threw his last shaft and heard a satisfying whump, but the man came on toward them with a shaft protruding from his chest. It was only then that Moctu realized dawn had come—he could see details of the man. He was a Shiv, and even with a shaft in his chest, he was more than Moctu could handle. The warrior slashed his spear sideways, carving a slice across Moctu's stomach. He brought the butt end of the spear up, connecting with Moctu's jaw, stunning him. Once again, Palo saved Moctu's life, spearing the man from behind as he swiveled to meet Palo's charge. The thrust took the Shiv at the side of his lower back, piercing through to project out his abdomen. He roared with pain, and one of his hands left his spear to attend to the side wound.

Without a weapon, Palo threw himself at the Shiv, the collision taking both men to the ground. Moctu was back in the fight and speared the Shiv in the side of the neck, causing blood to spray over both him and Palo, drenching them. The warrior finally lay still.

Gasping for breath, Moctu surveyed the fighting going on beside them. Sokum was down, and Seetu was backed into a rocky niche, waving his spear wearily at an advancing Shiv. Lehoy and Nabu were struggling with two burly Shiv, and Alfer and Petrel were nowhere to be seen.

There were a lot of Shiv and Mung bodies on the ground, but their warriors still outnumbered Moctu's force.

We're out of shafts and fighting hand-to-hand with more powerful men who outnumber us, he thought gloomily. Tabar's words came to him: "Die your best death." His teeth clenched and a fury swept over him. He ran at the closest of the two warriors that Nabu and Lehoy were fighting, screaming and growling. Hearing the noise, the Mung turned and almost dodged Moctu's spear thrust, which took him just above his hip, while Nabu thrust upwards with his spear, lancing the man through his shoulder, just right of his neck.

As the brute lost his balance and toppled, Nabu smiled briefly at Moctu before moving to help Lehoy with his assailant. The momentary satisfaction that Moctu felt dissolved in the next heartbeat. More Pale Ones had just arrived from the west.

82

IT'S ALREADY HOPELESS, AND NOW, a new batch of Pale Ones, Moctu thought dejectedly. We'll die and then be *eaten*. His attention was immediately drawn, however, back to the nearby fight as Palo shouted, "Moctu...help...I can't—"

Moctu fought off the wave of despair he felt. "Die your best death," he reminded himself savagely, and he charged toward Palo, who was cornered by two Shiv. Either Shiv would have been a match for Palo, but the two Shiv together were even more formidable. On the way toward them, Moctu saw a spear on the ground, and he flung the one in his hand at the back of the nearest Shiv while picking up the downed spear.

The brute moved as he raised a stone-tipped cudgel to club Palo, and the spear hit him in his backside, causing him to drop the cudgel. Moctu realized the spear he'd picked up had a broken point, limiting its usefulness.

Palo was covered with blood, but Moctu couldn't tell if it was his or Shiv. The other Shiv he was battling knocked Palo to the ground and raised a club while Palo raised his spear sideways to block the hit. There was a tremendous commotion from behind Moctu as the newly arrived Pale Ones reached the western side of the promontory.

It's over, Moctu thought, but we'll kill as many as possible. We'll die our best deaths...and then I guess...they'll eat us.

The Shiv above Palo brought the club down, and Moctu heard Palo's spear split in half as he blocked it. The Shiv raised his club again, and Moctu was too far away to stop the hit.

A shrill whistle blew twice, and the Shiv froze, then turned and began helping the nearby wounded Shiv down the hill.

"What the...?" Moctu muttered, cocking his head. "They'd won...just about to kill us off, and now they're—?"

He turned, and his eyes narrowed.

"That looks like...Spirits...it is!" Relief flooded Moctu as, from across the battle scene, he saw Hawk. His friend briefly smiled at him before turning to pursue a fleeing Shiv. The newly arrived Pale Ones from the west were Krog.

"And there's Da...and Ronk!" And there were three more of the Krog that he didn't know as well. The Shiv still outnumbered the newcomers, but they were tired, and fleeing men make poor warriors.

Hawk caught up to a limping Shiv and extended his spear, tripping him up. With a powerful thrust as he passed the fallen warrior, he severed half of the man's neck. Blood sprayed, painting Hawk's legs red. Looking downhill, he located his next target and moved on with brutal efficiency.

Da was far off to Hawk's left side, where two large Shiv had slowed and turned to meet him. Moctu worried for the fierce Krog leader as he watched the taller of the Shiv easily block Da's spear thrust. The Shiv swiveled and walloped Da's side with the butt end of his spear. The shorter, heavier Shiv, seeing an opportunity, lunged forward, fully extending his spear. But Da's initial thrust had been a feint, and being uphill of his enemy, he was able to spin, avoiding the thrust, and he hammered his own spear savagely into the heavy man's exposed flank. Then Ronk was by Da's side, and the taller Shiv turned and fled.

Da and Hawk were the two men that Moctu would least like to ever have to fight. They were both fearsome warriors, skilled, ferocious, and powerful, and he almost felt sorry for the Shiv and Mung.

Seetu called for him, and Moctu reluctantly took his eyes from the fight down the hill to the carnage around him. Sokum was dead, having been speared many times. Shaking his head with disbelief, Moctu knelt by his friend's body and, stunned to his core, looked into the young man's vacant eyes. His lips tight, and fighting the despair he felt, Moctu gently drew the young man's eyelids closed, then shut his own.

But there was more, much more.

"Petrel's dead," Palo said. "Spirits, Alfer's body is below his."

Avi's father, Moctu thought, grief falling even more heavily on him. And Alfer, my stepfather. Never really liked him, but Mother will be devastated. Her third mate dead. Spirits.

With a desolate heart and an immense weariness, Moctu rose to go to bodies of Petrel and Alfer. Lehoy knew Petrel was Avi's father, and he also went to the pile of bodies. Two large Shiv had fallen there, and it took some time to pull them aside. Blood covered everything, and it was impossible to know what had killed him, as he'd suffered several horrible wounds. As he leaned to touch Petrel's shoulder, Moctu felt pains from his own injuries and wondered about their severity. As they pulled Petrel's body to a position next to Alfer's, the lower man stirred and moaned.

"Alfer's not dead," Moctu shouted, and a small portion of the gloom lifted from the group.

83

THE SHIV WERE BEATEN, and they continued to run. Hawk, Da, and the rest of the Krog killed four of them and overran their camp, taking three camp women and a number of high-quality sleeping furs. Only one of the Krog, Ronk, was injured, suffering a serious slash across his shoulder and chest that crisscrossed the scar of an earlier wound. The wound was not life-threatening, and he'd be fine. The Krog, especially Da, were in great spirits as they approached the promontory just before dusk.

Moctu and the Nereans were mourning their dead and treating their wounded. Every single one of their group had serious wounds, but all felt lucky—and a little guilty—to be alive. Their heartbreak at the loss of two wonderful men was more than offset by the elation and relief they felt with the triumph over the Shiv. But with their dead companions lying nearby, such feelings just seemed wrong.

As he saw Hawk and the Krog safely returning, Moctu's spirits soared higher, and ignoring the pain of his injuries, he rushed downhill to meet them.

"Hawk," he yelled, and the big, red-haired man smiled broadly and extended his arms. Neither man attempted a solemn, dignified greeting, instead opting for a joyous bear-hug.

"Brud Moctu," Hawk said happily. "Brud Moctu."

"Brud Hawk…Da, Ronk." He paused, nodding at the other three Krog. "Spirits, it's so great to see you. You came…and you saved our lives. *You saved our lives!* Spirits, that was close." Moctu finally broke from Hawk to hug Da and Ronk and clap the shoulders of the other Krog warriors appreciatively.

Da smiled, revealing his vicious-looking canine fangs, and he pointed proudly to the three women, none of whom appeared to be Shiv. They all had straight, brown hair, and two of them looked like sisters. Moctu learned from Hawk that the women had been captured by the Shiv during an attack on a clan to the north. They huddled together nervously, but they seemed pleased to be free of the Shiv.

"I tell Da he get any women we take," Hawk said in explanation.

"And the Shiv?" Moctu asked. "Are they…?"

"We kill four…not many left. They run north. No more problems, I think."

By now, the group had ambled to where the remainder of Moctu's group was, and his men greeted and thanked the Krog profusely. His arm in a sling, Lehoy seemed genuinely appreciative, but curious, and not completely comfortable with the Krog.

"What changed your mind, Da?" Palo asked. "Last we spoke, you wouldn't let the Krog help us."

Da pointed to Hawk.

"I hear Brud Moctu in danger," Hawk said. "I come…is obvious." He stressed the last word, grinning broadly, and Moctu laughed. "Rah, Lok, me…we convince Da."

Moctu laughed again, and was flooded with a happy warmth, a glow of both friendship and relief, something he hadn't felt for several moons. It was finally sinking in that he was going to live… that he'd see Nuri and Elka and his other friends and family again.

The feeling didn't last long. His eyes fell on the two bodies covered with skins, and he became somber again.

"Let's give a few prayers and thoughts for Petrel and Sokum," he said.

The group became quiet, even the Krog, as Hawk and Da motioned for their men to be respectful. All silently viewed the covered bodies for a long time, each man saying their own personal prayers, then gradually, they looked to Moctu to speak a few words.

"Spirits, we thank you for helping us defeat the Shiv today, but the victory came with a great cost," Moctu started. "We lost two very fine men. We ask you to welcome Petrel and Sokum to your world. They were our friends, and they were great warriors. Both fought bravely, and our people will always honor them and cherish their memory. We'll take them back to Etseh, and bury them properly next to our other heroes." He paused for a long moment, and his voice caught as he said, "These were…good men, Spirits. Please treat them well in the next world."

84

THE SKIES HAD MOSTLY cleared, and a half moon rose on the darkening eastern horizon. Palo and Seetu, who were the healthiest, extracted shafts from the Shiv and Mung corpses, then dragged them to the part of the promontory where the embankment was steepest and rolled them off the edge.

Moctu heard his stomach growl and realized he hadn't eaten anything yet that day. The wound across his stomach was painful, but the hunger inside hurt as much. Worries about feeding his people over the coming winter resurfaced, and he closed his eyes.

Spirits, please don't let this be a winter of famine, he prayed silently. Help us to find game. We'll need a great deal, because we have so little. And we'll need it soon. The high-mountain snows came early, and the ash trees have already begun to drop their leaves, so winter is coming soon. Please help my people…don't let them starve.

Hawk sat beside Moctu and put his arm around his friend's shoulder. Moctu opened his eyes, and Hawk said, "I'm sorry…" pointing to the two covered bodies. He started to say something else, but instead just closed his mouth and shook his head. Moctu nodded appreciatively, and the two men stared respectfully at the bodies for a long time.

"Please eat with us, Hawk," Moctu said finally. "We have a lot to talk about." Then, getting up to address the rest of the Krog, he said, "Please come sit and eat with us. We have little to offer, but we'll share what we have."

Hawk eyed Da, and the fierce, scar-faced man smiled and nodded. Hawk grinned at Moctu and said, "We eat with you...is obvious, but we bring the meat."

Ronk snorted a laugh, and Moctu wondered why. The Krog spread out two skins, each carrying a large quantity of dried meat. After Hawk motioned to it, Palo, who was closest, took a piece and tasted it.

"Mammoth meat, right? Tastes fresh."

"Did you kill a mammoth?" Moctu asked, his eyes wide.

Hawk shook his head no and smiled enigmatically. Ronk laughed again, clearly delighted by something.

"A mammoth...you got a mammoth?" Moctu continued.

Hawk held up three fingers.

"Three mammoths?"

Hawk nodded, and Ronk and Da laughed.

Something was up. "You killed three mammoths?" Moctu asked, his excitement rising. "We...maybe we can trade with you for some of the meat. Did you run them off a cliff?"

Ronk burst out laughing, and Da and Hawk struggled to maintain straight faces.

Hawk again shook his head no, and struggled not to laugh.

"What's going on? You have meat from three mammoths, right?" Moctu asked.

Hawk nodded and said, "Maybe more."

Ronk laughed so hard that he had to clutch his wounded chest. Even Da and the other three Krog men laughed.

Finally, the story came out. Less than half a moon back, Krog hunters had been trailing a herd of six mammoths, looking for an opportunity to kill one. Violent rains had lashed the surrounding area and filled the upstream drainages with runoff. Downstream, the drainages had coalesced into a raging flash flood carrying tree trunks, large stones, and other debris. The hunters had narrowly avoided the flood by climbing to higher ground. The next day, they moved downstream until they saw vultures circling in the sky, and they found the remains of two mammoths among huge, jumbled piles of detritus and mud. Driving off the vultures and a pack of hyenas, they began pulling rubble and debris away from the two massive bodies, and that had exposed another one. Even now, most of the Krog women were involved in butchering and drying the meat for the winter.

Moctu remembered the storm, a powerful one that had dumped a great deal of water. Earlier in his life, he'd watched a flash flood, and he shuddered now thinking of being caught in one. The one he'd seen was led by an enormous debris flow—looking more like an avalanche than floodwater—as it powered its way downstream. Tabar had told him that rains in late summer were the worst, melting glacial ice and snow, which further filled the drainages.

"Could we trade with you for some of the meat?" Moctu asked.

Hawk nodded and in Krog had a quick verbal exchange with Da that Moctu couldn't follow. The two men nodded at one another, then Da smiled and leaned back. With his hands behind his head, chewing a piece of jerky, he looked contented and untroubled.

Hawk grinned at Moctu and said, "Da say we give meat from one mammoth to you...our gift."

Moctu's jaw dropped, and he looked from Hawk to Da.

Da chuckled, unintentionally showing his fangs. "You help find Zat," he said.

Still stunned, Moctu shook his head. "This is too big a gift. You're being too kind. We'll trade with you for the meat. When I helped you find Zat's body...that was...that was just what friends do."

Da motioned for Hawk to talk, and Hawk said, "You saved many Krog from disease. Good friend of all Krog...you Brud Moctu. This is gift."

Moctu was too overcome with shock and thanks to speak. An immense relief, a happy satisfaction spread through him as he realized his people were safe from a winter of death.

Hawk continued, speaking to him in Krog and looking stern. "Two conditions."

Moctu cocked his head, suddenly concerned.

Hawk put up an index finger, signaling the first condition. "You come to Uhda soon to pick up meat." He held up his second finger. "And you bring Elka and Nuri. Rah wants to see Elka, and Lok wants Nuri."

Moctu laughed and ran a hand through his hair. "Deal."

85

THEY SILENTLY WATCHED THE morning sun ascending radiant in the eastern sky as they stood together, about to part. Moctu was surprised at the level of emotion that swept over him. Hawk truly was a brother to him.

"I'll see you soon, and I'll bring Elka and Nuri," he said.

Hawk nodded, and in Krog he said, "You should also bring others with you…men to help carry all that meat back."

The two men hugged, patted each other on the back, then broke apart abruptly, each a little embarrassed at the depth of affection they felt.

"Safe travels, Brud Hawk."

Hawk was quiet for a moment, then smiled. "You too, Brud Moctu."

As the Krog headed west, Hawk slowed to look back and hold up a hand. Even Da, surrounded by his three women, stopped and waved.

As Moctu's group waved back, Lehoy said, "We'd be dead if not for them."

"Those are the people Devu wanted exterminated along with the Shiv," Moctu reminded him.

"I know. It's hard to believe now…and I understand why you fought it so hard."

"You helped me fight it, Lehoy…especially with getting Elka back. I can never thank you enough for that." After a long pause, he said, "Devu's still...out there. You can't go back to the Lion People. Come with us, Lehoy. We'd love to have a warrior and hunter like you in our council."

Lehoy shrugged. "That seems like the best option for me. Really the only option. Thanks, I think I will. I..." He shrugged again, not finishing the sentence. "Thanks."

"I think you've shown some interest in a young woman back at Etseh who'll need some...consoling," Moctu said, showing the hint of a smile. "Maybe you can help with that."

Lehoy eyed him, then nodded.

The sun was high when the men began their trek south toward Etseh. Two red hawks cavorted on the breezes above the lower hills to the south, and some of the men took them as a good omen. Palo scouted to the southwest while Nabu scouted to the east as Moctu took his turn pulling the travois carrying the bodies of Petrel and Sokum. There was little talking as the men walked, each reflecting on the events of the past few days.

Over the next day as they neared the lowlands, in spite of his grim task, it was hard for Moctu not to feel a sense of, if not happiness, then at least relief.

I'm on my way home to see Nuri and Elka...and Alta and Zaila and the others, he thought, smiling. But the smile faded as his thoughts quickly returned to the grisly cargo he pulled. Sorting through the tumult of emotions that swept him, he idly watched the hawks soaring and diving in the sky. They seemed to be having fun and enjoying life in the skies.

There'll be a lot of sorrow about Petrel and Sokum, and by now, they're already mourning Jondu. But there'll be rejoicing too. No more threat from the Shiv, and the tribe is safe.

And I'm going to live. He blew out a breath, shaking his head in relief. Spirits, it looked bad there for a while...really bad. But the Shiv—they're gone. The Lion warriors...they're not going to be bothering us anytime soon. And our food...we're not going to have a starving winter. Moctu was again flooded by an immense wave of relief that left him on the edge of happiness.

"Thank you, Spirits," he murmured. "Thank you, *Krog*." He smiled, recalling the delight that Hawk had taken in telling him about the mammoths. A long moment went by as he contemplated the Krog. As grateful as he was to them, it bothered him that his tribe's well-being had depended on their generosity.

"Why were our hunts so bad this year?" he murmured, his mind returning to Devu. "He's still out there, and he..." Moctu scowled and barely restrained himself from spitting in disgust. "He thinks we honor the wrong Spirits. Is he right?" Lost in thought, he continued to drag the heavy travois over the uneven trail. Each time it bumped over a rock, Moctu felt the pain in his wounded midsection. But the pain helped him focus.

The Spirits have been with us...at least recently, he reflected. So, I don't think Devu's right. We're not honoring the wrong Spirits. We overcame all our challenges. The Spirits *must* be with us. Still, we lost three good men, and many of us are wounded. And our hunting... it's been...just awful.

As Moctu continued thinking on the matter, he heard an excited call from Palo.

"Moctu...set the travois down and come. Hurry!"

Already tired from pulling the travois, Moctu was winded as he got halfway up the hill and neared Palo. Palo said nothing but excitedly motioned for him to follow as he raced farther up the hill. Moctu was gasping as they rounded the hill to a rocky outcrop that offered a view of rolling hills and lowlands.

There were caribou. Lots of caribou. Hands and hands of them... uncountable hands of caribou. Moctu stared in awe at the sight, overwhelmed by it, staggered to his core. After a long moment, he closed his eyes and shook his head, inexplicably close to tears.

"Thank you, Spirits. Thank you."

Notes and Annotated References

I WOULD LIKE TO thank the following sources for providing information critical to the prehistorical accuracy of *The People Eaters*.

1. Rougier, H., et al. (2016) "Neanderthal cannibalism and Neanderthal bones used as tools in Northern Europe." *Scientific Reports*. DOI: 10.1038/srep29005—**A third of the 40,500- to 45,500-year-old Neanderthal remains at Troisieme cave in Goyet, Belgium show cut marks or percussion crushing** (to extract marrow). The marks are identical to those on horse and caribou remains, indicating they were consumed in a similar way.

2. Johanson, D. and Edgar, B. (2006) *From Lucy to Language* p 225. More than 850 roughly 130,000-year-old Neanderthal fossils from up to eighty individuals in Krapina Cave in Croatia indicated 1) **Most Neanderthals died between the ages of sixteen and twenty-four years**, and 2) There is strong evidence that some of these **Neanderthals were butchered, cooked, and eaten**. Page 234: 40,000 to 50,000-year-old Neanderthal fossils from Amud Cave in Israel have features that are a blend of Neanderthal and early modern human. Page 238: 50,000-year-old fossils from La Chapelle-Aux-Saints, France, show one individual with a deformed hip, crushed toe, severe arthritis in the neck vertebrae, a broken rib, and a damaged knee cap.

3. Cavalli-Sforza, L. L., Cavalli-Sforza, F. (1995) *The Great Human Diasporas : The History of Diversity and Evolution*. Translated by Sarah Thorne. New York: Perseus Books. **Mounds of broken bones have been found that suggest Neanderthals ate brains and bone marrow of fellow Neanderthals.** It's unclear whether they killed their neighbors in order to eat them or whether they may have been necrophagous, meaning they ate their dead, a form of cannibalism still widespread in Africa and practiced in New Guinea until a few years ago.

4.   Yustos, M. and José Yravedra Sainz de los Terreros (2015) "Cannibalism in the Neanderthal World: An Exhaustive Revision." *Journal of Taphonomy* 13 (1), 33-52. This is a good article that summarizes Neanderthal cannibalism, with six pages of references and an excellent map of the seven scattered documented sites. Solid evidence of **Neanderthal cannibalism has been found at Goyet, Belgium; Gran Dolina and El Sidron in Spain; and Moula-Guercy, Combe-Grenal, and Les Pradelles in France**. Additionally, the La Quina and La Chaise sites in France show evidence of cannibalism as well, but it is less conclusive.

5.   Dannemann, M. and Kelso, J. (2017) "The Contribution of Neanderthals to Phenotypic Variation in Modern Humans." *American Journal Human Genetics.* Oct 5; 101(4): 578–589. Neanderthal DNA affects skin tone and hair color, height, sleeping patterns, mood, and smoking status in modern humans. Sun exposure likely shaped Neanderthal phenotypes, and more than half of the identified alleles are related to skin and hair traits. These **Neanderthal alleles contribute to both lighter and darker skin tones and hair color. This suggests that Neanderthals were variable in these traits.** Determined red hair was probably not very common in Neanderthals. The variation in phenotypic effects of Neanderthal alleles demonstrates the **difficulty in confidently predicting Neanderthal skin and hair color**.

6.   Cerqueira, C., et al. (2012) "Predicting Homo Pigmentation Phenotype through Genomic Data: From Neanderthal to James Watson." *American Journal Human Biology* 24(5):705-9. Evaluated the reliability of predictions of pigmentation phenotypes using a large database of genetic markers in individuals with known phenotypes. From this, attempts to predict the pigmentation characteristics of prehistoric Homo specimens. Except for freckles, prediction is difficult: the agreement in predicted versus observed was freckles—91 percent; skin—64 percent; hair—44 percent; eyes—36 percent; total—59 percent.

7.   Watson, Traci (2012) "Were Some Neandertals Brown-Eyed Girls?" *ScienceMag.* This article reports on the above study, which analyzed the nuclear DNA of three Croatian Neandertal females. The study used a simple additive technique that equally weighted genetic variables to give a crude estimate of genetic effect. Results suggest that **all three had brown eyes and a tawny complexion. Two had brown hair, and one had red hair**.

8.   Callaway, E. (2014) "Ancient European Genomes Reveal Jumbled Ancestry." *Nature.* Studies indicate that some **early modern humans had dark hair and an olive complexion**.

9.   Anthroscape Human Biodiversity Forum (2009) Dolni Vestonice ivory carving dating to ~26,000 years ago indicates EMHs had straight to wavy hair. The Venus of Brassempuoy figurine suggests that **EMHs had wavy hair or possibly braided**.

10.   Sankararaman, S. et al. (2014) "The Genomic Landscape of Neanderthal Ancestry in Present-Day Humans." *Nature* 507: 354–357. **Neanderthals have more genes affecting keratin filaments, suggesting that interbreeding may have helped modern humans to adapt to non-African environments. Their results suggest that Neanderthal genes may have caused decreased fertility in hybrid males**.

11.   Hirst, K. (2018) "El Sidrón, 50,000-Year-Old Neanderthal Site." *ThoughtCo.*. **There is evidence in Northern Spain of cannibalism of thirteen Neanderthals** (seven adults—three males, four females—three adolescents, two juveniles, and one infant). Seven have the same mDNA haplotype, but three of the four adult females have different mDNA haplotype. So the men were closely related, but the women were from outside the group, **indicating patrilocality**. The bones indicate nutritional stress from a diet mostly of seeds, nuts, moss, and mushrooms. The overall evidence leads most researchers to believe **the group was killed and cannibalized by another group**, and it was not just one group eating its own dead. Dates fall into a range of 43,000 to 49,000 years ago (roughly the time of this story). The dates fall within Marine Isotope 3 (MIS3), a period known to have experienced rapid climate fluctuations.

12.   Pääbo, S. (2014) *Neanderthal Man*. Basic Books. In Vindija, Croatia, bones had cut marks or were crushed into small fragments, indicating they were broken for nutritional value during cannibalism. Paabo called this typical of many, even most, sites where Neanderthal bones are found.

13.   Rodriguez, J. et al. (2019) "Does Optimal Foraging Theory Explain the Behavior of the Oldest Human Cannibals?" *Journal of Human Evolution*, Vol 131: 228–239. Evidence suggests that **cannibalism was a normal behavior for our ancestors, including *Homo antecessor*** (which evolved into both Neanderthals and *Homo sapiens*). Hominins were a common, highly ranked prey type.

14.   Hendry, L. (2019) "The Cannibals of Gough's Cave." Natural History Museum of London website. Evidence indicates that **modern humans at Gough's Cave near Somerset, England, likely cannibalized other humans as part of a ritual about 14,700 years ago**.

15.   Underdown, S. (2008) "A Potential Role for Transmissible Spongiform Encephalopathies in Neanderthal Extinction." *Medical Hypotheses*, Vol 71, Issue 1: 4–7. This article suggests that **Neanderthal cannibals likely**

ingested prions as they ate modern humans, spreading a mad cow-like disease that reduced populations, thereby contributing to their extinction.

16. Raffaele, Paul (2006) "Sleeping with Cannibals." *Smithsonian Magazine.* Korowai tribesmen in New Guinea have practiced cannibalism into recent times. Some isolated Pacific Island cultures, such as Fijians, have as well.

17. Rozzi, F. et al. (2009) "Cutmarked Human Remains Bearing Neandertal Features and Modern Human Remains Associated with the Aurignacian at Les Rois," *Journal of Anthropological Sciences,* 87: 153–85. A child's skull with Neanderthal features may have been used by modern humans as a drinking cup or for other ritualistic purposes. Cut marks on the skull, similar to those found on reindeer bones, could indicate human predation of Neanderthals or human skinning of Neanderthal heads for trophies.

18. Chagnon, N. (2013) *Noble Savages: My Life among Two Dangerous Tribes– the Yanomamo and the Anthropologists.* New York: Simon & Schuster.

19. Roser, M. (2013) "Ethnographic and Archaeological Evidence on Violent Deaths." *Our World in Data.* This fascinating compilation and comparison of violent death rates in various ancient cultures documents that many hunter-gatherer societies had high rates (e.g., 1,325-year-old Crow Creek site in North Dakota shows 60 percent and 13,000-year-old site in Nubia indicates 46 percent!).

20. Otterbein, K. (2004) *How War Began.* Texas A&M University Press. War was common in prehistoric cultures. The atlatl was probably the most important event in the last forty thousand years. It allowed for *Homo sapien* migration into Europe and elsewhere, the increase in our numbers, and the demise of Neanderthals and *Homo erectus.*

21. Pinker, S. (2011) *The Better Angels of Our Nature: Why Violence Has Declined.* Viking Books. This book presents volumes of data that demonstrate that violence has been in decline for many thousands of years. Hunter-gatherer societies had high rates of violent death. The change to an agricultural culture brought a reduction in the chronic raiding and feuding and resulted in a fivefold decrease in rates of violent death.

22. Ember, C. (1978) "Myths about Hunter-Gatherers." *Ethnology* 17: 439–448. Excluding equestrian hunters and those with 50 percent or more dependence on fishing, warfare is rare for only 12 percent of the remaining hunter-gatherers. Ancient hunter-gatherers were not peaceful, with most engaging in warfare every two years.

23. University of Hawaii at Manoa, *Pacific Island Newspapers: Papua New Guinea*. Papua **New Guinea has 848 languages** (12 percent of the world total), all in a country the size of Thailand.

24. ICRP. (2017) "The old ways are gone: Papua New Guinea's tribal wars become more destructive." *Medium.com*. **There is nearly constant skirmishing and warfare between nearby tribes.**

25. Adovasio, J. and Pedler, D. (2016) *Strangers in a New Land.* Firefly Books. This work estimates that **at the time of European contact, there were 1,000 mutually unintelligible languages in America, or a total of 2,500–3,000 if dialects are included.**

26. Martin, D., and Frayer, D. (1997) *Troubled Times: Violence and Warfare in the Past.* Gordon and Breach Publishers. **Twenty-five percent of men died from warfare during most of human history**. Documents evidence of violence in ancient bones, but also uses case studies in archaeology, ethnology, and osteology to show **prehistoric cultures were often violent.**

27. Shipman, P. (2017) *The Invaders—How Humans and Their Dogs Drove Neanderthals to Extinction.* Belknap Press. **Domestication of wolves may have helped modern humans overcome Neanderthals**, as well as other predatory species in Europe. Neanderthals were likely extinct by the time that "wolf-dogs" appeared. Modern humans did and Neanderthals did not survive the Campanian Ignimbrite eruption about 39,000 years ago.

28. Gross, M. (2015) "Are Dogs Just Like Us?" *Current Biology* Vol 25:17. DNA dates **dog domestication back 33,000 years**.

29. Thalmann, O., et al. (2013) "Complete Mitochondrial Genomes of Ancient Canids Suggest a European Origin of Domestic Dogs." *Science*, Vol. 342, Issue 6160, pp. 871–874. A comparison of the genomes of ancient dogs and wolves with modern canines concluded that **dogs evolved in Europe 19,000 to 32,000 years ago**.

30. Botigué, L., et al. (2017) "Ancient European Dog Genomes Reveal Continuity Since the Early Neolithic." *Nature Communications,* vol 8. The oldest, unequivocal evidence of a domesticated dog is 14,700 years ago in a German site. Using DNA, this study narrowed the **timing of dog domestication to 20,000–40,000 years ago**. According to their analysis, dogs diverged from wolves between 36,900 years ago to 41,500 years ago.

31. NOTE: Although there may have been earlier migrations into the Americas, the genetics appear to show that the ancestors of current Native Americans closely tie to migrants that arrived after 16,500 years ago.

32. Voormolen B. (2008) "Ancient Hunters, Modern Butcher Schöningen 13II-4, a kill-butchery site dating from the northwest European Lower Palaeolithic." PhD thesis, Leiden.

33. Richter, D. and M. Krbetschek (2015) "The Age of the Lower Paleolithic Occupation at Schöningen." *Journal of Human Evolution* 89: 4656. Using thermoluminescence, dated heat-treated flints, and determined the **Schönigen site to be 320,000 years old, making the wooden spears found there the oldest in the world.**

34. Milks, A., Parker, D., and Pope, M. (2019) "External Ballistics of Pleistocene Hand-Thrown Spears: Experimental Performance Data and Implications for Human Evolution." *Scientific Reports* 9, no. 820. In a deep dive into the Neanderthal throwing versus thrusting of spears debate, researchers recruited six javelin athletes to throw **replicas of the Schönigen spears.** They found the **athletes could hit targets as far as sixty-five feet away with sufficient impact to kill an animal.**

35. NOTE: Some previous researchers had suggested that Neanderthals only thrusted their spears, but it's probable that Neanderthals *did* throw them, at least sometimes. Even their ancestors were likely throwing spears long before. Ten of the Schönigen spears have been recovered from lignite mines amidst 40,000 horse bones that show cut marks. The spears are perfectly weighted for throwing, and were likely used by proto-Neanderthals as they ambushed the horses near a lake. The Neanderthal "Pale Ones" throw their spears in this book somewhat more than they did in *Moctu.*

36. Gibbons, A. (2016) Modern Human Females and Male Neandertals Had Trouble Making Babies. Here's Why. *Sciencemag.* Y chromosome of male Neanderthal from El Sidron, Spain, from 49,000 years ago weren't passed on to EMHs and suggests that female EMHs and male Neanderthals were not fully compatible.

37. Mendez, F. et al. (2016) The Divergence of Neandertal and Modern Human Y Chromosomes. *American Journal of Human Genetics* 98:4. Analysis of Y chromosome from Neandertal male from El Sidron, Spain, from 49,000 years ago suggests the most recent common ancestor between EMHs and Neandertals was 588 kya. This analysis identified several protein-coding differences, which could cause male Neanderthal/female EMH incompatibility and possible reproductive isolation. Hybrid males fathered by a Neanderthal had a greater chance of being miscarried.

38. Serre, D., et al. (2004) "No Evidence of Neandertal mtDNA Contribution to Early Modern Humans." *PLOS Biology*, 2 (3): 313–17. The absence of Neanderthal-derived mtDNA in modern populations suggests that

hybrids are the result of Neanderthal male/modern human female pairings.

39.   NOTE: References 36, 37, 71 and 72 versus 38 demonstrate the controversy about which sex pairings worked. Concerning the offspring, it is becoming clearer that hybrid males may not have survived or were infertile, so **the genes we carry today probably came from female hybrids.**

40.   Hublin, J., et al. (2020) "Initial Upper Palaeolithic Homo Sapiens from Bacho Kiro Cave, Bulgaria." *Nature*, 581 (7808): 299–302. Evidence of **modern humans in Bulgaria dates to 46,000 years ago**.

41.   Higham, T., et al. (2011) "The Earliest Evidence for Anatomically Modern Humans in Northwestern Europe." *Nature*, 479 (7374): 521–524. **The oldest modern human fossil in northwestern Europe is about 43,000 years old.**

42.   Pearce, E., et al. (2013) "New Insights into Differences in Brain Organization between Neanderthals and Anatomically Modern Humans." *Proceedings of the Royal Society.* **Neanderthals had bigger eyes and more brain space dedicated to vision, so they probably could see better than modern humans.** They also may have been able to see better in low light.

43.   Weyrich, L., et al. (2017) "Neanderthal Behaviour, Diet, and Disease Inferred from Ancient DNA in Dental Calculus." *Nature*, vol 544: 357–361. **Neanderthals discovered penicillin more than 40,000 years before we did. Analysis of the DNA of dental plaque of a Neanderthal from El Sidron, Spain, shows that he used poplar bark (which contains an aspirin-like compound) and fungus containing penicillin to treat an abscessed tooth.**

44.   Buckley, S., et al. (2013) "Neanderthal Self-Medication in Context." *Antiquity* 87 (337): 873–878. El Sidron **Neanderthals likely also used yarrow and chamomile** as medicines.

45.   Ríos, L., et al. (2019) "Skeletal Anomalies in the Neandertal Family of El Sidrón (Spain) Support a Role of Inbreeding in Neandertal Extinction." *Scientific Reports.* 9 (1): 1697. **The thirteen inhabitants of Sidrón Cave collectively exhibited seventeen different birth defects, probably due to inbreeding, which signals low population densities.**

46.   Shroomery website: The Liberty Cap (Psilocybe semilanceata) is the most widespread wild **psilocybin mushroom** of the world. It grows in north temperate areas but it has been found even in Peru, India, and also at altitudes of **4,000 meters in Italy**. Its effects include pupil dilation, spontaneous laughter, and delirium. Higher doses cause visual effects and a calming of the body.

47.   Bailey, M. (2013) "Ice Age Lion Man is World's Earliest Figurative Sculpture." *The Art Newspaper*. The Lion Man of Hohlenstein Stadel is an **ivory carving of a lion-headed figure and is known as the oldest anthropomorphic animal carving in the world**. Discovered in Stadel cave in Hohlenstein Mountain in southwest Germany, it has been dated to approximately 40,000 years ago. Other important carvings discovered there include the Venus of Hohle Fels (33,000–38,000 years old), the earliest ivory carving of a mammoth, and several bone flutes.

48.   Guatelli-Steinberg, D., et al. (2016) "What Teeth Reveal about Human Evolution." *Cambridge University Press*. **Thirty-nine percent of Neandertals had hypoplasia** (grooves in tooth enamel), which **indicates periods of famine or poor nutrition**.

49.   Villa, P. and Roebroeks, W. (2014) "Neandertal Demise: An Archaeological Analysis of the Modern Human Superiority Complex." *PLoS ONE* 9(4): e96424. The cognitive/cultural/technological gap between Neanderthals and EMHs was much smaller than previously hypothesized and not large enough to explain their demise. **Neanderthals made use of ocher**, personal ornaments, bone tools, and complex hafting techniques before the arrival of EMHs in western Eurasia.

50.   Churchill, S. and Rhodes, J. (2009) "The Evolution of the Human Capacity for Killing at a Distance." *The Evolution of Hominin Diets* (J. Hublin and M. Richards, eds.). Analyses of Middle Paleolithic points suggest that long-range projectile weaponry (most likely in the form of spear thrower-delivered darts) was developed in Africa sometime between 90–70 ky BP, and was part of the tool kit of modern humans who later expanded out of Africa.

51.   National Geographic Society Genographic Project (2012) Basque Roots Revealed through DNA Analysis. *Press Room*. A comprehensive analysis of Basque genetic patterns indicates their uniqueness that predates the arrival of farming by 7,000 years. The results of the study support **a genetic continuity of current day Basques with the earlier Paleolithic or Mesolithic settlers** of their area. NOTE: Since **Basque is probably the language most similar to what early modern human migrants into Europe spoke,** I have used many Basque words or derivations for the Nerean and Lion People cultures.

52.   Hovers, E., et al. (2003) "An Early Case of Color Symbolism: Ochre Use by Modern Humans in Qafzeh Cave." *Current Anthropology* 44 (4): 491–522. Among its many other uses, **red ochre was likely used by females to fake menstruation, making them less available sexually.**

53. Stratton, J. (2019) "Waco Mammoth National Monument: Viewing Mammoth Bones In Situ." *National Parks Traveler*. **Eighteen mammoths were killed 65,000 years ago in a flash flood** or other natural catastrophe near Waco, Texas. In addition to the first event, there were two other calamities in the next 15,000 years that caused animals to die and be covered by mud in this area (these included other mammoths, camels, and saber-tooth tigers).

54. Pfizenmayer, E. W. (1939) *Siberian Man and Mammoth*. Blackie and Son, London. The mummified Berezovka mammoth from Russia shows evidence of having been buried in a mudslide.

55. DOE/Pacific Northwest National Laboratory (2007) "An Ancient Bathtub Ring of Mammoth Fossils." *ScienceDaily*. Pacific Northwest National Laboratory researchers have identified **sixty-two known or suspected sites of mammoth** and other fossil remains **from repeated ice age floods** of ancient Lakes Missoula and Lewis in Washington State.

56. Malakowski, L., Snowflake Obsidian. *The Learning Series,* Wiregrassrockhounds.com. **Snowflake obsidian is black volcanic glass with white inclusions** of cristobalite, which form a snowflake pattern.

57. Pliny the Elder (circa AD 77) *Naturalis Historia* (translated by John Bostock, Henry Thomas Riley, 1857). Among other places, **snowflake obsidian is found in Italy**. Obsidian was first named by Pliny the Elder (the Roman historian-scientist who died at Pompeii).

58. Walker, R, et al. (2010) "Evolutionary History of Partible Paternity in Lowland South America." *Proceedings of the National Academy of Sciences*. 107 (45): 19,195–19,200. **Many Amazon tribes (up to 70 percent) believe that any men who have intercourse with a woman during her pregnancy are partial fathers of the child**. The theory also shows up in New Guinea, and elsewhere, and is called partible (or shared) paternity. A common belief is that the offspring will grow to express the characteristics of the men who contributed the most semen. Therefore, **a good mother will have sex with several men so her child will enjoy the best qualities of her partners (and be partly the best hunter, best napper, or best storyteller, etc.)**.

59. Caesar, J. (circa 52 BC) The Gallic War. Wrote about the **Celts in England who had beliefs and followed practices related to shared paternity**.

60. Nakahashi, W. (2017) "The Effect of Trauma on Neanderthal Culture: A Mathematical Analysis." *Homo*, 68 (2): 83–100. **Neanderthals suffered a high rate of traumatic injury, with an estimated 79–94 percent of specimens showing evidence of healed major trauma. Researchers**

speculate that this is from close-quarter, ambush hunting, i.e., thrusting versus projectile weaponry.

61. Trinkaus, E. (2012) "Neandertals, Early Modern Humans, and Rodeo Riders." *Journal of Archaeological Science*, Vol 39, (12), 3,691–3,693. Former studies suggested that Neanderthal injuries were similar to those of rodeo riders and indicated close-quarter hunting. In fact, **Neanderthals and Paleolithic modern humans show similar injury patterns, and evidence of effective throwing spears has been emerging for Neanderthals**.

62. Elliott, Barkeater, UrbanDictionary.com. Barkeater is the English translation of the Mohican word "Adirondack." Mohawks used it derisively for Algonquian-speaking tribes who **ate the inside bark (cambium) of the white pine when food was scarce**.

63. Pontoppidan, E. (circa 1752) *Attempt at the Natural History of Norway*. Vol I and II. The **inner bark of trees, including white and scotch pines, elm, ash, birch and aspen, is edible** and can be ground into flour for use in bread.

64. Qiaomei Fu, et al. (2014) "Genome Sequence of a 45,000-Year-Old Modern Human from Western Siberia." *Nature*, vol 514, 445–449. Researchers sequenced a high-quality genome of a ~45,000-year-old **modern human male from Siberia. Substantially longer genomic segments of Neanderthal ancestry than those observed in present-day individuals indicate that Neanderthal gene flow into his ancestors occurred 7,000–13,000 years before**.

65. Romandini, M., et al. (2020) "A Late Neanderthal Tooth from Northeastern Italy." *Journal of Human Evolution*, Vol 147. A 48,000-year-old child's canine represents the most recent evidence of Neanderthals in Northern Italy.

66. Karafet, T. et al. (2008) "New Binary Polymorphisms Reshape and Increase Resolution of the Human Y Chromosomal Haplogroup Tree." *Genome Research* 18(5) 830-838. The **haplogroup R1b originated during the last ice age** at least 18,500 years ago and **is most frequent in the Basque Country (91 percent)**.

67. Papagianni, D., and Morse, M. (2013) *The Neanderthals Rediscovered— How Modern Science Is Rewriting Their Story*. Thames and Hudson. This work discusses how **cannibalism was relatively common with pre-Neanderthal hominins, Neanderthals, and modern humans**. It says the Gran Dolina, Spain, early human cannibalism "makes them more, rather than less, human." It also discusses the fast pace of recent anthropological discovery.

68. Gibbons, A. (1997) "Archaeologists Rediscover Cannibals." *Science*, Vol. 277, Issue 5326, 635–637. There is **strong evidence for cannibalism among our ancestors** (as early as 800,000 years ago) **and Neanderthals**; and more recently, among the Anasazi, the Aztec, and the people of Fiji.

69. NOTE: Some researchers have sought to explain away the cut marks on human bones as de-fleshing for ritual or for purposes of easier burial. But such an explanation does not adequately explain percussion marks to extract marrow, or the fact that the human bones are commonly found among bones of prey animals that show similar cut marks. The human bones were processed in the same way as animal carcasses, and many show charring similar to that of the game animal bones. The high degree of disarticulation and fragmentation that is typical refutes the argument that the bones were purposefully buried. Additionally, some of the human bones show animal gnaw marks *after* the human-made cuts, suggesting the bones had been discarded, not ritually buried. Cannibalism is by far the simpler, more elegant explanation.

70. Frayer, D. (2014) The Routledge Handbook of the Bioarchaeology of Human Conflict 4 Trauma in the Krapina (Knusel and Smith, ed.). This is an excellent and lengthy summary of Krapina research to date. Cranial **trauma at Krapina is likely due to interpersonal violence. The disarticulation and fragmentation of human bones argues against ritual or ceremonial burial.**

71. Mendez, F., et al. (2016) "The Divergence of Neandertal and Modern Human Y Chromosomes." *American Journal of Human Genetics*, vol 98(4): 728–734. **The Neanderthal Y chromosome has never been observed in modern humans and it's probably extinct.** This may be due to women's immune systems attacking male fetuses due to protein-coding differences between modern human and Neanderthal Y chromosomes. **Women may have consistently miscarried male hybrid babies.**

72. Petr, M., et al. (2020) "The Evolutionary History of Neanderthal and Denisovan Y chromosomes." *Science*, Vol 369, Issue 6511, 1653–1656. Analysis of Neanderthal Y chromosomes indicates they are more similar to that in modern humans than to the more archaic Denisovans. This is likely due to interbreeding that happened before 100,000 years ago. The **modern human Y chromosomes may have been selected because of faulty Neanderthal DNA compromised by inbreeding due to small population size.**

73. Haws, J., et al. (2020) "The Early Aurignacian Dispersal of Modern Humans into Westernmost Eurasia." *PNAS*, Sep 2020. Early modern human artifacts found in Portugal date from 41–38K years ago, 5,000 years

earlier than previously known. Our overlap in time with Neanderthals becomes briefer as more evidence comes in.

74.   Marginedas, F., et al. (2020) "Making Skull Cups: Butchering Traces on Cannibalised Human Skulls from Five European Archaeological Sites." *Journal of Archaeological Science*, vol. 114. This work documents **evidence of bowls made from human skulls** at five widely distant locations in Europe including the UK, Germany, Spain, and France. The abundance of separate sites indicates that the practice was relatively widespread.

75.   McCauley, B., et al. (2018) "A Cross-Cultural Perspective on Upper Palaeolithic Hand Images with Missing Phalanges." *Journal of Paleolithic Archaeology* vol. 1, 314–333. Multiple European caves feature **handprints that are missing digits**, which likely represent sacrifices to appeal for supernatural help, mourning practices, or amputations for frostbite or disease.

76.   NOTE: Neanderthals were named after a German valley in which some of their bones were found in the mid-1800s. The valley was named for Joachim Neander, a German theologian from the mid-1600s, who wrote more than forty hymns and poems for the Church, some of which are still sung today. Ironic fact: "Neander" means "new man" based on the ancient Greek translation of Neander's name, so Neanderthal means "valley of the new man."

77.   Sykes, R. (2020) *Kindred: Neanderthal Life, Love, Death and Art.* Bloomsbury Sigma. A wonderful book full of facts about Neanderthals with delightful anecdotes and side comments such as how **Neanderthals might have been named "Awirians" or "Calpicans" if the earliest-discovered fossils of these humans (in Belgium or Gibraltar, respectively) had been recognized as a new species.** Sykes documents that **Neanderthals were clever, technologically inventive, and adaptable** to many terrains and climates. She weighs in on Neanderthal spear thrusting vs. throwing, citing studies that indicate spear thrusting was common, but Neanderthals likely threw spears as well. Her comment on page 70—about how early humans, like more recent hunter-gatherer cultures, probably allowed or encouraged their young to play with sharp tools—dovetails nicely with our storyline. Another of her comments on page 142—about how hyena packs typically show up to scavenge kill sites within thirty minutes—also ties to a scene in this book.

78.   Von Petzinger, G. (2016) *The First Signs: Unlocking the Mysteries of the World's Oldest Symbols.* Atria Books. Von Petzinger has visited dozens of European cave art sites and compiled a database of 350 Ice Age localities that indicate **thirty-two symbols are used repeatedly in prehistoric art around the world.**

79. Pajovic, G. (2015) "On CI Eruption as a Factor of Cultural and Demographic Changes on the Turn of the Middle to Upper Paleolithic on the Eastern Adriatic Coast." *Independent Academia.* The **Campanian Ignimbrite eruption undoubtedly had a negative effect on human populations, but it was probably not the key factor in the extinction of the Neanderthals.**

80. Hardy, B., et al. (2020) "Direct Evidence of Neanderthal Fiber Technology and Its Cognitive and Behavioral Implications." *Scientific Reports* 10: 4889. **Neanderthals in France had cord-making technology.** Roughly 45,000-year-old fibers from the inner bark of what was likely a conifer were S-twisted, then plied together with a Z-twist to form a three-ply cord.

81. Crevecoeur, I., et al. (2021) "New Insights on Interpersonal Violence in the Late Pleistocene Based on the Nile Valley Cemetery of Jebel Sahaba." *Scientific Reports* 11: 9991. Remains at Jebel Sahaba, Sudan date to 13,400-18,600 years ago, and show **evidence of multiple acts of warfare among hunter-gatherers.** Seventy-five percent of adults show a healed or unhealed lesion, with projectile impacts the most common form.

82. Wolpoff, M. and Caspari, R. (2006) "Does Krapina Reflect Early Neandertal Paleodemography?" *Periodicum Biologorum* 108 (4). This work analyzes teeth and other remains of **eighty-three Neanderthal individuals** and **determined high child survivorship but low adult life expectancy. Few lived past age thirty.**

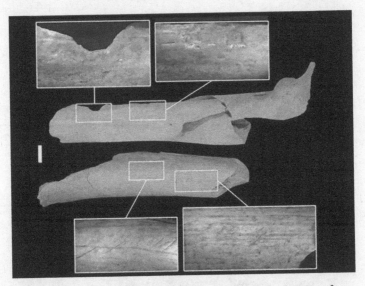

From Reference #1—Bones from Goyet Cave in Belgium showing signs of
cannibalism.

The different categories of anthropogenic modifications found on Neanderthal
bones at Goyet. Femur I (left) displays signs of having been used as a
percussor for shaping stone, and femur III (right) bears cut marks indicating
the processing of remains during butchery activities. Scale = 1 cm.

Splendid but chilling watercolor by Emmanuel Roudier.
Photo by Don Hitchcock.

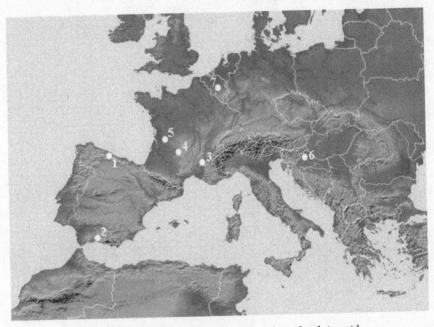

From Reference #4—Geographical location of the analyzed sites with evidence of Neanderthal cannibalism: 1) El Sidrón; 2) Boquete de Zafarraya; 3) Moula-Guercy; 4) Combe-Grenal; 5) Les Pradelles; 6) Krapina; 7) Goyet. With permission—from Yustos and Yravedra (2015).